THE SILENT CANARY

A NOVEL

ANGELA BRICKER

The Silent Canary

Cover design by Alena Nelson @drippedinrose

To Princess Alena, the living heartbeat of this story.

To the one hundred thirty-four men and women of the Chilwell National Shell Filling Factory; may you never be forgotten.

And to Elsie Lavinia Gibbs.
This book is for you.

One for sorrow,
Two for mirth;
Three for a wedding,
Four for birth;
Five for silver,
Six for gold;
Seven for a secret,
never to be told...

— MAGPIE NURSERY RHYME
VARIATION

THE SILENT CANARY

POPPY

BEESTON, NOTTINGHAMSHIRE, ENGLAND
FEBRUARY 21, 1916

FEAR HOLDS MY HAND AS IF I AM ITS CHILD.

I lean in and trust it unwaveringly. Listen to its warnings. Heed its call.

It has never abandoned me before.

A train whistle pierces through the bustle of morning patrons who meander about the train station platform looming before me. The large wheels of the transport squeal in protest against the metal tracks as the black locomotive slides into the station right on time.

Beads of sweat appear on my palms in an instant despite the cold rain that falls.

Father, a distinct head shorter than nearly everyone who surrounds him—myself included—stands beside me with his shoulders squared and his chest puffed beneath a khaki British military uniform. His winter trench cap dangles from fingers that tap a solid rhythm against his leg, while his other hand holds his departure ticket firm against the pull of the wind.

He glances in my direction, then releases a sigh drenched in irritation. "War is hard for everyone, Poppy. We all must make sacrifices." The condescension in his voice, while familiar, slides down my core with all the finesse of a snake devouring a rabbit.

"I just don't understand, Father." I take a step closer to him and lower my voice. "You're four years older than the age conscription even allows for, and the war will surely be ending soon; why enlist at all? I wish you would—"

"Remember your place, Poppy Pemburton." Father's words turn sharp, and they prick my spine like a touch from an unwelcome man.

"My place?" I step back, aghast.

His thin, auburn eyebrows slope in an accusing slant, and he leans into my space. "You are a twenty- two- year old woman for goodness' sake. Behave yourself." I open my mouth to speak, but he continues, "Hold your tongue. It's high time you obey the rules of society. Stop your childish war protests and fear mongering throughout Beeston." His hand waves through the air as he works himself up, the paper ticket crinkling beneath the pressure of his clenched fist. "Settle down so you can find a decent man willing to marry you. That Luca Whelan boy isn't going to wait around forever for you to grow up."

My belly swoops at the mention of Luca's name, but the sensation isn't enough to distract me from the way my jaw clenches as a growl claws its way up my throat. Behaving is for dogs.

And saints.

I am neither.

I'm just about to say as much when the departing train's first boarding call rings out across the station, silencing my rebuttal. My chin juts forward in open rebellion, my only way of communicating the intent to defy Father's wishes of societal obedience, but it's likely best that's all I can do. I shouldn't say things I know I'll come to regret before Father embarks upon the train that will likely carry him to his death.

My shoulders shudder at the thought, and fear settles between the blades. None of the men who have left our small town of Beeston for the front lines of the Great War have come home. Not in one piece anyway.

War tears families apart. That's why I've devoted the past year of my life to protesting its deadly clutches at every enlistment location and street corner within Beeston. I often march alone, but that doesn't make my voice any less valuable.

Somehow, I truly believed that my collection of anti-war signs, worn-out marching boots, and filth-laden frocks coated in the spit of those who don't see things quite the way I do would be enough to pull my father away from the siren call of Kitchener's Army. Somehow, I thought it would be enough to make him stay.

But that was foolish. I should know better by now; nobody stays.

Not for me.

In the pocket of my dress, I slide the smooth, gold ring that once belonged to Jane, my mother, between my fingertips.

Rub, rub, rub.

The cool metal turns warm as I rub it, and the worn places on the surface of the ring calm me.

"Someday I might tell you why I chose to enlist, but until I do, I trust you will respect my silence." Father retrieves his satchel from the cobblestone walk and thrusts it over his shoulder as though it has offended him somehow. "You have secrets too, do you not?" His eyes, blue and large like mine, are a midnight storm.

Of course I have secrets. Don't we all?

But I don't try to understand Father's secrets. I don't ask questions. Because secrets are just that: secret. They belong only to their owner. They're not meant to be open. Not meant to be discovered. Not meant to be shared.

Keeping secrets is how you survive. Father taught me that.

But it's not Father's secrets I want. It's his truths.

I turn away from him and watch as raindrops leave tiny, wet circles on the sleeves of my lace-factory dress, blurring the dark oil stains left there from years of working the lace machinery. A gust of winter wind prickles my neck. I pull my black shawl tighter around me, but the threadbare fabric does little to block out the cold.

"Goodbye, Poppy," Father says to my back. "Take care of yourself."

When I turn to look over my shoulder, I only see Father's retreating form climbing up the station steps and onto the platform. His wavy, red hair flops messily about as if it's the only piece of him willing to acknowledge me.

Instinctively, I reach up and pull on my own matching strands.

"Goodbye, Father," I whisper.

A lump rises thick and heavy in my throat.

No, I will not cry. If I cry, I care. And I cannot care. Caring leaves me vulnerable. Emotional. Weak.

I swallow around the sob begging to escape. Sharp needles of pain pierce my throbbing throat from the attempt.

Fear. Lean into the fear, I command myself. Fear protects me from harm. From pain. From abandonment. Because fear reminds me of what and whom I've lost so that I never get close enough to anyone to risk losing more. Fear comforts me because it's the only emotion that offers me safety.

If I stay afraid, I stay vigilant.

A shrill whistle cuts through the air, announcing the final boarding call.

Father places his trench cap on his head right before he disappears through the open train car doors. They close right behind him, sealing his fate.

And mine.

My heart thuds hard within my chest. My breath comes out in short gasps. Pain fills my lungs as they constrict.

I turn away from the departing train and, with shaking hands, push through the mass of bodies that have made their way down off the platform. I can scarcely breathe as people press in on all sides of me, stealing my air. I break into a run, a desperate need for space fueling my body.

"Miss, are you alright?" I hear a woman ask as I narrowly avoid running into her large traveling case.

I gasp for air but cannot seem to find it. I vaguely register the worried looks of strangers as I pass them. I want to tell them I'll be fine, but the words escape me. A hand grabs onto my wrist, but I manage to shake myself loose and press forward.

If only I could get away from everyone, I would be able to breathe.

"Poppy!" a familiar, strong voice shouts from behind me.

I whip around to see Luca reaching out to me.

"I'm here," he says.

I let Luca grab hold of my shoulders. I tilt my head up and gasp desperately at the air above me while my hand taps fiercely against my exploding heart.

"Count with me," he commands, and I do my calming counts as he taught me.

"Ten, nine, eight, seven . . ." I manage to recite with him.

When we get to three, I can breathe somewhat normally again. By one, the shaking in my hands has nearly stopped.

I lick my lips and take a desperate breath in, then slowly exhale. I close my eyes and let the soft rain trickle down my face. The cool water caresses my heated cheeks, and I concentrate on its feathery touch against my skin. I take another deep breath, my chest loosening with each passing second.

When I open my eyes, I find myself staring up into Luca's concerned ones.

"Better?" His eyebrows raise along with the question.

"Much. Thank you," I breathe out. My attention gravitates to my feet to avoid Luca bearing witness to the flush I can sense creeping into my cheeks.

"I knew you were fast, but wow." Luca whistles through his teeth. "That might be a new record. Remind me not to race you." He winks.

At that, images from summer days of our childhood when Luca and I would spend our afternoons racing barefoot up and down the banks of The Weir, sweat dripping down the edges of our flushed, happy faces flit through my mind like snapshots of a picture reel. I know as well as he does that while I could always beat every girl my age in a foot race, Luca was still faster. But I think he senses my embarrassment, and I'm grateful for his attempt to make me smile.

Although the rain has begun to subside, water drips steadily from Luca's hair onto his face as he peers at me through the dark, wet strands. His blue-green eyes—the color of a tropical lagoon—framed by thick, black lashes swiftly pull me in.

But fear reminds me to push away the flutter in my chest, and I obey.

I don't love Luca. I don't.

I can't.

He's been my closest friend since he came to Beeston, England, from Italy to live with his aunt when he was seven—his parents and brother tragically lost in a drowning accident. Although he's two years older than me, I taught Luca how to speak English, how to read, and how to climb the vines that ascend the wall of the church to the roof. He taught me how to draw, how to spin on the twirly rides at the fair without getting sick, and how to protect others with my words instead of my fists.

He's the only person who has never left me. So I can't love Luca. Because if I did, he would leave me someday too.

I clear my throat when I realize I've been staring at this man for a length of time that is entirely inappropriate for our friendship. Chuckling awkwardly, I glance down at the cobblestones I'm hoping are still firmly beneath my feet.

That's when I notice that Luca is completely soaked through. His brown trousers sag beneath the grip of his suspenders, and his white button-down shirt sticks with valiant loyalty to his body. I try not to stare at the outlined muscles evident beneath the translucent fabric and instead wonder how he ended up in exactly the right place at exactly the right time.

"Where did you come from?" I ask, taking a step back.

His foot becomes interested in a small rock. "I waited across the street for you to say goodbye to Thomas." Luca slicks back his wet hair with both hands and clears his throat before continuing. "In case . . . um . . . in case you needed me."

I want to obey fear more than anything, but it's devastatingly hard when Luca can mend my broken heart in seconds. *He could shatter it just as quick,* fear is eager to remind me.

"Oh." Luca snaps his fingers together and reaches toward his back pocket. "You dropped this when you were running." He slides my black shawl out of the deep confine and holds it out to me, smiling as though he has won first prize at the fair. The worn shawl is the first item I made on my own at the Beeston Lace Factory. I was only eight years old—too young to be allowed to work the machinery alone—but I labored beneath Jane's work desk, hidden from the owner's view. If I'd lost the tattered work of art, I would be devastated beyond words.

"You're always saving me, Luca." I smile.

He wraps the lace around my damp shoulders. "You're worth saving, Firebird." He taps the underside of my chin with the curve of his finger, and his eyes bore into mine as if his gaze alone could imprint those words onto my soul.

I wish it could.

With his thumb, he wipes a streak of water from my cheek, then stuffs his hand in his pocket before speaking again. "Do you want to talk about it?"

I slip my hand inside the pocket of my dress, and my fingers move along the smooth metal of Jane's ring again.

Rub, rub, rub.

Raw thoughts of failure build a wall of shame around me, but I choose to give them a voice. "No matter how many protests I ran, how many prayers I uttered for Father to stay away from the war, how many nights I waited for Jane to walk back into our cottage, my family still slipped through my grasping fingers. It's the one thing I've feared since the day Jane left."

"Your mother—"

"Jane," I interrupt him.

Luca sighs but concedes. "*Jane* isn't your father. Thomas will be back." But the way his eyes lock on the thumb he's poking through the hole of his trouser pocket makes me believe otherwise.

Jane traded Father and I in for a lavish life of fame and fortune as an actress in America nearly a decade ago while Father, Luca, and I were away at The Beeston Spring Fair celebrating my thirteenth birthday. Only a short note wishing us well in our future endeavors and her gold wedding ring were left behind as proof of Jane's existence in our lives. Proof that there was once a woman whom father and I loved desperately but who never saw either of us as anything more than rocky stepstones from her past to her future.

My shoulders lift into a shrug. "What if he dies in France?"

If Luca hears the quiver in my voice, he doesn't comment.

After Jane left, my once adoring and playful father became a slave to his anger and grief. For ten years, I have waited for grief to give my father back to me and held on to the hope that he believed our relationship was worth saving. That the weight of his digging insults and sharp words would one day soften. But if he dies in France, our relationship—our *family*—dies too.

"If he dies in war, he dies a hero," Luca says with conviction.

"Pfft, heroism," I scoff. "Men romanticize war, what it will be like to join up and go to battle, how they will defend freedoms and come home a hero. But none of them think about the people they leave behind. Husbands leave their wives, sons disappear in the dead of night, brothers leave the bodies of comrades killed on the battlefield. Most men never to return home." I chew the inside of my lip until I regain control of my emotions. "Families here are torn apart because men in other countries decided they couldn't get along. How is that right?"

"Most of them want to serve their country, Poppy. They're making the noble choice to put duty before comfort." Luca shrugs as if that's a perfectly acceptable reason for the poor choices of men.

"It isn't noble! These young boys line up in droves to enlist in a war they understand nothing about, and if they don't serve, they're called unpatriotic. You yourself"—I wave in his direction —"have first-hand experience with the putrid white feathers that flutter around those who don't enlist and serve. Those whom the government deems *cowards*."

I pause in front of him for a moment and throw my hands in the air when he shows no response to my outcry. "How does that not ever bother you?"

"I never said it didn't." Luca works a finger back and forth along the hem of his shirt, unsuccessfully fighting a smudge of charcoal valiantly clinging to the cotton fibers.

"Then tell those pompous girls who shove the feathers in your pocket *why* you haven't enlisted, and they can stuff the white feather upside their back end and be ashamed of themselves for trying to make the bravest boy I know feel like a coward."

Luca's cheeks grow pink at the compliment, but he brushes it off. "I'm not brave, Poppy. I'm not even close to brave. But shouting in their faces that I'm the sole caretaker of my loony, elderly aunt isn't going to ward them off."

My shoulders droop. I know he's right. "I have disliked all the commotion surrounding the Great War since the beginning. The propaganda posters, the newspaper headlines, the white feathers." I count on my fingers as I continue. "I have protested, I have marched, I have stood in front of the enlistment doors and refused to move. But until now—until this very moment— protesting was about keeping *other* families together. Now the war has its disgusting hands on mine."

Luca raises his eyes at my declaration. "What are you going to do about that, Firebird?"

What can I do? How can *I* take a stand against the injustices of war? What more can I do than I already am?

Then, a comment my employer made the previous week—a comment I had not paid much attention to at the time—trickles into my thoughts: *"Once Lloyd George sees to it that ammunition factories are built throughout England, it's going to right change the tide of this bloody war. Just you wait and see that it doesn't."*

I begin to pace in front of Luca, an idea brewing. "How many ammunition factories are already built in England?" I ask.

"I couldn't say exactly, but they recently completed the one in Chilwell." Luca points in the direction of the town southwest of ours. "Rumor around Town Square is that they have already begun to fill TNT shells." A handsome smile, bookended by dimples, appears on his face. "Are you going to seek employment there?"

"Of course not," I huff. Father wanted me to stop my childish protesting. Fine. There will be nothing childish about my next protest.

If I stop the production of ammunition, I stop the war.

If I stop the war, Father comes home. Alive.

And then, someday, if Jane comes home too, we can finally be together as a family.

"What I am going to do, Luca," I say, looking him right in the eye, "is shut these factories down one by one. Starting with Chilwell."

Luca's eyebrows stretch upward beneath the long hair splayed across his forehead, the wet strands hiding their skeptical arch.

"My birthday is coming up." I find the edge of my shawl and thread my fingers through the frayed strands. "A protest should keep my mind busy enough."

Luca's face relaxes, and he pulls me into his chest. His lips tickle the skin along my forehead as they cradle the whisper in his voice. "Absolutely."

2

LUCA

BEESTON, NOTTINGHAMSHIRE, ENGLAND
MARCH 8, 1916

MY COLLECTION OF WHITE FEATHERS STANDS AT ATTENTION IN the large, green vase on the fireplace mantel flooding my field of vision. I should refute the tokens of cowardice, as Poppy suggested that day at the train station—return the feathers to the girls charged with stuffing them in my pockets—and explain why I am not an enlisted soldier of brave heroism, but I don't.

Because what Poppy doesn't know is that I deserve each one.

To the left of the vase, the second hand of a clock ticks loudly, a hollow echo against the sitting room walls that display my charcoal works of art in the quiet one-bedroom cottage I share with Aunt Elizabeth.

Each strike of the clock is a reminder that if I don't leave soon, Poppy will surely get herself into so much hot water trying to protest the Chilwell ammunition factory that I might not be able to get her out.

I throw another log on the fire and poke the dying embers as the ticks of the clock intersperse with my aunt's heavy breaths while she situates her overly large frame into our one remaining rickety chair at the table in the humble kitchen behind me. I glance over my shoulder as the wooden chair creaks in protest at the request to be used.

Aunt Elizabeth swears at me through crooked, yellow teeth to mind my business and then waves her walking cane in the air as if it, too, is scolding me.

"Where is my tea, Lucas?" Aunt Elizabeth hollers. My name is not nor ever has been Lucas, but she refuses to call me anything but the Latin derivative of my given name.

The tea kettle shrieks in response, as if understanding Aunt Elizabeth is not to be trifled with. I take a quick look inside the green vase to make sure the alcohol bottle I confiscated from her yesterday is still hidden away beneath the feathers until I can properly dispose of it. Then, I make my way to the kitchen and retrieve her favorite teacup—the glossy white one with the chip in the handle—and pour the tea quickly, careful not to let the scalding liquid splash over onto the open blisters on my fingers and palm.

Normally my fingers callous, but the extra work at the Sweet Shoppe in the evenings after my day shift ends at Humber bicycles hasn't allowed my blisters the time they need to heal. But I have no complaints. The shifts keep me out of the cottage and away from my aunt, and the additional labor is how we make ends meet during the winter months, when I can't sell our garden vegetables to the town grocers.

The work doesn't remove me from Beeston, a town I have wanted to flee since the moment I arrived, nor does it provide me what I crave the very most: permanent freedom from Aunt Elizabeth's oppressive clutches. But the extra time away serves as enough of an escape. That and the moments I'm able to steal away with Poppy. The thought of the unconventional girl with hair as red as the blaze of a setting sun, freckles that smother her face in kisses, and eyes so deep blue they would drown me if given the chance trickles through my mind, and I almost drop the cup of tea.

I steady my thoughts and place the cup and saucer before Aunt Elizabeth. "I mixed the herbs for your headache into the tea. Be sure to drink it all," I tell her. "The pills for today are in the pocket of your sweater. Take them before you finish the tea. And for all that is good and holy, please do not leave the cottage without a coat," I remind her as if I don't repeat these same childlike instructions to her every day. The one day I didn't, I found her half frozen to death, walking in circles around the fountain in the town square. "I will be home in time to start your supper, but I need to leave for a few hours."

In response, Aunt Elizabeth begins to sing her favorite nursery rhyme—the one she personalized just for me the day I arrived in her home seventeen years ago as a seven-year-old orphan:

"Little coward Lucas is going to start to cry.
Better find his Mami to make him a pie.
But Mami won't be coming back; Papi took her away,
To the bottom of the ocean where they live with little Giovanni to this very day."

"I started a fire for you," I say and point behind myself toward the fireplace, ignoring her attempt to goad me. "It should have enough logs in there to keep you warm until I return."

Aunt Elizabeth merely grunts in response.

As soon as I step outside, I take off in a run toward Chilwell National Shell Filling Factory No. 6, which is nestled in the quiet agricultural civil township of Chilwell less than five kilometers southwest of Beeston. Wincing against the sting of the cold wind on my cheeks, I try to shake the insecurity that always rises in my chest with the rhyme I would do well to forget. I know it was not my father's fault that he, my mother, and my little brother, G, drowned off the coast of Italy. *If anyone is to blame it is I.* But the singing lyrics burn all the same.

Aunt Elizabeth was my only living relative willing to take me in. And she only agreed for the sole purpose that at the age of sixty-two, she was alone, aging, sick, and in need of someone to help bring in income—a fact she reminds me of often. But she has never taken a liking to me, an unfortunate truth that stems from a disagreement she had with my father, her younger brother, when my parents married. A disagreement I was never privy to but ultimately drove her from their childhood home in Italy across the water to England, where she became a sorry spinster who despises everything and everyone—me most of all. Particularly so when I became the warden of her alcohol several years ago, after which she made it her personal mission to turn my life into a stunning reflection of her misery.

But whether she took me in all those years ago out of love, duty, or pure selfish need doesn't matter to me. Her willingness kept me from growing up in an orphanage. For that, I owe her my loyalty and protection.

Any abuse I suffer at her hand is only the penance I willingly pay for letting my fear of water keep me from getting on the boat with my family. For letting G, whom I promised I would always watch over and protect, climb aboard without me.

At that thought, the image of the white feathers on the mantle flutters in. I know I'm not a coward for my inability to serve in the war; Aunt Elizabeth would die if left alone. But my aunt isn't wrong when she calls me *little coward Lucas*. Not wrong at all. And I will never stop accepting the white wings of the devil that remind me of such. I only pray God will see fit to end my penance soon.

When I arrive at the Chilwell factory a little over twenty minutes later, I'm out of breath but no longer cold. I stop to catch my breath and stare in awe at the incredible two-hundred acre site sheltered quite impressively between the neighboring hills reaching toward the sky. I remember hearing rumors that the placement here was to hide the buildings from the attention of potential enemies. I'm not sure where those rumors came from, seeing as the location is undisclosed anyhow, as are all ammunition factories throughout England. The War Office forbid the printing and publication of such addresses to keep the locations out of the hands of our opponents. Unless they are employed there, even most of Beeston's citizens have only a general idea of its whereabouts. It was only last week that I, myself, saw the grandeur that is the Chilwell factory for the first time when I accompanied Poppy on her scouting mission to learn the size and location in preparation for today's protest.

I move down the length of the multistory, wrought iron fence that encloses the factory site toward the gated entrance, expecting to see protestors and signs, women with banners slung across their chests, and angry factory employees shooing them all away, but there is nothing of the sort. Instead, I find Poppy facing off with a man by herself, their bodies bent forward at sharp angles, their faces only inches apart.

I jog faster toward them.

The man is no taller than she is without his top hat, which stands askew on his head, showing thick, gray hair beneath. His round face is quite purple, a color I don't think is normal for this man's skin tone, seeing as the hands he's flailing around are as white as the snow threatening to fall.

I'm close enough now that I can hear the high-pitched octave of Poppy's voice. When she has reached this level of projecting, I know she is moments away from combusting or saying something she *should* regret but won't.

Standing behind the feuding couple, I stick out my hand and touch Poppy's elbow to alert her to my presence.

She startles at the touch, and her head whips around to face me. "Luca!" Her jaw loosens for a brief second before her neck swivels back toward her rival.

I keep my hand at the small of her back as I take my place beside her.

At the same moment, a woman exits the factory gate and approaches us. The short bob of her dark hair brushes the top of a brown, collared shirt that is tucked as tightly into her black skirt as her lips are into her teeth. Her face says she is terribly put out by the inconvenience of being called down to deal with a toddler's tantrum during her busy workday.

When she glares at Poppy, her nose scrunches beneath her spectacles, and I instantly recognize this woman as Mrs. Cecilia

Fischer, owner and resident of the building that houses the Beeston Lace Factory where Poppy has worked for nearly her whole life. *Does Mrs. Fischer work here at the filling factory?*

"What is all the commotion out here about? Do we need to call the authorities, Mr. Ashby?" asks Mrs. Fischer, drawing the angry man's attention her direction.

"Mrs. Fischer, thank heavens you are here. I need you to deal with this insubordinate child." The man pulls a handkerchief from his vest pocket and mops his forehead.

"I am not a child," Poppy snarls.

"What problem is Miss Pemburton causing, Mr. Ashby?" Mrs. Fischer stands beside him, hands calm and shoulders poised.

"You know this wretched girl?"

Mrs. Fischer simply nods as her eyes roll up into her eyebrows, and she sighs deeply, as if she regrets to admit such recognition. She likely does, seeing as Poppy and I used to wreak havoc throughout the Lace Factory building while Jane worked. The Lace Factory business itself occupies only the second floor of the three-story building, but we would play hide-and-seek throughout the entire structure—taking extra special delight in scaring Mrs. Fischer near to death as we popped out from behind boxes in the storage rooms on the third floor, where her apartment also happened to reside. To escape her pursuit of our capture, we would slip in and out of windows, only ever breaking one in the five- or six-year timespan we spent playing there. And that was my fault, not Poppy's—a painful lesson that one should never run forward while looking backward over one's shoulder.

"This child, Mrs. Fischer," Mr. Ashby says drawing out the word *child*, "has thought she might hold a protest at our factory, *my* factory, and has done so by throwing rocks at my windows, yelling untrue nonsense at my employees as they enter the factory, and even going so far as to call me, the manager of this fine establishment—an establishment that is meant to bring our men on the front lines of France the ammunition they need to defeat Germany, mind you—'a Kaiser-loving scumbag.'" Mr. Ashby's shoulders shake with the energy of a penned-in bull, and his face turns an even deeper shade of purple as he relates the last offense through tight lips, spit spewing in all directions.

My fingers itch to take hold of his handkerchief and wipe his chin, but I refrain. Instead, I cast a sidelong glance at Poppy, trying to catch her response to these accusations, and I see nothing but pride etched into her features. I'd hoped the man was exaggerating, but clearly he is not. I want to both shake Poppy's shoulders for being so foolish and shake her hand in celebration of her strong-willed audacity.

"A protest?" Mrs. Fischer says. I watch her eyes narrow in what must be confusion as she looks around and notices, as did I, that nobody else is here.

Mr. Ashby continues undeterred. "She is a belligerent girl who doesn't know her place and has no desire to support our troops fighting overseas."

Anguish flashes in Poppy's eyes. I increase the pressure of my supporting hand around her waist and give a gentle squeeze.

Flames of fire rekindle in her gaze and swallow the sorrow as though it never existed. "My place, sir," Poppy squares her chin, "is wherever I can stand the tallest. The troops shouldn't be overseas. They should be home with their families."

"That is precisely why we do what we do here, Miss Pemburton," Mrs. Fischer says, her voice as sharp as the angles of her jaw. "We provide the ammunition our soldiers need to defend themselves so they can come *home* to their families. We ensure there is a way for our men to defend Britain." Somehow, Mrs. Fischer straightens even more, standing tall with a certain pride in her stance. "Working here at the Chilwell National Shell Filling Factory is a great honor. A noble way to serve your country. It is a privilege to walk into this factory every day and do our bit to support the war effort." Mrs. Fischer lowers her voice, and her words soften slightly. "We are all in this war, Poppy, whether we like it or not. The only choice you have now is to join or to sit by and watch the men you love die, knowing you did nothing in your power to bring them home."

Poppy's eyes widen, and she sucks in a breath.

Mr. Ashby crosses his beefy arms across his chest and nods in something like triumph as if he were the one who put Poppy in her place. "Mrs. Fischer, as the women's supervisor of this establishment, I trust you will take care of our little problem here." He points an accusing finger just a breath away from Poppy's nose.

I ready myself to grab that accusing finger if it gets any closer to her.

He continues, "I had better never see you on these grounds again. As manager over this factory, I will have no choice but to have you arrested for trespassing if I see so much as one of your abhorrent red hairs in my line of sight." Spittle dribbles down his chin as he fires the last few words through teeth clenched so tight I fear he might break a tooth.

"Oh, I wouldn't dream of trespassing on your little bomb-filled land mine, Mr. Holy One," Poppy taunts as she mockingly bows before him.

Mr. Ashby lunges toward her with a bellow right as I pull her swiftly away. In one motion, I sweep her up into a cradle position in my arms and run.

"Wait, I'm not finished!" Poppy protests as she struggles futilely against my hold.

"Oh, you are definitely finished, Firebird."

Over my shoulder Poppy yells at a now distant Mr. Ashby, "I hope you sleep well at night knowing you are blowing up good men who have wives and children back at home."

Mr. Ashby's gruff voice carries on as well, but the wind rushing past keeps us from hearing it. While her verbal attack on this Mr. Ashby fellow may not have been the best way to handle her anger at her father for enlisting to fight, Poppy must always have something tangible to hold on to when her world erupts, and this protest of sorts was hers.

Once the factory is out of sight, I slow to a walk. Poppy jumps out of my arms, but when her feet touch the ground, she pulls me into a fierce embrace.

"Thank you for coming." Her breath tickles the hairs along the side of my neck, and I hold very still so she doesn't sense the shiver it sends dancing down my spine. I've learned how imperative it is to our friendship to keep those desires to myself. "Those goons were unbelievable," she huffs.

I slide my hands around her waist and hug her to me. "Happy Birthday, Firebird," I whisper into her ear. "I'm sorry I was late. I came as soon as I could." Then I ask, "Where were all your supporters? All the women with the signs and the banners? You wanted to celebrate your birthday with your favorite anti-war signs and these well-loved marching boots." With my shoe, I tap the edges of her brown leather boots, which are coming apart at both the seams and the laces. "Did you not invite anyone else to your party?"

"Nobody showed." I can't see her face, but the straight spine of her back arches softly beneath my fingertips as her shoulders droop against me, telling me everything I need to know. I want to keep talking like this, holding her in my arms, offering my support, feeling the weight of her against me and the closeness of her lips, but she steps back, and I'm forced to let her go.

"Well, should we celebrate your birthday, or was that enough excitement for one day?"

The corner of her mouth pulls into a smile. "What did you have in mind?"

"Fry's Five Boys chocolate bars and the church roof."

Poppy spins away from me, laughing. "Race you there!" She takes off down the dirt road.

I watch as her hair plays with the wind and listen as her laughter lights up the space around her like fireflies in the dark, and I know I would chase after her all day to any location in the world, if only she would let me.

3

CHARLES

BEESTON, NOTTINGHAMSHIRE, ENGLAND
MARCH 29, 1916

EVERY PART OF MY BODY ACHES, BUT IT'S THE DELIRIUM THAT threatens to kill me. Either that or the boredom.

After rolling my shoulders back, I stretch my arms out in front of me and admire the way my muscles flex beneath my thin, white cotton shirt. I steal a glance at the Glashutte on my wrist, a handmade gift from my late father who was a German watchmaker. Ten minutes and I can flee this cramped office and debilitating chair for home. Not my home, of course. Never back to my home. That is not an option. To whatever "home" Gukenstein, my intelligence superior, arranged for me in this poor excuse of a town.

Apparently, I'm to share living quarters with one of the village preachers, Jerimiah Jones, and his wife, Mabel. When I met Gukenstein at our rendezvous in Marseille, France, before we crossed to England, I overheard him discuss the arrangement with my new mission contact, N18, who will be operating under the cover of "cousin."

I scoff at the irony of *me* living in the back of a church with a man of God. But right now, after being yanked from my previous mission without warning, thirty-nine hours of rushed, sleepless travel, followed by immediately reporting to my new assignment as the Beeston Nottinghamshire Post Office manager, I would crawl into bed with a Frenchman if it meant I would get a moment of sleep.

I force my attention to the identity papers on the desk in front of me in the small, cramped closet I'm told is my manager's office, as if I haven't studied my new life with religious vigor since they were handed to me twenty-four hours ago. I know the drill: commit the new information to memory until I no longer remember my previous identity, Monsieur LeBlanc. Or the identity that died before that one, Petrus Goossens. Or my training identity, Aleksy Balinski, which should be so far from memory I shouldn't be able to recall it. Gukenstein would be livid if he knew. Most importantly, I should not remember my real identity: Jakob Kirtchner, age twenty-seven, of Munich, Germany.

It has been easy to forget Jakob.

Every spy has something they do to keep themselves grounded during missions; otherwise, they would lose their sanity along with their identity. Remembering is my thing; it's both a blessing and a curse.

I repeat the facts of the new character Gukenstein has created for me over and over with my eyes closed until I can speak the words forwards, backwards, and with conviction.

Until I am, indeed, *Charles Andrews*.

Identity: Charles Andrews. Twenty-seven years old. Far West Texas, USA. Postal employee.
Family: Mother and Father: Sarah and Alfred Andrews (father deceased), Cattle farmers
Older brother: Timothy (twenty-eight)
Younger brother: James (twenty)
Occupation: Post office manager of the Beeston, Nottinghamshire Post Office.
Reason for move from USA to England: Wanted to escape the pressures at home to run the family ranch with my older brother Timothy. When my cousin from

Clifton, Nottingham, a town just southeast of Beeston, mentioned the elderly man who ran the Beeston Post Office was going to be retiring soon, I put my hat in the ring for the job in hopes of getting as far away from home as possible.

I study the photographs attached to my character profile, all at a cattle ranch in Far West Texas, USA. I visualize myself there, and I must say I don't hate what I see. A setting sun blankets the wide-open grassy plains with golden light that highlights my tanned skin as I help Timothy herd the cattle to pasture. Imagining the strong thunder of horse's hooves beneath my saddle, the tough grip of the leather reins in my hands on the long cattle drive, and the cool sweat dripping from my brow beneath my cowboy hat after a long evening at the round-up has me ready to head straight to Texas after my stint in England. And I have to admit, I *am* a very attractive cattle hand in my imaginary cowboy hat and boots.

The bell above the post office door out in the lobby tinkles a faint welcome to whoever just walked in, and I glance again at the time on my Glashutte. Five minutes until the post office is officially closed. I close my eyes and place my head on the desk in the tiny back room. If I'm silent, hopefully whomever it is will go away.

There is rustling around the desk out front, and I debate giving up my silent treatment, but I hold to my resolve when I hear a female voice yell out, "Hello? Mr. Johnson? Excuse me? Hello? Is anybody here? I have only three letters to post, but they must be on this evening's outgoing train, so do hurry." Her voice is whiny, and it grates on every nerve I have left within me.

Is it too late to pretend I don't know the English language?

I grip the edges of my identity papers, remembering three nights ago when Gukenstein told me my mission in France was over—my cover blown—and I'd be speaking English for the remainder of the war. Now I'm here in this forsaken town as punishment.

"This isn't a punishment, Kirtchner," Gukenstein had said, slamming his fist against the wall of the safe house minutes before the French police invaded. "This is an opportunity for you to earn the transfer out you've been asking for and not be dishonorably dismissed from duty. I had to pull strings to get a post office manager position this close to where we believe the biggest ammunition factory in England lies." He thrust a map at me. "If our intel is correct, the shell filling factory has been running operations for several months somewhere within a twenty-five-mile radius of the post office. I've been waiting for the right soldier, a soldier who already speaks the language fluently, to send in for the job."

England takes me even further away from Mutter. I can't protect her from my tyrannical stepfather with an ocean between us. But I also knew refusing Gukenstein on the brink of my arrest in France was not an option.

My knuckles burned white and hot against the pressure of my closed fists as I asked, "What's the job?"

"Use the position as post office manager to intercept and censor all incoming and outgoing mail on Germany's behalf. Make nice with the townspeople; get them to talk. Find where the factory is located and then infiltrate it." He looked me in the eye. "You want the coveted position as liaison interpreter for the German Empire? Do this last job in England. When the war is over, so is your life as a spy. You have my word."

That's all I want: to be out of the world of spies and espionage that keeps me constantly on the run.

I sigh and come back to the present. "We're closed," I call down the hall to the woman I can hear making exasperated sounds.

N18 spent the entire journey from Marseille to London helping my practiced English become thick with a Texan drawl. *"It's passable." N18 shrugged as I shook her hand goodbye in London before catching the train on to Beeston. "But passable isn't good enough. Perfect it as though your life depends on it. Because it does."*

"Closed?" The woman in the lobby lets out a harrumph, followed by a grunt, and then says, "Who's there? Who am I speaking with, please?"

I ignore her. I've made a decision, and I will not rescind.

"The cuckoo clock standing behind me shows that it's not quite five o'clock, so you can't be closed yet. Mr. Johnson never closes before the cuckoo bird runs five times around the clock. I have some mail from the Beeston Lace Factory that must go out today, sir. If you'd be so kind as to come process these letters and get them postmarked, I'd be much obliged."

I run a hand across my face and say every swear word I know in all five languages I know them in before calling out as definitively, and as Texan, as possible, "We're. Closed."

This time there is silence on her end. Beautiful, sweet, perfect silence for several minutes. She was easier to shake than I anticipated.

I release a deep breath.

Finally. This day is finally over. I need whiskey, food, and sleep. Preferably in that order.

I gather up my leather satchel, stuff my identity paperwork inside, grab the cowboy hat Gukenstein insisted I wear in public, and flick off the office light.

Three steps into the hall that connects the manager's office to the help desk in the lobby, I see mounds of black fabric atop the white service counter. As I move forward a few more steps, I realize there is a woman amid the fabric. A tall woman with hair the color of spilt blood is standing on my counter. She is bent over at the waist, tugging at the hem of her black dress, which appears to be caught on the heel of her boot, muttering profanities to herself. *Classy.*

I exhale slowly, place the cowboy hat on my head, and silently curse Gukenstein for the hundredth time in twenty-four hours.

This woman is the very definition of the word *punishment*.

"I beg yer pardon, miss. Git down off my counter this instant."

The woman jolts at the sound of my voice and nearly falls from the counter before glaring at me with large, blue eyes nearly hidden behind chunks of red hair that catch around her face. I'm tempted to pull her hair back so I can see more of her, but I keep my hands pressed firm and unmoving on my hips.

"I most certainly will not remove myself until you promise that you will postmark these letters," the woman says. "They must go out this evening." She yanks the struggling piece of hem from its prison, then stands to her full height and crosses her arms defiantly.

My jaw tightens as I consider how much work this clearly unhinged woman is going to be. I just want a stiff drink. And at this point, I will do anything to get her to leave.

"Miss—"

"Now. Right now," she interrupts sharply, glancing around the room, avoiding eye contact with me. "Immediately." She matches my posture, placing her hands on her hips, and juts out her chin.

My head flops forward in defeat. I pull the hat from my head, toss it on the counter, and run a hand through my short, cropped hair. A long, slow sigh escapes my lips. "Fine. Just get down from there, alright. I can't have ya gettin' hurt in my post office and then tryin' to harass me for yer own misconduct."

I set down the bag I was carrying and turn around to gather postage supplies, leaving the woman to her own devices to climb down from the tall counter. If she found a way up on her own just to make a point, she can certainly find her way back down.

From behind me a loud flop echoes as she hits the floor, followed by the less enjoyable sound of a crack, then a pop.

"Ohh," she wails.

I rush around to her side of the counter. *Women!* It doesn't matter what country you're in, they're all the same. So deter-

mined to be independent until they are and then realize they can
do nothing without a man.

"See. This is exactly what I was talkin' about. There ya go
gettin' hurt all because ya chose to do somethin' silly like climb
up a counter. Very unlady-like too, I might add." I kneel next to
her on the ground and survey the situation.

She pulls off her boot, the heel of which broke off in the fall,
but nothing on her foot looks swollen.

"Yer fine, right? Nothin' broken?"

She looks me square in the eye, as if challenging me to a
battle of wills.

I hold her gaze steady, accepting the challenge while I gently
move my hand around the edges of her ankle bone to determine
the severity of her injury. This close to her, I notice the smattering of freckles across her cheeks and nose. I want to think
they're ugly. Yet they're anything but, and somehow they cause
the blue of her eyes to deepen.

"It's not broken," I tell her. "It'll just be bruised for a few
days. If ya keep yerself out of trees, *and peoples' hair*, ya shouldn't
have any problems with it healin' up just fine." I stand up and
offer her a hand.

She angles her neck in different directions, glancing around
the empty post office as if to find another offer of help, then
reluctantly stretches her hand out to reach mine.

I pull her to a stand, and after making sure she is balanced
against the counter, I sweep down and pick up three crunched
envelopes from off the floor. "Might these be the very important
letters that need sent?" I look doubtfully at the crumpled mess
in my hands.

"Indeed, they are."

I scan the writing on the outside of the envelopes, then
slowly walk back to my side of the counter. "Well, let's see what
we can do, then, Miss Pemburton." If she's bothered that I
addressed her by her name, she doesn't show it.

"I am delivering these for the Beeston Lace Factory, where I work. It is crucial they are on the outgoing train this evening," she says. "Mr. Barstow, my employer, has a running tab with Mr. Johnson, the post office manager, which he pays at the end of each month. You can add the required postage fees to the tab."

"I'm sure ya know, miss, but Mr. Johnson no longer works here. He retired this mornin'. I am the new manager, and I've had no such discussion with a Mr. Bastard regarding this transaction agreement."

"Mr. Barstow," she corrects me. "And what do you mean, *retired?*"

"Ya, that's what I said: *Barstow*. Retired, you know . . . when you get old and don't want to work no more. Can't say I blame him now that I've spent a day here." I give her a pointed look.

"I know what retired means; I just can't believe he's gone. He's managed this office since I was a child." The woman looks genuinely baffled by this new information.

"Uh huh. Anyhoo," I say moving things along, "I obviously can't just take yer word for the postage fee, now can I? How do I know you can be trusted? All indications of our encounters thus far have shown me that you, as a matter of fact, should not be trusted. You'll need to pay in full for today's transaction if ya'd like those posted today. Otherwise, you can wait until I have a convenient time during which I can meet with yer Mr. Bastard and make such arrangements."

At my response, air flies in and out of her nostrils in rapid succession.

"Careful there, or ya might start a tornado with all that crazy breathin' ya got going on." I run my finger in a circle motion around her nose.

"Fine." The woman breathes out slowly, her eyes lingering on my face. If daggers shot from her eyes, they would certainly hit their mark.

Then, it appears she silently counts down from ten. For some reason, getting under this woman's skin is bringing immense joy back into my life. I smile happily back at her as if nothing about this evening has phased me. She digs through her coin purse.

"How much will it be then, please?" she asks, pouring her coins onto the counter between us.

"Ooh." I make a clucking noise with my tongue and look over at the clock standing against the wall. "It's after five o'clock now, as ya can see, so I'll no longer be able to process yer transaction on this business day, as the office is now closed. I'm truly sorry for any inconvenience, ma'am, but I'll be happy to serve ya tomorrow at nine a.m." I cock my head to the side and smile the smile every other woman on earth swoons at, but judging by the look on her face, makes her want to vomit. Mission accomplished.

"I beg your pardon?" The words stutter from her lips. "It's just hardly after the hour, and . . . and if you hadn't . . . hadn't, well, you know." She begins waving her arm around the room like she's conducting an out-of-tune marching band. "And besides, the cuckoo bird has not come forth yet cuckooing the hour; therefore, it musn't yet be five."

"The cuckoo bird hasn't come forth yet because he no longer comes forth anymore. So, you see, it must be the hour."

"Are you mocking me?" She looks at me astounded.

"I found the little bird thing annoyin', so I cut it out of the clock and took out the springs. Much better not hearin' that little chirp every hour, don't ya agree, Miss Pemburton?"

She huffs. "You will be hearing from my employer tomorrow. He will not be pleased with how you have treated me or the way you have chosen to run this place of business. You disgust me," she spits out.

"How *I* have treated *you?* Was it not yerself who came into *my* place of work, yelled offensively loud demanding to be served, jumped up on *my* counter, tried to break yer own leg to harass my business, and then got angry I wouldn't do the dishonorable thing by postmarking something today that indeed cannot go out until tomorrow? I think the disgust, my dear, lies with you." I place the cowboy hat back on my head and nod definitively.

"Ahh!" The woman shoves her coin purse into the crook of her arm and sweeps up her letters and discarded broken boot with the opposite hand. With her head held high, she flips around and hobbles on her one good boot to the front door.

As she swings the door open, she turns back toward me. "Don't ever call me 'my dear' again, Farm Boy," she calls out coldly before letting the door slam closed behind her.

Farm Boy? I don't hate that. And somehow, I'm not nearly as desperate for that sleep anymore.

4

POPPY

A JUNGLE OF LUSH, GREEN ENGLISH IVY VINES RUN UP THE backside of the Beeston First Church of God. The thick evergreen plants twist together like ropes from the green ground, covering below to the top of the roof and creating the perfect secret ladder to scale the length of the two-story building. When Luca and I were children, the vines were thin and sparse. We had to train our young muscles to pull us up the length of them. Now, it takes only a moment for me to maneuver my body from the ground to this hidden portion of the church's roof, where Luca instructed me to meet him this evening for some sort of surprise.

At the top of my climb, I am met by a four-foot-tall stone wall that runs the length of this portion of the roof. It, too, is covered by the woody climbing vines, but a gap approximately two feet wide in the stone wall opens to a flat, square landing.

I pull myself up over the roof's edge onto the platform and squeeze through the vines' branches that nearly cover the small opening.

Luca stands in the center of the space with his hands behind his back and a smile so big, both dimples adorn his face.

My heart warms at the sight of him.

"Happy Birthday," he says the moment I draw myself to a stand. From behind his back, he pulls out something about the size of a child's doll that's wrapped in what appears to be some sort of canvas cloth.

"My birthday was last month," I say. "Remember the whole ammunition factory protest debacle? I think you saving me from arrest was gift enough, don't you?"

"Indeed. But lucky for you, I am the gift that keeps on giving." He hands me the package as I laugh. "I would have liked to surprise you with these weeks ago, but Aunt Elizabeth poured a vile of her medicine down the basin because she didn't like the taste of it, and I had to purchase a new one with the money I'd saved," Luca says.

My stomach flips when I begin to unravel the cloth and see a pair of brand-new, beautiful black leather Victorian boots—nicer than any I have ever owned. Shiny, black buttons run up the length of each boot, not one button missing. The canvas drops to the ground, and the scent of genuine leather wafts around me. I trace the intricate stitching, my finger gliding along the smooth material.

"Luca," I breathe out. "I . . ."

He knocks his hand against the heel of each boot. "The salesman said these boots are made to last. I made him take a hammer to each heel just to make sure he wasn't scamming me."

"Luca, you shouldn't have. I can't even imagine how much this pair cost. You need new shoes more than I do."

"Since your heel snapped off your dress boot, you've been attending church services in your protest marching boots." He tries to hide his left shoe with only half a sole that's been missing laces for as long as I can remember. "My shoes do me just fine."

"I don't know what to say. This is the nicest gift I've ever received." I hold the boots tight to my chest. "Thank you, Luca. I love them."

He shrugs. "No need to thank me. I'm sorry the new American bloke at the post office didn't help you down off the counter, but I'm not sorry it gave me the opportunity to spoil you just a bit." His tone is thick with warmth and affection, and I find myself wanting to inch closer to him. Wanting to step into the comfort and safety the look in his kind eyes is offering me. And try as I might, which perhaps is not very hard, I can't look away.

His gaze travels in slow, deliberate movements around my face as if he is memorizing every feature, and my skin buzzes with the strange curiosity of what being kissed by Luca Whelan might be like.

Fear escorts me a few steps back, and I sit down against the stone wall and begin removing my old marching boots while searching my mind for a safer topic to explore. "That American is the rudest man I have ever met," I say once I've composed myself. "Well, next to that Mr. Ashby fellow from the ammunition factory. But I will never let him get the better of me. Either of those men for that matter."

"You certainly won't." Luca laughs as he walks toward me, his hands casually tucked in his pockets as if completely unaffected by the way his eyes just held my heart.

"Can you believe all those dreadful things Mr. Ashby said to me that day? What a wicked man. He nearly had me arrested simply for telling the truth. Had you not been there, who knows what else I would have done." Although the incident at the ammunition factory was several weeks ago, Luca and I still had not discussed it further. Once we'd raced up to the church roof and I'd eaten my weight in chocolate bars, I wasn't in the mood to rehash the confrontation. I hadn't brought it up again, so neither had Luca.

"You verbally assaulted the man, Poppy," Luca says. "He very well could have had you arrested for speaking to him that way."

"So you agree I won that argument, then?"

Luca rolls his eyes, but the corners of his mouth lift into a smile.

"Okay fine; it was a tie," I concede.

Luca sits down next to me, pulls out a piece of paper and charcoal from his shirt pocket, and begins to sketch.

"Did you accomplish what you hoped to at your protest?" he asks me.

"Well, it's just as awful of a place as I imagined it would be, but am I ever going to be able to stop the ammunition factory from production as I intended? Am I going to shut the entire factory down like I wanted? As well as every other factory in England?" I sigh. "No, I suppose not. But it felt good to do something I believe in. To use my voice to tell people that I disagree with this war and everything it touches."

"You're never afraid to stand up for what and who you believe in. That's admirable." He gives me a quick look before returning to his sketch. "But remember that they, too, are fighting for something they believe in. The people who work at the ammunition factory, that Mr. Ashby fellow who manages it, our men on the front lines, your father—they all believe in something too, or they wouldn't be where they are. Even the enemy believes what he's doing is right. What makes one of us right and one of us wrong? One of us better and one of us worse?"

My conscious pricks at his words, and an unsettled feeling steeps low in my belly. I don't want to think about the war anymore.

I slide my new boots over my stockings, a perfect fit. When the buttons are securely fastened, Luca helps me stand, and we make our way to the ledge of the roof. Luca leans his back against the stone wall and faces inward, continuing his drawing, while I lean my stomach against the wall's ledge and face out toward the trees surrounding us.

A thick forest of English Oak, Spruce, and Scots Pine stands large and tall, defending our little twenty-square-foot hideaway here. The bare branches of the oaks above us create a natural wood ceiling during the winter. In the late spring and summer, when the leaves are in full bloom, the luscious greenery creates a most gorgeous canopy with leaves in every size and shade of green. But the way the trees come alive in autumn transforms the rooftop into another world altogether.

When I was ten and Luca was eleven, we made a blood pact never to divulge our secret hideaway. I trace the pink scar that runs from the base of my ring finger down the length of my palm, wincing as I remember the way Luca sliced through the flesh of both our palms with his pocketknife. He slammed his hand against mine and squeezed my fingers tight between his as we recited our pact, our small voices etched in pain:

> *"Where the thick vines crawl and God watches over all,*
> *where the stone wall cannot crumble and the patrons will not assemble,*
> *lies a place just for us, only our souls here we will trust."*

A sense of overwhelming nostalgia burns through me at the memories I share here with Luca. "I can't ever imagine leaving Beeston. Can you?" I tilt my head in his direction.

"Every day," he says.

"Pardon me?" My nostalgia deflates.

His cheeks flush, and his eyes widen, as if he hadn't meant to say that out loud. His gaze drops then, and he studies the ground before speaking again. "Beeston isn't to me what it is to you, Poppy."

"Home? Beeston isn't home to you? Because that's what Beeston is to me." I hear the defense rising in my voice as I turn fully to face him. Whether Luca meant to say something or not, he did, and there is no way I can let this conversation slip away now.

"Beeston will always hold a special place in my heart because it's where I met you, but someday I would like to, in the far, far distant future when Aunt Elizabeth is . . . you know, when she is gone. Which won't be for a *long* time . . ."

He's scrambling, and I want to scream at him to just spit out whatever it is he would like to do.

Rub, rub, rub.

"I would like to leave Beeston and move back to Italy." He says the last part so softly it lands on my ears like the brush of a rose petal.

Italy. My mouth drops open. Luca has an adventurous spirit, and I always knew Beeston was too small for him, but Italy?

"Life isn't the same for me here as it is for you, Firebird. I'm not waiting for any family members to return, and I don't have a home that holds special memories or a job with any potential for growth. You have built a life here—a future. But for me, this town is . . . is . . ." he trails off and lets out a long, slow exhale. He licks his lips and traces the scar beneath his chin with his finger. His nervous tell.

I try to prepare myself for the fallout of what his words will do to me.

Because Luca is right about Beeston. This town *is* home for me, and I will never leave its safe borders. Every goal I have for myself and my future is here. I want to live forever in the cottage I grew up in, the cottage my father's parents built with their own hands. I dream of owning the lace factory that I currently manage under the direction of Mr. Barstow, the owner who is rumored to be announcing his retirement this year—the same owner who turned a blind eye as I sat beneath Jane's skirts as a toddler, hidden away until I was old enough to sit beside her and work the machines myself.

Jane. What if Jane were to return to Beeston someday and I had moved away? How would she find me? And I want to continue healing my broken relationship with Father if—when— he returns.

I want all these things, but I want Luca to be here too.

In the distance, the sound of alarm bells ringing on a Beeston Fire Brigade truck slices the silent air between us, bringing Luca and I back to the present moment.

"What is this town to you, Luca?"

"It's my prison." His shoulders inch upward and slowly ease back down as if they're voicing an apology.

The truth stings my heart. How is my haven Luca's prison? I know Luca feels somewhat trapped as Aunt Elizabeth's caretaker. That he takes care of her because he is a good Christian man. I was not aware, however, how desperate he is to be free of her. I was not aware that he hated our town so much he plans to flee the entire country the first chance he has.

Truth be told, I'd have let Aunt Elizabeth sit in that cottage and rot until she's deader than dead because she deserves nothing less. And I am quite certain the good Lord agrees, but I guess I should be grateful she's still alive if it's the only thing keeping Luca here.

"I want to go back to Italy," he says, his voice pleading for me to understand. "To make something of myself, yes, but also to learn more about my parents, my grandparents, my heritage. More about who I am." Luca turns to face out toward the tree line, tucks the paper and charcoal stick back into his shirt pocket, and rests his forearms on the ledge of the stone wall, his side pressed against mine. "And I need to face what I did." His jaw is clenched.

"What did you do?"

"I let cowardice win. I didn't get on the boat."

"You couldn't have saved them, Luca. No one could have."

"Maybe not. But I shouldn't have stayed behind."

My heart aches for him. For the weight I sense he is feeling. I reach out and pull him into my arms.

He molds to my body, and I wish I knew how to ease his burden. I'd assumed he made peace with the tragic loss of his family. He never talks about it. Once he learned English, he settled into Beeston comfortably. Or so I'd thought. And although I knew he didn't love his Aunt Elizabeth, I thought he'd made a life here he loved.

I had no idea how wrong I've been—how much guilt he's carried. How long has he been suffering alone? Could I have done something, said something, that would have made a difference?

Luca steps out of my embrace and tucks a strand of hair behind my ear. His finger traces a soft line down my cheek before he gives me a silly, dimpled smile and says, "Don't worry, Firebird. I will be here to bother you for a very long time. You'll surely be married off and too busy for our crazy antics by the time I leave Beeston anyhow."

"Oh no, I am *never* getting married," I say. I see the tight flinch behind Luca's eyes when I emphasize the word *never*, but he blinks it away quickly. I continue, "Loving people makes you vulnerable. Weak. I can't love anyone. I won't." I shake my head. "I saw what that kind of love did to my father when Jane left us. When you love people, you give them power over you. Power to hurt you. Power to break you." I look down at my hands, embarrassed by my truths. "And I don't have any pieces of myself big enough left to break."

I sense Luca's gaze on my face, studying me.

"What if love could put those pieces back together?" he asks.

My heart skips its next beat and slams into my throat unannounced. If anyone could put my heart back together, it would be Luca.

But fear reminds me that I can't let him do that just to let him shatter it again when he leaves someday. Saying yes to loving him now would be as if I handed him the hammer myself. If my own mother couldn't love me, who could?

"I am not worthy of that kind of love," I say.

Luca raises my chin until I'm looking in his eyes. "You are more than worthy."

I want to look away, but I'm mesmerized by the way his eyes speak to me in a way they never have before. Mesmerized by the way my soul comes alive and yearns for him with merely a look.

He takes my face in his hand, and his thumb grazes my jaw so softly I'm not positive I'm being touched at all. "You don't have to earn your worth, Poppy. Your worth belongs to you. It's already yours independent of what anyone else thinks or says." Luca bends his head and rests it against my forehead, our noses nearly touching. His breath dances along my lips as he speaks. "I would never allow anyone to tell you otherwise—not even yourself."

"You can't protect me from everything, Luca."

"But I want to anyway." His hand cradles my face, his fingers soft against my cheek.

My heart pounds on the door of my resolve, telling me to loosen the strongholds within me, and my fortifications weaken ever so slightly. His eyes are so close I can see the incredible mix of blues and greens that make a shade of color that exists only for Luca Whelan.

Come in for a quick dip, his pools of sea glass urge me. *Nothing bad will happen here.*

"Poppy," Luca whispers my name. A plea. The word hangs heavy in the air between us, as if it's somehow made of glass. Neither of us speaks, not wanting to cause the inevitable shatter we both know will come with more words.

Rub, rub, rub.

No, I can't do this. I cannot afford to fall. Not with Father gone. Not with Luca's desire to leave hanging in the balance.

It's not the right time, my resolve says, pounding back on my treacherous heart and commanding the bloody organ to fortify its strongholds. I can't lose Luca the way I've lost everyone else. And eventually I *will* lose him; he said so himself. And if I love him when I do, I will never recover. Because even if I could trust him with my heart, he has to leave Beeston, and I have to stay. I can't give Luca my heart, no matter how much I want to.

Because if I lose Luca, I lose everything.

"I need to go. I'm sorry." I step away from him and run toward the opening in the church roof. "Thank you for the boots."

"Wait, Poppy. Please don't leave." He crosses the space and pulls the sketch paper from his pocket. "Look." He lays the artwork flat on his upturned palm.

I glance down at the drawing.

My own freckled face stares back at me, only it isn't my face exactly. The lines are too soft and curved, my eyes too light and hopeful.

"That doesn't look like me." I shrug.

"It's what you look like when you're up here with me." Luca takes my hand in his and strokes the back of it with his thumb. "Please stay."

My heart races at the husky sound in his voice and the heat of his touch, but when moisture fills my eyes, I know it's time to go.

"I'm sorry." I pull my hand from his, push my way through the small opening, and scale down the vines.

When I reach the ground, I look up. Luca's lips are pulled tight together, his jawline sharp. He puts one hand up in a small goodbye over the ledge, while his other hand worries the underside of his chin.

I turn and run, letting the chill of the spring night air erase the chill in my veins. *It was your own fault*, fear chastises me. I know better than to be vulnerable with Luca. I know better than to share intimate thoughts and touches. I need to get back home. To ground myself.

As I round the corner of the street that leads to Aunt Elizabeth's cottage, one street away from my own, sounds of the Beeston Fire Brigade alarm bells get louder, and a heavy scent of smoke permeates the air.

My heart freezes within my chest in the same moment that my feet begin to fly.

Aunt Elizabeth's cottage is drowning in flames.

5

POPPY

BEESTON, NOTTINGHAMSHIRE, ENGLAND
APRIL 25, 1916

A GENTLE SPRINKLE OF RAIN MIXES WITH THE SOFT, YELLOW haze emanating from the oil-lit street lamps in the early evening air above me. I move down the vacant street that leads to my cottage and push through the wooden gate. A large, brown basket with a blue cloth placed over the opening sits on my doorstep. After a long day of trimming fabric ends and settling petty squabbles at the lace factory, whatever is on my porch is a welcome distraction to my weary mind.

I run up the dirt path, eager to peek beneath the cloth. My mouth waters instantly when I pull it off and see piles of Fry's Five Boys milk chocolate bars. There must be nearly a hundred chocolate bars in here!

Luca.

What is he getting at? He always brings me a Fry's Five Boys bar from the Sweet Shoppe on Friday—*Five Boys Friday* we call it—but it's only Tuesday. And why are there so many?

"Are there enough?"

I drop the cloth, surprised at the sound of Luca's voice behind me.

"Enough to feed a small army." I laugh and turn to face him.

The laughter falls dead on my lips the moment I catch sight of him.

A khaki military uniform dons his body. The same military uniform my father wore the day I watched him walk onto the train two months ago.

Air becomes strangled behind the lump in my throat.

"Why are you wearing that?" I hear the accusation in my tone.

Luca sobers quickly and looks down at his hands, avoiding my gaze. "One chocolate bar for every Friday that I will be gone."

"Luca." When his name leaves my lips, I'm not certain if it's a statement, a question, an accusation, or a warning.

"I depart on the next outgoing train this evening."

This evening? My hands clutch the skirt of my dress as I lean back into the wooden door of my cottage, allowing it to hold me upright.

It's only been seven days. Seven days since Aunt Elizabeth died, cremated in a fire that took her, the cottage, and everything inside of it. Luca didn't own much—only a few items of clothing, his charcoals, and his artwork—but what he'd had he loved.

The mortician said Aunt Elizabeth's body was found half inside the fireplace with a shattered bottle of alcohol next to her. Luca suspects she was reaching for a bottle of brandy he'd hidden away from her inside the large, gaudy green vase that sat atop their mantle. It was pushed to the far back corner where he knew she couldn't reach it. He didn't know how she knew the alcohol was in there or how she thought she was going to retrieve it, but darn it all if she hadn't fallen flat into that fire trying to get to it. Stupid woman.

For seven days we have avoided the conversation of what Aunt Elizabeth's death means for Luca's future. For seven days we have pretended the conversation we had on the church roof only hours before the woman's death did not happen.

I thought we would have more time. More time to talk. More time to plan a solution that worked for both of us.

I never considered the possibility of Luca enlisting in the very war I despise. He was there when my father left. How could he do the same thing?

Words fumble around in my mind, running into one another. Thoughts collide hard with feelings. Questions rush forward so quickly I can't process how to ask them.

"I . . . I don't understand."

"I went into the army office this morning to enlist. Officer Gentry said they still had a few spots open in the infantry leaving this evening. This is the last train running from Beeston to London for several days." His bottom lip quivers with a tremble so slight I almost miss it before he catches it between his teeth and presses on, "Now that I have made this decision, I know if I don't get on that train tonight, I won't be able to do it. I can't stand next to you every day with a departure like that hanging over us."

Rub, rub, rub.

The ring in my pocket warms quickly between the strength of my fingers. Fear laughs at me in her mocking way.

I push off the door and pace in the small space beneath the thatched awning. "What about Italy? What about me? You can't do this, Luca. You can't leave me here alone." My voice is thick with emotion I can't hide.

Luca stills me with a warm hand on my wrist, and guides me back to him. His green eyes bore into mine as he holds me firmly in front of him. "Poppy, you are so much stronger than you realize." His voice is strong. Confident.

"Please don't leave," I plead, softly reaching up to touch his face. "I need you." The next words rush out before I can stop them: "Marry me, Luca. If you love me, stay and marry me."

"No."

"No?" I can't keep the hurt out of my voice.

He doesn't speak for several moments.

When he does, every last string holding my heart in place breaks. "I will not marry you, Poppy Pemburton." Luca pulls me into his chest and wraps his arms around my waist. "I love you," he whispers. "I have loved you since the moment you put your hand in mine, led me to the back of the church, and told me that if I didn't learn how to properly climb vines, I was no kind of boy you wanted to be friends with. I love your passion to achieve, your ability to hope, and your courage to stand back up when you fall." His lips brush as light as feathers against my ear, and his voice deepens. "But what I love most about you are your scars. The scars I can see—" he pulls my hand up between us and traces the scar from our blood pact on my palm—"and the ones I can't." He moves his finger to my heart and taps gently.

I nearly come undone at the soft pressure of his touch.

"There is nothing I want more than to marry you, but *I* am not everything to *you*. Until you can truthfully say that I am—until you can say that you love me—I will not marry you."

"But I . . . I do. Of course I do," I say. *I could.*

"No, Poppy, you don't." He says it with so much kindness I want to cry. "You can't even pretend to say the words." He offers up a soft smile. "You're afraid of losing me, and that's not the same thing. We both deserve to marry someone who loves us—not someone who simply fears our absence."

I know he's right, and I want to despise him for the truth he speaks, but I can't.

I drop my head and pull my black shawl tighter about my body as if the familiar threads could create a shield around me.

"There are some things I need to figure out too. Things I need to overcome on my own," Luca says, fidgeting with the scar beneath his chin. "But one day I *will* marry you, Firebird."

Chills race up my spine at the conviction behind his words. Chills I find I don't want to push away—don't want to run from now.

Luca places a soft kiss on my forehead and lets his lips linger against my skin as he speaks. "Because one day, you won't be afraid to love me back. And one day, I will come back to you as the hero you think I am."

"I wish you could see yourself the way I see you, Luca," I say. "Then you would know you already are a hero. If my scars are what you love about me, why can't you love your scars too?"

Luca studies my face for a few beats before taking several steps back. He fiddles with the cuffs of his uniform sleeve and after a moment says, "Mine aren't scars. Mine are still open wounds that I can't heal here." He reaches into the satchel slung over his shoulder and retrieves a white feather. He holds it out in the space between us and absently twirls the plume between his thumb and forefinger as he speaks. "This morning as I was walking into Humber for my shift, a girl handed me this white feather. Typically, the girls thrust them in my direction and simply yell at me to do my bit. But this girl planted herself in front of me and slowly tucked the feather into my shirt pocket as she blatantly questioned how I could allow my fellow chaps and classmates to stand tall next to their rifles while I cower behind the women left behind. She told me to stop being a coward. To serve my country by standing for myself and for those who need my protection."

Luca shakes his head, and his eyes gloss over. "In that moment, Poppy, I knew I had to go. Not to Italy but to France. And not because of the girl's opinion of me, or the feather, or even because I'm grateful for this country, although I am. I made the decision to enlist because I need to know if I'm able to stand for *myself*. I need to know if I truly am a coward." His voice is so low, I can hardly make out the words. "I have the chance to prove Aunt Elizabeth wrong. To prove to myself that I'm not the worthless boy who will never amount to anything." He looks everywhere but at me. "Someday, I want to go back to Italy and make peace with what happened, but I need to find out the truth about who I am first. I suppose it's time to face the enemy."

"Who's the enemy?"

The forlorn shrug of Luca's shoulders as he tucks the feather back inside the satchel nearly breaks me.

"I don't believe in this crazy war one bit," I say, "but I believe in you, Luca. I always have. If this is something you think you need to do . . ."

Rub, rub, rub.

My bottom lip starts to tremble, so I bite down hard to keep my emotions in control before I continue. "I won't try to stop you or make you feel bad about going." I try hard to smile for him.

His eyes explore my face before settling intently on my lips.

There isn't a fairground ride in the world that compares to the way my stomach drops as Luca studies my mouth like it's a treasure map that will disappear at any moment. Beats of fear mixed with desire flutter through my chest so rapidly I scarcely register the steps he takes to close the remaining space between us.

My heart is the switchboard, and Luca is the conductor, flipping all the switches at once as he places both of his hands on the sides of my waist drawing me to him. This train is going completely off the rails, but all I want to do is hold on for dear life and see where it takes me.

His eyes, an intimate shade of soft green in this light, lock onto mine longingly.

Luca Whelan is going to kiss me, and I am not going to stop him.

"When I do fall in love with you, Luca," I say, "how will I prove it to you?"

"You won't have to prove it, Firebird. I'll know."

My cheeks grow hot, and my hands move of their own accord to Luca's chest. I notice my fingers trembling against the rough collar of his uniform, so I grip the fabric of his shirt to steady them.

His strong hands pull me even closer to him, then slide slowly up my back, leaving a path of yearning everywhere he touches. Fear must have abandoned its guardian post, because everything in me is desperate to know where Luca's touch will take me.

He bends his face to mine and waits patiently for permission, his mouth no more than a breath away from my own.

I close my eyes and bring him to me.

Luca kisses me gently at first, his lips caressing mine tenderly, carefully, as if I'm a priceless heirloom. The movement of his mouth against mine is slow, deliberate, and soft, but it speaks volumes. It's as if he knows this is his last moment to tell me he loves me in a way only one's soul can communicate. I will never be the same after this kiss. There is no one and nothing outside of this space that matters.

Luca cups my face, and as he deepens the kiss, I memorize the way my chest explodes with joy and warm desire. The way my body melts against his. The way he tastes slightly of mint, and hope, and just a whit of sadness. The way he smells like the color blue—fresh, clean, alive. The way his soft hair feels tangled between my fingers. The way my heartbeat thuds in my ears, my fingertips, my chest—a rhythm only Luca will ever know. In mere moments, my heart has created a melody for only him. For only us.

Slowly, he pulls away from me. I look into his eyes and am in complete disbelief that this is the same man who walked up to me only minutes ago. Because I am not the same woman. I have been on a trip around the world with that kiss, and I never want to return.

Luca smiles down at me, his eyes more alive than I have ever seen them. "Oh, Firebird, what have you done?"

"I'm quite certain I have just left you something to remember me by."

He laughs. "Indeed, you have. As long as I live, I shall never forget that kiss." He pauses a moment and then pretends to look around frantically. "Wait! Oh no, I'm starting to forget already! I think we must do it again to keep it fresh in my memory." Dimples break out beneath his presumptuous smile.

He brings his lips back to mine, and this time they are full of a passion I want to explore, a desperation I want to understand, a promise I want to believe. I'm almost convinced I'm going to walk straight to the Beeston chapel, where I will force Preacher Jones to marry Luca and I while his wife, Mabel, plays a love song on her harp, when the sudden horn of an automobile beeps in loud succession as it rolls down the street past my cottage.

Time rushes in without warning, a ticking clock swinging on a pendulum between us. Luca slows our pace, and I know the moment our kiss of discovery, longing, and promises turns into a kiss of goodbye.

"Firebird, Firebird, Firebird." Luca chuckles as we break apart. "How am I supposed to leave after a kiss like that?"

"You know, you never have told me why you call me Firebird."

Luca shakes his head, and his face reddens, and now I must know.

"Please," I say when he continues to keep quiet.

"Okay. It's silly though. Keep in mind I was only seven." He takes a breath and starts: "My father used to tell G and I a story of a large bird with majestic plumage that glows brightly, emitting red, orange, and yellow light like a bonfire that's just past the turbulent flame. The firebird. It is beautiful but dangerous. In Russian folklore, he told us, the firebird represents a treasure that is rare and difficult to possess. A marvel that is highly coveted but both a blessing and a bringer of doom to its captor. The fact that even just one of its feathers contains magic suggests the great power of the bird.

"With that, Papi would pull a long, bright-red bird feather from out of his hands as if by pure magic. Giovanni and I were wowed, our tiny minds enthralled by the concept of this mythical creature. 'Every magical story begins with this feather, Luca,' my papi had said, smiling, loving how he'd enraptured us with his tale.

"The first day I saw you in Beeston, I was a shy seven-year-old boy who couldn't speak your language, but your hair reminded me of my father's red feather and the story of the firebird. I didn't know your name, so I called you Firebird."

I grin. "Luca, that's not silly at all! I consider it an absolute honor that you bestowed upon me such a powerful nickname. I truly could not love it more." My heart melts within my chest at the thought of Luca's sweet seven-year-old face looking at my crazy, untamed red hair and being reminded of such a tender, special part of his childhood. "But," I look into his eyes, trying to gauge his reaction, "do you think I'm a bringer of doom?"

Luca narrows his eyes as if thinking deeply. "You are beautiful but dangerous. A marvel and a blessing. A bringer of doom though? I couldn't say. I'm not trying to capture you, so I suppose I'm safe from your fiery clutches." Luca winks, then takes hold of my hand and leads me out from under the porch awning.

We walk toward the wooden gate in silence, the cool drizzle of rain unapologetically robbing us of our warm, intimate moment.

"I love you," he says and squeezes my hand.

"I know." I squeeze back.

Luca takes a deep breath. "I'm going to leave now, Poppy. I'm going to turn away from you and run all the way to the train station. And I'm not going to look back, because I don't trust myself to keep moving forward if I see your face again." He smiles, though there's a sadness that fills his eyes. "And don't tell me you love me now, because I won't be able to get on that train if you do." Luca kisses the backside of my hand, picks up his traveling case, and disappears through the gate.

Tears slide down my face, and I don't try to stop them. I stand frozen to my spot, my hand pressed to my lips to keep from crying out, my head shaking back and forth as if the movement itself could refuse the heavy ache settling in my chest.

For the second time in as many months, the word *goodbye* slips through my lips, unnoticed to a man in uniform.

As I watch him run until there's no more khaki in view, I know I will do anything in my power to bring him home because now I know, beyond any voice of reason, a truth I have never allowed myself to hold.

I love Luca Whelan.

There is no other option than Luca coming back home safe. Because the only thing worse than the thought of Luca dying in the war is the thought of Luca dying without hearing those words from me.

6

LUCA

TRAIN EN ROUTE TO THE CANNOCK CHASE
TRAINING FACILITY IN STAFFORDSHIRE
APRIL 25, 1916

THE TRAIN CAR JOSTLES ME FROM SIDE TO SIDE AS IT HURTLES down the track, my head bouncing along in rhythm with the movement. It's hard to get any rest this way, but I wouldn't be able to sleep anyhow. Not with the way my stomach is twisted in knots.

The past seven days are a blur of questions and decisions smeared with guilt. How did my aunt know the alcohol was in that vase? I should have emptied the bottle sooner—a regret I will carry with me for the rest of my life. I take responsibility for what befell her, but am I a sinner for the relief that cascaded down my being the moment I realized I will never be abused at her hand again? Will God cast me aside for my complete lack of sorrow at her death?

Freedom was on my doorstep for the first time in seventeen years, and I wanted it with such desperation my soul physically ached for reprieve, yet even then, enlisting as a soldier was not an option I considered at first. I knew the passion with which Poppy despised this war. But when the white feather was tucked over my heart and my cowardice was called out, the verses of Aunt Elizabeth's special nursery rhyme repeated in my mind. And as it did so, I realized that before I could go to Italy and face my past, before I could relive the days of my childhood innocence and return to the home where I was taught by my father to live bravely amongst the bandits who surrounded our village and by my mother to honor and care for the people I love, and before I could promise Poppy that she could trust me with her heart, I needed to discover what kind of man I was. I needed to put myself to the test. I needed to fight—my own demons if nothing else.

The hardest thing I've ever done in my life was walk away from Poppy. Putting one foot in front of the other all the way to the train station was only possible because of the hope I hold that going to France will make me a better man. For myself and for Poppy.

Our kiss goodbye slips into my thoughts then, and I welcome the memory of her hands tangled in my hair, her slender, soft skin beneath my touch, and her warm breath tickling the sensitive spots along my neck. The way her voice whispered my name with desperation echoes within me, a sound I will replay over and over as to never forget. And her ever-loving, perfect red lips. I nearly groan out loud in my seat, remembering the way they tasted, sweet like ripe strawberries, and the way they moved along mine, timid and careful at first and then full of confidence and hunger as she let down her guard.

"It's only a woman that can put a smile like the one you're wearing on a bloke's face," a voice says from above me as a weak fist slugs my arm. I glance up to see a scrawny, young chap with jagged-cut, light-brown hair and small eyes leaning over the top of my seat. While he's dressed exactly like me, he's a good head shorter and has the face of a young man barely old enough to hold a gun, much less use one.

"Pardon me?" I'm not exactly sure what to say, but I'm none too happy that my thoughts of Poppy and her lips have been interrupted by this goofy looking boy.

Without an invitation, he slides into the vacant seat facing opposite me and sticks out his hand. "Samuel Davies from

Whitby. Or Sam as my mates call me, or Sammy as my mum calls me. Please don't call me Sammy."

I wonder if calling him Sammy would get him to leave sooner but decide to use my manners. I place my hand in his open one and am surprised by the firmness of his handshake. "Nice to meet you, Sam. Luca Whelan from Beeston."

"Luca." He repeats my name over and over while studying my face. He gives a decisive nod after the fifth utterance, as though my name has been approved to match my looks. Then, he draws out a long "Hmm" while rubbing a hand through his hair. A smell wafts up from him, and it's not pleasant, though I can't seem to place it.

I don't allow myself to squirm under the boy's scrutiny. I want to be left alone to return to my daydreams of Poppy, but Sam doesn't seem to notice my discomfort with his presence. I clear my throat to disrupt the silence and hopefully the staring. "So, Sam, what do you do in Whitby? Or *did* you do before enlisting, I guess."

"I'm a fisherman like my Pa and like his Pa before him and his Pa before him. And if I had any brothers, they'd be fishermen too. Ninety percent of the male population in town have the same occupation. That's just what we do in Whitby."

Ah, the smell: fresh fish.

I wrinkle my nose in the least offending way possible and ask, "And the other ten percent?"

"The other ten percent eat our labor because they're too old to catch it themselves."

"And what do the women of Whitby do?"

"They drive the fish loads into the cities further inland and sell at the markets because they know how to bat their eyelashes." Sam flutters his eyelashes as if there's something attacking his eyeballs. "And move their bodies." He starts shimmying his torso awkwardly in a way I think is supposed to portray a woman walking. Maybe Sam doesn't know very many women. "They get triple the price any of us blokes could ever get for our catches," he says.

It takes every ounce of strength within me not to erupt in laughter at his antics, but I don't know Sam well enough to know if that would hurt his feelings.

He settles into his seat and continues, "Whatever the women don't sell, they bring back home and cook for the men. My two younger sisters can sear and fry a fish better than any girl on the coast," he says with pride.

"I take it you like the ocean, then?" Just saying the word *ocean* makes my tongue feel weird. Like it's swollen and made of lead.

"It's more home to me than the four walls I live in on land. There's not a problem in this world that a day out on the water can't solve."

I would beg to disagree, but I won't get into that with this strange boy.

Without warning, my mother's face swims through my vision. I change the subject. "How long is your deployment for, Sam?"

"Shortest one conscription allows for. I don't plan on staying away from my wife any longer than I must."

Before I can even respond to the word *wife* coming from this boy's mouth, he lets out a yelp. I look up to see a small group of young men who look to be slightly older than Sam walking down the aisle between the rows of seats. Each of the boys let the butt of their rifle hit Sam on top of his head as they pass, letting out guffaws with each of his weak protests. When the fourth and final bloke passes, he calls out, "Sorry, Sammy. Better go back home and let Mummy kiss you better."

The train car erupts in laughs around us, and when I look down at Sam, his face is a color of red so deep Poppy's hair would dull in comparison. Sam may not be someone I would have picked out of the crowd as a mate, but my older brother instincts kick in intrinsically. In fact, Sam is probably about Giovanni's age. Or how old G would be if he were still alive. I absently finger the scar beneath my chin—the only remaining physical token I have left of G.

"What wankers," I mutter. "Are you okay?"

He rubs the back of his head lightly and chuckles. "Oh, that?" He points toward the front of the train car where the boys have disappeared into the next car. "Yeah, that was just some of my mates messing around. I met them on the train yesterday. They're a group from Norway. A little rough around the edges, but I don't mind. We're all a little tense right now, going off to war and all that."

"You *should* mind, Sam," I say. "You shouldn't let people treat you like that. Those Tommies are not your friends."

Sam's face starts to redden again.

"Let's go to the food car," I suggest. "I'll buy you some supper and a drink. Are you old enough to drink?" I ask, wondering if he may have been conscripted by mistake.

He laughs. "If I'm old enough to shoot a gun. I'm old enough to drink."

I can't argue with that. As I follow Sam to the food car, I watch his narrow shoulders slump beneath the weight of his gun. His feet trip down the aisle in shoes that are obviously too big, and his eyes take in every sight and sound around us as we walk. Every boy I know wants to suit up and go to war, but it seems like this poor kid wants to be anywhere else than on a train taking him to the front lines. He probably assumes he's as good as dead.

I decide right now that I will never allow that to happen. Sam might only have two sisters, but whether he likes it or not, he just got himself an older brother too.

7

CHARLES

BEESTON, NOTTINGHAMSHIRE, ENGLAND
MAY 10, 1916

THE TELEPHONE IN THE BACK ROOM OF THE POST OFFICE RINGS out through the empty building, signaling the first call in the code.

One ring. Silence.

No matter what problem I'm handling in the Post Office, whom I am with, or where I am within the four walls, I am to pick up immediately following the last singular ring in the series.

Two rings. Silence.

I, myself, have no way of contacting my mission contact agent, N18, nor my intelligence superior officer, Gukenstein. I haven't spoken with him since he left me under the care of N18 in Marseille, France. N18, or "cousin," as I am to refer to her now, calls at the same time every Friday afternoon. If I don't answer, she will assume I have been compromised.

Three rings. Silence.

As per the information I was given during my last contact with N18, the rate at which ammunition factories are being constructed, and therefore putting weapons into the hands of our enemies, is escalating exponentially. Gukenstein believes there are over one hundred fifty national factories within

England at this point, and our spies are infiltrating only four of those factories.

Two rings. Silence.

One ring.

"Hello. Beeston Post Office, Charles Andrews speakin', could ya hold for a moment?" I say for my part of the coded communication.

"I can only hold for a moment. My dog needs to go out for a walk. Be quick, please," N18 says for her line, agitation evident in her voice.

"Yes, of course. My 'pologies." I utter my required line without conviction and study my Glashutte.

Sixty seconds of silence to deter any allied forces or switchboard operators trying to tap into the call.

My head begins to throb above my eyes. I don't want to have the same conversation as last week. I understand that we need the location of the ammunition factory, but I have nothing for her. Nothing. As it would turn out, the townspeople here aren't keen to share information with newcomers. The shell filling factory may as well be a locked down prison on the bottom of the ocean for my lack of ability to get inside information or find anyone who works there *and* get them to talk.

I sigh and rub a hand down the front of my face.

"Cousin Charles," N18 barks into the earpiece.

"Yes, ma'am."

"How is the post office today? Busy?"

"It's the end of the day, so most of the town is closin' up shop. Not too many folks come 'round at this time."

"No? That's unfortunate. Are there any new town events I should know about? I would just love to get some information about *locations* of important events to put on my calendar."

My jaw clenches. I force it to loosen before speaking again.

"I'm not 'ware of any as of yet, ma'am, but I'll be happy ta send ya a telegram when I have some information 'bout where the next town fair will be held."

"A fair? Well, that does sound exciting. I do love a good party. I'll tell you what: if the town doesn't put an event together by a week from today, I'll send our cousin over from Clifton to do it. She has quite the personality. I'm sure whatever she works out will be dynamite, and you'll be able to head back home to America immediately with exciting stories to tell."

I slam my fist into the desk and choke back bile, barely able to get my words out: "I understand."

"Good day, Cousin Charles. I look forward to speaking with you next week."

I jam the earpiece back onto the cradle of the telephone holder and let out a string of swears.

One week. I have one week to get something worth holding Gukenstein off from sending another agent, or perhaps even N18, herself, down to replace me.

I cannot go home a dishonorably discharged soldier of the Deutsches Heer.

I was fifteen years old when my vater died and Uncle Hans, Vater's brother, stepped in and married my mutter. Although it was necessary for us to have the financial support of Uncle Hans's income, he was brash and offensive, and out of youthful, arrogant stupidity I often told him so. Unfortunately, Mutter typically paid the price for my unbridled tongue.

So at seventeen, when my best mate chose to end his formal education and follow his elder brother's path of training in German intelligence at the spy school of the Kriegsnachrichten-stelle in Antwerp, I eagerly joined him. Vater had been dead for two years by that time, and my only sibling—my sister, Greta, who was two years my senior—had recently married and moved to west Germany. Greta said Hans was kinder to Mutter after I left, so it was easy to stay away. I never returned home.

The German intelligence agency became my home. It has been ten years now of a life on the run in the shadows of reality. Perfect for a young man avoiding his past. Unacceptable for a grown man who has a responsibility to care for his mutter.

But if Gukenstein transfers me out of intelligence and into interpretation, as he promised upon completion of this mission, I can stay in Germany for good. Find home again. Watch over Mutter. Languages come more naturally to me than breathing, a fact I didn't know until a year into intelligence training. By the end of my second year, I was fluent in French, Italian, German, Spanish, and English. "A gift of tongues," my instructor had called it. Between that and my ability to remember and recall intricate details and facts, I would be the perfect liaison inter-preter for the German Empire.

I will do *anything* to receive that transfer from Gukenstein.

If I am going to infiltrate this factory, what I truly need is someone on the inside. Someone who is employed there whom I can get close to. Build a relationship with. Someone who will trust me.

"Hello? Anybody here?" a woman's voice echoes down the hallway. "Farm Boy, are you working back there or just drinking yourself silly?"

Poppy Pemburton.

"Either way, I need you to stop and come retrieve some boxes I brought over from the lace factory. I placed them right outside the door. There are three of them. You did learn how to count on the farm, right?"

After my hat, Poppy is the next best thing about this mission. The brief interactions we've shared over the last six weeks when she pops in to deliver the occasional post for the textile factory she works at always leave me invigorated. She challenges me in a way nobody ever has, and I find I quite like the game of making her miserable. She is the first woman I have interacted with who is not affected by my charms, my golden-brown eyes, or my ability to make women swoon—a fact I find fascinating. It also doesn't hurt that she's beautiful.

I place my hat on my head and take my time sauntering out to the lobby. "Unfortunately, I stopped drinkin' alcohol. It's bad for the liver."

"Ah, there you are. I'd hoped your missing presence meant you were no longer employed here. Shame." Poppy pouts. "Please collect the boxes and send them out first thing tomorrow."

"Ya sure ya don't need the packages on the five o'clock evenin' train, Miss Pemburton? We still have an hour till close today, so if ya don't talk too much, I could prob'ly swing that for ya." I lean across the counter into her space. "And it was a cattle ranch, my dear, not a farm." I wink at her.

She doesn't move back even a breath. Her blue eyes come alive as she glares into mine. "No, Farm Boy. I don't need you to *swing that* for me."

Poppy tries to mimic my Texas accent, and I laugh out loud at her miserable attempt, which earns me a wicked glare.

"If I wanted them posted today, you would know, and you would comply." She squares her shoulders and reaches into her bag before thrusting two small sealed and addressed envelopes into my chest. "These, however, I would like posted today." She clears her throat and adds a soft, "Please."

I look down at the letters pressed against my chest and see one addressed to a Thomas Pemburton, who I assume is either a brother or her father.

The second one I can't see, so I pull the envelope from her fingers. Luca Whelan. The handwriting on the outside of that envelope is soft and curvy, not like the one addressed to Thomas, where the letters slope hard and to the right. I have seen a couple letters come in for Poppy from Luca but none from anyone named Thomas.

"Sure thing. It'd be my pleasure." I tip my hat toward her, and she studies me intently. Beneath her stare, I grab the metal letter opener out of the drawer, then slice open the letter addressed to Luca.

Poppy gasps and lunges for the letter, but she's not quick enough. "What in heaven's name are you doing?"

I make a tsking sound at her and take a step back.

"Stop it this instant," she says. "You have no right to open that; it's private." She reaches far over the counter, her arm swinging out toward me, and her hand brushes against the envelope.

I catch her fingers in mine so she can't grab hold of the letter.

She tugs hard to pull her hand free from my grasp. The momentum causes her vibrant hair to swish around the milky white skin of her face. The sunlight streaming in from the window behind her strikes a match against the red strands, and they glow like fire embers across snow. I am stunned into momentary silence at the sight.

"These have ta be censored," I finally say, steeling myself.

"Censored?"

I grab hold of Poppy's shoulders and slide her backward off the counter until her feet touch the floor and the counter separates us once again.

"Remember what happened last time you were on my counter?" I shake my head at her the way a parent would reprimand a child. "That was embarrassin' for ya, Miss Pemburton. Let's choose to behave appropriately and avoid snappin' a heel off another pair of boots, shall we? Those ones look purdy and new."

Her eyes are ablaze. "You don't have to censor my private letters. I understand why you must do that for mail coming in and out of Chilwell but not my personal posts."

My heart thuds within my chest, and it takes every second of the ten years' experience I have as a spy to control the way my eyebrows are begging to fly upwards. *Is the ammunition factory in Chilwell?* A town less than five kilometers from where I'm standing. I swallow and nod my head, looking down at the envelopes until I'm sure my voice—and face—will be normal when I look up.

"Oh 'specially the personal ones. Who knows what kinda secrets you spill in these personal letters to yer loved ones that the filthy Germans would just love ta git hold of. You women never know when to keep yer mouths shut."

"I beg your pardon." Her fists form into balls on the counter, and her eyes narrow into fierce slits. Heat radiates off her in waves. "Besides the fact that everything that comes out of your mouth is insulting, you are completely misguided in your think-ing. I would never divulge secrets in my letters. I'm not as daft as you make me out to be."

"No? Hmm. Let's see 'bout that." I slide the thin sheet of paper from the envelope and unfold it. "I was given strict new instructions by the War Office just this week to open, read, and appropriately censor every letter that comes into this office from anyone *suspicious*. If sensitive information gets past me and is placed in the wrong hands, I could not only lose my job but also be arrested for treason. You wouldn't want me to lose my job now, would ya?"

Poppy leans forward against the counter, her palms flat and her fingers stretched along the white surface. "You're telling me that for the next, however long my father and my . . . my . . . my Luca are out serving, *you* will be reading every letter I send them?"

I pull a black marking device for censoring mail from the same drawer the letter opener was in and smile at her in response before beginning to read aloud in my best British accent:

"Dear Luca."

Poppy groans, and I look up to see her face in her hands.

Her cheeks are pink, but I'm not certain if it's because speaking of this Luca has her flustered or if the idea of me reading her private letters still has her angry. Probably both, and I give myself a silent pat on the back and continue reading out loud.

"I hope this letter finds you well. Your training schedule sounds rigid, but I'm sure it's much better to be busy working, as it helps the time pass faster.

"Blah, blah, blah. Borin', borin', borin', and more borin' stuff." I want to poke my own eyes out with the blackout censor tool as I scan over the next several paragraphs. I consider tossing the letter into the garbage to spare the poor recipient the tedious read.

"I don't think censorship requires commentary of my personal life," Poppy quips.

I continue.

"Due to the war, the demand for lace has decreased so drastically Mr. Barstow has had to let all but three of us go. And even then, there's hardly enough work to keep the three of us busy for a full day. I find myself spending an embarrassing amount of time staring out the window daydreaming about ▬▬▬. *The way you* ▬▬▬▬▬▬ ▬, *and* ▬▬▬▬▬, *and* ▬▬▬▬▬▬▬ ▬▬ *is something I will never forget. I must run now if I want to get this letter posted, but I think of you always and miss you in every moment.*
Yours, Poppy."

"What are you doing? Those parts don't require censorship." She points to the black slashes marring the white page. "I said nothing secret or sensitive that the Germans can't read."

"Can't or shouldn't? Trust me; I'm doin' all of us a favor. Nobody wants to hear the way you describe intimate details of your *relations* with a man."

Poppy's face flames red. "I did no such thing. You can't . . . you can't just—"

"Can and did, I'm afraid."

"Mr. Andrews, you are positively infuriating."

I smile at her with delight. Mission accomplished.

"I want nothing more than to jump over this counter, put my hands around your neck, and—"

"Thank you for the compliment, but that seems a little forward, even for you, Miss Pemburton. I haven't even bought you dinner yet."

Her eyes narrow at me, but she continues as if I said nothing. "But since strangling you is not a viable option, I want your superior's contact information so I can report you."

An idea strikes me then. An idea so good, I truly wish I could kiss myself.

"Miss Pemburton, you don't seem like the type of woman who sits idly by, waitin' for others to fight your battles for you, so how is it that you find yourself laborin' at a dying lace factory, mindlessly daydreamin' of kissing this man," I say, waving the envelope addressed to Luca in front of her, "instead of actively doin' your bit to bring him home so you can actually kiss him?"

I draw her attention to the War Office advertisement calling for women munition's workers in the front window of the post office. "Seems to me if you really loved this Luca fellow as much as your letter attests to, you would be working over at the Chilwell Shell Filling Factory like all the other women in Beeston." I hold my breath in anticipation of her response to the name of the factory.

"You don't know anything about me," Poppy says as she flips her hair over her shoulder defiantly, but I don't miss the way her eyes cloud over or the way she works her bottom lip between her teeth as she studies the sign.

I exhale and silently rejoice. The factory I have spent nearly two months searching for is so close I could drive there in a quarter of an hour in the Wolseley automobile Gukenstein had delivered to me just last week.

I let the silence in the post office settle around us for a moment before speaking again. "Perhaps you're not as brave of a girl as you pretend to be," I say, shrugging my shoulders. "That's okay; we can't all be heroes." I square my shoulders and flex my arm as I point to the door. "Also, I *am* the superior, so feel free to leave a complaint in the box by that door."

Poppy's clenched jaw loosens, her shoulders drop, and the fight dissipates from her eyes. She walks to the door and stands with her hands pressed to the glass, looking out to High Road, which runs in front of the post office.

It's not until another patron swings the door open, startling her, that Poppy moves. She turns back to look at me as a mustached man with a cane pushes past her, hollering that he needs the newest collection of war stamps. Poppy makes eye contact with me and points outside the door.

"I'll take care of the boxes," I assure her. She nods her head, then disappears without a word into the foot traffic outside.

I place postage on the two envelopes Poppy brought in and throw them in the outgoing post pile. That poor lad. Luca Whelan has no idea what's coming for him. The Germans are going to win this war, and I'm going to make sure his lovesick lady friend is the one who pulls the trigger.

8

POPPY

METAL PINGS IN A METHODICAL RHYTHM BENEATH THE strokes of hammers. Steel howitzer shells of all sizes clang together as munition workers, dressed in saxe-colored boiler suits and matching head caps, load them onto trolley carts. The grinding of machinery I have yet to discover the purpose of is equal in volume to the endless chatter amongst the hundreds of Chilwell factory employees swarming about me.

Following close behind Mrs. Cecilia Fischer, I make my way through a building I don't know the name of and am tempted to squish my hands over my ears at the onslaught of noise. This is nothing like the steady buzz of sewing machines, snipping shears, and quiet whispering of the ten gossiping women I'm accustomed to managing at the lace factory.

"Quickly now," Mrs. Fischer says, marching at a pace so fast I'm inclined to call it running.

She was assigned to accompany me from Mr. Ashby's office—where, after the incident of my little protest in March, I had to beg Mr. Ashby in a most humiliating way for employment here—to the changing rooms, where I am to dress for my new job as a munitions worker. It's a thought that still makes my stomach twist.

I promised myself I would do anything in my power to bring Luca home. I didn't think that would include setting aside my morals, but Mr. Charles Andrews's comment at the post office about doing my bit rather than sitting idly by until Luca returns struck me. I could scarcely breathe as I left the post office that day with the revelation that the uneducated farm boy from America was right—as much as I hated to admit it. In the days following that uncomfortable interaction, similar comments Mr. Ashby and Mrs. Fischer made at my protest about providing soldiers with ammunition to defend themselves also filtered through my mind and nagged at my conscious until I was nearly overcome with guilt at the thought of doing nothing while my father and Luca flirt with death every single day.

So I made the choice I had to. If the men I love can sacrifice, so can I.

Gaining employment here today, however, proved to be a battle I was not prepared for. Despite having my papers from the employment office with me and verifying my ability and acceptance to work munitions war work, Mr. Ashby would not accept them. He wouldn't even look at them! He called Mrs. Fischer in to his office to escort me off the premises, but rather than do that, she simply said, "There are vacant spots in the danger house, sir. The dangerous weapons don't load themselves." She chuckled and then turned a sour, patronizing face toward me. "Although it would be such a pity to have this young, sweet beauty working in such a filthy and dangerous facility."

I didn't know what the danger house was, but I was smart enough to know, if I was going to follow through with my predetermined decision, I was going to have to accept any offer. I wasn't going to let Mr. Ashby or Mrs. Fischer get the better of me. "I'll take it," I declared.

Mr. Ashby didn't like the arrangement, but he conceded upon one condition: in addition to my danger house twelve-hour shift, I must agree to make myself available to do whatsoever task he asks. Clean the toilets, wash the floors, take postage to the post office, shine his shoes, bring him tea, etcetera as often as he requires it. Even after I've worked a full shift.

I paused then. Took a moment to process what employment here would cost me. I'd been prepared to swallow my pride and become a munitions worker—not to become a slave to a man I despise.

It's not too late to walk away from this, fear whispered with her beckoning call. I could go back to my simple life at the lace factory. Back to my comfortable, predictable job. Back to what I was good at, what I loved doing. Back to Mr. Barstow's promise of ownership upon his retirement this year.

But when Mr. Ashby yelled, "Do you agree?" with a slam of his large fist against his wood desk, I raised my face to his and forced myself to smile.

"Agreed," I said.

"Mrs. Fischer, as the woman supervisor over the danger house day shift, this girl is your responsibility now. See to it she doesn't disappoint me, or you will both lose your jobs," Mr. Ashby said. That didn't make Mrs. Fischer all too happy, but here we are.

My new supervisor directs me into the changing room. "This is where you will come when you arrive for work," Mrs. Fischer says, handing me a boiler suit. The one-piece garment is made of a thick, textured material and is drawn in at the waist with a soft belt. The idea of wearing trousers is revolting. I want to help the men fighting, not look like them.

"You will come into the danger house dressed in this uniform every day with your hair pulled back and tucked into your cap." She hands me the cap as well as a pair of soft, black booties with no treads nor laces with hooks and eyes—just a thin, pliable boot that slides on and off the foot. "You take off your outside shoes," Mrs. Fischer points down to the marching boots that adorn my feet, "and keep them in your locker."

I wore my protest marching boots so I wouldn't dirty the new boots Luca gave me as I made the walk from Beeston to

Chilwell, but I think I truly wore them as an act of defiance against my bending morals. To me they say, *I still believe war tears families apart, but for now I'll do what I must to keep them together.*

Mrs. Fischer continues, "Once you have removed all hairpins, jewelry, metal pins, metal buttons, any hooks and eyes, cigarettes, and/or matches from your person and placed them in your locker, you may jump over the barrier onto the clean side in your stockinged feet." Mrs. Fischer leads me to the barrier line in the room. "When on the clean side, you may then slide on your danger house shoes, proceed to the timecard machine, and punch in for your shift. Do not, under any circumstances, ever bring anything metal into my danger house. At best, you could be written up and suspended from work. At worst, you could be dead."

I let out a little chuckle but wipe the smirk off my face the moment I look into Mrs. Fischer's serious eyes.

"There is nothing funny about factory explosions."

"No, ma'am," I agree.

Mrs. Fischer glances at her wristwatch. "There is one hour remaining on day shift. Change into your uniform, and I will take you over to the danger house so you can meet the canary girls you will work with on shift and learn the basics about what we do here."

"Canary girls, ma'am?"

"You'll see." Mrs. Fischer smiles.

Once I change and clock in, Mrs. Fischer provides verbal directions to the closest washing facilities, toilets, and canteen as well as outdoor rest areas, where she says there are often music bands entertaining during mealtimes and games played on the different recreation fields during breaks.

Then, Mrs. Fischer ushers me through the door of the danger house. I freeze the moment I step over the threshold. If the sound from the first building I walked through won't kill me, the smell in this building certainly will. Sulphur, metal shavings, oil, and some sort of bright yellow powder sitting in open tubs are just a few of the smells choking the air. The walls and floors are coated in yellow, and to my horror, so are the hands and faces of several of the women working in here.

I try not to let disgusted thoughts of their appearance show on my face and instead search the vicinity for vented windows or fans to blow out the dust, only to find there are none. Does one just become accustomed to these sorts of working conditions? I bring the collar of my uniform in front of my face to cover my mouth and nose, but it doesn't make the tickle in my throat disappear.

This is the danger house? This is where I agreed to work?

"Your employment at Chilwell involves working with the picric acid we melt down into liquid to fill the shells with," Mrs. Fischer says as we make our way through the house. "That is what turns everything the canary-yellow color you see in this space."

My throat begins to itch, and I force myself to hold in the sneeze tickling my nose. Several clusters of women and a few small groups of men work alongside one another at long rectangular tables that are lined parallel throughout the space of the room. Each person has their head down, focused on the task before them, and they pay no attention to Mrs. Fischer or me.

"Clara," Mrs. Fischer says once we reach the center of the room.

A small girl who can't possibly be older than fourteen or fifteen snaps her head up. Her cheeks still have that soft, youthful look, and her chin comes to a gentle point, her face creating an almost heart-like shape. In her hands, she holds a small, wooden tub filled with the bright yellow powder.

"Yes, Mrs. Fischer?"

"This is Poppy Pemburton. She will be joining our day shift beginning tomorrow."

At that, heads all around the room swivel my direction, and that's when I notice many of the workers are coughing and sneezing. I take a deep breath to calm myself, then instantly regret it.

Rub, rub, rub.

"Please see to it that you spend this last hour of shift teaching Poppy what she will need to know for tomorrow. I expect her to be trained and ready to work by shift start at seven a.m."

"Yes, ma'am," Clara says. The girl offers me a large smile that takes up nearly her entire delicate face. Dark, short hair pokes out beneath the bottom of her cap, and even darker eyes peer at me with an almost twinkling sort of shine. I've never seen eyes that quite literally sparkle.

"Sophia." Mrs. Fischer addresses a yellow-faced, slender woman that looks to be a few years older than myself. "Tomorrow, I would like Poppy to shadow you."

"Yes, Mrs. Fischer," the woman says with a nod, then goes right back to work.

At that, our woman supervisor turns on her heels and vacates the house.

For as friendly as Clara's face is, Sophia's is quite the opposite. Fine by me. I'm not here to make friends. Never had them before; not interested in having them now.

Clara runs up to me and takes me by the arm, eager to lead me back to the table where the others work. "Let me introduce you to the canary girls," she says. "There are about fifty people on shift here in this house at any given time, but the four of us here," she points to herself, Sophia, and two other women standing across from us at the rectangular table, "have worked together since the factory began filling shells in February. That's why we're more yellow than the others."

"So this bright yellow powder is what turns your faces and hands yellow?" I ask.

"It turns *everything* canary-yellow," the girl across from us says, rolling her blue eyes. She pulls her blonde hair, colored nearly green—from the powder I suppose—out of her cap for me to see. Then she flashes her yellow-crusted fingernails at me and says, "Everything you touch, everything you sit on, everything in your dreams at night—yellow."

"That's Annabelle," Clara says, "and she's being dramatic. Yes, everything we touch in the house turns yellow, but once you go to the washroom and clean up after shift, only your skin remains yellow."

"For now," Annabelle says, laughing. "Just you wait till you have dreams of handsome yellow princes tonight."

"Of course a prince is what you would dream about," a girl with fair skin and freckles almost as numerous as mine says as she nudges Annabelle's arm and laughs. "Hi, Poppy," she says. "I'm Nessy. Don't let Annabelle scare you. The doctors say we will be yellow while we are working directly with the acid, but after a few years, the pigment of our skin should return to normal."

My head jerks back. *A few years? Should?*

Nessy offers me a warm smile. "We're happy to have you on shift with us, Poppy. I hope you choose to stick around."

"Back to work, girls," Sophia says with a clap of her hands. "I don't want to be slowed down by Poppy tomorrow because Clara didn't do as she was told."

Clara's pale-yellow cheeks flash pink, and she ducks her head.

"It's fine," I whisper to Clara. "If I slow her down tomorrow, I'll just blame it on my late-night fraternizing with the yellow prince of my dreams."

Clara bursts into giggles, and something squeezes my heart at the sound. *Don't get attached*, fear reminds me. I don't have time for distractions or for the heartache friendships bring. I'm not here to make friends. I'm not here to be noticed. I'm not here to make a mark.

I'm only here for Luca and Father.

"This is picric acid," Clara says as she holds out the tub full of bright yellow powder, and I force myself to pay attention. "It comes to the factory in wooden tubs. First it's sifted."

"Is it the sifting that disperses the powder into the air, making everyone sneeze and cough and bringing that horrid bitter taste to the back of your throat?"

"It is," Clara says cheerily, as if I answered a question right on a very difficult test. "Then, after sifting," she goes on with a level of excitement that should be reserved for first kisses or Five Boy Fridays, "the acid is put in cans and stood in tanks, where it's boiled until it melts into a clear fluid like vinegar." She walks me over to another table. "Then it's poured into the shell case, but a mold is put in before it has time to solidify. This mold, when drawn out, leaves a space down the middle of the shell. But before it's drawn out, beeswax is poured inside and several cardboard washers placed inside."

We move to another table, where men and women are removing molds and placing something in the now vacant space. "The mold is replaced by a candle-shaped exploder of TNT. After this," she points to yet another table, "the freeze cap is screwed in and then two screws must be put in to hold it firm. The holes for these screws must not be drilled straight into the detonator. If they do, the thing explodes."

Clara turns to me with her hands on her hips, her face beaming. "And that's what we do here."

"Is that all?" I ask. "Pfft, easy." I wave my hand through the air.

Clara laughs again. "I know it's a lot, but you pick it up quickly. Each day, we rotate stations so that we're all proficient at every station in the house. That way, we can easily fill extra shifts if asked, and our hands get a break from contact with the picric acid. You'll shadow one of the canary girls at each of the stations until you're ready to work on your own."

"Nessy said she hopes I stick around. What did she mean by that?" I ask.

"Most women don't stay in the danger house. They transfer over to the factory shell store when positions open. That's the building with the trolley cars and ceiling cranes you probably saw when you arrived. It covers almost nine acres and can hold up to six hundred thousand filled shells and one hundred thousand empty shells ranging in size from fifteen inches to sixty pounders." She divulges the information to me with an almost reverent awe.

"Why do the women prefer to work there?" I ask.

"Because they get to drive train car trolleys across the floor and climb ropes like monkeys from the floor up to the ceiling. Then, they climb into the ceiling cranes so they can transport the shells around the building. I suppose another reason is because it's a good bit safer to work there than in the danger house. But," she says, smiling, a mischievous glint in her brown eyes, "they don't have nearly as much fun as we do."

"Mrs. Cecilia Fischer allows for fun?" I ask with a skeptical laugh.

Just then, as if saying the woman's name conjures her up, Mrs. Fischer barrels through the danger house door, clapping her hands together and shouting, "This isn't the Red Lounge, ladies. Let's get to work! We have shells to fill and men to kill."

My eyes widen, and my hands tingle with what I hope is not regret at my choice to become employed here.

"She's joking," Clara whispers to me.

"I don't know the meaning of the word," Mrs. Fischer says directly behind my other ear.

Every little hair on the back of my neck salutes in response. When I glance down to hide my grimace, I see a very faint, very finite smattering of yellow powder decorating the back of my hand.

Two hours ago, I was Poppy Pemburton: Beeston Lace Factory manager, war protester, and happy recluse with pale, unstained skin that, quite truthfully, I very much admire about myself. Now, my heart races, and my mind spins with fear as I wonder who I am about to become.

9

LUCA

NO ONE SO MUCH AS BLINKS. SIX PAIRS OF EYES HOLD MY GAZE as I let out a long, slow breath. I almost lick my lips, but out of the corner of my eye, I see Private Adams staring right at me as if he's waiting for me to wet them. That must be my tell.

I'm so close to taking home the pot. The joy I would feel in taking the week's worth of coffee rations Private Johnson threw in the middle of the table is worth every ounce of strain to keep this poker face. I glance down at my hand again and keep my features stoic. I know I've got all of them beat except Adams. I can't read him at all. I have yet to learn his tell.

Everyone's gaze swings to Adams as he takes his turn. With a growing smile and puff of his chest, he lays down three jacks and two kings. A chorus of chanting and congratulatory slaps on Private Adam's back begins around the table, but my glands salivate in anticipation. I can nearly taste the bitter coffee in my mouth.

Sam sits to my left, his leg bouncing up and down. He chose to fold, as he does almost every time, and his eyes plead with me to come through for him. He threw a stack of Ethel Warwick photographs in the pot and whispered to me the moment he laid them down that I had to win them back for him.

I look around the table slowly, making eye contact with each player, letting the anticipation build. Johnson is likely to flip the table when he sees what I've got—four eights—so I get ready to seize the coffee rations before they get lost in the scuffle of greedy men.

As I raise my arms in the air to throw down my cards in triumph, Captain McDaniel blows through the hut door, sending the cards on the table shooting into the air.

"Ladies, get your arses to the trenches now!" Captain shouts. "You are to report to your station in less than five minutes from this second, or everyone in this hut will be on latrine duty for the remainder of the week."

Johnson lunges for the coffee rations at the same time Adams reaches into the middle for his gold watch, and Sam stuffs his photographs in his uniform breast pocket. The other three Tommies each take their meager antes, and I glare at every man in turn before I chuck my winning hand onto the table, gather my charcoal sketch of our infantry that I gambled and surrender to Captain McDaniel. Johnson laughs, but at least the others look appropriately guilty. Sam pats me affectionately on the back. He hands me one photo of Ethel and gives me a creepy wink as we walk out of the hut.

"That's alright, Sam," I say. "I know you need it more than I do." I wink back at him, and he laughs as I return the photo to his pocket.

"My Sarah is plenty of woman for me, but it wouldn't be right to leave all those photographs just lying on the table for any dirty scallywag to take off with, now would it?"

"That would be a true shame, indeed," I say.

Rifles fire off to our left in the weapons training field as we make our way to our afternoon training post in the trenches. The faint voices chanting marching orders in rhythmic waves echoes over the patch of wasteland between us. The weapons fire again, and I notice Sam's shoulders flinch ever so slightly at the sound. Our rifle training hours are my favorite hours of the week, but I saw Sam stuff cotton in his ears yesterday on the field. I didn't ask him about it, but everything I've learned about Sam over the number of weeks we've been in training together tells me weapons training is his least favorite.

Field Major Frederick greets us at our training post. For the next several hours, we train in the rows and rows of trenches dug along the west side of camp.

We run in and out of the deep, muddy crevices. We train our legs to move in every direction with rapid fervor. We train our feet to pull through the mud without losing a boot and our bodies to hide out of sight on command. My muscles scream for relief, but still we move. My throat burns with the need for water, but still we chant. My feet are wet with blood-soaked blisters and sweat, but still we run.

Field Major Frederick blows the whistle at the hour mark, signaling a ten-minute break to rest and drink before we complete our final hour of training for the day.

I slurp water from my canteen before handing it to Sam for a swig. He drank all of his in the first hour. Sam chucks his helmet to the ground and guzzles while I wipe the pooling sweat from my brow. Unfortunately, there's nothing I can do to cool the June heat that seeps through every other part of my uniform.

Sam holds the canteen out to me. "I saved the last for you. I'll go fetch more somewhere if you need it," he says.

"That's alright, Sam. Drink what you need."

He eyes the canteen still in his grasp and offers a quick thanks before downing the remaining drops.

"I have never hurt this bad in my life," I groan. I lean down and rub my hand along the back of my leg while I continue to complain. "Muscles I didn't know I had—in places I didn't know was possible to have them—feel as though they have been replaced by flames."

"Was somebody in poor health when they enlisted in the army?" Sam asks, teasing me. "It's a good thing you have me here to train you since Field Major Frederick is going so easy on us."

I look up at Sam. His face is a shade of red so deep it could be classified as purple; his overgrown, floppy, brown hair is plastered to his forehead as if he were just caught in a London rainstorm; and his dry, cracked, blood-stained lips are quite literally terrifying to behold.

I start to laugh. "How is it, Sam, that at the end of the hottest day of the year thus far, during the most rigorous training we have experienced to date, with nothing but a few drops of water holding us together, you are all smiles and jokes? Does nothing ever bother you? Are you truly this happy and easygoing all the time?"

"I am now," Sam says, a goofy grin on his mouth.

"Now? So it's just rigorous training that takes us to the brink of death that has you all giddy for life?"

"Not the training, exactly, no. But there is something about facing death that teaches you what life is and what it isn't." Sam sobers and looks at the ground a moment before speaking again. "I lost my best mate, Anderson, two years ago. On December 16, 1914, five minutes past nine in the morning, two ships of the Imperial German Navy opened fire along the coast of Whitby. Anderson lived in a cottage near the coastguard station on the edge of the east Cliff. He had just walked outside his home to head toward the dock to meet me for our day of fishing when a shell burst close to one of the outbuildings next to him. Anderson died instantly."

"Sam, I am so sorry."

I take a minute to process Sam's story. His flinching at artillery noises on the fields begins to make sense. But this is just training. How is he going to survive the battlefields of France?

"I was angry at first," Sam says. "That's the reason I didn't enlist during the first couple years of the war." He hands the canteen back to me and wipes his dirt-covered hands down the length of his trousers. "I couldn't be a part of something that would constantly remind me of losing my mate. They took his bloody life." Sam swears and spits into the dirt. "I didn't want them to take my life too."

A little patch of spittle sits on his lower lip and slowly moves down his chin as he continues speaking. "I swore I would never give the Germans the chance to take more from me than they already had. But the anger I held from Anderson's death was changing who I was." He sighs. "My sisters kept their distance. My father stopped taking me on his fishing expeditions. I no longer recognized myself in the mirror. The person I was turning into wasn't anyone Anderson would have been mates with." Sam wipes his forearm across his brow and squints his eyes against the sun. "I knew I needed to let go of what I was carrying and try to forgive the men who killed him."

"Why would you care about forgiving them?"

"Cause if we let anger over the injustices of life overtake our spirits, we become nothing more than the people who hurt us, you know?" Sam elbows me lightly in the arm.

But I don't know. I've never let go of the injustice of my past, and I never will. Holding on to that is what gives me purpose. Knowing that I must spend my life making right what I did wrong so long ago is what motivates and drives me to protect those I love now.

"I don't know, Sam. I think when we let go of the past, we forget." I finger the scar beneath my chin, grateful for the reminder it is. "And if we forget, what was the point?"

"You don't forget. You never forget, I don't think. You just forgive," he says with a shrug of his shoulders.

"You've forgiven the Germans who killed Anderson?"

"Yeah, I have."

I give Sam a look that I know conveys skepticism. How does one just let go of anger? Of guilt? Of pain? How do you do that and still hold onto the memories that you want to have?

"Luca, the anger controlled everything in my life for two years. That's a long time to sit with the devil. I knew I needed to make peace with it, but I didn't know how. Then I met Sarah."

He smiles. "She emitted so much bloody light and joy; it made me see my life for what it had become. It was like her light held up a mirror to my darkness, and I truly saw myself for the first time since Anderson died. I didn't want to be that person anymore. I wanted to be with Sarah, but I couldn't be with her the way I was." Sam leans over and ties up the undone laces on each of his boots. "Forgiving someone doesn't make what they did okay. It just makes it okay for you to move forward."

"You said you were conscripted. Did you not enlist after you forgave them?"

"Nah." Sam laughs, and his hands fall to his hips. "Because then I fell in love, and love makes men weak, doesn't it?" He raises knowing eyebrows up at me. "Sarah and I fell hard and fast. I mean look at me." Sam waves a hand up and down his body. "She said she wanted to start a family with me and all that, so she convinced me to stay and marry her instead of leave."

"But married men were conscripted anyway," I say, understanding.

"So they were."

The whistle blows near the trench, signaling the end of the break. I scoop Sam's helmet from the ground and shove it back on his head. He grins up at me with the stupidest of smiles.

"What?" I ask.

"You can let go of whatever you're holding onto. Then maybe you'll stop trying to take care of me all the time," Sam says, clicking the straps beneath his chin into place.

"I'd take care of you no matter what, Sam. Who else is gonna make sure your ugly self gets home to Sarah?" I smack him on the top of the helmet good naturedly, and he takes off in a lopsided jog.

I say it jokingly, but I mean every word.

Protect Sam. Prove I'm not a coward. Don't die. And if I accomplish all those things, convince Poppy to marry me.

We leave for the front lines of France next month, and I am all in.

10

CHARLES

BEESTON, NOTTINGHAMSHIRE, ENGLAND
JULY 21, 1916

"It has been a month, Cousin Charles, since you provided me with the location coordinates of Chilwell's upcoming fair, and you assured me you had an inside scoop on the specifics of the event, but I have heard nothing," Intelligence Agent N18 says, annoyance clear in her tone. "I have been more than generous with my patience. I need to know these particulars, Charles, so I can prepare for my arrival. After a whole month, I don't even know one detail about the inner workings of the fair. How ridiculous is that?" N18 laughs with wicked abandon into the telephone.

"I understand. I do," I say when her cackles subside.

"I'm beginning to think you lied to me about how much you are involved with the towns' affairs, and I don't like being lied to."

"I have an inside scoop," I say firmly. "The previously laid plans were . . . interrupted, but I assure you new plans are in action as we speak."

"It's past the planning stage, Cousin. The planning stage was last month. If you are still planning, you are far behind schedule, and I have no use for you."

"I will have specific information next time you call with an inquiry. I'm very close to obtaining the details of the fair's operation. It would be ill advised to change groundwork now."

"I want to have the time of my life at the fair, Cousin Charles. Make sure you don't disappoint me." The click of a telephone followed by silence echoes in my ear.

I slide the earpiece back into its cradle and remove the coarse camel-hair blanket from the crack below the office door. The post office lobby was full of patrons this afternoon when N18 made her Friday phone call, and I didn't want to chance anyone overhearing our conversation. We speak in code, but I don't think it requires a genius to crack it. In fact, I'm quite certain even a Neanderthal would understand. Thank goodness I had the foresight last month to hire an extra set of hands to cover our afternoons. I would've had a building full of eavesdropping customers otherwise.

I told the old man I hired that I have a weekly call home with my mother each Friday afternoon and appreciate my privacy. He patted my back and told me that I was a beautiful boy and that my mother must be very proud of the man she raised.

I don't know about that.

I fold the blanket and place it beneath my desk. When I enter the lobby, the rush of customers has nearly ended, so I begin working my way through the mail, specifically searching for letters from women and men who I have discovered work at the Chilwell factory, hoping to come across something useful as I censor.

When I had the idea to plant the seed of ammunition factory work into Poppy's mind, it felt brilliant in the moment. Put Poppy in the factory; use her to gain information.

My plan worked so quickly, I had to bite my tongue to keep my mouth from dropping open when Poppy came in the very next week to post letters straight from Chilwell factory itself as an *employee*. How she came to be the exclusive post office liaison for the Chilwell ammunition factory, I have no idea, but I saw it as an absolute gift from the war gods and an omen for Germany.

N18 sent me a box of my favorite German chocolates repackaged and sealed in an American chocolate box that week.

In the two months since, a few useful details have popped up in letters Poppy has written to Luca and Thomas, but once she realized I was censoring out information related to the ammunition factory, she stopped writing about it altogether. And the factory mail Poppy brings in has not been the gold mine I was hoping for when I encouraged her to work there.

"Mr. Andrews?" the old man I hired calls to me. "These tools we have here to slice open envelopes and packages are all quite dull." He runs a blade over his finger to show me. "Would you like me to take them down to the Beeston Lace Factory and ask Mr. Barstow, the owner, to sharpen them for us?"

"The lace factory?"

"Oh yes. The factory has the very best sharpeners for shears in Beeston. Most of the folks in town take their shears to him. Mr. Barstow charges a small fee and then your blades are good as new. I've been taking my knives there for years. I'm sure he'd sharpen these tools right up."

After my conversation with N18, fresh air and movement is exactly what I need to get rid of my building frustrations. "I find myself needin' a walk about now anyway, sir," I say. "Thank you for the tip. I'll take care of the sharpenin'." I roll the tools into a dark blue cloth, place my cowboy hat on my head, and nod farewell.

When I reach the end of High Road, which runs in front of my business as well as most of the businesses in Beeston, I turn the corner and make my way across the cobblestone street, when a group of yellow-faced women on bikes nearly run me over.

"Whoa." I jump out of the way as their bikes come to a halt around me.

"What are *you* doing here?" Poppy asks, breathless.

Her eyebrows narrow, and her blue eyes darken to a dangerous shade of storm as if I have personally offended her by being in the outdoors.

"Good evenin', canary girls." I tip my hat to the other four ladies who surround me. "What am I doin' where?" I ask Poppy, innocently. "In Beeston? Workin' at the post office. *Runnin'* the post office," I say, emphasizing my position of power, and wink at the blonde woman next to Poppy.

"Gross. Don't do that to Annabelle." Poppy follows her words with a gagging noise.

"He can do that to me if he wants," the blonde says, twirling her long braid around her finger.

"Why are you here, as in, in the middle of the road," Poppy says, ignoring the blonde. "As in, right now when I'm coming home from my shift. Messing with me in the post office isn't enough for you? Now I must worry about you accosting me outside as well?"

"Who says he's here for you?" Annabelle smiles at me coyly. "He could be here for any of us. Who are you waiting here for, Mr. Andrews?"

The girls on their bikes giggle.

How do I always manage to irritate Poppy so quickly? I wish she'd relent a little bit. Maybe I should try to get intel from this Annabelle girl instead.

I am quite positive Annabelle would tell me anything I want to know, but she would be entirely too clingy and likely end up blowing my cover. On a mission like this one, I need plenty of privacy. The entire point of my uneducated rancher character cover from Texas is to stay *off* everyone's radar.

At this point in the game, Poppy, as the ammunition factory post office liaison, is my best and only bet.

"Wish I could say I was here to meet one of you purdy ladies, but it was just my good fortune to cross your path. I'm headed to the Beeston Lace Factory to ask that nice gentlemen who owns the business if he would be so kind as to sharpen the tools we use to slice open letters and packages for censorin'." I wave the rolled-up cloth holding the tools before them.

"Maybe Poppy should go with you," exclaims a young teenage girl with short, dark hair. "She worked there for basically her whole life. I'm sure she would love to help you."

Poppy smiles over at the girl, but I notice the tight pull around the corners of her lips.

"Oh yes, Poppy would have those sharpened for you in no time," says a different girl. "She's amazing with her hands." She has almost as many freckles on her nose as Poppy, but her hair is a drab brown color instead of Poppy's vibrant red. "We watched her mend a boiler suit for Sophia here." The freckled girl points to another girl whose lips are pinched so tight, I wonder if she's just sucked on a lemon. "And she finished in a matter of seconds. It was incredible."

"Thanks, Nessy," Poppy says, clearly uncomfortable with all the praise.

"Not too long ago," I say, smiling, "Poppy promised to do something to me with her hands—"

"And that is enough of that," Poppy interrupts, but the pink on her cheeks is reward enough. "Ladies, why don't you go on ahead to the Red Lounge. I'll meet you there in a moment," she says.

The teenage girl speaks up again. "The lace factory owner even offered Poppy ownership of the factory, but her beau left for the war, so she's making ammunition instead to help bring him home. Isn't that the most romantic thing you've ever heard?" She brings her hands up to her chest and swoons.

Ownership? I am impressed. "Ah, yes, young love." I make my voice go soft and sweet. "Nothin' better."

"And after Poppy put all her hopes and dreams on hold for someone else, mean Mr. Ashby treats her like his slave. Making her clean washrooms, and fetch his tea, and make all the post office runs. It's terribly unfair." The teenager's dark brown eyes brew in testament to her words.

I'm curious as to why this Mr. Ashby chap chose Poppy for that role, but instead of asking, I make a mental note to thank him for his choice in *slave labor,* as the girl put it, if I ever have the pleasure of meeting him. "Life is rather unfair; better you learn that lesson now when you're young," I tell her.

Poppy glares at me before turning to the girls. "Clara, make sure you stay close to Sophia on the way to the lounge. I know Annabelle and Nessy like to race, but your bicycle is on the fritz, so I don't want you trying to keep up with them."

"I don't need an escort, Poppy. I'm old enough to be out on my own," the girl that must be Clara says.

"Come on, Clara. Let's go," Sophia says. Clara complies with a pout.

When the girls ride off, I turn to Poppy and try to break the icy air between us. "I don't know if you knew this or not, but the lace factory has an open tab with the post office, so I never have to collect payment when an employee comes in to make a transaction. I just send the owner an invoice at the end of every month. It's quite wonderful. You should have told me that the first time we met. Things between us could have been much different."

Poppy ignores my sarcastic comment completely, but somehow, it's just as satisfying as one of her biting remarks.

"Mr. Andrews, you and I are not friends. I don't like you, and I would appreciate if you didn't insinuate otherwise in front of those impressionable young women."

"What if we're not around impressionable young women?"

"Good evening, Mr. Andrews." Poppy begins to pedal away.

"May I ask you a question?"

Poppy doesn't turn around, but she stops pedaling, so I keep talking.

"Did you really turn down the opportunity to become the owner of a business to be someone's servant girl? For a boy?"

Poppy drops her bike, turns around slowly, and walks straight back to me. Each step methodical. Deliberate. I have never cowered to anyone in my life, but something sharp shoots straight through my chest as she approaches.

She stops only a step away from me, our faces inches apart.

"I am *no one's* servant," Poppy says through clenched teeth. "I work in the danger house, where I spend my days filling up so many shells with explosive powder, I could take out an entire fleet of Germans by myself. In one twelve-hour shift, our team fills seven thousand five hundred shells. The expectation is that every employee fill forty-five shells during their shift. I fill at least one hundred thirty a day." She pauses, adding a dramatic flip of her wrist as though she's giving me time to compute the numbers and expects an answer, which I will absolutely not give her the satisfaction of getting. When I don't so much as blink, she sneers. "Since I know you're slow, that's triple what every single person on my shift outputs. The factory's output to date is three million, two hundred sixty-six thousand, six hundred sixty-four. I am a slave to no one. And Luca isn't just a boy; he's the man I love."

I keep my mouth firmly locked. If I say something, I fear I will scream out in celebration. I nod and take small steps backward. The numbers Poppy spewed are worth gold. Relief eases every tight muscle in my body.

But as I watch Poppy turn around and bike away, a frightening realization freezes my joy.

The secrets I need aren't going to be found in the packages Poppy brings in from the factory or the personal letters I censor a few times a month.

No. All the secrets I need are locked inside the head of a beautiful, feisty, nearly always angry girl-child. I can't make her upset every time I need more intel. In fact, I'll be lucky if she speaks to me again after tonight.

If I didn't entirely burn the bridge to the ground, I'll be forced to persuade the only female in the world that hates me to like me. Or to at least tolerate me.

Chilwell National Shell Filling Factory No. 6 is no longer the target for my mission.

Poppy Pemburton is my target.

My entire future rests on winning over an infuriating redhead with a temper from the underworld. Fantastic.

Mission accepted.

11

POPPY

CHILWELL, NOTTINGHAMSHIRE, ENGLAND
AUGUST 14, 1916

THE COARSE FABRIC OF MY BOILER SUIT RUBS AGAINST MY inner thighs, chaffing the tender skin as I move through the danger house toward the exit. I decide I will never—no matter how long I must wear trousers while working here—enjoy them. Even three months' time has not been long enough for me to adapt to the unflattering menswear that is my munitions uniform.

"Stop scratching your legs. You look as if you have insects crawling inside your trousers," Sophia says, stilling my hand.

"I can't help it. I don't know how you all love these things."

"What? The trousers you mean?" Nessy laughs. "Oh, Poppy, you're so vain. These change everything about the way we can move! I wish I could wear them home after shift." Her hands trace the outside of her uniform affectionately.

"I don't mind the trousers; they make my back side look fantastic," Annabelle says with a grin and a flick of her hip. "But one thing I wish I could get rid of after shift is the burn in my eyes and throat."

I glance at her face and notice her soft, blue eyes are a tinge red and swollen.

"My throat burns at the start of shift," Nessy skims a hand

down the length of her freckled neck, "but then the blend of smells settles in my stomach, and it stops bothering me. However, I am having severe aches in my chest. Sometimes at night, while I'm trying to fall asleep, I notice it's hard for me to get a full breath of air. It feels as though a small child is sitting on my chest." She worries her bottom lip between her teeth.

While the side effects of working in an ammunition factory are known by all who don a boiler suit, this is the first time I've heard concerns over them spoken aloud.

I, myself, have yet to become accustomed to the air-filled stench of the poisonous yellow powder we fill the shells with. Not to mention the way the oily machinery somehow coats the inside of my mouth with a metallic taste that lasts for hours. Or the staunch odor of sweating bodies in the ventless space. Or the masses of people and the constant noise they make.

It's all so different from my work in the small, quiet textile factory where I spent my days with soft lace, the sweet hum of a sewing machine, and only ten women employees who all but ignored me. It was positively ideal. While producing lace for household textiles is perhaps not as meaningful a work as this one, I miss it every day.

"Pains in my abdomen have increased over the last several weeks," Sophia says as the last wagon of filled ammunition shells for our shift rolls past us on the track that will take it to the store house for packaging. "Has anyone else experienced that? I thought at first I might be pregnant." The other canary girls close to the danger house exit all spin around at once and stare at Sophia. She wipes a hand across her abdomen. "My husband came home on leave last March." Her cheeks blush beneath the yellow of her skin. "But my doctor confirmed there is no pregnancy."

"You're married?" Annabelle's head snaps forward.

I can tell from the wide, gaping mouths of Nessy and Clara that this is news to them as well.

"Was," Sophia says. "We were married for six months. Robert died in the line of duty in April."

Nessy gasps, and Annabelle's eyes grow large and round. Clara is at Sophia's side in an instant, her arms wrapped tightly around Sophia's frame. Sophia stiffens at the touch but doesn't push Clara away.

"Why didn't you say anything?" Nessy's sorrowful voice echoes the feeling in the space.

"For this very reason." Sophia waves a hand in front of the lot of us. "I don't need the theatrics. The sad condolences. Death is a part of life. We live; we die. That's how it has always been and how it always will be. Grieving is pointless. It doesn't bring your loved one back."

"But why didn't you tell us you were married?" Annabelle shakes her head in disbelief.

"Nobody ever asked. And frankly, it was no one's business." Sophia's chin points forward.

"I'm so sorry you lost the love of your life," Clara says with tears in her big, brown eyes.

"There's no such thing as the love of your life, Clara. That's a childish notion." Sophia's voice clips the words, but I hear the wobble in them.

"Anyhow," Sophia clears her throat and blinks hard before allowing her gaze to bounce between the four of us women, "do you think the pains could possibly be from the work here?"

Sophia gets only noncommittal shrugs in response.

I look over my shoulder, hoping Mrs. Fischer has somehow made herself appear in the house. She practiced nursing for decades before her husband passed away last year from tuberculosis. After his death, she packed her medical equipment away for good and began work at Chilwell. At least, that's what the rumors say. But I'm certain she would have some sort of answer.

But it's not Mrs. Fischer I see when I glance behind me.

A small crowd of women have gathered, listening to our discussion.

As we make our way to the washroom, all the women begin to share stories of their own health ailments and medical troubles in hushed whispers. How doctors either ignore their concerns altogether, or tell them there isn't enough data to understand why this is happening to them, or don't have the knowledge of how to fix it.

Twenty basins line the walls, and a small mirror is placed above each one. We hurry and take turns washing our hands, faces, and arms as best we can, then pat ourselves dry with towels.

A finger gently taps my shoulder. I turn behind me to see a woman, at least two decades my senior by the looks of her, whose hair is so dark and rich it reminds me instantly of a Fry's Five Boys chocolate bar. Her skin is pale and yellow, her eyes sunken in with dark circles beneath them, making her appear quite sickly.

"My name is Martha Roberts." Her voice is raspy and desperate. "I have abdomen and chest pain nearly every day. I cough all night long and can hardly sleep for the burn that sets in when I close my eyes. I want to quit working here, but my children need my wages while my husband is in France." She stifles a sob. "We need to do something about our working conditions. I'm not sure how much longer I can survive this."

"I'm sorry." My eyebrows slant down in confusion. I'm unsure why a woman I don't know believes I'm the person her concerns should be addressed to. "I don't make the decisions regarding the conditions in which we work."

Martha takes a step closer to me. "I watched out the window the day you came protesting our factory." She takes hold of my arm, all five of her fingernails emphasizing her desperation. "I couldn't hear what you were discussing, but I could see that Mr. Ashby's temper did not intimidate you. You stood your ground. And the moment I saw you square your shoulders and take a step into Mr. Ashby's space instead of out of it, I knew you were somebody who would fight for change.

Somebody who would make a difference. Please help me. Please help us."

I glance up and am surprised to see many of the women nodding their heads in agreement with Mrs. Roberts.

Their opinion of me sends a wave of pride burning through my being. A being that is consistently reminded to remember my place, to close my mouth, and to dutifully obey the men who walk before me.

While I am grateful to finally be *seen*, and while I understand the fear behind the unknown ailments, there is nothing I can do about any of them. I don't know the first thing about medical care. Furthermore, if Mr. Ashby were to somehow catch wind of *me* leading an uprising of angry, yellow women, he would certainly fire me.

Besides, there are a plethora of explanations for all their ailments that don't involve the factory.

"I'm sorry you have experienced health concerns, ma'am." I pat the chocolate-hair woman on the arm, then turn my attention toward the rest of the danger house employees. "I'm sorry you are all experiencing ailments, but let's calm ourselves for a moment and think these things through. Perhaps the abdomen pain is coming from eating meals in the canteen rather than what you are used to eating at home. Perhaps the chest pain is because you have a slight illness in your lungs." I take a breath. "Or perhaps we are all simply anxious due to a period in our lives filled with overwhelming unknowns. When will the war end? Will our men survive? Will *we* survive? How much worse will things get? If the Germans win, what will that mean for us? For our lives? Our families?"

I look around at the women. "An unknown future is cause enough to send our stomachs clenching, our hearts fluttering, and our chests heaving with fear. But let's not overreact. I would suggest that if any of you are feeling ill, you reach out to the factory physicians and see what they have to say on the matter.

As for our yellow skin, be sure you are using Oatine cream on your hands and face and drinking milk every chance you get to combat the picric acid, as Mrs. Fischer has instructed."

A prick of guilt tiptoes across my heart as Martha Roberts shuffles silently toward the washroom exit, her head drooped and her shoulders curved in. I wish I could do more.

Before I see her arms opening, Clara has them wrapped around my middle.

My body tenses without warning at the physical touch. Besides Luca, this is the first time another person has embraced me since the night Jane ran away, and I can't decide if I want Clara to stop touching me or to never let go.

"I'm so glad you came to work at the factory with us, Poppy," Clara says as she squeezes me even harder against her. "You are the best big sister I've ever had." She tilts her face up to mine, and her eyes shine with warmth.

I've decided. I never want her to let go. Fear warns me to be careful—reminds me what happens when I let people in—but for the first time in a very, very long time, I don't care to listen.

"Thank you, my little canary," I say, squeezing her back, and Clara beams at the nickname.

"I despise my yellow skin," Annabelle grumbles as she finishes washing in the basin, and although I don't say as much, I agree with her. Jane would be appalled if she saw me. She used to take the backside of a wooden hairbrush to my derriere if my hair was in tangles. I can't imagine what she'd do to me if she saw this staining upon my skin and hair.

Shame twists my insides.

"I don't know," says Clara studying her hands, "I kind of like my yellow skin. It's a mark of who I am and what I do. A mark of devotion to my country. A mark of sisterhood. I'm proud of my yellow markings."

I look into the mirror as I dry my face and notice the yellow tinge that has been ever present along my fingertips and palms for the last three months is now beginning to color my cheeks and forehead as well. I scrub harder.

The rough cloth leaves red lines scratched into my cheeks, but the canary yellow remains.

Dear Father,

It has been quite some time since I've heard from you. I pray to God for your safety as you battle along the Western Front.

The British newspapers cry out, "All Goes Well for England and France." The press boasts of our success—of the strength of our valiant soldiers—and declares with some boldness that although the fighting is intense and the resistance fierce, we are winning the war. However, the casualties from the Battle of the Somme fill pages upon pages of newspaper columns, and the stories from the injured men returning from war are sickening. It doesn't sound at all like winning to me.

I don't know what to believe, but I choose to hope "all goes well" because I cannot afford to entertain the thought of anything else. I have lost Jane for now; I shouldn't lose you too. I'm not ready to let go of my dream of having our family together again. It's a hope I've held onto for ten years. If you die, Father, you take my dream to the grave with you.

It was selfish of you to enlist. To leave me here wondering why fighting in a war was more important to you than fighting for a better relationship with me. Why it was more important than fighting to bring Jane back home to us.

I want to fix everything, but you must come home for me to do that. Don't die.

—Poppy

~

September 4, 1916

Dear Firebird,
We made it to France last week. They positioned our squadron immediately on the north side of the

Somme River to provide relief to exhausted soldiers who have been fighting here since July. There is immense bloodshed on every side; there is no victory found here. Training prepared us for nothing. War is the vilest of all human emotions. Every day, I try to find God. He isn't on the battlefields of malice or in the trenches of despair, but I carry Him in my heart as best I can and pray that is enough. Enough to keep my heart from turning as black as my hands.

I'm sorry that American is bothering you. He sounds like a dodgy bloke and certainly not worth your time getting worked up over. If this fellow continues to assault you, perhaps you should suggest Mr. Ashby find another employee to run factory posts to the post office.

It kills me that I'm not there to protect you. Not that you have ever needed my protection—I know you take care of yourself—but I find that for as long as I have known you, that is all I have ever wanted to do. To protect you from every bad thing and person in this world and ensure you are happy.

Your smile and laughter are pure magic, and if I'm being honest with myself, I daydream of those two things an embarrassing amount. As well as your perfectly shaped lips against mine. But I only tell you that because I can hide behind this paper and pen while doing so.

Whether or not you decide I get to be a part of your life in the way I am most hopeful to be, please know I only want what is best for you. Your happiness is all that matters to me.

*No matter where the obligations of life or the
desires of our hearts take us, you are a part of me today
and always.*

Forever. Forever and always, I will love you,
Luca

*P.S. If you miss me always and think of me in every
moment, as you say in your letters, does that mean you
love me? If I was a betting man, which I am becoming,
I would say yes. Sam agrees with me, and he's married,
so he probably knows.*
*P.P.S. I cannot believe poor Mr. Barstow had to close
the lace factory. I suppose it makes sense what with
the war going on. That was nice of Mrs. Fischer to
turn the building into a dormitory for you canary girls
to live in for the time being, but I must say, I am indeed
laughing at you living with that many women. Good luck
in there. Try to take it easy on them; they're probably
terrified of you.*

∽

September 22, 1916

Dear Luca,

Nobody is terrified of me. That is just silly nonsense. I might be a
head taller than any of the women in the dormitory, but I am as docile as
a rabbit.

Don't worry about me, Luca. Mr. Andrews, the American, is harmless. All muscles and no brain. He is easily duped and moves slower than a
sinner walking to church. Between you and me, I feel sorry for him. It
would be difficult to be so inept at life. But if he bothers me any longer,

you have my word that I will put in a request to Mr. Ashby to be requited of factory post office duties.

I would never wish you to be away, but I must say I am quite glad you are not here to see my abhorrent skin. It is good you can only dream of me in memory because I'm certain if you saw me now, you would cringe at the sight. My skin has become stained with a yellow tinge that no amount of suggested milk or Oatine cream has been able to remove. I fear the condition will only worsen the longer I work at the ammunition factory.

It is this way for all the women who work at munitions factories across England. People have labeled us "canary girls" because we quite literally resemble the color of the canary bird. It is truly a sight to behold. When we walk to and from Chilwell to Beeston, when we are in the grocers, when we ride the train, or when we go to a picture show at the theater; people whistle, and clap, and congratulate the "canary girls" as we pass. Men pay for our food, women praise our efforts, and children stare at us strangely—and I can't say I blame them.

At first, it was quite embarrassing to be the center of that kind of attention, but now I feel rather proud to be a "Chilwell canary," to be recognized as a woman of sacrifice. I don't accept my yellow skin, but I suppose I will take it in exchange for honor.

I am sure the American will censor out nearly all of those previous paragraphs, so I guess you'll just get to be surprised by the color of my skin when you next come home.

Do you get to come home on leave at all now that you're in France? It's been so long since I've seen you, I think I might be starting to forget your face. You have unevenly placed eyes and a large, round nose, correct? Are your eyes blue or brown? Hmm ... wish I could remember.

War sounds as awful as I always believed it to be. I am sorry you witness such travesty every day. Perhaps the only victory one finds in war is the victory within. Your heart could never be black, Luca; the devil is afraid of you.

My heart is yours, Luca,
—Poppy Pemburton

P. S. Do I love you? I guess time will tell. Sam seems like a smart sort of fellow. I would certainly keep him around for all the romantic advice he is clearly knowledgeable about. Take care of one another and give him a hug from me for keeping you in line while I can't be there to do so.

P.P.S. You do protect me, Luca. You protect my heart.

12

LUCA

ALONG THE SOMME RIVER, FRANCE
OCTOBER 8, 1916

I should be so tired that exhaustion takes me like a baby and rocks me to sleep. Twenty hours on duty defending our trench along the Somme River in the sleet and rain should have me begging for respite, but my frozen body is swimming in adrenaline. At Captain McDaniel's order, I obediently move to a makeshift cot dug into the sides of the trenches, but I am unable to close my eyes. I know I need rest to be prepared for what's to come, but Sam's face lined with worry at the order given to take my place on watch has my heart seizing. He shouldn't be defending the trench without me.

When McDaniel ordered us apart, the panic that shot through my core reflected in Sam's eyes. Sam always plays it safe —never volunteering for first round on watch, or for packing the explosives into the trenches, or for cleaning and loading the weapons. He sticks close to me, and for that, I'm glad.

The other soldiers tease him for being a coward, but Sam doesn't have a cowardly bone in his body. The fact of it is, he didn't choose this life. The war path thrust upon him is far outside the comfort lines he has drawn for himself. Guns, explosives, loud noises, blood; it all causes his shoulders to flinch, but that doesn't make him cowardly. He shows his strength in a different way. A quieter way. The only way that matters, really.

Every day, Sam shows up.

The lot of us would let the silent cold of night wrap us in death's bow and deliver us into the next life, but every day, Sam wakes us up, songs from his time aboard the fishing boats tumbling from his lips. Where we are wont to bury ourselves beneath piles of coats and boots, huddled together in the muddy trench for the sake of warmth, Sam puts his helmet back on and encourages us to do the same. Every day, Sam stays in the fight. He climbs up the trench walls and holds his weapon at the ready when he would rather be anywhere else in the world.

Instead of closing my eyes, I pull the sketch I drew of Poppy on the church roof the night I almost kissed her out from my breast pocket. I haven't been able to draw for weeks since I ran out of my supply of charcoal, and my fingers ache for the feel of the smooth stick in my grasp. I slip the folded paper I keep close to my heart out next and reread Poppy's latest letter for what feels like the hundredth time since it arrived. I have it memorized now, but I want to see her handwriting, to touch the ink on the page, to ground myself as I picture the words on the paper trickling from her lips.

"Aren't you supposed to be sleeping, mate?" Johnson calls out to me, ripping me from thoughts of staring into Poppy's eyes as he leaps into the dirt-made bunk above me.

"Not tired," I reply.

"You're insane. I'm sleeping until Sunday." He kicks off his boots and is snoring before I can finish telling him to put his boots back on. Captain will rain torture upon Johnson if he catches him out of full uniform. Then it'll be trench runs for all of us in the morning.

I roll out of the nook I'm lying in and grab Johnson's shoes.

As I stuff Johnson's mammoth-sized foot back into his army boot, a chilling sound ricochets through the air above. Before I can do anything but cover my head with my arms, a German shell explodes at the edge of our trench.

The explosion reverberates through my chest, the vibrations tearing me nearly in two as the blast forces me to the ground. Dirt mercilessly rains down, creating a cloud of brown so thick, trench dust coats my eyes. The blow continues to ricochet in my ears, the hollow of my throat, and the beat of my heart, which thunders like lions chasing their prey.

But it's the deafening silence following that paralyzes me. It's as if the gift of sound has been sucked from my body.

My ears ache beneath the pressure.

When heat and smoke fill my lungs, I know I must move. Large, red-hot flames swallow the brown dirt in nearly one gulp. The orange fire parades down the trench walls, inching toward me.

I must move, but the silence pushing in on every side renders my muscles incapable. I stretch my mouth wide in an effort to open my eardrums, but still nothing. I throw Johnson's boot to the side, and when I attempt to stand, I realize a blackened foot is all that remains of the man who spoke to me less than one minute ago.

I lose the contents of my stomach. My head swims with fog as I heave, but afterward, sound rushes in with great fury.

I wish it hadn't.

Screams fill every corner of the trench. Screams that will never, as long as I live, leave my mind. Men are lying every which way in the dirty mud at the bottom of the trench. Many are missing limbs, and those are the lucky ones.

I hold onto the edge of the bunk until the space around me stops spinning. Debris floats through the thick, brown air as if in slow motion. I pick a piece of charred paper floating toward the top of the trench to focus on and make my way to it.

Sam!

I must find Sam. He was at the top of the trench. If he survived this, that's where he'll still be. The volume of noise will likely have him curled in a ball with his hands over his ears, so I look for bodies that look round—and alive.

Giovanni feared loud noises too. I stroke the underside of my chin, searching for the familiar, smooth stretch of scarred skin. "I'm sorry, G. I'm so sorry," I mumble just as the trench goes black.

I worry we've been struck again, but in seconds, everything is the same as it was before. I must be blacking out.

I graze my hand along the cool mud wall in case I lose consciousness again and let it guide me toward the last place I knew Sam to be, but my legs are slow and unwilling to comply.

"Luca!"

I hear my name, but I can't seem to place the voice.

Blackness encroaches.

I welcome its peaceful promise.

"Luca!" the voice shouts near my ear this time. Hands grab my shoulders.

I want to sit down. I'm ready to sleep now. I can't remember where I was going, anyhow.

"Medic!" the voice calls.

I know that voice. A smile breaks across my face. "G?"

"Your brother isn't here, Luca. It's me, mate."

Disappointment blankets me at the response, but I try to focus on where I am. Pain explodes in my arm. War. I'm at war. There was an explosion. Everyone is hurt.

G isn't hurt anymore. He's fine. He's in heaven with my mami and papi.

But Sam! Sam is hurt, I remember. I must find Sam.

"I need Sam," I hear myself say.

"Yeah, mate, it's me. I'm right here. I've got you. Medic!" I hear Sam's voice scream again. He must be really hurt.

"Can we sit down, Sam?" I ask.

Sam holds me firm against him. "Nope, we can't do that. We have to keep moving, mate. We need to get you to a medic."

Me? "I don't need a medic. I'm fine. I just need to sleep for a minute. McDaniel told me to sleep, remember?"

"Can't sleep now, Luca. You have shrapnel in your arm. You're bleeding. An awful, awful amount of blood."

Sam loses his insides next to me. Poor Sam. Maybe he needs some sleep too.

"C'mon, mate, lean over my shoulder," Sam says as he pushes me onto his shoulder, and for some reason I want to laugh, but I'm not sure why. It is nice to relax though.

I let my body fold over his.

"That's it. Good job," Sam grunts beneath me. I feel him moving slowly forward. Then everything around me disappears.

When I come around again, the air is cooler, lighter. But the noise is much louder. Exploding sounds of gunfire, shells, and bombs come from every direction. I open my eyes to see we are no longer in the trench, but the world spins, so I quickly shut my eyes again.

"Sam?"

"I still got you, mate," he says as if he's speaking with an elephant on his chest. Then he swears. "We need to get past the line without getting shot at. There's too much gunfire right now, so the medics can't get through safely. We are going to have to go to them. Luca, I need you to stay awake for me, okay? Picture that pretty redhead of yours. Can you do that?"

I blink my eyes, trying desperately to focus on what Sam is saying. Is Sam carrying me right now? To a medic because I'm wounded? Too wounded to walk on my own? That can't be.

I save Sam.

Sam doesn't save me.

Sam can't walk through a bloody German attack to get me to a medic. "I'm okay, Sam. You stay here. I'll run to the medics, and they'll take care of me."

"No. I've got you," Sam says beneath me. "I might be small, but don't take my lack of height for lack of strength. It ain't no easy task being on a fishing expedition. I've been preparing for this moment my entire life. I'm going to run, and all I need you to do is stay still and awake. Perfectly still so the shrapnel doesn't move and cause more damage. Okay?"

I don't know how to respond. I don't know if it's the lack of sleep, the horror at what I've seen, or the loss of blood causing me to lose consciousness, but I can't seem to make sense of what Sam is saying. I'm here to protect Sam. I enlisted in this war to fight my cowardice so that I could return to Poppy a hero.

But if I'm not invincible, if I can get hurt, if someone has to save *me*, what makes me a hero then?

"Okay," Sam yells above the thundering wave of bullets exploding somewhere close by. "On the count of three. Stay awake, and count with me, Luca," Sam commands.

Immediately I'm back with Poppy at the train station the day her father left for war. "Count with me," I had commanded her in much the same way. I picture her beautiful, fearful face trusting mine as I count with Sam now, and in this moment I realize, maybe I'm not here to save Sam. Maybe we're here to save each other.

"One. Two. Three," we count together. And Sam runs.

13

CHARLES

BEESTON, NOTTINGHAMSHIRE, ENGLAND
OCTOBER 20, 1916

"GOOD EVENING, COUSIN CHARLES," N18 SAYS THROUGH THE telephone after we've recited our lines and waited in silence for the required sixty seconds. "Uncle and I are having the most glorious holiday with your family at your beautiful ranch in Texas."

"Is that right?" I say into the mouthpiece. Over the past couple months, the calls with my contact have been rather pleasant in nature. Either Germany is winning the war, or N18 wants to win me.

I glance at my Glashutte. It's later than N18 typically calls, and I know Poppy will be arriving shortly, so we need to make this quick. Poppy's factory shift ends at seven p.m., after the post office closes, but I stay late to wait for her. In an effort to rebuild the previously crumbling bridge between us—which I'd burned to the ground when I called her a *servant*—I offered Poppy an apology deal: the six days a week she works, I stay as late as needed at the post office until she arrives after her shift. I process all the factory mail she needs posted so it's on the first outgoing train every morning. In exchange, Poppy agreed that she will "maybe, one day" forgive me. Three months later, and I'm happy to say that the mutually beneficial relationship between Poppy and I is heading in the right direction. We're certainly not friends yet, but she tolerates me with many less huffs and puffs than were present upon my arrival in England.

"You would be so proud of the way your brothers are taking charge back home while you are away," N18 says with pride in her voice.

I have only the British newspapers and letters from the Beeston men overseas to receive war information from. Both are highly skewed in favor of the allied soldiers, and the men writing home to their mothers and wives write only of their bravery and strength, so I take most of what they write as rubbish.

The only exception to this is Luca. He doesn't hide behind his paper when he writes, so Luca's letters are my main source of information—before I censor it all out, of course. But it's good to hear it straight from another German's lips now.

According to Luca, there are two battles that have been a blood bath for both the allied and central powers for many months now: the battle at Verdun and the fight along the Somme River. The allies tried to wear down our German offensive at Verdun by forcing them to split their defenses and send reinforcement to the Somme in July, but Luca said the German soldiers don't move. They're able to hold their ground for weeks at a time despite the heavy rains, dense fog, sleet, and snow they have experienced throughout October. Yet the weather has affected the allied soldiers in their march to push the German line as their soldiers struggle to cross muddy terrain under fierce fire from our artillery and fighter planes. Supposedly, the British have advanced less than twelve kilometers since the Somme battle began on July 1.

Is it too naive to believe Germany will be victorious by the end of the year?

"You should be very proud to be an American, Cousin Charles. I know I am," N18 says. "While I'm sure you wish you were here with us, you're doing good work over there in England. Keep it up. I haven't been able to make my way over to you as I'd hoped. Uncle keeps me quite busy, but I will come visit soon; I hear the yellow lemon pastries there are to die for." N18 cackles that wicked laugh of hers, and spiders crawl the length of my spine at the sound.

"I don't know if I'd die for them, Cousin, but they are indeed tempting." A certain yellow face flashes through my mind.

"What wouldn't you die for?" a woman's voice calls out from the lobby as if my thoughts conjured her forth.

I quickly end the conversation with N18 and replay my end of it, ensuring there's nothing I'll have to smooth over in case Poppy overheard the entirety of it.

"What wouldn't you die for, Mr. Andrews?" Poppy repeats as I round the corner into the lobby. A slew of packages from the factory litter the counter as if Poppy walked in and threw them from her arms. "Because Martha Roberts just died for freedom," Poppy says as she steps out from behind the boxes. "Martha Roberts just died for Britain. Martha Roberts just died because of me."

Poppy is sobbing. Her face is streaked with tears, and her shoulders are shaking as if she has a horrendous case of the chills.

"Whoa, whoa there now." I tear the cowboy hat from my head and rush to her side. I take her by the elbow, lead her to a chair behind the lobby desk, and urge her to sit. Her hand is working something furiously within the pocket of her dress.

"Why don't ya start from the beginnin'," I say, pulling up a chair. In the eight months I've known Poppy Pemburton, I have never seen her wear anything other than a coat of confidence and a shield of fire. Sometimes both simultaneously. I'm not quite certain what to do with this version of the woman sitting next to me.

"A couple months ago, a lady named Martha Roberts who has a husband serving in the war, and children, and pretty hair the color of chocolate," Poppy says with a tremble of her lips, "came to me and told me she was feeling very ill. She said we needed better working conditions, but I brushed away her concerns, Charles. I ignored her!"

I bristle at my cover name coming from Poppy's mouth for the very first time. It's odd but not terrible.

"I told her it was likely due to stress," Poppy continues. "Everyone who works in the danger house is sick in one way or another, and I didn't know how to help. But now a woman is dead because I didn't help her." Poppy's head drops into her hands.

"There's nothin' you could've done. You can't blame yourself for this, Poppy." I hand my white pocket hanky to her.

"I could have talked to Mrs. Fischer or Mr. Ashby sooner. But Mrs. Fischer has been in London on business for the last two weeks, and Mr. Ashby ran me out of his office without listening to a word of my concerns for our safety. He didn't even know who Martha was." Poppy balls the handkerchief in a fist.

"So you did talk to Mr. Ashby about your safety, then?"

"Just now, when I went to his office to gather the daily posts to bring here."

"What did you say?"

Poppy stands from the chair and starts to pace. "Well, I said, 'Mr. Ashby, enough is enough. Yellow skin, painful abdomens, difficulty breathing, and now death? Something needs to be done, and it needs to be done now.' To which he replied that if he needed his coffee filled or his office dusted, he would send a supervisor to fetch me. So then I said, 'I am not a dog, Mr. Ashby. Nobody fetches me.' And then I told him I would be saving him a great deal of trouble down the road if he would just listen to me."

"And did he?"

"Of course not." She stops pacing and whips around in my direction. "He told me he didn't have time for my dramatic antics and accusations. He said that Martha could have died for any number of reasons. That there is no proof the cause was from working there. Then he yelled at me to get out. But I can feel in my bones that I'm right about this, Charles. I must make him understand."

I stand from my chair and lean back against the counter. "I've heard Mr. Ashby doesn't take kindly to women with opinions."

Poppy scoffs. "He said I had no place speaking to a *man* the way I did and reminded me I was as replaceable as the next woman. I wanted to scream at him that I quit—that I refuse to work for chauvinistic men—but the image of Martha's mother-less children, of her husband who won't discover the death of his wife for weeks, flashed through my mind, and I knew I couldn't leave." Poppy turns to me, her blue eyes full and heavy. "I have to help the women left. All of them."

I think I have an idea that will make this experience work in both our favors.

"Miss Pemburton, where is the next closest ammunition factory?"

Poppy glances around the post office and scrunches up her nose as if she isn't sure she should tell me.

I don the most charming of all my smiles. "I have a plan."

Her curiosity must get the better of her, because she caves, her voice turning to a whisper. "I only know the location of one other factory. One of the girls who works in the danger house with us has a relative who works at a factory in Leeds. It's the Barnbow National Shell Filling Factory. Why?"

I know Leeds to be approximately one hundred kilometers away. It would take a full day to drive there and back, but I am positive N18 is unaware there's a factory there. My heart pounds at the possibilities.

I plop my cowboy hat on my head. "Let's go."

"Go where?" Poppy's face instantly frowns, and she pulls back from me.

"Let's go to Barnbow."

"Right this moment? Whatever for?" She flounders for a beat, odd sounds coming from her lips. Her hand moves to the inside of her dress pocket and then she says, "How would we even get there?"

"We can take my auto. Then you can see firsthand how they run things there. All the girls in England are bein' called canary girls for their yellow skin, right? Well, if that's true, the women in Barnbow are probly' fillin' shells the same way you girls in Chilwell are. But they might have some safety precautions in place that help them avoid ailments. Precautions you could inform Mr. Ashby of."

"You have an automobile?" she says doubtfully.

"A 1912 Wolseley. It was issued as somewhat of a bribe to accept the post office position here in England. They were desperate to fill the position quickly what with all the qualified men bein' gone, so they sweetened the deal a touch. C'mon, now; let's go see what we can find out for ya. If we leave right now, we should be home by the start of your next shift."

Poppy stares at me for a long moment. She looks as though she's calculating every possible outcome of this proposal, but I hope my idea is so good—so tempting—that whatever risks present themselves in her mind, a trip to another munitions factory will be worth the gamble. That the chance of possibly solving her dilemma will outweigh her mistrust in me.

"Mrs. Fischer will be back in a few days. I should just wait and let her take care of things. She's a retired nurse, and Mr. Ashby listens to her."

"But how much time could you save Mrs. Fischer, and by consequence the canary girls sufferin', by already havin' traveled to a different factory so you are able to offer your supervisor concrete solutions she can then take directly to Mr. Ashby?"

"Why are you so eager to do this? What's in it for you?" Poppy asks me with a skeptical cross of her arms.

I love and hate her poignant honesty. What's in it for me is finding the exact location of another ammunition factory for N18 to report back to Gukenstein, which gets me one step closer to everything I want: A transfer to the coveted spot as the

German Empire's liaison interpreter. The opportunity to live in Germany for good and watch over my mutter. A happy contact agent. Perhaps even another box of German chocolates.

"I've been itchin' to take that beautiful automobile out for a long drive, but I haven't had anywhere to go." I say. "You'd be doin' me a favor." That's not even a lie.

"I don't know," Poppy says, a look of twisted confusion on her face. "What if the Barnbow factory isn't taking any safety precautions either, and it's a waste of a trip?"

"But what if they are? What if there is somethin' to be discovered that could save somebody's life? What if this trip changes everythin'? Isn't it worth a chance?"

She sighs as one who's been defeated in a race. "Let's go, then."

We've driven quite aways from Beeston in silence, when I glance over and notice Poppy's arm is extended out of the auto, resting on the door frame. Her fingers dance slowly in the wind as if the air rushing past is tickling the tips. Her shoulders are relaxed back against the seat, her chin tilted toward the cold night air. She has a faint, almost peaceful smile on her lips, and I get the feeling this is the first time in a while she has felt at ease.

I did something to bring that smile to her lips. And I don't hate that thought.

I decide to take a risk.

As we approach the top of a steep hill, I use the hand lever to shift gears and step down on the accelerator pedal. The car lurches forward in response.

Poppy's body jolts at the force, but she squeals in delight and breaks into laughter. It's a sound I would never tire of hearing.

When we begin our swift decent down the hill, Poppy pushes herself out of the automobile till her waist rests on the frame of the door. She leans out like that for a moment, her hands holding herself balanced against the auto, and sets her chin at an angle that lets the wind whip at her face. Tendrils of hair pull loose from the bun tied at her neck until the bun gives way and hair shoots out around her in sparks of red. The free strands swish through the air like she's been caught in a tornado, and her laughter trickles through the air between us. I slow the speed to make sure she doesn't fall out, and when I do, she raises both arms up in the air, throws her head back, and lets out a long scream as we careen down the dark, empty road.

Everything inside me comes alive at the sound. Alive in a way I have never experienced. I want to push the unknown feeling away, but it's there in the pit of my stomach, going nowhere, and I find I'm as curious about it as I am embarrassed.

A few minutes later, she shimmies back into her seat and smiles over at me. It's a small smile but so genuine it catches me off guard. The blue of her eyes shines with moisture beneath dark, wet lashes. Her cheeks glow with life. The tip of her nose is red, and her hair . . . well, her hair is a perfect mess.

"Thank you," she says, exhaling. Her breath shudders, but her voice is strong and full of energy.

I nod at her and return a much-too-genuine smile of my own. I clear my throat and silently repeat the details of my Charles Andrews identity card until I have no feelings of any kind within me.

"I know this excursion was simply an excuse for you to drive this fancy auto," Poppy says, interrupting my third round of memorization recall, "but you're doing me a huge favor by driving me. I've never lived or traveled outside of Beeston; I can't, really." She twists her fingers together in her lap, and I make a mental note to ask more about that statement later. "But if I find some answers to the factory's safety problems while in Barnbow, this is going to save lives. You're helping me make a difference. I truly can't thank you enough. And . . . um . . ." She looks down at her lap, untwists her fingers, and then looks back at me, her gaze soft and playful. "I forgive you."

"Forgive me?"

"For calling me a servant." She chuckles.

I laugh and tip my hat to her. "All it took was a drive in the Wolseley? I should have done this ages ago."

Her light laugh sounds like the noise I imagine a twinkling star makes.

"You're one of the good fellows, Charles. I may have misjudged you."

Something erratic moves through my chest at her words. Every time I'm around Poppy, I feel things I've never felt before. Joy? Desire? Life? Excitement? I'm not certain.

But there's a discomfort sitting within this stirring too. A discomfort to what I'm not quite sure yet. I am nothing if not a loyal citizen of Germany. It's the country I was born, raised, and educated in. I love my country. I love my people. Same as Poppy does hers. Same as anyone fighting, I suppose.

But now I'm wondering, what makes one of us wrong and one of us right?

My head begins to ache.

I can't do this. I can't go down this road.

There are no answers here—just unknowns and trouble. I would do best to stick to my plan. Whether I like this spy life or not, I'm good at it, I remind myself. I just need to keep Poppy from getting in my head. That's the job.

Poppy is the job. The enemy. The target I must align in the crosshairs of my scope.

While sometimes that means the job will require us to enjoy one another's company, I must remember that every time we're together, I have the sole purpose of collecting more information.

Remembering facts and regurgitating them is how I stay grounded. Remembering facts is how I'll keep my head straight in this mission. It has worked in every mission before.

I am Charles Andrews, a rancher and post office manager.

I am Jakob Kirtchner, German spy.

I begin talking, trying to distract myself. "I'm startin' to git rather sleepy, so to keep me awake till we git to Leeds, how 'bout you tell me exactly how it is you fill a shell?"

Poppy side-eyes me and balks. "I'm not telling you how we fill shells. We're not allowed to speak about details like that outside of the factory. They have reminder posters saying as much plastered to nearly every surface throughout the buildings."

"They swear you to secrecy with magical rituals or somethin' like that?"

"Something like that," she says and laughs.

"Okay, Silent Canary. As you wish."

"Silent Canary?"

"If you can't talk about your work as a canary girl, doesn't that make you a silent canary?"

She contemplates for a moment and then a large smile grows across her face. "Yes. I'm a silent canary. I like that."

Eventually, I'm going to have to make this loyal canary sing.

"I think you're doin' the right thing by tryin' to get answers," I tell her. "No matter what the outcome at the Barnbow factory, it's brave of you to try." My own ulterior motives aside, I mean every word. The yellow pigment of her skin does nothing to mar her beauty, but it does have me concerned for her health. She's not coughing all the time like many of the other women, but whatever is happening inside her body from the chemicals she's working with cannot be good.

The thought strikes a protection chord somewhere deep in my core, different from the way I feel about Mutter, but I don't have time to find the string and cut it before Poppy reaches over and squeezes my hand.

"Thanks, Charles." The touch is warm and soft, and something inside me shifts at the tenderness. Weakens. I make a mental note to never think about protecting or coming within touching distance of my British enemy again. And I put it right next to the note that says, "Jakob Kirtchner, GERMAN spy."

But as Poppy settles into her seat with a satisfied smile and closes her eyes like she trusts me to take her anywhere in the world, my spirit warms with a feeling akin to peace. An emotion I haven't experienced in years.

Then I have a strange yet not unwelcome thought: if I play this game carefully, perhaps we can both come out unscathed. Poppy Pemburton may be the target, but that doesn't mean I have to keep the little yellow bird lined up in my sights with the intent to shoot her down.

I just need to ride on her wings and let her lead me back to the nest.

POPPY

CHILWELL, NOTTINGHAMSHIRE, ENGLAND
OCTOBER 25, 1916

CECILIA FISCHER PUSHES HER CHAIR BACK FROM HER makeshift examination table and stands. "This is unacceptable." Her voice is sharp, and it cuts through the clamor of the danger house like a saint speaking unholy words in a chapel.

Clumped in small groups throughout the house, women rise to their tiptoes and edge closer to observe the scene before them. Sophia is lying flat on her back on the table, her palms gripping the edges while Mrs. Fischer runs her fingers along Sophia's abdomen, pushing gently, pausing, then pushing again.

Sophia lets out a sharp cry at each touch. She is the twentieth woman our factory supervisor has examined this morning.

Mrs. Fischer's brown bob shakes with vigor, and her eyes swivel to mine. Although I'm standing on the opposite side of the table, her gaze penetrates the air between us as if she's close enough to feed off my soul.

"I agree," I say. "Unacceptable. I believe the handling of poisonous chemicals without protection is the ultimate reason for Martha Robert's death and the cause of suffering for so many other canary girls."

I motion toward Sophia and out toward the women that surround us. "Mr. Ashby wouldn't listen to a word I said when I approached him with requests for improved working conditions, but I believe I'm right." I have yet to suffer any ailments other than a tickle in my throat, a constant metallic taste in my mouth, and yellowing skin, but Sophia's stomach cramps and Nessy's chest pain have only increased since the day they first voiced their concerns in the washroom.

"Tell me what you discovered during your *unauthorized* visit to Barnbow," Mrs. Fischer says.

"They have the same basic rules as we do here: each employee must remove all metal items of any kind from their person and be dressed in their overalls and rubber boots before they can enter the filling room. But once on the factory floor, the workers put on gloves to protect their hands" —I mimic the action of sliding on gloves— "and wear masks over their mouths and nose to keep from breathing in the dangerous chemicals. Masks and gloves, Mrs. Fischer! Think of the problems we could avoid simply by asking Mr. Ashby for those things."

Cecilia Fischer nods as she removes a stethoscope from around her neck, places the ends in her ears, and presses the metal circle onto Sophia's chest.

"The factory also has proper ventilation in place," I continue. "Windows and fans are in every building in the factory, and the windows are always vented and fans always running in the filling house, even during the cold months. I was there during their night shift hours, and the fans were running even then."

Mrs. Fischer helps Sophia down from the table, hangs the stethoscope over her shoulder, and places her hands on her hips. "There are definite signs in every woman I examined today that show poor health with possible permanent damage to lungs, abdomen, and skin, but without any other data or proper medical equipment, it's impossible to know to what extent. Even with visits to the factory physicians, there will be no definitive answers," she says. "We don't know if the pains will subside once employment at the factory ceases or if there will be lasting ailments beyond our time here. But I agree that the severity each of you is experiencing is likely due to the lack of care in our working conditions. I will speak to Mr. Ashby on behalf of the danger house employees and see to it that we have the same safety precautions Barnbow National Shell Filling Factory does."

Murmurs of gratitude ripple throughout the house.

Mrs. Fischer faces me, slides her spectacles down her nose, and lowers her voice. "Authorized or not, you did good work here, Miss Pemburton. You should be proud." She returns her stethoscope to her bag. "I'm not sure how many more women we would have lost before I thought to travel to another ammunition factory and do some investigating."

I almost tell her it was, oddly enough, Mr. Charles Andrews's idea, but I think better of it. In hindsight, I shouldn't have allowed an American civilian to be my chauffeur to an undisclosed British munitions factory, but after news of Martha Robert's death, all that mattered to me was justice for her and protection for these women.

And I can't say I regret it. I haven't ridden in an automobile in ages; it was positively thrilling, and Mr. Andrews wasn't a terrible riding companion.

Clara, Annabelle, Sophia, and Nessy circle around me, and Mrs. Fischer slips from the house.

"Poppy, you did it!" Clara cries as her slender arms circle about my waist.

I don't want to become used to her overt displays of affection, but when my body naturally leans into hers and my chin rests atop her head without a second thought, I know my mind and my heart are not in agreement.

"Oh, I did nothing," I say with a wave of my hand through the air. "Mrs. Fischer will finally get Mr. Ashby to see reason so we can continue to move forward and do what we came to the factory to do: fill ammunition for our boys."

"I wish I had a boy," Clara says dreamily in my arms. Her thick black lashes flutter with dramatic gusto, and I laugh at her girlish romantic antics.

"You are much too young to be worried about having a man, Little Canary," Sophia says. Everyone in the factory has taken to the nickname I awarded Clara, as it suits her perfectly.

At Sophia's words, Clara's back straightens with sudden force, and her cheeks flush. "Am not. I'm eighteen," Clara says a little too loud with a little too much protest in her voice.

"I'd believe that lie just about as soon as I'd believe my husband was still alive." Sophia looks at her with pointed accusation.

Clara's eyes dart about the room. "It's not a lie. Sophia, you're—"

"As we were saying," Nessy interrupts loudly, "Mrs. Fischer couldn't have spoken to Mr. Ashby without your proof, Poppy, so we are grateful to you. Did you take a night train to Leeds to visit Barnbow?"

With the attention off her, Clara relaxes back into me but I tuck away her panicked reaction to Sophia's remarks into my memory to ask one of the women about later.

"Night trains are my favorite," Annabelle says. "One time, I met a fellow traveling from Scotland to England on the night train. Let's just say . . ." She pauses and giggles. "He took a detour to Annaland that night."

Sophia gags. "For crying out loud, Annabelle. Do you have any sense of decorum?"

I scratch my neck and think about how to respond to Nessy's question as Annabelle and Sophia argue over the definition of decorum.

Had I been in a better state of mind that evening at the post office, a night train would have been the better option of transportation. But at least I can be thankful it was only Mr. Andrews who was with me. *He, of all people, knows the high value of government secrets and censorship,* I think as I internally roll my eyes, remembering the way he all too eagerly blacked out portions of my letter detailing my passionate goodbye kiss with Luca.

"Yes, a train car," I say, my mouth seemingly full of marbles.

My gut flips at the lie. Lying is the one thing I never, ever do. Jane lied to me. My father lies by omission. Lies destroy lives. Even simple ones have the power to hurt others beyond repair.

I open my mouth to rescind the lie, but at the same moment, Clara says, "I've never been on a train." Her thin bottom lip curves into a pout.

"You've never traveled by train?" Nessy stammers. Her mouth drops dramatically when Clara shakes her head in the negative.

"Never had the reason to, I guess," Clara says.

"How'd you get to Chilwell?" I ask. "Didn't you come from Wales?"

"Caught rides with passing autos when I could." Clara shrugs. "And walked the rest."

"All the way from Cardiff?" Annabelle raises her eyebrows in disbelief. "In the winter?"

"Took me just over two days," Clara says with pride. "Didn't have the money for a train."

Just then, Mrs. Fischer blows back through the danger house door, her hands clapping for our attention. "Ladies, we will be taking our meal break early today. Please close out your stations and move to the washroom. While you are eating, maintenance employees will be opening windows and installing fans throughout the buildings, starting here in the danger house. Masks and gloves will be here by the end of the week."

A cheer goes up, and the canary girls move quickly to obey Mrs. Fischer's orders. Nessy and I go back to the detonators station and finish screwing in the freeze cap for the shell we were working on before Mrs. Fischer began her health checkups.

"Nessy, can I ask you about Clara," I say when I'm sure the little canary is out of earshot.

"What about?"

"She isn't eighteen, is she?"

Nessy glances around and lowers her voice. "Clara turned fifteen two months ago."

My eyes widen in disbelief. "She was fourteen when she was accepted for war work? Fourteen?" Her looks and behaviors clearly testify of a younger age, but the thought of a fourteen-year-old girl signing on for this type of work breaks my heart. What could have possibly led her to do this?

"Stop screeching," Nessy scolds me. "She lied on her paper-work. She had to."

"Whatever for?"

"Because the minimum age requirement for girls to work munitions is eighteen."

"I know *that*," I hiss. "Why is she here at Chilwell at all? What caused a fourteen-year-old girl to become so desperate that she would travel over two hundred kilometers from home, alone, to work at a dangerous factory that required her to add four years to her age?"

With steady hands, Nessy places the final screw into the freeze cap of the fifteen-inch howitzer shell and loads it onto the wagon that will transport this load of filled shells to the store-house. Back at my side, she stands so close to me I could count all the freckles that dance across her nose if I wanted to. "Mrs. Fischer and I are the only ones who know the truth about Clara's age," she whispers.

"Mrs. Fischer knows?" Somehow, I can't see Mrs. Fischer knowingly breaking any rules.

"She's the one who found Clara, cleaned her up, and helped her fill out the paperwork at the war office to become employed here."

"Found her where?"

"A little bundle of rags shivering outside the war employment office in Beeston back in February. Clara's left eye was black and blue and nearly swollen shut, her arm was broken, and she was starving. Poor girl didn't have a pence to her name."

"That's terrible," I say, turning to look at Clara. She laughs at something Annabelle says as they work together to pour beeswax into a shell. Clara's sweet face is full of joy, optimism, and a youthful energy so vivid that the image Nessy described seems near impossible.

"Who hurt her?" I ask, my skin prickling beneath my uniform.

"I know Clara wouldn't mind you knowing the truth; I've seen how you've taken to one another, but please don't mention her age to anybody else. Clara is terrified of being sent back home."

"Who hurt her?" I repeat.

"Her father. There was a pub down the street from their house. Most of the time, he couldn't remember which one he lived in—the pub or the house. Clara was the youngest of five children—all girls—and was often the only child home, so she received more *attention* from her father than anyone else."

"You are the best big sister I've ever had," Clara had said to me a couple months ago, and my heart aches.

Fear reaches out, but I ignore its offering of protection. It's not dangerous to love a child.

"Why did she choose to run to Beeston?" I ask, both sickened that she had to leave and astonished that she made it here at all.

"The primary school she attended turned into a war hospital in 1915. Gossip among the nurses and soldiers was that the large ammunition factory in Chilwell was hiring thousands of women and paying eight shillings a week with free meals. An older girl assured Clara the factory was so desperate for women workers that she could lie about her age and no one accepting applications at the Beeston War Office would notice. She ran away from home the next day."

"She's so brave," I say. "I don't know that I could have left home. Left my mother."

"Mothers don't look the other way while their children suffer."

I don't know what to say to that.

Rub, rub, rub.

I worry the ring over and over between my fingertips as thoughts of Jane spark forgotten memories.

Jane forbade me from calling her Mother. I thought everyone called their mothers by their given name until I heard a child at church address her mum as Mother. When I asked Jane why I didn't do the same, she said she never wanted to be a mother and that calling her such would only remind her of her failures. She was Jane and would be addressed as so.

At the time, I had no idea what she'd meant by *failures*. I'm not sure I do even now.

"Mrs. Fischer promised Clara that if she was a hard worker and kept her age a secret, she would see to it that nobody knew anything about her past," Nessy says, pulling me from my memories. "She told Clara she could start over after the war. Rebuild a life for herself with the money from working here. And Mrs. Fischer would ensure Clara never had to return home if she didn't want to."

The sound of something metal tinkling across the floor freezes our conversation.

I search my pocket with frantic fingers.

No!

I know I'm not supposed to bring metal into the danger house. Ever. *I'm the one preaching safety standards for goodness' sake.* But Jane's gold ring is a part of me. There has not been one day —not one—since the night Jane left that the ring has left my person. It was never supposed to slip from my boiler suit pocket.

I look up right as Mrs. Fischer bends over and retrieves the ring from the ground.

"Whose is this?" she asks quietly. Not one person speaks.

"The rightful owner of this metal band will be dismissed from the factory. Owner, you have five seconds to come forward, or the whole of you will spend your meal hour cleaning the men's toilets until I find out who it belongs to. Five, four, three—"

"It's mine," Clara shouts, and my heart nearly tears in two.

I take a step forward to tell the truth, when Nessy yanks hard on my arm and tells me to shut up. I whip around to face her, ready to give her a piece of my mind, when she whispers through clenched teeth, "Clara is the only person in this room Mrs. Fischer won't fire. Let her take this one for you. Mrs. Fischer knows that's not Clara's ring. She knows Clara would never do something that stupid."

Mrs. Fischer's eyes narrow in Clara's direction before they pivot to me and hold my gaze.

All feeling drains from my hands and face. How could she possibly know it's mine? I don't even think Luca knows what that ring looks like. It's never outside my pocket.

The tip of Clara's nose turns pink, but she steps forward and holds out her palm, effectively tearing Mrs. Fischer's stare from me. "It's mine. I'm sorry. It was on a chain around my neck, and I forgot to take it off in the changing room. It must've broken when I was working."

"This ring could have created a spark that in turn would set off an explosion at any moment, and none of us would be standing here contemplating cleaning men's toilets," Mrs. Fischer says. Her voice is light, yet her face is anything but.

"I understand," Clara says.

The whole room watches as our little canary stuffs Jane's ring into her boiler suit pocket and runs from the room. My insides shake with remorse. I'm sick with regret for letting Clara take my punishment, but Nessy's right. If Mrs. Fischer tells Mr. Ashby I brought metal into the danger house, we will both be fired, as per his "conditions" when he hired me, and I will never fill another shell again. And then what would I do? The Beeston Lace Factory closed its doors months ago.

"This is the first time metal has ever been found in our danger house," Nessy says near my ear. The hint of threat in her voice accompanies her pointed look.

"I understand," I say, guilt coursing through me. "It won't happen again."

"See that it doesn't. I'll never let Clara take the fall for you again."

"Neither will I."

While that promise seems to satisfy Nessy, my not one but *two* lies—one outright and one of omission—plus the absence of Jane's ring from my pocket has my stomach in an unsettled mess, and panic squeezes my chest. I focus on counting backward from ten, my finger discretely tapping the beats against my heart.

"The rest of you wash up and go eat," Mrs. Fischer says. "I'll see you back here in an hour." She nods her dismissal before quickly retreating after Clara.

I'm too upset to eat, so rather than make my way to the canteen with the canary girls, I head outside for fresh air. I walk the perimeter of the iron fence near the entrance of the Chilwell factory grounds that guards the factory buildings when I see a gentleman leaning against the fence, watching me. The man isn't wearing a boiler suit, but he is wearing a uniform.

A British military uniform.

I see him then. Green eyes that reflect the afternoon light. Eyes that look like a soft storm in a blue lagoon. Eyes that look like coming home.

Luca.

15

LUCA

CHILWELL, NOTTINGHAMSHIRE, ENGLAND
OCTOBER 25, 1916

POPPY PEMBURTON'S WARM BODY WITHIN MY ARMS TAKES every conscious thought and breath from my being. Her face is buried in my neck, her arms wrapped tightly around me. My hands grip her to my chest, as if an unseen force could at any moment try to rip her away from me. Nothing in the world matters more than this moment.

Her frame shakes with sobs against mine as I spin her around, and around, and around outside the Chilwell factory gates, creating a centripetal world for the two of us to disappear in. The shrapnel wound near my shoulder screams in protest at the movement, but I would hold her in my arms like this until my arm fell off if it meant I never had to let her go.

Tears prick the corners of my eyes at the familiarity of *her*. At the sight of the freckled face and blue eyes I have dreamt of for six months. My fingers itch for a drawing pad and charcoal.

I slow our spinning and twist my head to better see her. She raises her eyes from the crook of my neck, and her face, wet with tears upon yellow-colored skin, sends my heart straight into her hands. I kiss each individual tear that caresses the soft skin of her cheeks before my brain approves the action my lips have taken.

She doesn't push me away. She holds tighter to me still, and more tears fall. I greet them with my lips, and she leans into each kiss.

I move my mouth beside her ear and whisper, "It's good to see you too, Firebird."

"I can't believe you're here. You're really here." Her eyes glisten with fresh moisture, and her fingers run up and down my face, over my lips, and into my hair as if she's confirming she isn't in a dream.

I memorize the feel of her touch on my skin.

It's the memory I know I will hold onto when I lie in the dark trenches. It's the memory that will keep me standing when I want to surrender to the darkness. The memory of this gentle, loving caress.

I release my fierce grip around her and let her slide carefully to the ground. Her hands trail down my arms, and even through the thick fabric of my khaki uniform, my skin comes alive beneath the pressure of her touch.

I lean forward and press a gentle kiss to her forehead. "Surprise."

"When did you get home?" she asks. "How long will you be here?"

"I just walked off the train. Came straight to Chilwell to find you. I have three days leave in Beeston."

"I wish you would have sent me a telegram so I could have requested some holiday to spend with you while you're home. I'm working the next three days." I hear the anguish in her voice.

"I would have, only I didn't get a chance to write before Captain gave me orders to travel home while my wound heals."

"Your wound? Luca, you're hurt!" Poppy grabs at my body, searching. "Where? What happened?"

I calm her hands in mine. "It's just a slight prick of the skin in my upper arm is all." I point to the place near my shoulder. "There was an explosion in our trench. There were many men hurt much worse than I was, and they needed all the beds in the medic tent for those with serious wounds. Because mine were nearly all healed up, Captain McDaniel ordered me to take one week's leave. I am of no use to them until my arm heals because I can't hold my gun properly. With travel time, I'm allotted three days here in Beeston."

"Did you lose any men you were close with?" Poppy's voice is soft. Respectful.

My mind flits to Johnson and his large boot left empty in my hand. "Yes. We lost some very good men."

"Sam?"

"Sam is fine, thank the good Lord above. Sam saved my life." I can almost feel Sam's strong hands holding me up even now, and my heart swells with pride at the memory of Sam, my brother in arms, carrying me across his back to safety. "I would have passed out from blood loss in the trench if Sam hadn't found me and carried me out of the trench and through the gunfire to the medics behind the lines."

I will never forget how the whiz of flying bullets assaulted my ears as he ran with me. How the eruption of dirt in the air sprayed upon my flesh as a bullet missed us. Trepidation emanated off Sam in waves, but still he ran. He never stopped. Not until he knew I was safe.

"Sam will forever be in my prayers of gratitude," Poppy whispers.

Her reverence for Sam causes a lump to build in my throat. "Mine as well."

Poppy cups my face in her hands. "I'm so grateful to have you home for as little or as long as possible. I must run now or Mrs. Fischer will have my hide, but can we meet in our spot when my shift is over?" She raises her scarred palm up to me. "Seven thirty?"

"Seven thirty," I confirm and place my scarred palm against hers. Her yellow-stained fingers press against my brown, dirt-stained ones. Our two hands, once clean with innocence and laced with benign fears, are now inlaid with sacrifice and molded to carry suffering the other knows nothing about. These hands once knew the weight of every boulder the other carried, but whose hands are these that touch now, I wonder. What more will they endure? How differently stained might they become as the war carries on?

But when Poppy slowly interlaces our fingers, her soft skin skimming mine until our hands are clasped, I know these two imperfect hands will always find their way back to one another. These hands, no matter the stains upon them, will always be a safe place for the other's heart to land.

I slide my arm around her waist and press a quick kiss just below her ear. "I'm grateful to be home," I say. "Nowhere else I'd rather be."

She sighs deeply, and her warm breath tickles my neck, creating a sensation there that sends my heart racing.

I debate throwing her over my shoulder and running into the thick forest of trees behind the factory, when she says, "I'll see you tonight." She flashes me a quick smile as if she knows exactly what my thoughts are and takes off in a run back to the factory.

BEESTON IS MAGICAL AT NIGHT FROM THIS HIGH UP ON THE church roof. The familiar way in which the town falls asleep echoes like the chords of a homecoming song against the stone walls of our fortress, a beat all its own that draws you in and lulls you into a cozy trance. Shop doors slam closed, friends holler salutations, boot heels click along cobblestone streets as couples wander hand in hand beneath the flare of gas lamps. Below us, Preacher and Mabel Jones click the locks of the church doors securely into place, and as if on cue, the autumn night insects begin their evening melodies.

Poppy and I look out over Beeston now from behind the ledge of the church roof, arm in arm, leaning against one another silently. We watch as heavy clouds fill the night sky, a cocoon of moonless black above the trees that shield our heads.

In the subdued light, Poppy looks breathtaking in a blue, floor-length silk dress with billowing sleeves. Her hair is twisted up behind her head with a few rebellious tendrils spilling around her face. She sidles closer to me and squeezes my arm gently.

I try to camouflage my grimace by tucking my arm carefully around her waist and drawing her in front of me, holding her so we're both facing out toward the town.

"I'm sorry; did I hurt your arm? You don't have to move it if it hurts too much," she says.

"And miss a chance to hold you? Never."

She leans slowly back into my chest. We sit in companionable silence for a long while, and as I hold this quiet girl in my arms, I realize how much Poppy has flourished in the time I have been away. Where there was once fear in her eyes, now there is confidence. Where there was once despair in her heart, now there is hope. Where there was once faltering in her actions, now there is surety.

"Tell me about it," Poppy says, breaking the silence. "About the war. What it's really like."

"You don't want to hear it."

"Yes, I do." Poppy turns in my arms, facing me. "I gave up owning the lace factory to put my own two hands to work alongside you and Father. I want to know that what I'm doing is making a difference. I see the newspapers and listen to the war gossip, but I want to hear it from you, Luca. I want to feel what you feel." Poppy places her hand over my heart. "Please."

The strength in her voice pricks my soul. I know she can handle the weight of my heart, and suddenly I want her to know. I want to share this part of my life with her too. I want to walk this new adventure of our lives together as much as we can while serving thousands of kilometers apart.

"Battles are exhausting, fatigue all encompassing, and death a constant reality and sometimes, even, a privilege," I say. She doesn't flinch at my words, so I continue. "The freezing temperatures of the muddy trenches keep our bodies and feet in a state where one is never fully dry nor warm. Many men have acquired trench foot and have lost their appendages. Hunger is a near-constant reality. Red liquid colors both our daydreams and our nightmares. Gunshots are the backdrop of our lullabies, yet sleep is a luxury of the past. The cries of grown men in the night are enough to strip a child's innocence." I drop my head, shame and embarrassment fighting for center stage. "I'm not fighting in France to prove myself a hero anymore. I'm simply there to support the allied troops and endure. There is no glory to be had; only evil laughing victoriously over those who remain."

If Poppy thought I was a hero before, she will certainly see straight through that facade now, but I cannot lie to her.

Poppy lifts my chin. "Long before you stood on a battlefield, you stared evil in the face and survived. You can't prove yourself a hero, Luca, because you already *are* one. You beat the devil once; you can do it again."

"That doesn't make me a hero, Firebird. That only makes me a survivor," I tell her, biting back the tears that choke the inside of my throat.

"They are one and the same." She cups my face with her slender hands and pulls me closer until our noses are touching. "You don't have to chase the world to save it, Luca. You just have to keep standing back up. *That* is what makes you a hero."

Everything in me wants to jump from the roof we're standing on and run from the girl who just opened me up and examined each part of my wrecked soul with merely a few spoken words. My embarrassment at the trickle of tears that betrays me burns hot against my cheeks.

I try to turn away from her—I would like to keep *some* dignity—but she holds me firmly in front of her.

"You are not the evil of your aunt," Poppy whispers. Her soft lips press against my cheek as she kisses away a tear in the same manner I did to hers this morning. "You are not your pain."

Another kiss. "You are not at fault for what happened to G or to your parents." Another kiss, this one right on the scar that curves beneath my chin. "Nobody—not even God—holds that against you. It's okay to forgive yourself now."

A sob escapes me at that. At that permission to forgive myself.

Can I? Can I let this go?

I have already forgiven Aunt Elizabeth; maybe I can start to forgive myself too. Maybe I have paid enough penance.

I take several deep breaths and wipe a hand across my face as if I could possibly wipe away all traces of embarrassment. "Sheesh. I don't know what it is about leaving everything I know behind, facing battles every day, and laying my heart on the line that has made me this weepy pile of feelings." I shudder dramatically, and Poppy laughs.

"Do you want to do counts to calm yourself? I am pretty good at those now."

I chuckle at her smirk. "Well, I usually use these to get me through tough days and nights in the trenches." I pull out a stack of letters she's written to me and the picture I drew of her the last time we stood here together, and I lay them on the ledge for her to see.

Her mouth drops open at the sight of them. "You carry those around with you?"

"Of course. Right next to my heart. They're my most prized possessions."

Poppy rises on her tiptoes and grabs hold of my shoulders as if there's more energy in her body than she can contain. "I love you, Luca!"

Her sudden declaration catches me off guard. I do a double take and watch her face, looking for signs that she said what I, indeed, think she said.

Her eyes dance as her smile grows.

I'm positive she said the word *love*, but selfishly, I want to hear it again. I want to be ready for the words when they come so I can hear the way they sound in the timbre of her voice. So I can watch the way her mouth moves when she says them and memorize the way they cause my heart to race.

"What did you say?"

Poppy laughs and moves in close to me. She wraps her arms around my neck and looks up at me with great intent, as if she understands I need this. Her eyes go soft and pull me in. There isn't a pair of dark-blue eyes more beautiful in this entire world.

Along the back of my neck, her finger traces a slow, deliberate path from the collar of my shirt up into my hair, setting every molecule of my body on alert.

"I said," she says, her lips so close beneath mine, one could hardly slide a piece of paper between them, "that I. Love. You." She declares each word slowly and with purpose. Her bottom lip grazes along mine as her mouth forms each word, sending fire shooting through my being. I am both alive and dead in this very moment. Is my heart beating out of control, or has it stopped altogether?

I am confident nobody has uttered those three words with more integrity, passion, or belief than Poppy Pemburton has in this moment.

My bottom lip skims the freckle on the top of her mouth. "I love you too, Poppy."

Can she sense the near explosion within my chest? Feel the pulse of my heartbeat throbbing for her? "More than any man has loved a woman."

"I know," she whispers back. "I'm going to kiss you now, Luca, but I'm going to take my time."

Everything within me freezes and warms in the same breath.

I want everything I do to testify that I will always be here for her. From the words I speak, to the way I hold her, to the way I kiss her. She can trust me to be her rock no matter how near or far I am to her. And when our lips meet, that's the message I want them to send to her.

A promise from my soul to hers:

I will love you always and forever.
You can trust me with your heart.
I will never betray you.
I will never walk away.
You don't have to be afraid.

The look I see in her eyes is one of longing and desire. How am I the man lucky enough to be on the receiving end of that desire?

She closes her eyes, her dark lashes splayed across her creamy, yellow skin, and she pushes up onto her toes. Her nose caresses mine, and her breath—warm and sweet—exhales in soft tumbles across my lips. She licks her lips so slowly I think the gesture might kill me.

Finally, her mouth meets mine for the briefest of moments before pulling back the slightest amount. Then she comes back, confidently finding my lips again, and the sensation of her soft mouth feathering mine knocks me nearly to my knees. Over and over she does this, each kiss lasting a moment longer than the last one. Each placement of her lips moving to a new location on mine. The kisses are slow and careful but not timid, or unsure, or teasing.

She kisses me as if we're conducting an intense study of one another's new strengths, weaknesses, and heartaches. As if we have a mutual understanding that although these lips have met before, they have never met in *this* way, because we are, each of us, new and different from how we were then. And I find I very much enjoy being under her observation.

Her body shivers against me.

I slide my fingers up her sides until my hands cradle her back, stabilizing her.

She arches into my touch and then her lips melt into mine. Her hands make their way up my neck and into my hair as I nibble along her bottom lip. She tightens her hold around me and presses closer into me still, and my body responds instantly. Everything about this woman undoes me.

I let my fingers travel with slow purpose back down the length of her, memorizing every curve and bend along the way, then wrap my arms firmly around her waist. She opens her mouth slightly, and I deepen our kiss at the invitation.

Her hands move down my shoulders and over my arms, then grab hold of my suspenders. She pulls tight against them, the fabric of my shirt gripped in her fists, her mouth moving with increasing fervor against mine.

I pick her up by the waist and set her on the ledge of the brick wall, never losing the taste of her kiss. I grab her face in my hands, needing something firm to hold on to so I can respond to her desire with all the fire raging inside of me.

My body is so alive with want for this incredible woman who truly loves, knows, and understands every piece of me and of my heart. My hands make their way into her hair, freeing the delicate twist from her head.

She groans softly into my mouth as my fingers become tangled in the soft strands that have broken free.

I stop breathing entirely when she utters my name as if she is starved and I am a feast laid before her.

I know if I don't slow down now, my message to her will not be one of integrity. But I want her to know, I *need* her to know, that she can trust me.

I untangle my hands from her hair and slow the kiss. When I can feel my heart again, I pull my lips from hers and place a quick kiss to the tip of her nose followed by a long, firm kiss on her forehead. I release her from my grasp and take a succession of steps backward until I have put a decent amount of cold night air between us.

"I must stop kissing you now, or I will never be able to stop."

"I don't want you to stop, Luca," she whispers across the space. Her lips are swollen and red, and the sight of them causes my heart to tremor.

"I don't want to stop either; trust me." I laugh and duck my head so she won't see my cheeks flare.

When she giggles, I know it's too late.

In three days, I must leave Poppy again, but this time I'm heading back to war-torn France armed with the power I need to 'stand back up,' as Poppy admonished. Because I am going to marry Poppy Pemburton.

I will take down whatever stands in the way of my returning home in one piece—body *and* soul—to do that.

16

CHARLES

BEESTON, NOTTINGHAMSHIRE, ENGLAND
OCTOBER 27, 1916

"WE TRAVELED TO AND FROM LEEDS IN THE MIDDLE OF THE night, so it was dark when we arrived," I tell N18. "Therefore, I don't know the exact coordinates of the new post office location, but I am certain I could find my way back there if I needed to."

"And your travel companion was unaware of your goals?"

"Completely unaware," I assure my contact.

Poppy's bright eyes and infectious laugh weave their way into my thoughts. Her genuine gratitude for the ride to Leeds and the smile I've found myself replaying in my mind over the last week make my insides twist.

"Were you able to see inside the new post office for yourself?"

"There are guards placed around the perimeter of the land. Only those whose names are on the list and who have a badge are allowed through the construction gates."

"Exceptional work, Cousin," N18's voice purrs through the earpiece of the telephone. "Uncle will be thrilled to hear this. We had five post office locations within England staffed with the highest-trained men to help Britain maintain stability during these treacherous times of war. Thanks to you, that number is now six. Slowly but surely, we will be staffed all throughout England."

I've deduced N18 is using the term *post office* as a cover for *ammunition factory* in this particular conversation, but I'm not certain if she's saying that those five munition factories now have a German spy somewhere within their walls or that we have German spies in the five actual post offices closest to a munitions factory, performing a similar cover job as mine.

Either way, that knowledge doesn't bring me the same amount of pride it once did, because I don't know what the end goal is with infiltrating these factories. Does N18 know? Does my direct superior intelligence officer, Gukenstein, even know? Are we simply spies reporting information back to Germany so the Kaiser can keep an eye on the allies' production of weapons —as I was told when given this assignment—or are there different plans in the works?

Surely not anything harmful. This isn't the front. The battle isn't in England. Those who work in the factories are civilians.

Unfortunately, on the ground level, I'm told next to nothing. I know only the job I am required to perform, without receiving the why or the how.

I'm beyond ready to be done with this puppeteering world of espionage.

I rub a hand through my hair and hurry to cover the exasperated puff of air that escapes my lips. "Glad to be of help," I say through the mouthpiece. "Goodnight, Cousin."

I hang up, thoughts of Poppy still rolling through my head. She dropped off the Chilwell Factory mail earlier this evening and rushed out before I could ask her if the gloves and masks that arrived for the canary girls a few days ago were working out. Apparently, she had "big plans" tonight and didn't have time to talk.

I lock up the post office and walk toward the church, where I'm eager to share a nightcap with Preacher Jones, as we do most evenings, then head to bed, where I will not dream of Poppy's hand touching mine.

When I start up the walkway toward my room at the back of the church, I see the young girl from the factory, Clara Whittaker, I believe, and a man in a British military uniform walking toward me. I almost turn around before they catch a glimpse of me, when I hear Clara say, "When you two get married, can I please be invited to the wedding?"

Then, laughter I'm becoming rather fond of makes its way to my ears. Poppy moves out from behind the man and into my line of sight as he says, "If I have the pleasure of marrying Miss Pemburton here, we wouldn't dream of getting married without you there." The man looks at Poppy over Clara's head, and Poppy looks back at him as though she may just melt right there into the sidewalk.

Married? A marriage—even an engagement—could cause this whole operation to slip from my grasp. It would be inappropriate for a married or engaged woman to continue to spend the kind of time with me that is needed for my mission. And while I wouldn't have a problem with that sort of inappropriate behavior, *my favorite kind of behavior*, I know Poppy well enough to know she would.

The man must be Luca. I heard he was home on leave for a few days.

I groan inwardly at the complications his being in Beeston is going to cause me. The relationship between Poppy and I is mutually beneficial in a big way. We can both win here. But for us to keep winning, I need to keep her in my sights—and out of Luca's.

It's time to ruffle some feathers.

"Good evening," I say, walking up to the three of them.

The yellow pallor of Poppy's cheeks turns near gray when she sees me, and she comes to a halt.

"Good evening, Mr. Andrews," Clara greets me warmly.

"Nice to see you, Miss Whittaker. You are lookin' radiant today, as usual."

She giggles as I pivot to address the man at Poppy's side and offer my hand to him. "Charles Andrews, Beeston Post Office manager from Texas, USA."

Luca takes my hand without hesitation and offers a firm handshake. He looks me dead in the eye as he speaks: "Luca Whelan, proud soldier of the British Army."

"He's returning to France this evening," Clara states proudly.

"Is that right?" I ask, looking at Luca.

He offers a quick, firm nod of his chin in response.

"Well, that's mighty fine of you to fight for yer country. As noble a calling as one can have, fightin' for the country you love and believe in."

"It is indeed," Luca says taking several steps closer to me. "Say, Mr. Andrews, you planning on suiting up if America finally gets its act together and joins this thing?"

I don't miss the edge in his voice, the hint that he is brave, and I am a coward hiding in England. "I'm always the first one to defend my country and my family if duty calls," I respond.

"How noble and brave of you."

We stand eye to eye, neither of us blinking or moving, our breath marching forth from our nostrils in perfect synchrony.

"Yes, we all love the country we're from, don't we now?" Poppy pipes in. "It's a good thing we're all on the same side, then, isn't it?" Her voice is strained. She steps forward, placing a hand on Luca's arm. "Luca, let's go visit with Mrs. Christmas before it's time to depart to the station." She pulls him in the direction of the Sweet Shoppe.

Clara's fingers twist together, and she looks back and forth between Poppy and me, her eyes wide and concerned.

I wink at her and smile, and some of the tension leaves her face. Poppy wraps an arm around her, and the girl's shoulders instantly relax.

"Good evenin', then, my silent canary." I tip my hat toward her and let my eyes trail up her body.

Poppy's face burns bright. "Not *your* silent canary; *a* silent canary," Poppy hisses. "*A*."

I talk to Poppy, but my eyes don't leave Luca's as I speak: "I'll be seein' you 'round the post office soon, I suppose, Poppy. Once yer no longer *occupied*." I put strong emphasis on the last word. "I've missed spendin' my evenin's with you."

"Goodbye, Mr. Andrews," Poppy says with an air of dismissive authority.

Luca's eyes are glued to mine, green flames of rage billowing beneath slanted eyebrows. When he makes a small growl sound deep in his throat, I know I've hit my target.

I never miss when I aim.

October 28, 1916

Poppy,

The only selfish thing I've done in my life was marry Jane. In my heart, I knew she didn't love me. I knew a beautiful woman singing in a lobby at a French hotel couldn't have fallen in love with the likes of me after one wild, frivolous night together, but I was desperate to believe her lies. Desperate to take her away from her controlling father in France and marry her as she begged me to do. Desperate to bring a wife home to my parents before my mother passed away. I thought that after Jane came to England, met your grand-parents, and settled in Beeston, she would grow to love me the way she professed to.

After Jane left, I couldn't bear to look at you. I had failed you. I know I have been hard on you over the years, but it was for your own good. Life breaks those without backbones.

I didn't enlist with the intent to die or survive. My reasons are my reasons.

Stop waiting for Jane. Stop waiting for me. Neither of us deserve you.

Take care of yourself,
Thomas Pemburton

November 9, 1916

Dear Father,
      Life also breaks those without hope. Whom I deserve and what desires I cling to are not for you to decide. You never failed me; you've only ever failed yourself. You can have your secrets. Just come home.
      —Poppy

November 16, 1916

Dear Firebird,

I'm coming home! I'm coming home to Beeston! I have been given special permission from Captain McDaniel to have leave for Christmas. After nearly four months of bloody conflict along the Somme River, word along the front is that this battle should be coming to an end any day now. The Tommies have relieved the French soldiers under siege at Verdun, the main German forces have been held along the Western Front, and our enemy's strength has been significantly worn down. It is time to stop the heavy bloodbath on both sides. Once Commander in Chief, Sir Douglas Haig, finally calls off the offensive, we can begin pulling our troops back.

When we have cleaned up from this mess, Captain says he can afford to let me slip away for one week's time. After that, I likely will not return home again until the war's end. We are losing too many men to death and capture; all able-bodied men are needed to stay on.

Sam will have leave for Christmas as well, even though he was just home in September—lucky bloke—so we will travel back and forth from France together, which I much prefer, since I detest traveling over the waters without him. He is great for distraction as he can talk on any subject for any amount of time, in any circumstance—and he knows my fear of water well. My travel home in October was my first time on the waters without Sam, and suffice it to say, my shipmate donated every bottle of liquor he acquired to me free of charge.

Just a few weeks more and I'll be holding you in my arms, doing everything I can to mess up your lipstick.

Forever. Forever and always, I will love you,

Luca

November 28, 1916

Dear Luca,

Ah, my love! The newspapers say that the battle along the Somme has officially been terminated. Christmas together! I can't believe the luck of it. I had Clara pinch me three times to be sure I wasn't dreaming. Even Mrs. Fischer had a good chuckle at our shenanigans.

I'm glad you will travel home with Sam and that Sarah will get to have her husband home as well. A true Christmas miracle! I love Sam already, and I can't wait to meet he and Sarah someday.

I don't know how I will survive not seeing you again until the war's end, though. But I won't think of that now, it doesn't help to worry about that which we do not yet know. I suppose we'll just have to make the most of our time together next month.

My heart is yours, Luca,

—Poppy

P.S. You know quite well that I do not ever wear lipstick unless it's a very special occasion. Come to think of it, I can't remember the last time I experienced an occasion worthy of lipstick.

P.P.S. Do you prefer red or pink lipstick?

December 11, 1916

Dear Firebird,

I hope the evening of my return will be the most special occasion of both of our lives thus far. I am beginning to pack my things already.

My ship departs from France on the twentieth of December. I should arrive in Beeston on the evening train the night of the twenty second. Bring the red feather I have enclosed here (it's not a real firebird feather, but it's as close as I could get while in France) with you to the station when you come to greet me. I want to make sure I'm kissing the right girl the moment I step off the platform.

Forever. Forever and always, I will love you,

Luca

P.S. Red. Always red.

17

LUCA

ARGONNE FOREST, NORTHEASTERN FRANCE NEAR THE MEUSE RIVER DECEMBER 14, 1916

MUDDY, WET LEAVES CLUMP BENEATH MY BOOTS AS OUR infantry makes its way through the thick trees of the Argonne Forest in northern France near the Meuse River. The sky is nearly black with night and heavy with cold rain and sleet, but still we march.

Captain McDaniel received orders for our unit to reach Aubréville, a city approximately twenty-five kilometers west of Verdun, by nightfall. There, we will join another British military unit and, in the morning, move on to Verdun to offer relief support to the exhausted French troops. Inside my boots, the heels of my feet are raw and blistered—my toes surely frozen— but it's nothing compared to my cracked, bloody hands, which are coated in dirt and grime.

In front of me, shoulders shiver with cold, backs slump forward beneath weighted packs, and jaws clench inward, but no one stops or complains.

Six more days. Six more days and Sam and I will be on a ship home to England, I encourage myself.

Sam, who brings up the rear next to me, moves alongside me slowly, cheerfully humming "It's a Long Way to Tipperary," as if we're on holiday at the beach rather than freezing our back ends off in the middle of a war. The Tommies in front exiled Sam to the rear march after he broke out into an off-key rendition of the chorus several hours ago. Sam ignored their grievances at first, but when Private Andrews swore to mop the German's faces with Sam's blood if he didn't move his loudmouth to the rear of the group, Sam complied.

"So, you're going to propose to your girl when you go home, are you?" Sam asks between verses of song. "Ask her to spend the rest of her life with your sorry self?"

My lips, numb with cold, scarcely move as I speak. "That's the plan."

"Think she'll say yes?"

If Sam had asked me that question just a few months ago, I wouldn't have been sure of the answer, but now I know. "Without a doubt."

"Well then, I apologize for taking the most perfect woman on earth to be my wife, but I'm sure Poppy is a close second." Sam slaps my back in a brotherly manner. "Congratulations, mate. I'm happy for you. Being married is the greatest. I'm the best thing that ever happened to Sarah."

"Is that so?"

We follow a narrow, winding path through a heavy patch of trees, making sure to keep the last soldier in our infantry within our sights.

"I mean, if we're being technical, she seems to work out okay for me too. I guess we have what you would call mutually benefi-cial nuptials because . . ." Sam pauses, and his face breaks into a wide, lopsided grin, "Sarah is making me a father."

"Sarah is with child?" I grab him about the shoulders and shake him. "You're going to be a father, Sam."

"That's what I said."

I yank him into my chest and wrap my arms around him. "Congratulations, mate. I can't believe you didn't tell me before now." I release him, and he grins up at me stupidly. For just a moment, I let myself wonder if Giovanni would have wanted a wife. If he would have been excited to be a father, had the option ever presented itself.

"Just got the post today. Baby should be born next summer, doctor says. June most likely," Sam says, pride beaming from his face.

An echo of weapons firing from several yards ahead startles both of us, and we freeze in place.

Sam's eyes grow large and round and fix on mine, his smile replaced by a deep frown. At the celebration of Sam's announcement, we lost sight of anyone in our unit.

The captain's voice shouts commands, but from our location in the rear of the unit, the commands are muffled, absorbed by the thick trunks and falling sleet.

Shots ricochet through the trees, the yells of men ring out around us, and feet thunder the ground. A body runs toward us, but in the dark, I can't see his uniform.

I yank Sam behind me, but we don't have time to take cover.

Then, an English voice I recognize as Corporal Adams shouts, "Run!"

As Adams flies past me, his always-perfect poker face is stripped away. Fear, I now realize, is his tell.

Our infantry has been ambushed.

I survey the scene, trying to decide if it would be best to flee or hide. The dark forest is on our side, so I choose to hide. I don't want to be a moving target. There's a large bush a few yards to our left with a mound of leaves beneath it. We can dig a small mud cave.

Silently, I motion to Sam where to go. He nods his head, confirming my proposal.

We run, pausing behind large trees for cover until we reach the bush. We have yet to see any German soldiers, but the gunfire has not ceased, and voices are drawing closer.

"Quick." I pull Sam to the ground. "Start digging under here."

The muddy earth seeps through the knees and legs of my worn uniform. Our hands move together in unison.

The cold dirt numbs my palms and fingers, but we pause only when it sounds as if someone is approaching.

After several minutes, we've dug a sort of mud cave just big enough to hide our legs. Hopefully the leaves and bush will cover the rest, because we're out of time.

Sharp German voices ring out through the trees nearest us.

We climb into our makeshift hole, our two curled up bodies squished together, and cover ourselves as best we can and wait.

Sam's body is pressed in front of mine. He shakes violently, and I can think only of Giovanni. *If only I had been there.*

Gun shots break up the shouts of men somewhere near our hiding spot. Sam tenses in front of me at the sound, and his teeth chatter loudly against one another.

The voices get closer, and soon boots are stomping against the leaves all around our hiding spot. Something heavy, possibly the butt of a gun or maybe even a large man's boot, hits the bush above my head, and dirt sprays down against our cheeks. Sam flinches and whisper-yells a string of swears.

"Hier," a German voice shouts. "Ich habe einen gefunden." *I found one.*

Sam twitches in my arms, and all I can think about is Sarah and Sam's unborn child. Nobody is going to take the life of that child's father unless they take me first.

I shift my body to cover Sam's just as the remaining muddy leaves that hide us are swiped away.

18

CHARLES

BEESTON, NOTTINGHAMSHIRE, ENGLAND
DECEMBER 22, 1916

"FROHE WEIHNACHTEN, COUSIN CHARLES." N18 SHOUTS THE German words through the line. Either she's too drunk to care, or she assumes no one is tapping into the phone lines this close to Christmas.

"Merry Christmas to you too, Cousin." I return the sentiment with zero emotion.

Although the small town of Beeston is doing its best to prepare for a wartime Christmas—small, decorated trees outside shop doors, wreaths of green and holly adorning windows, and the Beeston Carolers rehearsing along High Road—the sky tonight is dark and pregnant with clouds. The nighttime cold seeps through the walls of the old post office building and bites bitterly at the flesh beneath my black blazer. A grumpiness I can't shake eases its way down into my bones, where the chill of the room lies and taunts my moody spirit. Even my favorite carol, sung boastfully and with an accompaniment of bells by an onset of carolers outside the post office door does nothing to lift my gloom.

"I have to go back in to the party now—schmooze a few Englishmen, if you know what I mean." N18 laughs with her entire drunken soul, and I am rather displeased that I know exactly what she means. That's how I worked past missions as well, except with *women*, not men. "Good work in England this year, Cousin. I can't wait to see what the new year brings for us," her voice rings out.

I return the phone to its cradle and wander out to the empty post office lobby, a letter I came across hours ago still gripped in my hands. A letter from Luca that changes everything. A letter that Poppy will never read because I must make it disappear.

December 15, 1916

Dear Poppy,
    I don't know how to tell you this. My heart aches at the turn of events and the thought of you sitting at the station alone, waiting for me. I hope this letter reaches you before then, or I will be crushed that I have unintentionally caused you more pain and heartache as you wait and wait for me to arrive. Please know I did everything I could to avoid capture. But it was either go willingly with the German soldiers to their prisoner of war camp or take a bullet on the floor of France.
    Our infantry was ambushed by German troops last evening on our way to Verdun. Myself, Sam, and three other men from our unit were apprehended and taken prisoner. The rest of them were either shot for fighting back—God rest their souls—or were lucky enough to escape. I know you will receive an official Prisoner of War notice from the army, but I wanted you to hear it from me first, if possible. Prisoner status aside, I am

safe and healthy—no need to worry about me.

You told me I didn't have to chase the world to save it, and I think you were right. So then, while I am forced to labor in this stationary place, I will never stop standing back up. Not until I am home with you where I belong.

Forever. Forever and always, I will love you,

Luca

P.S. Picturing your lips swiped in red is saving my life right now. Merry Christmas, my love. I hope we are together for the next one.

WHILE NEWS OF LUCA'S CAPTURE, AT FIRST, SEEMED beneficial for my mission, I soon realized it would likely pull Poppy even further away from me. As long as Luca is alive, Poppy will cling to him. Her thoughts will become loyally transfixed to his—his letters home her guiding light, all my efforts of a friendship with her terminated.

A simple prisoner of war letter is not going to bring Poppy to me the way I need it to. Not when they're practically engaged to be married.

So when a Killed In Action notification arrived earlier today for the family members of another soldier from Beeston, a rather unfortunate idea took root. An idea that was as impossible as it was possible. An idea that made me squirm as I attempted to wrestle it into submission. Is it right? Wrong? Do I have a choice? Would I even falter if I didn't know Poppy the way I know her now? Would I hesitate if her feelings weren't a priority to me?

Her feelings shouldn't be a priority to me. But the moment N18's coded telephone signal rang through the post office for our weekly call tonight, I knew it wasn't a choice at all.

This is war. Nobody has a choice. All we have is duty. And mine is to Germany.

Luca has to die.

While N18 rambled on in my ear about Christmas back home, I got to work.

It was almost too easy. The Beeston man killed in the line of duty was not a war officer, so the notification card for his death was preprinted. Only the rank, name, regiment, date, and cause of death were written manually with ink. I've created false documents, altered identity cards, and forged authentic certificates many times, so smudging the ink and changing it to say Luca Whelan and his regiment took just minutes. The rest of the information already handwritten in for the slain soldier works for my needs. Rank: Private. Date of death: December 16 1916. Cause of death: killed in action on the field of France. Perfect.

The notification was not delivered to the soldier's family today, and the addressee did not come into the post office to collect their mail, so they will never know anything is amiss. Their loved one is dead. Not receiving the notice doesn't change that.

While I wait for the smudged ink on the postcard to dry, I twist the brim of my cowboy hat around and around in my hands until the felt has nearly creased itself into oblivion, thinking about how my decision will affect Poppy.

Luca's death will be painful for her in the moment, sure, but it's harmless really . . . in the end. Luca won't actually *be* dead.

And I *will* tell her the truth, or at least some of the truth, as soon as I am able to. Whenever I need to for that matter. If Luca's death proves too much for her to bear, I can always pretend a letter from Luca just made its way to her and save the day. I am sure there are death mix-ups along the front lines and in the trenches all the time.

I decide I will hide all his incoming correspondence inside the empty back portion of that ridiculous grandfather cuckoo clock in the corner of the post office. And when I leave England, I'll give Poppy all the hidden posts, and she'll be overjoyed to discover the truth.

I'm not lining the Silent Canary in my crosshairs, I remind myself; I am simply following her to the nest. I might have to take out some predators along the way, but this is the only way we both win in the end. This is the only way I ensure *I* become her closest confidant.

I touch a finger to the postcard. The ink is dry.

It is done.

I ignore the way my heart thuds heavily and swells uncomfortably within my chest as I tuck the card into my shirt pocket and make my way to the train station, where I know Poppy waits for Luca.

19

POPPY

BEESTON, NOTTINGHAMSHIRE, ENGLAND
DECEMBER 22, 1916

ONCE SPECKLED WITH SHARDS OF ICE, THE IRON BENCH WHERE I sit is now thoroughly warmed beneath my green silk dress, Luca's favorite.

The evening train came. Soldiers exited in droves. Mothers cried, lovers kissed, babies crooned.

The evening train went.

Luca did not come.

It is half past ten now, but still I sit. My white fur coat, a splurge I paid Mrs. Fischer to purchase for me during one of her trips to London, has the red feather Luca sent me tucked safely inside the pocket next to Jane's ring. Clara mercifully returned the jewelry to me the day following the accidental drop in the danger house. Despite the predicament I'd put her in, she restored the ring to my pocket without so much as a hint of displeasure toward me. "Sisters take care of each other," she'd simply stated with a smile.

The raised platform in front of me stands empty. Besides the barely audible patter of snowflakes as they layer the ground inch by inch, the world is silent.

I do not cry.

Luca will come. I will sit here until morning because I know my Luca is coming home.

I spin a strand of hair around my fingers and choose to hold onto hope. *We always have a choice,* I remind myself. And I choose hope.

I pull a small mirror from my purse and reapply my lipstick. The next train won't be here until five a.m., but in case I fall asleep here, I need to be ready.

Red. Always red.

But it's not Luca who walks forlornly down the tracks toward me nearly an hour later.

It's Charles Andrews.

His cropped blonde hair and golden-flecked brown eyes catch in the light beneath the gas lamp he walks under, and my breath hitches at the sight of a single postcard gripped in his hand and the stoop of his shoulders.

There is only one reason he would seek to find me at the abandoned train station on the same night I am to meet Luca.

Luca who never came.

Fear reaches for my hand.

I almost reach back. Almost lean into fear's unwavering promise as I have so many times before. The promise that it will never leave me alone. But as my fingers move to find the cool metal ring in the pocket of my coat, the soft feather tucked inside glides across my palm.

I pull Luca's gift from my pocket and hold the red feather against my heart. Then I stand to meet Charles.

Without words, he offers me the postcard in his hand, his eyes avoiding mine.

As I open my hand to take the card, the bird feather falls from my fingers. I watch it float to the frozen ground in what seems to be slow motion, as if my whole life is riding on the back of that singular, light feather. The red plume lands with a whisper on the white winter snow, marring its innocence.

As my eyes flit across the postcard, I wonder if it is possible to break an already broken heart. If there is a world in which I can live without my Luca.

I already know. There is not.

20

POPPY

WHEN WE'RE STRIPPED DOWN TO OUR CORE, TO OUR SOUL, TO the very essence that makes up the human body, what do we have left besides the love we carry there?

Pain. Heavy pain the love walked away from and left behind.

But perhaps they are one in the same: love and pain. Two sides of the same damaged coin. Can you ever truly have one without the other?

I close my eyes and let those thoughts move freely around my mind as I lie curled in three-day-old clothing on the sofa in the dark sitting room of my cottage, mourning Luca. The same sofa on which I mourned the loss of Jane on the night of my thirteenth birthday and then my father's departure ten months ago.

I have every intention of burning the horrid piece of floral furniture once I am willing to move from this spot. I refuse to mourn the loss of another person in my life upon its itchy fabric. Too bad Aunt Elizabeth isn't here to start a fire.

My cottage sat empty after I moved into Mrs. Fischer's dormitory in the renovated lace factory building with the other canary girls months ago. But I have hid away in here three solid days now, and it smells and feels the way a closed-up house would: stuffy and slightly wet with perhaps a smidge of regret, longing, and complicated memories.

The canary girls have been in and out, taking care of me with religious dedication over the last seventy-two hours, but it's Christmas evening, and I shooed them out to attend Christmas service together.

I take the few moments I have alone to unpack sacred memories of Luca that belong only to me. To turn them inside out and study them. To hold and reverence them. To miss the way his green eyes bored into every corner of my soul, pleading with me to understand how deeply he loved me.

The pain is so heavy, I could lay here on this couch for the remainder of my days and never feel a morsel of guilt or desire for change. It is a pain that resides in the depths of every part of my body. I may have only accepted my love for Luca a very short time ago, but knowing I also lost the only person who has not left my side in seventeen years—who has been there for me through every loss and heartache—captures nearly every remaining breath in my body.

A soft knock sounds at my cottage door. I freeze. I'm not ready for guests.

The knock repeats, followed by: "Poppy? May I come in?"

The thick wood door muffles his words, but I recognize Charles's voice.

I rise from the couch and wrap my black shawl around my shoulders before making my way to open the door.

"Clara got word to me that ya sent the canary girls down to the church," Charles says, his hat clenched in his hands, his back ramrod straight. "But she didn't want you to be alone, so she asked if I could be here with ya until Mrs. Fischer arrives after day shift."

Charles looks as uncomfortable to be on my front porch as I am with him standing there.

"It was kind of you to stop by, but you needn't stay," I say. "I am quite fine. I don't need a nanny. I am sure you'd rather be . . .

be . . . well, I don't know where you like to be on holidays, but I'm certain it isn't at the side of grieving women."

"Oh, on the contrary. I make a habit of comfortin' grievin' women on all my holidays." He breaks into a small smile, and although his attempt at humor has no effect on me, I widen the door for him to come in.

"Suit yourself," I say, shrugging. "But I am rather boring company right now." I make my way back to my mourning spot.

Charles adds a log to the fireplace and spends a long time stoking the fire and staring at the embers, neither of us putting forth an effort to make conversation.

"Does the pain of loss ever go away?" I ask into the stretched-out silence of the room.

"The loss of my father comes in waves. And while some days are more bearable than others, the pain is always there under the surface of everythin' ya do. Every decision ya make. Every layer of protection ya try to place over yer heart to keep it from breakin' again."

We stare at one another as the words sink into the empty spaces around us.

I let his honesty move through the sour places of my soul— the places where Jane's abandonment, and father's absence, and Luca's death lie—and resign myself to the understanding that I will never be free of the pain of losing my best friend and the man I loved. If I accept that truth for what it is, will that make moving on from Luca's loss easier?

But what if I don't want it to be easier? What if I don't want to move on without him? I don't want to laugh without him next to me. I don't want to dance without his arms around me. I don't want to sit on the church roof if he isn't next to me, paper and charcoals in his hand. I don't want to be in a world that doesn't also hold Luca. I want to miss him every day. Because if I miss him, he is still a part of me. I can still feel him. And I never want to *not* feel Luca.

"I miss him," I say simply. The words are heavy with both too much meaning and not enough.

"Missin' is good. It's the forgettin' that's bad. Forgettin' the way they shook yer hand or hollered yer name when you knew you was about to get a beatin', or forgettin' the weight of their palm as it collided with yer shoulder before they told ya how proud they were of ya." He drops his chin. "I'm startin' to forget, and I hate myself for it."

Charles clears his throat. "Anyhow." He shakes his head and stands up. "I got this here thing." He pulls a small box wrapped in red and gold paper out from his overcoat pocket and hands it to me.

"For me?" My eyes widen in surprise.

"I just wanted to give you a little somethin'. Merry Christmas, Poppy."

I push myself to a sitting position, peel the wrapping from the box, and open the lid. Inside is a small, pocket-sized Atlas.

"Um, thank you?" I say, not quite understanding the gift.

"Ya mentioned on our trip to Leeds that ya haven't traveled or lived outside of Beeston. That you *couldn't*?" He raises one eyebrow, and it slightly quirks as if he needs confirmation of that statement before he can continue.

I nod slowly, trying to keep up with where this is headed.

"Maybe one day I'll know more 'bout yer story and why that is, but I thought that if ya can't leave to see the world, maybe you can hold it in your hands until yer ready to."

My skin prickles up and down my arms as my heart swells. I don't know that I will ever tell Charles about my trepidation about leaving Beeston. About my history and complicated feelings with Jane. About my irrational worry that the day I leave might be the exact day Jane comes home to find me. But Charles seems to pick up on little details, comments, and feelings in an impressive manner for an uneducated farm boy, and I am rendered speechless.

"Charles." I can barely speak. "That is so . . . thoughtful."

"You sound surprised."

"I am," I admit.

He lets out a chuckle.

"It's just that I wasn't expecting anything," I say. "And this is
. . . I mean . . . and you are . . . and what I mean to say is . . .
thank you." I look down at my hands running across the Atlas
cover and command them to stop immediately. "Thank you very
much. It's perfect."

There is a knock on my front door, and as Charles leaves to
answer it, I think about his kind gift. I think about the death of
Sophia's husband and about Clara's choice to run away from
home at fourteen to assist with war work. I think about Mrs.
Fischer's strength to supervise the danger house and about
Luca's life and death.

I realize something then as thoughts of my friends and their
lives swirl around my mind:

In war, there is no victor.

Not one person comes out unscathed. Unchanged.

What makes my losses greater than those of any other
Englishman, Frenchman, or German for that matter? We're all
fighting the same war. The only thing of consequence to any of
us is what's left of us when the fighting ends. When the weapons
are packed away, when the ammunition factories close, when the
men who survived come home, what will be left of all of us?

What will be left of me?

21

LUCA

PRISONER OF WAR LABOR CAMP,
HENDECOURT-LÈS-CAGNICOURT, FRANCE
MARCH 8, 1917

THE HUT DOOR BLOWS OPEN, AND A GUST OF COLD MORNING wind, along with the shine of a flashlight on each head in the tent, accompanies a German guard's sharp order: "Aufwachen!" When the bright light swings across the guard's own face, I jolt at his youthful appearance. His small build, fair skin, and yellow hair don't match his murderous voice.

The tent becomes a flurry of blankets, clothing, and men with bad breath groggily muttering expletives. We have five minutes to make up our cots, organize our surroundings, and be dressed with shovels and picks in hand before punishments are executed. Sometimes there's food available before we leave for the day's work; sometimes we don't eat until the afternoon. My stomach grumbles its demands, and I hope it's not the latter.

Sam swings his legs around his cot and moans when his bare feet hit the cold floor.

"Good morning, Sunshine," I greet him, to which he grunts in response.

Today's task will have us working on the railway sidings for the Germans in Croisilles, unloading trucks of all sorts of material. When we first arrived, we were tasked with building roads for German convoys along the Western Front, but our allied forces have blown up most of them.

Sam and I join the other prisoners at the meeting spot to hike the six kilometers to the railhead. Then the guards give the order to begin marching.

No breakfast, then. The pit in my belly cries out.

Sam slides an apple into my hand. I don't know where he got the red fruit, but I bite into it as quietly as possible. We pass the apple back and forth until we have eaten everything but the stem. And then we each get one seed to suck on until it loses its flavor, at which point, I crunch that between my teeth and swallow it as well. It's quite a deal better than the snail-like creature that was stuck to the bark of the willow trees, which we cut up and then boiled with nettle leaves for last evening's supper, so I can't complain.

As we make the trek to our assigned post, light begins to illuminate the sky with a grayish-blue hue that promises a new day. Another day in which I am alive. In which Sam is alive. And in which Poppy loves me . . . I hope. Because hope is all I have.

I have no way of knowing for certain if my captors send the letters I write. I'm told they do, and I've seen the riders come to deliver and collect the camp's posts, but perhaps my letters are not with the others. Perhaps mine are burned in the nightly fires that warm the Germans hands and feet. I know it's a far-fetched theory, but that's the only explanation I can come up with for the three months of silence from Poppy. Or perhaps she has responded, but her letters can't find me.

"Cheer up, mate," Sam says with his signature slug against my shoulder as we find our places in the line of prisoners along the trench. "We'll eat again soon."

"It's not that." I chuckle despite the tightness my thoughts have created in my chest. "Today is Poppy's birthday."

"Still haven't heard back from her?" Sam grunts as his shovel hits the frozen ground.

I shake my head.

"The letters will come," he reassures me. But I'm not so sure. He's already received two from Sarah.

"Sei ruhig!" The commandant shouts in my face to be quiet. His blue eyes bore into mine, and while I see no humanity reflected there, they are so similar in color to Poppy's that the edges of my anger soften. He must mistake it as submission because he leaves me to shovel and walks farther down the line to bark out more orders.

On Poppy's thirteenth birthday, I told her that her eyes were my favorite color.

It was March 8, 1906—the opening day of the Beeston fair. Poppy's father took Poppy and I every year because the fair always fell on, or near, Poppy's birthday. Jane never went with us, always saying, "Fairs are for peasants." But it was something the rest of us looked forward to with great anticipation every year. And that particular year was going to be better than any other. That year, I had worked up the courage to tell Poppy I was sweet on her.

After a full day of knocking over milk bottles, saddling ponies, riding the Ferris wheel till we were dizzy, laughing at turtle races, and eating so much blueberry pie we were sure to have stained-blue fingers and mouths forever, night finally fell. I grabbed Poppy by the hand and ran with her until we were hidden behind the large Ferris wheel. I can still remember the way her giggle spilled melodiously as we ran, making the air come alive as if with magic. The fair music tinkled quietly in the distance, and the stars were soft against the black of the night.

It had rained on and off throughout the day, and the night air was chilly and damp. Poppy shivered beneath her black shawl, which was a good deal thicker then than the sorry thing is now, and her lips trembled. The little freckle on her top lip shook as she tried to still it with her teeth.

I could do nothing but stare at her, all the words I had practiced instantly gone from my fourteen-year-old mind as she stood shivering in front of me. I shifted my weight from foot to foot, the nervous silence building between us.

Then Poppy laughed. "What is it, Luca?"

"I wanted to give you your birthday gift."

"Behind the Ferris wheel?"

I had no words that could possibly explain everything I wanted to say. So instead of speaking, I grabbed her small hands in mine and leaned into her, planting a quick kiss on her cold lips.

I backed up immediately and looked down at the ground, too embarrassed to look her in the eye after my impulsive action. But then she grabbed me by the shoulders, came up on tiptoe, and kissed me back. Right on the lips.

It was as quick as mine had been, but it was perfect.

"I will love you forever, Poppy." The admission came pouring from my lips. I hadn't meant to say it; I didn't even have a clue what love was, but I found I meant every piece of whatever kind of love a teenage boy was capable of feeling.

"Forever? Forever is a long time, Luca." She laughed adorably. "I might get weird or ugly or do something to make you hate me. Maybe you shouldn't say *forever*. Maybe you should just say *today*. I love you today."

"You could never do something that would make me hate you, and you will never, ever be ugly."

"What if I stay blue like this forever?" She held up her blue-stained hands from the blueberry pie and wiggled her fingers.

"Blue is already my favorite color. Your eyes are my favorite color."

She blushed, then grabbed my hand, pulling me out of our hiding spot. "Come on. Father will be looking for us."

I tugged her hand and gently pulled her back into my arms. "Forever. Forever and always, I will love you," I whispered in her ear.

The tips of her ears turned pink, and she placed a quick peck on my cheek. "My heart is yours, Luca." Then she was off again, running and laughing, the white ribbon that was tied in her hair dangling loose and trailing down her back.

We never spoke of that kiss or of our childish confessions ever again. When we arrived at the Pemburton's cottage that night, Poppy and Thomas found the letter Jane left them on their kitchen stove, and nothing was ever the same.

Suddenly, a gunshot fires to my left, pulling me from the past. Instinctively, I look about for Sam. He's about three yards from me and flat on the ground, as are most of the other prisoners along the line. I duck and crawl on my belly until I reach him.

"What happened?" I yell.

"Some bloke was talking back. I don't know. The commandant ordered him to do something, and our Tommie retorted that he'd rather die than listen to a bloody German. And then the gun went off." Sam's eyes are wild. "I saw him get bloody shot, Luca. Commandant just pulled his weapon and fired. Can they do that? Can they just kill us off like that?"

"I think somehow we thought that as long as we were in this camp, we were safe from the bloodshed of war," I mumble.

"It's war; we aren't safe anywhere," Sam hisses.

I get to my feet and pull Sam to me. "But if we give up, the enemy wins. We must keep standing back up." Poppy's encouraging words ring through me.

"Stand back up," Sam says with a firm nod. There is an unfamiliar yet inspiring fire in his eyes.

I repeat the mantra with my own accepting nod, a silent agreement between two captive soldiers. "Stand back up."

22

CHARLES

BEESTON, NOTTINGHAMSHIRE, ENGLAND
MAY 25, 1917

"I HEAR RUMORS THAT THERE ARE NOT ONE BUT *TWO* POSTAL locations less than one hundred kilometers south of you, Cousin Charles," N18 says with greed. "Two!" I can almost hear her salivating through the earpiece of the telephone. "Have you been made aware of such information?"

"The one in Leeds is the only location I have knowledge of."

"Leeds is to the north. Have you taken the opportunity to travel south, Cousin? You really should be taking advantage of that pretty auto Uncle gifted you." Her voice is clipped now, a tone that grates against my spine. "We need to ensure we are working in conjunction with as many postal office locations as possible; don't you agree?"

"Yes, Cousin."

"Good. Then see to it you find out the coordinates for the two southern locations as soon as possible. Uncle and I don't care how you do it—only that you do. Don't disappoint us."

The telephone disconnects. I take a deep breath before setting the receiver down.

I know I need to finish this job, and most of the time I even want to, but is the mission still the only thing that matters to me? Is the transfer into interpretation my only future goal? I want to take care of Mutter, but perhaps that doesn't have to be in Germany.

The month after Poppy received word of Luca's unfortunate demise, she left her cottage only once outside of her work obligations to attend a candlelight vigil the canary girls held in honor of Luca's death. I knew Poppy was going to mourn, but I was unprepared for the level of devastation she suffered. I had hoped for a few quick sorrowful nights at best, a few weeks at worse.

By the end of January, when there was still no change in Poppy's demeanor, I thought my plan to drive Luca away had completely backfired. She was no closer to sharing ammunition factory details with me than she was previously; in fact, it was worse.

Thankfully the canary girls, Clara in particular, as well as Thomas still serving along the Western Front, were reason enough for her to not give up.

Now, while Poppy still speaks of Luca often, she and I spend nearly all our evenings together after her shift ends at the factory, and our connection sends my heart spinning like a top. That connection is the exact reason I forged the little document about Luca dying, but feelings I did not expect nor want to have for her have surfaced because of it.

But even more dangerous than developing feelings for my target is the fact that my target is bringing me, *Jakob*, back to life. Jakob—a boy who had hope. Who had light. Who had love.

While remembering details and regurgitating them keeps me grounded, remembering Jakob and resurrecting him makes me vulnerable. It's dangerous. There's no space for my boyish frailties in the spy life.

For years, it has been easy to forget Jakob. To obediently dive into my cover identities and assume new life roles one after the other. I've followed a blessed pathway of feigned heroism designed to forget the pains of my past. And it worked until I met Poppy, a girl who, simply by being, living, and thriving as a red rose among thorns, has reminded me who I am and the things I wanted before. Before I trained to become a spy. Before Uncle Hans became my stepfather. Before Vater died.

I finger the Glashutte on my wrist, and my chest grows heavy as memories of Vater's face come into view—his smile whenever Mutter entered the room, his laugh when I tried to clasp the Glashutte around my skinny arm, only to have the heavy face swing downward and slip right off, his eyes when he watched Greta dance across the kitchen floor. He loved us, his family. And we loved him.

Poppy's passionate way of living reminds me that I hoped for that. For a family. Love. Stability. A home filled with laughter.

But do I know how to live a life that isn't built on pillars of lies and manipulation?

Poppy can fall for Charles, the farm boy from America. Charles can even, somewhat, fall for Poppy. But for now, Jakob— the man whose goals are shifting—must remain neutral. I must keep my identities separate in my head—and heart. It's better for both her and I that way. Safer.

"Farm Boy, are you talking to someone back there?" Poppy's voice calls to me from the lobby.

I check my Glashutte. She's right on time with the evening factory posts. I pick up my cowboy hat. *Show time.*

"I telephoned my mother for her birthday," I tell Poppy as I spin my cowboy hat around the tip of my finger, coming down the hall. Half-truth, half-lie. It is Mutter's birthday; I only wish I could have called.

"Oh, how wonderful!" she exclaims. "How's the farm back home?"

I place the cowboy hat on my head. "The *ranch* is just dandy, thanks for askin'. My brother's doin' a swell job keepin' things going without me for now."

"How long has the ranch land been in your family?" Poppy asks as she levels a stack of brown boxes on the counter.

"As long as I can remember." I mark the boxes and parcels and separate them into the outgoing bins for tomorrow as I carefully think about how to add a sliver of truth into my cover story. Lies become easier to tell the more truth you add into them. "Although I may not want to take over the ranch," I say, "I'm proud of where and who I come from. My ancestors did what they needed to do to make their dreams come true."

"And do you plan to do the same?" Poppy asks.

"Make my dreams come true?" I lean forward and place my forearms on the counter, my hands in a clasp. "I s'pose I do."

Poppy bends at the waist and mimics my folded arms on the counter, her face just inches from mine. "And what are your dreams, Charles Andrews?"

I look at her for a long moment, and my stomach flips over itself as her blue eyes hold my gaze steady. I love that she is never afraid to ask the question she wants an answer to. That she lets her instincts guide her. If she weren't the enemy . . . . *But she is*. And that's all that matters.

I know she's talking to Charles, but I can't help but process the question as Jakob. My only option right now is to return to Germany. And I do that by serving the German army. Is that *my* dream though? Unfortunately, I don't have the luxury of exploring other options. Not yet, at least. Not until this war is over.

"I don't know just yet," I admit.

"You don't have to have it all figured out right now," Poppy says, her eyes watching me. "But it is your life," she whispers gently. "You don't have to do anything you don't want to do, Charles."

Don't I though? I want to ask her. Don't I have to walk the path I started? Don't I have to complete this mission? Don't I have to do that to protect Mutter from Hans? What would I do if I didn't stay with the German forces? Where would I go? Who would I become?

But still, her words stir something within me. *It's my life.*

I don't realize I've clenched my jaw until Poppy's warm finger runs tenderly down the side of it, loosening every muscle there in the wake. Sensation shoots down my arm at the touch, and desire pulses through my fingertips. If I moved forward two inches, I would be close enough to kiss her. Her full lips are pink and slightly parted, and I am certain they are the softest thing I've ever laid eyes on. I desperately want to know if they taste as incredible as they look.

I close my eyes, take a deep breath, and push backward off the counter, putting space between us. I can't kiss Poppy Pemburton. Not until I can do a better job of separating Charles and Jakob when I'm around her.

Focus.

I am a spy in the German army, and until that fact changes, I have a job to do.

"You know what I want to do, Poppy?" I ask with a clap of my hands. *Don't disappoint us,* N18's words ring in my head.

Poppy raises her eyebrows in question as her cheeks flush pink atop her yellow skin. Perhaps she was thinking of kissing me too.

I try not to let that go to my head, but I fail.

"I want to go on a drive with you again. South this time, though. Perhaps I can teach you how to drive. What do you say?"

"I couldn't possibly drive." Laughter trickles from the most tempting lips I've ever beheld. "But I'll think about it, Farm Boy," she says with a smile that guts me. "I'll think about it."

23

POPPY

CHILWELL, NOTTINGHAMSHIRE, ENGLAND
JULY 14, 1917

I WAIT UNTIL I'M ALONE IN THE WASHROOM OF THE ammunition factory to scrub at the yellow tinge on the back of my hand. Beneath the force of my fingers, the thin cotton rag tears at my skin until it's raw and bleeding, but red is better than yellow, even if for only a few hours. Eventually the specks of blood will drain away, and the yellow will take back its rightful place.

Our safety precautions of face coverings and gloves are well in place, and the masks have helped the employees' chest and lungs show significant signs of improvement, according to the on-site physicians. And while the gloves haven't lightened the yellow staining already upon our hands, they have certainly slowed the rate in which the yellow deepens. Unfortunately, the yellow tint is already deep on the backs of my hands and the hollowed-out part of my neck. My face carries the worst of it.

Jane would be appalled at the sight of me.

Out of habit, I reach for the metal ring in my pocket, but the fabric lining is empty of jewelry, as per safety protocols. I will never make that mistake again.

I close my eyes now and slowly count down from ten with a tap against my chest for each number. I remind myself that the ring is tucked safely away in my locker and wait for my breathing to slow.

When I open my eyes, exhaustion burns behind my lids. How long has it been since I slept properly?

Nightmares of men lying in pools of blood fill my sleep world. They all carry Luca's face and sometimes even Father's. Sleep is no longer a reprieve.

Last I heard from Father, nearly eight months ago now, his troop was fighting along the Somme River in northern France, but the battle there ended months ago. I write to him, but there is never a response. He likely believes if he stops writing, he can slip out of my life unnoticed. That it's better for me that way, as he all but said in his letter.

Stubborn fool.

I take a deep breath and rinse out the rag in my hands. There's no yellow that runs from its fibers into the basin. I knew there wouldn't be, but a defeated grunt slips from my lips anyway as I hang the rag to dry.

"There you are!" Clara runs into the washroom, breathless, her football kit hanging loose around her thin frame. "Mrs. Fischer needs you to clock out now. You're the only one not in a motorcar yet, and we need to head out if we're going to make it to our match on time."

My spirits lift instantly. "I can't believe our first game is finally here." I run to her, and we hurry to the locker room so I can change into my kit.

Last month, Charles and I drove south, as he'd suggested, and he did indeed teach me how to drive. Or tried to, at any rate. It's not an activity I will ever be trying again—not that Charles would encourage it after nearly losing his precious auto into the depths of a very murky pond when I mistook the accelerator for the brake. But seeing Charles's face drenched in terror had me laughing in a way I haven't in a very long time.

I agreed to travel with Charles because of a conversation I overheard between Mr. Ashby and Mrs. Fischer while I was dusting the factory owner's office the afternoon following Charles's offer. They were discussing happenings at another munitions factory near Banbury, arguing over whether Chilwell should allow the women working in our danger house to form a football team like the woman at Banbury National Shell Filling Factory No. 9 had. Mrs. Fischer, of course, being in favor of the idea due to the need for the canary girls to get proper exercise and fresh air to help with their lung ailments, and Mr. Ashby not being in favor due to his desire for no one to be happy—ever.

When I'd returned to my cottage that evening, the thought struck me that if Charles could drive me down south, I could talk to the Banbury women and see what information I could learn about how and when they play football. Despite America's decision to join the fight a few months ago and newspapers testifying of the tides of the war turning in the allies' favor, the people here, having lived in a country at war for three years now, don't know what or who to believe anymore, and the energy throughout the danger house had been low since the beginning of the year. We were mentally exhausted and physically overwhelmed with war work, so I hoped football could bring some life, some fun, back into our world.

Sure enough, the women in Banbury had formed a football team months ago and were all too eager to help me gather information to start our own team at Chilwell. They sent me home with a ball, a pile of extra kits, a pamphlet detailing a series of matches we could enter to play against other ammunition factory teams throughout England, and a secret: their production of ammunition had increased by one thousand shells a week once they started playing football together!

When Mr. Ashby realized that he was missing out on increased shell production and that the women's factory football teams played for war charities, he changed his tune and ordered us handsome new matching kits that very day. The canary girls loved the idea of creating a Chilwell football team, and Mrs. Fischer agreed—without too much persuasion—to be our team manager. She gave me another one of her "well done" sentiments but then followed it with, "If you ever go to another ammunition factory again without permission, though, I'll fire you."

So I guess Charles and I won't be taking any more trips of that nature. At least without Mrs. Fischer.

When we arrive at the pitch where we're to play, the one thousand spectators in attendance are already settling into their seats, and the outdoor arena is abuzz with excitement. Mr. Ashby saw to it that our factory was responsible for advertising this match to the arena's surrounding local towns, so most of the audience is here today in support of Chilwell.

We stretch our limbs and practice passing until the game whistle blows. There are eleven of us on the pitch at a time, and after only a few weeks practice, I'm elated to be one of the eleven starting girls. I have always loved to run, but wearing trousers while doing so (the *only* time I prefer trousers to frocks), kicking a ball as hard as I can, and being encouraged to be aggressive is an entirely new level of euphoria.

"Pemburton, faster! Move to your left. Move, move, move!" Mrs. Fischer shouts at me from the sideline as the opposing girls, the *Leeds Ladies* from the Barnbow factory, run at me, their faces—yellow like mine—hungry for my ball.

The *Chilwell Canaries* spread themselves out around the pitch, finding their positions as I search for Little Canary. The score is two to two with one minute remaining in the game. If we score this goal, we'll see victory.

The spectators are on their feet. The crowd is chanting "Chilwell girls" over and over. Their faces are a blur, but their voices echo in my head with pure clarity.

My heart pounds within my chest, my pulse thrums in my fingertips, and my feet control the ball with perfect precision. If I could freeze any moment, it would be this one.

This is the moment I love. This moment where I'm wildly alive on the football field, aware of every breath, every beat of my heart, and every movement of my body.

Two girls in Leeds's navy-blue-and-white-striped kits narrow in on me.

I turn my back and run sideways down the left side of the pitch and keep the ball moving between my feet. I slow my pacing as I approach center field. Sophia and Nessy flank me on the left and right. I dribble the ball back and forth and wait for Little Canary, our center forward, to get open so I can pass to her.

"That's it; now wait for your open shot, and pass it to Whittaker," Mrs. Fischer directs as Clara brushes around her opponent.

"Now!" our manager shouts from behind me, and I obey. The round, brown leather ball sails toward Clara beautifully.

Annabelle guards the other team's half-back, leaving just enough space for Clara's feet to capture the ball and kick it right past their goalkeeper into the net.

As the white net encloses around the ball, our team lets out a cheer, deafened instantly by the roar of the crowd. We run to encircle our little canary as the final whistle blows.

"The Chilwell canary girls from Chilwell National Shell Filling Factory No. 6 win 3–2 in today's match against the Leeds munition ladies from Barnbow National Shell Filling Factory No. 1," the announcer boasts to the press clamoring for our photographs. Our team photograph will be in every newspaper in the surrounding cities tomorrow, but our ammunition factory name and location will be noticeably absent. Those in attendance at the matches know where the teams are from, but as war office protocol currently dictates, it is never to be printed.

Hands are in the air, and voices all around us are chanting, "Chilwell! Chilwell! Chilwell!" Nessy is crying with the biggest smile I have ever seen upon her freckled face. Annabelle and Sophia are celebrating with the six other women who make up our team, and Little Canary's arms are tight around my neck. Mrs. Fischer is standing on the sidelines, clapping with perfect refinement, the dangling whistle around her neck bouncing in rhythm as we celebrate our hard-earned game-winning point.

Annabelle leads us in our victory song, swaying her hips a bit more exaggerated than the rest of us, and we sing together boldly.

"Great job, Pemburton. You're a natural," Sophia says to me when the song comes to an end. "I'm glad we're doing this together." She gestures toward the field. "You were right; it's been good for us. It's been good for me."

We share a knowing look, one that is somehow both stricken with grief and lined with hope. How those two emotions can coexist in the same moment, in the same heart, I couldn't explain.

Sophia has been a surprising but welcome friend over the last several months. The only person in my world, it seems, who understands the depth of my pain. With just a look, or a word, we know when the other needs a change in conversation or activity.

"Me too," I say with a nod of my head.

Sophia smiles, and for just a moment, her sour demeanor disappears. Her face is lovely.

I wish Luca were here to draw her this way. Luca was amazing at drawing people and things as they could be. It was his gift. He saw the potential in everything—the magic of an ordinary moment, the possibility of a beginning—and somehow captured it on paper.

I ache to be with him again. The grief comes in waves, as Charles told me it would. Sometimes the pain is bearable and I can smile without trying, but sometimes it's so debilitating I can't move for hours.

To some, women's factory football might be a silly game, but to the canary girls, it's a light in the darkness. It is relief from pain. It is healthy bodies beneath yellowing skin. It is happiness despite the heavy hearts that hold it. And what is all that if not hope?

I step away from the celebrating women and reach for my canteen in the grass. I drink greedily from the mouth and let the cold water replenish me.

I don't know a lot right now. I don't know how I will continue to survive without Luca. I don't know where my father is. I don't know when the war will end. I don't know if the allies will be victorious. I don't know if Jane will ever come home. I don't know what will happen today, or tomorrow, or next year.

But what I do know is that this feeling right here, the one stirring low in my belly that is warm and peaceful as I watch the excitement of playing football bounce off each smiling woman, is one I want to last.

War does not bring happiness. Death does not bring happiness.

I must find it anyway.

Maybe there is no such thing as a lifetime of happiness. Maybe we only get moments in between the grief, but I am determined to make *those* moments matter. Moments like the motorcar rides with Charles, and Clara's arms around my neck, and a ball between my running feet, and memories of Luca and I that play over and over in my mind.

I will never not miss Luca—never stop wishing he were still here—but as long as I'm still alive, I am determined to find joy. Luca would want me to be happy. I know he would. It's all he ever wanted for me.

After a long day working our factory shift and then winning our football match, Clara, Nessy, Annabelle, Sophia, and I walk home from the Beeston train station together, tired but happy. I wave goodbye to them as they go west toward the lace factory dormitory, and I head east toward my cottage.

Needing some space and privacy to grieve, I'd moved back home after Luca's death, but now I think I might be ready to go back to the dormitory. It's been nearly seven months, and I find I need the support and comfort being around these women offers me.

I push through my cottage gate, and a beacon of light streams through the small window in my kitchen onto the grass below.

I'm certain I did not leave the light on when I left this morning.

A dark, shadowed figure moves through my kitchen past the glass pane, and I scream out. I clamp a hand over my mouth and turn to run, when my front door opens, and a familiar voice stops me in my tracks.

"Poppy, I'm home."

24

LUCA

PRISONER OF WAR LABOR CAMP,
HENDECOURT-LÈS-CAGNICOURT, FRANCE
SEPTEMBER 9, 1917

SWEAT GATHERS BITTERLY BETWEEN MY SHOULDER BLADES, THE drops of moisture running together in streams beneath my uniform. I run a hand across my forehead to catch the drips there before they make their way into my already clouded eyes, then lean over and lift the next crate of German shells onto the convoy. All the ammunition needs to be transported to the front lines by sundown.

Next to me, Sam swears as the cargo he carries slips from his grasp. I lunge forward and catch the crate of shells a hairsbreadth from the ground.

"Thanks, mate." Sam's breath is shallow and tight.

"My hands are slippery too. Working in this heat is going to be the end of me."

Sam glances around, then lowers his voice. "There's a stream just half a click south of here. I guess some of the fellows have been taking turns keeping watch so a few blokes can run in for a quick dip to cool off."

"And you think that would be a good idea? To sneak off under the noses of the German guards for a jaunty swim?" I ask.

Sam eyes me carefully before responding, his words slow and calculated: "Do you think it would be a good idea?"

"I think it's a right foolish idea, Sam."

"Yeah, you're right." Sam shakes his head and scrunches up his face as if he smells horse manure. "Those other blokes are bonkers. No way I would chance getting caught for a simple moment of relief." He wipes his hands down his trousers and reaches out to take the crate back from me.

"Sometimes, though," I say, "right foolish ideas make the best stories."

Sam's head whips up to look at me. "Yeah?"

"Yeah." I smile.

Thirty minutes later, I'm sitting on the bank, my legs plunged into the cool water and my aching, blistered feet numb with relief, believing I might survive the rest of the day running German ammunition to the front after all.

"Wahoo!" Sam yells as he kicks past me. I shield my eyes as he glides positively naked through the shallow stream.

"Luca, you have to get all the way in. It feels amazing."

"I'm good right here."

"Ah, I get it. You're worried I look better naked than you do. It's okay, mate. I won't tell anyone I have more muscles than you."

I lean over and use my hand to spray a stream of water into his face. "Don't you worry about what I look like naked."

"Luca, look at my bloody arms." Sam flexes. Although the lack of food and nutrition have erased his soft, round cheeks and made hollow marks beneath his eyes, Sam is no longer the scrawny boy he was when we met. Nine months in a prisoner labor camp digging trenches, carrying ammunition, building roads, and all the other physical labor the Germans need completed have formed muscles beneath our uniforms that didn't exist before. I haven't looked at my reflection too much, but I can feel the change in myself as well.

"You better stop working so hard, mate. Sarah isn't going to recognize you when you get home with all those big, new muscles."

Sam's grin stretches the width of his face. "She won't be able to keep her hands off me. Can't say I'll be sad about working on baby number two."

"There's a nauseating image. But speaking of babies, how is little Evelyn Davies?"

"Plump and as adorable as me, according to Sarah's last letter. She said she'll include a photograph in the next parcel she sends. I can't believe my little girl has been on this earth for three months, and I've never seen her." Sam stands from the water, and I avert my eyes just in time. He trudges over to the bank and grabs his uniform. "You don't want to take a quick dip before we head back?" he asks as he slides his legs into his trousers.

"I'm all cooled off now, so no need." I pull my legs from the water and inch the hems of my trousers down. When I stand, I notice Sam staring at me. "What?" I ask.

"What's your deal with water?"

"My deal?" How do I tell my best mate, a man who makes his living and finds all his joy being on water, that I despise it? That I don't trust its cool, alluring waves and endless depths that swallow people whole.

A hearty slap against my shoulders jolts me. "It's nothing to be ashamed of, mate. Lots of people are afraid of water."

"I am not afraid," I bark.

Sam steps back and throws his hands up as if I'm about to attack him.

"Sorry," I mumble. "I *was* afraid. A long time ago. Now I just have bad memories."

We walk in silence back to where the other prisoners are loading shells on wagons and slip behind a large bush to wait for a space in the guard's patrol big enough for Sam and me to sneak back into the group unnoticed. Despite our cool off, sweat is already beginning to form along the creases in my eyelids and pool in the crevices of my folded arms.

"What bad memories?" Sam eventually asks, as if my past is an open book for his reading pleasure.

I look at him, hoping my gaze of annoyance at his prying question will clue him into changing the subject, but he continues to stare back, oblivious. I look around the bush, but there are still too many Germans lining the path between us and the prisoners. We won't be going anywhere for a bit.

I sigh, giving in. "When I was seven years old, my parents and little brother, Giovanni, drowned off the coast of Italy. They were traveling in a small ship when a storm kicked up, and the waves capsized their boat. All but two people aboard died."

"That's terrible, brother," Sam says, placing a hand on my shoulder. "Ghastly story. What was your family doing traveling up the coast of Italy without you?"

"Finding somewhere new to live. But I didn't want to move away. I was happy living among bandits. Unfortunately, my parents felt otherwise."

"Bandits?"

I show Sam the scar beneath my chin.

"That's from bandits?"

I nod. I'm thankful every day for the scar and its physical reminder of both G and my responsibility to protect others. "I grew up with my papi, Max; my mami, Luci; and my little brother, Giovanni, in Castelmezzano, Italy, a tiny village located in the heart of southern Italy's mountains. Because our little town was surrounded by mountains, there was an abundance of hiding places, and the town became a refuge for bandits.

"One summer evening, when I was seven years old, G and I were playing a game of hide-and-seek with some neighbor children before supper, and we wandered a little too far outside the area Papi and Mami allowed us to play. Before I knew it, we were surrounded by bandits.

"It was my fault; I knew I was supposed to protect G. I'd promised Mami I would keep him safe when we played outside.

"The bandits poked their guns into our sides and ran their knives down our necks." I trace my finger along my scar, remembering the way the sharp metal cut softly into my tender flesh.

"How did you escape?" Sam asks, his eyes glued to mine.

"Papi came looking for us and saw the bandits. He got us out of there by popping off a few bullets into the air, but that night, Papi and Mami made the decision to leave Castelmezzano. The next day, they boarded a small passenger ship that would take them up the coast to find a new home in northern Italy, but I was terrified of the dark, open waters." I take a breath, pushing through the hard feelings that always come up when I think about that day. "I begged Mami to let me stay with my mate for the days they would be gone and promised her that if she allowed me to stay behind this time, when the time came to make the move, I would come without a fight." I shake my head. "That was the last time I saw my family. It was my fault G and I ran into the bandits, my fault my parents decided to move north, my fault they embarked on the boat that day."

Sam licks his lips and cocks his head to the side, his eyes in narrow slits. "If you had gone, you would be dead too." He says it as though he is speaking to an incompetent child. "You need to let that guilt go, mate. Sometimes things just happen." His tone is callous as he offers a shrug of his shoulders. "You are in no way responsible for their deaths. Crikey! You weren't a coward; you were *seven*. You've got to stop torturing yourself." He lets out a puff of a laugh.

My neck cracks at the force with which it flails back as I glare at Sam. All three people I've told my story to before— Poppy, Mrs. Fanny Christmas, and Preacher Jones—have each respectively wrapped their arms about me in compassion and nodded in understanding at my feelings of loss. I'm unprepared for Sam's bluntness, and my defenses rise.

"Sam, you don't know what-"

"Don't be daft, now," Sam presses on, throwing his hands in the air like this is the most exasperating conversation he's ever had. "Think of the good that has come from your life since then. Would you give up a life with Poppy in exchange for dying just so you don't have to feel sad sometimes?"

"No," the word rushes out of me without a thought, "but . . ." But nothing, I realize. There is nothing I would trade a lifetime of memories with Poppy for. Nothing. Not even for having my family back.

The moment the truth registers, I want to take it back. It feels like betrayal. Disloyalty. And truthfully, it makes my skin crawl with embarrassment. But now that the notion exists, there isn't a thing I can do to dissuade my mind from believing it.

"Okay, then," Sam says with finality. "If you wouldn't give up the life you have now, stop carrying the guilt for the accident that brought it to you."

And in that one moment, beliefs I have held onto for years dissolve and crumble like rusted metal chains along the ocean floor.

I am not responsible for their deaths. I am not a coward. I am thankful to be alive.

25

CHARLES

BEESTON, NOTTINGHAMSHIRE, ENGLAND
NOVEMBER 20, 1917

"ENGLAND IS AWFUL," N18 SAYS WITH ALL THE SELF-righteous flippancy of a socialite. "I don't know how you've survived, constantly surrounded by these verminous people. No wonder you were so angry Gukenstein dropped you here." She gives a flick of her wrist, and a red hand fan with intricate floral designs flares open.

The middle-aged woman I've spent nearly two years speaking with over the telephone is now standing across the lobby counter from me in the empty post office. An elegant, black, wide-brimmed hat adorned with long, red feathers, sits atop short blonde hair that curls around her petite face. Long, black gloves don her arms, and she holds a sleek, black clutch. N18 is beautiful in a striking way. A woman no one would suspect of espionage. A woman who will now live less than two hundred kilometers from me.

My blood boils.

"I've only been here for a week, and my skin feels as though it's crawling with filthy Brits. I don't know how I'm going to survive the remainder of the war in this dreadful place," she says.

Once I found the coordinates for the two filling factories south of Chilwell—Banbury and Coventry National Shell Filling

Factories No. 9 and 21, respectively—it took Gukenstein another four months to make the arrangements for N18 to become employed in England as a munition's worker at the Banbury National Shell Filling Factory No. 9.

"You'll get used to it," I tell her, spinning my cowboy hat around my finger, feigning nonchalance at her presence. "Somehow this place grows on ya."

"Hopefully it's only the *place* that's grown on you and not the people." She shivers dramatically. "But, alas, I didn't travel to Beeston to complain. The reason for my visit this evening is to tell you that my cover name is Liza Humphries. I am to be your dear cousin, an English nanny who momentarily stepped away from that line of work to do my bit in serving my country at Banbury. It isn't safe to communicate over the telephone any longer, so all our forthcoming communications will be in person."

At that moment, Poppy bursts into the post office, a stack of boxes from the factory in her arms, hair that's escaped the bun at the nape of her neck sticking out in different directions, and her thin, black shawl sliding sideways off the long, black dress hugging her body.

She's already talking as she walks under the tinkle of the bell above the door. "You would not believe what Mr. Ashby had me doing during our dinner hour toda—"

The sentence dies on her lips the moment she notices N18— *Liza*. Her body stiffens beneath the postage she bears.

The post office is always vacant at this hour, so I understand her confusion. I'm none too thrilled myself that N18 is meeting Poppy in person. It's bad enough that my superior, Gukenstein, sent Liza to infiltrate my life; I don't want Liza anywhere near Poppy's.

Liza turns to face Poppy and, with dramatic flair, fans herself with her red hand fan like she's at the oceanside in June rather than indoors in November.

"Well, well, well. Who do we have here?" N18 croons.

"Liza, this is my friend, Miss Pemburton," I say, motioning with a swing of my hat to Poppy, who's making her way toward us, her eyes narrowed and calculating. "Miss Pemburton, this is my . . . cousin, Liza. The one who lives south of here who notified me of the Beeston Post Office manager opening."

Liza takes in Poppy's yellow face and hands, then breaks into a Cheshire cat of a smile. "Ah, yes. Pleasure to meet you. I've heard *so* much about you."

"A little chilly outside for a fan, is it not?" Poppy says coldly.

"A lady always carries a fan. You never know when you might need to smack a gentleman's hand away," Liza replies in a perfect English accent. "But then again," she says, looking Poppy up and down, "maybe you don't have that problem."

"I don't need a fan to smack a gentleman," Poppy retorts. She drops her packages onto the clean surface of the counter.

"Oh, I like her." Liza smirks. "Well, I certainly know when three is a crowd, so I'll be on my way. You two have a good evening. I'll see you soon, Cousin." With that, she snaps her fan closed and exits the post office.

"Let's get these posted for ya," I say in an effort to pull Poppy's attention away from N18's retreating figure. I toss my hat onto the counter, open the drawer that has my censorship tools, and reach for a knife to cut open the parcel, when a letter that came in today for Poppy from Luca stares up at me from the drawer.

The moment the writing registers as Luca's, I slam the drawer closed, my heart racing.

I was in the middle of reading the letter when N18 surprised me with her visit. I tossed the letter in the drawer and forgot about it. I can't afford to become lackadaisical. Not when we're almost to the year mark of Luca's "death" and Poppy is finally moving on.

"Everything okay?" Poppy asks. "Find a mouse in there or something?"

Even though I'm certain my face has lost all its color, I keep my expression stoic. "Nope. Not a mouse."

Over the past eleven months, I have managed to keep every one of the eighty-seven letters Luca has sent home hidden from Poppy in the back of the cuckoo clock that stands only steps away from us. He has written her faithfully at least twice a week every week since his capture late last year. No matter that she has never written him back, the poor bloke won't give up. It's embarrassing really. At this point, I'm certain I'm doing Poppy an enormous favor by keeping away this man who clearly has an unhealthy obsession with her.

The clock has a door the height of the clock in the back that can be opened with a key, but I threw the key away so nobody could ever fix the bird. There is also, however, an almost imperceptible crack near the base on the backside that can be opened by inserting and then twisting the thin blade of a knife. The inside of the clock is hollow, about eighteen inches wide, and nearly six feet high. It's the perfect place to store unwanted letters.

"Well, now I have to see what has frightened you as much as my driving did," Poppy says, laughing as she walks to my side of the counter.

I stand firm in front of the drawer and fold my arms across my chest. The thought of Poppy seeing a letter from Luca dated two weeks ago makes my heart thump vigorously. I'm certain I could power a motorcar with the amount of energy my body is exerting in this precise moment.

"There's nothin' in there."

"Oh, there is absolutely something in there—something you don't want me to see—and I am not moving from this spot until I know what it is."

Poppy plants her body so close to me, her arms lightly brush against mine as she crosses them. Her breath inhales then exhales across my neck. I fixate on the faint spots of purple in her blue eyes.

"You're right. There's somethin' I don't want ya to see. It's top secret. If you saw what's in there, I'd have to kill ya," I say, shrugging my shoulders.

"Charles Andrews, if you don't show me what's in there, I'll be forced to kill *you*."

"That's a chance I'm willing to take."

Poppy uncrosses her arms, steps closer to me, and places one hand on either side of my body against the counter, trapping me in front of her.

Now my heart is accelerating for reasons that have nothing to do with what's inside the drawer behind me. She tilts her face up, her lips inches from mine, and says, "Are you sure about that, Farm Boy?"

Right now, the only thing I'm sure of is that I want to grab hold of Poppy Pemburton and kiss her senseless. But that's a line we haven't crossed yet. A line I have kept myself teetering on the edge of for months now, waiting until I know for certain that a physical relationship with her won't jeopardize my mission. Waiting until my heart can decipher between Charles and Jakob.

Poppy slides one hand around my waist, and my body reacts instantly to the touch. She rises onto her tiptoes, and her breath strokes my lips. I lean forward, tempted to close the minute distance between us, when the drawer behind me slides open.

My hand flies behind my back, and I grab hold of her wrist just as she pulls something from the drawer.

"Tsk. Tsk. Tsk. Drop it," I growl into her ear. "Drop what's in your hand."

"Not a chance," she says, laughing. She tugs against my grip, but her wrist is locked in my grasp.

"One. Two. Three," I count in warning. When she still doesn't release what she stole, I bring my other hand to her side and tickle my fingers against her ribs as quick as I can.

Poppy erupts in laughter, her body jerking back and forth beneath my dancing fingers, but she doesn't let go of what she's holding.

"Last chance," I warn as she thrashes about, her hand still locked behind my back.

I don't relent, and between gasps of breath she finally shrieks, "Fine! Fine, I give up!"

When I stop tickling her sides, she collapses against me. Behind my back, I slide a piece of paper from her pinched fingers, and I turn back to the drawer, careful that she doesn't get a glimpse.

It is, indeed, Luca's letter. I bite my bottom lip to keep from cursing, slam the drawer closed, and fix my hat to my head to buy time for the grimace on my face to ease.

"It's somethin' I'm workin' on for you," I lie. "You can't see it yet, though," I say, facing her.

"For me?" she straightens to a stand in front of me.

"No more questions, Miss Silent Canary. This time it's my turn to keep a secret from you."

"Okay, fine," she says. "I'll let you have your secret this time." She smiles up at me, and her eyes glow with life. When she looks at me like that, all I want to do is scoop her into my arms and kiss her until I can't breathe. "But next time, you won't be so lucky," she says.

"There won't be a next time."

Poppy wags a finger in front of me. "Good. I don't like secrets."

Secrets is not a subject I'm comfortable with. "How is your father?" I ask finding safer ground. "Any better?"

Poppy moves to my side and leans her back against the counter, matching my posture, our arms hanging loose at our sides. "Not any better, but not any worse." She looks over at me. "I just want my father back. The man he was before Jane left, but at this point I'd even be happy with the man he was before the war."

Thomas came home from the war four months ago with trench foot, a disease Poppy says took his mind instead of his life. The few times I have been around him, which I try never to be, he stares into the corner, mumbling things to himself that we don't understand and swearing that he will find his revenge on the Germans. It's a miracle he made it back to Beeston in one piece since he is as delirious as he is angry.

Rather than return to the dormitory with the canary girls, Poppy decided to live with Thomas in their cottage so she could care for him—a decision that she doesn't regret but that I know exhausts her.

"I'm sorry," I say. "I would do just about anythin' to get my own father back. It's hard to hold sufferin' in your hands and not be able to relieve it."

Poppy studies my face, her eyes darting back and forth between mine. I hold her gaze. I am terrified of this dangerous creature, yet I have a burning desire to know what holding her in my arms would feel like.

She turns slowly toward me. Her little finger brushes against mine, and she freezes.

I wrap my finger around hers, and the sensation of this simple caress causes my heart to race, but she may as well be worlds away for the desperate way in which my hands ache to pull her to me.

She licks her bottom lip, and the freckle on her top lip dips down. My chest squeezes at the temptation to cross enemy lines.

I almost take a step away like the good spy I should be, when she reaches her other hand to my face and, with slow deliberation, pulls my face toward hers.

Heat explodes through me. I try to say something, to swallow, to move, but I can't.

In the silence, Poppy turns all the way in to me, and my hands disobediently find their way to her waist. I pull her to my chest, my fingers gripped around her, my eyes never losing sight of the lips I want on mine.

"Charles." Her voice is a murmur that sends my heart erratically beating, but my lips freeze above hers as I register her utterance of my cover name, effectively shocking me out of my Poppy trance.

It's not Jakob she wants but Charles. And that's what *I* should want. That's the purpose of everything I am building and working toward within the mission: a relationship between Poppy and Charles. But the moment the word left her lips, the truth of my feelings stabbed me in the back.

I wanted her to say "Jakob." I want it to be *me* she is desperate to kiss.

Closing my eyes, I take the step away I should have taken before.

Poppy's arms fall to her side, confusion and hurt swimming in clouded eyes.

She has real feelings for me. Feelings I manipulated her into having. Feelings that only exist because of what I have done.

My feelings for her are real too, but they are real with no manipulation on her part.

I don't want to fall for the real her while she is falling for the fake me. *I* want to be the man she desires. So maybe . . . maybe I'm done being fake. Maybe now I know what I want for my life. And maybe what I want isn't a transfer within the German army.

What I want is Poppy.

26

POPPY

CHILWELL, NOTTINGHAMSHIRE, ENGLAND
APRIL 27, 1918

THE FALL OF 1917 PASSED BY IN AN ENDLESS BLUR OF FOOTBALL matches, filling shells, friendly evenings with Charles (much to my dismay after our near kiss last November), and nursing Father. The winter into 1918 brought more of the same routines, minus the football since the frozen ground and sleet made the playing conditions too dangerous.

While I am grateful Father is alive and has returned home, he is still lost to the war for the most part. There are moments of coherency and stillness that were not there when he came home last July, but they are still few and far between with more bouts of anger and fits.

Spring has brought our first football match of the year. The changing room inside the ammunition factory is brimming with nerves and excitement as we dress in our football kits—a long-sleeved green-and-white-striped jersey top; short, black pants that graze our knees; black knee-high stockings; and black leather football booties. The look is completed with a green cap pinned over our tied-back hair.

Little Canary tucks her arms through mine and Nessy's as we exit the changing room, chattering and giggling in anticipation

of the match, while Annabelle and Sophia bicker over the placement of the oversized cap sliding off Clara's small head.

Playing football has benefited our physical health, perhaps
even more than the gloves and masks have, but it has also saved
the spirit of every one of the canary girls during this war. We bring
all our troubles and bottled-up fears onto the pitch and leave every
emotion right there on the grass we trample, or stuck to the ball
we send sailing through the air, or in the sweat that drips from our
pores to the earth below us, ready and willing to take our pains.

Although we fight hard against the Coventry National Shell
Filling Factory, the Coventry Ladies secure the win over us 4-3,
taking both the victory and the joyous smiles we wore only an
hour ago.

"No celebration at the Red Lounge now." Disappointment is
written all over Annabelle's face as we reconvene in the dressing
room of the Chilwell factory post-match. "I made the most
beautiful dress to wear out tonight in anticipation of our win."
Annabelle apprenticed as a fashion designer in London before
the war, so whenever she can scrape some fabric ends together,
she works on new designs.

Nessy places a hand on her stomach. "Well, I'm famished.
Save the dress for our next victory, and let's go to Mrs. Christmas's Sweet Shoppe for tea and biscuits," she says to Annabelle,
who agrees with a reluctant smile.

After we've changed out of our football kits and back into
our street clothes, we fetch our bicycles and begin the ride back
toward Beeston.

"I'm going home to sleep until next week." Sophia yawns.
"Little Canary, come on back to the dormitory with me. You
need your rest too."

"Can't I go with Poppy? She's just going to meet Charles at
the pond."

"Yes, and she doesn't want you there." Annabelle winks at me
over Clara's head.

"I'd love to take you, Little Canary, but I think we'll be out late, and it's already been a long day with filling shells and playing football. Next time, okay?"

Clara pouts for only a moment before shrugging her acceptance and waving goodbye as she pedals away.

The pond sits atop a hill surrounded by a deep grove of trees. It's on the far side of Beeston near the Weir where Father used to work controlling the arrival and departure of small boats along this portion of the River Trent. Not many people know about the pond since it's in a secluded location on the outskirts of town, but Father and I used to swim there in the summers after he was done working when I was little girl. Charles and I have taken to having late suppers there quite often since the weather began to warm in March. Many evenings, Clara comes with us, but tonight I'm going to tell Charles how I feel about him.

Luca has been gone for nearly eighteen months now, and the only regret I have is that I missed out on loving him for longer because I was afraid of losing him. In the end, I lost him anyway. I don't want to make that mistake again. Loving Luca was worth every ounce of the pain I endured to say goodbye. His death taught me that nothing is promised to us. That every day we're alive is a blessing. A gift to be opened and used.

I want to *live* my life, not be a spectator.

For a year now, Charles and I have spent nearly every moment together after my day shift at the factory. But he has kept his distance physically since our near kiss last fall. Perhaps because he thinks I'm not ready for a new relationship, or perhaps because he's not interested in me outside of a friendship, or perhaps because he's planning to return home to Texas when the war ends and he knows I will never leave Beeston. But I'm done waiting.

I like Charles. Very much. He makes my chest spasm with laughter and my stomach swoop with nerves. He makes my body tingle with desire and my heart speed with excitement anytime he is near. He listens to everything I have to say and asks more questions than I sometimes even have answers to. He challenges my intellect and praises my victories. He makes me feel safe amidst a war-torn world, happy despite the despair of enemy fire, and excited for a post-war future. I suppose I don't simply *like* Charles. I love him.

Loving Luca was familiar in a way I will never experience with another soul for as long as I live. Loving Luca was like cocooning myself in my black shawl, or ducking into my favorite bookstore on a rainy day, or simply breathing. We knew each other in a way nobody else ever has or ever will know us. He was my first best friend and the forever love of my life.

But I'm beginning to believe it might be possible to love more than one person. To experience love again, though in an entirely new way. Because loving Charles is exhilarating. Loving Charles is like driving an automobile for the first time, or seeing lightning bolts before the crack of thunder, or forgetting to breathe altogether.

I don't want to worry about what-ifs or futures unknown anymore. I want to live in the now that we have.

And right now, I want Charles.

When I arrive at the pond, it's nearly dark. Charles is already there, but instead of sitting on the blanket, reading or snacking on whatever he picked up from the market as he usually is, he's submersed in the pond, his back to me.

I watch him for a moment, trying not to admire the way his shoulders flex beneath the full moon as the light refracts in fragments on the ripples of the water. Then I stop trying and just enjoy the way his strong arms thread through the shimmering ribbons of blue.

Flutters of desire start low in my belly and work their way up into my chest until my heart feels as though it's beating in my throat.

Rub, rub, rub.

Fear tempts me to turn around and run away. *It will hurt in the end*, fear warns me.

I know, I reply.

Without making a sound, I loosen the black laces from my boots and slide them off along with my stockings. I drop Jane's ring into one of the boots and place my black shawl on the ground next to my shoes, and when I'm certain Charles isn't looking, I move to the bank and slip into the water unnoticed. My long-sleeve, navy cotton dress pulls heavy against my body, but the cold water is magnificent against my flushed post-match skin. I make my way to where Charles lies floating in the shallow water on his back, and I'm thankful to see that while he has momentarily lost his shirt, he still dons trousers.

I get as close to Charles's ear as possible without him noticing me and say, "Nice night for a swim?"

Charles startles at the sound of my voice. His arms flail about, causing his body to break through the surface of the water with a giant splash and then disappear beneath the ripples. He resurfaces with water sputtering from his lips and large droplets running down the contours of his face. He wipes a hand across his eyes and shakes his head from side to side, water flying in every direction.

Laughter bubbles up within my throat, and I can't keep it in another second.

"Oh, ya think that's funny, do you? Scarin' me near half to death? How 'bouts I sneak up and scare you half outta *yer* wits next time?"

The cold water and proximity to shirtless Charles has officially affected me. Through shivering teeth, I rattle, "Nothing scares me, Farm Boy."

Charles studies my face, a serious expression etched along his handsome features. He gulps, and his chest flexes as his arms move out slowly toward me, as if he isn't sure he should touch me but can't stop himself. "Nothin'?" His hands grab me firm around my middle, and he pulls me in close to him, then rubs his hands up and down my arms. His eyes drink me in, and in the moonlight, they turn to liquid pools of gold.

I lick my lips to keep them from trembling, and Charles's gaze moves to my mouth.

Fire ignites the sensitive places throughout my body. *Please stay this time. Please don't back away from me again. I want this. Please want me too.* I will my eyes to translate the message.

Water laps in small waves around our waists, pushing us closer together. Charles presses his hands into the small of my back and dips his mouth below my ear. His lips tease my skin as he says, "Ya know what scares me, Silent Canary?"

Hairs along my arms and neck prickle in response.

"You." His lips graze my earlobe.

My breath shutters, and the words are out before I can stop them. "I'm in love with you."

I close my eyes to his reaction, but when warm, full lips press mine, that's all the answer I need.

His mouth moves fast and hungry against mine as if I'm going to vanish at any moment and he will be left starving. His kiss is passionate, wild, dangerous. And the longer I lose myself in his want of me, the more I want to know exactly what is behind each door I know he keeps his secrets firmly locked behind.

I scarcely have time to respond to his desire before his fingers trail over and down my hips, and I nearly lose consciousness. Every sensation in my body erupts simultaneously when he lifts me up and guides my legs around his waist, drawing me in closer. Strong arms hold me tight to him, and my body pulses with a longing for his lips to discover every part of me.

I arch backwards as Charles presses his mouth against the soft flesh of my neck, and the inky black night overhead lulls my fears away with the tide. There is no space between our bodies and endless space above us as time both stops and bends like eternity.

"Why do I scare you?" I whisper.

"I think the better question is, Why don't *I* scare *you?*"

"Should you?"

"Yes."

Shivers prickle down my spine, but I stand my ground. "I'm done being scared, Charles. Fear doesn't get a say in my life anymore."

27

LUCA

PRISONER OF WAR LABOR CAMP, HENDECOURT-LÈS-CAGNICOURT, FRANCE APRIL 28, 1918

PLAN. PREPARE. EXECUTE.

That is the goal.

Fail. Rethink. Try again.

That is the reality.

For eight months, Sam and I have meticulously planned every part of our escape, down to the last minuscule detail.

We had to lie low after a prisoner attempted escape in January. The escapee was caught, and the guards took his life without question. Nobody has attempted an escape since.

Prisoners often come and go, transferred between camps and placed as needed to fill German labor shortages. When they roll through this camp, they swap prisoner camp stories and tell tales of how our commandant is widely known as the worst in France —a man who plays war by his own set of prejudiced rules with nobody to question them.

There was an incident one evening involving my spurning of Commandant's advances toward me when I was trapped in his living quarters on an unfortunate cleaning assignment. Commandant did not appreciate my rebuff, and had I not been faster and more agile than he, he would have had his way with me. Clearly not a man who is familiar with the embarrassment of rejection, he has since attempted to harm and humiliate me at every opportunity, telling others I am being punished for attempted seduction of a superior officer.

Humiliation is a cowardly tool that does nothing but seal my decrepit box of calloused scars. What does cause my bosom to burn, however, are the whispers around camp that the commandant is going to transfer Sam out on the lorry coming through Hendecourt-lès-Cagnicourt tomorrow.

Some details of our plans have failed, and some preparations have shifted, but at last we are ready to execute. Failure tonight is not an option.

Silently now, Sam and I dress inside the trench we spent eight months digging with two stolen kitchen utensils from cooking duty. The hole lies hidden beneath the latrine behind our hut. Every day, when he or I visited the toilet, we removed the floorboards and dug for a few minutes at a time until we had a hole big enough to store our escape items: a German soldier uniform and boots for each of us, civilian clothes to change into after our escape—which we obtained from transfer prisoners— enough food to last each of us three days, a bag in which to carry everything, and one map each in case we get separated.

I am ready. My boots are laced, my drawing of Poppy is tucked into my shirt pocket, and the last letter she wrote to me is wrapped around the picture to keep it safe. I have no way of knowing if Poppy stopped writing because something has happened to her, or perhaps she believes something has happened to me, but I've written her every week regardless. The writing is therapeutic for me at worst and a beacon of hope at best. The singular white feather that prompted my decision to enlist, my symbol now of the guilt I have overcome and the courage I strive to carry, is also pressed to my chest beneath my shirt. I won't be taking anything else.

I tap Sam's leg lightly with my foot three times, signaling my readiness. My swollen ankle aches beneath my boot at the movement. I was forced to jump from the second story window of the guard's quarters last night into the bushes below after stealing the uniforms Sam and I don.

Sam returns the leg tap. It's time.

Despite the excruciating pain in my ankle, my palms tingle with anticipation.

Sam reaches up to push open the floorboard above us, when sounds of soldiers approaching outside the latrine prick my ears. The guards' whistles blow with wild abandon, and their boots hit the ground like a stampede of angry buffalo.

My hands ball into fists, and my jaw aches from the pressure of my clenched teeth. It's likely sometime between two and three in the morning, but somebody must've noticed our empty cots and called the guards. The whole camp—prisoners and guards alike—is going to be swarming with excitement now. Guard frenzy like this in the middle of the night can only mean one thing in a prisoner of war camp: attempted escape. It's too late to change our minds now, but perhaps we can use the mayhem to our advantage.

Sam picks up his bag and slides it across his chest.

I hold out a hand to Sam. "Stand back up."

"Stand back up." Sam's hand shakes mine, his fingers trembling but strong.

"I'll climb out first and make sure the coast is clear," I say. "Then we'll run to the fence line on the east edge of the field."

"Follow the fence in the shadows until we reach the north gate," Sam continues, speaking our plan out loud as we've done every night before we fell asleep.

"I will slide the sign over and bend down the cut wires." I mimic the actions with my hands.

"Then I will jump through and pull you after me," Sam finishes.

I take a large breath, my chest exploding with nerves. "And then—"

"We run," we say in unison.

We pry open the floorboard above us and move.

Everything outside is chaos.

Prisoners are running amok, hollering and whooping. German guards are in the mix as well—some trying to control the prisoners, some shooting their weapons into the air, some running along the outsides and insides of the gate, swinging flashlights. Some already searching the surrounding fields.

But Sam and I stick to the plan. It's all we know.

We move silently in the shadows, always keeping an eye on the nearest guards, allowing the chaos to provide our cover. My ankle throbs, but I keep moving, always keeping Sam in my line of sight. We make it all the way to the north gate without so much as a scratch. French and British prisoners run from us, mistaking us for the German soldiers they fear.

Every day for the last two months, as we made our walk back and forth through the north entrance gate to and from work duty, Sam would slip out of line a couple paces to the connected barbed wire fence. There, he would slide his hand behind a large metal sign that boasted the name of our camp in splattered red paint and make one slight cut into the barbed wire with a knife he whittled out of stone the first week we were here. Once bent down, the snipped wires should create a hole big enough for one man to slide through.

There's only one guard stationed at the north gate. He wears an eyepatch over one eye and swings a walking cane from side to side, whistling. Apparently, they don't believe someone would waltz out the front gate, so they sent a cripple to guard it.

I almost laugh at the thought.

There are no guards patrolling outside this portion of fence now, so I urge Sam forward along the fence until we reach the sign.

Just like we planned, I slide the sign to the side and fold down the precut wires. They bend easily into the perfect sized hole. I turn to tell Sam he did an impeccable job cutting these wires when I see *him*.

Commandant.

I see a glint of his sharp, spiked blond hair behind a tree that sits maybe twenty meters away. My eyes rove quickly, but in my heart, I already know there are no other guards hidden in the trees. Just Commandant and the cyclops guard.

Commandant wants this job. He wants this kill.

I imagine the way his thin lips curled with anticipation the moment he discovered my empty cot. The way he likely tracked Sam and I to this gate, allowing me to think I had won just to strip me of my victory. Between his shoulder and the tree, the tip of his rifle slides out like an evil tongue sticking itself out to taunt me. Only it's not aimed at me, it's aimed at Sam.

This is how Commandant is going to make me pay for my rebuff of him.

I don't even think. I grab Sam and shove his shoulders through the hole.

"What are you bloody doing? Stop it. This isn't the plan," Sam protests.

A bullet ricochets off the metal sign a breath away from my head, and I push harder. "The plan is changing," I grunt.

Sam struggles against me, but it's futile against the force of my adrenaline and my upper body strength. He has no choice but to slither the rest of his body through the hole, landing with a thud on the ground. In seconds, he is back up, reaching for me through the hole.

"Let's go." His voice is near hysteria as he yanks my uniform.

But I know we aren't both making it out of here alive.

If I stay, I can at least create a diversion. I can give Sam a fighting chance.

I know I wasn't responsible for G's death—that there was nothing I could have done to save him—but now I have a real chance to save another brother, and I am going to take it.

"Follow the plan, Sam. Get to England." I thrust my bag at him through the fence hole and will my fingers to stop shaking. "Go home to Sarah. Make more beautiful babies. Find Poppy. Tell her I loved her."

Sam grabs my shoulders and shakes them with such force my teeth chatter. "Luca, I am not doing this without you," he hollers. "I can't."

Another bullet ricochets, but this one hits the fence near my hip. Near my head, another bullet pings, and I duck.

"Sam, I twisted my ankle when I was getting the uniforms out of the guard's office last night; I can't run. I will slow you down. The guards will catch us, and we will both die. You know we will. The soldiers can hear the bullets hitting the fence; they're going to be here any minute. Please, Sam. Go."

Sam knows I'm right, but I see the hardness in his eyes. The squared defiance of his shoulders. He won't leave me here.

"Sam," I yell at him now, needing him to understand, "I don't have anything to go home to! There is no one there waiting for me. I have no home. Poppy has forgotten about me. My family is in heaven. I'm going to be with them now. You go to yours. Please do this for me. Sam, I can't lose another brother." Wet tears coat my face and neck, choking my speech. "Please run."

"God be with you till we meet again, Luca," Sam says as my right leg explodes with fire. My body thrashes into the fence, and I grip the wire to keep from falling to the ground.

"Luca!" Sam grips my hand through the barbed wire. His eyes are wide and crazed, but his voice is determined and thick with emotion.

Dark waves move through my brain, but I try to focus on his words.

"I love you, Luca," he says. "I will find Poppy. I will tell her she was in love with a hero. I will tell her that you saved my life."

I drop to my knees, no longer able to hold myself up. "Run, Sam."

"Luci," Sam yells at me as he backs away from the fence. "We named our daughter Luci. After your mother."

I blink in confusion. The pain is so severe. "No, you named her Evelyn."

"After you told me the story of your family, we gave her a middle name. Evelyn Lucille Davies. We call her Luci."

Sam turns then, and he runs, and runs, and runs.

I watch until I can't see him anymore. I watch until pain sends waves of black into my vision. I watch until the cool metal point of Commandant's gun connects with the back of my head.

And then, because I will not die sitting down, I stand back up.

28

CHARLES

BEESTON, NOTTINGHAMSHIRE, ENGLAND
MAY 18, 1918

NOTHING MATTERS TO ME MORE IN THIS MOMENT THAN memorizing the way Poppy Pemburton looks as she makes her way, slow and purposeful in a floor-length black charmeuse dress, through the crowds of people dotting the dance floor of the Red Lounge. The neckline comes up in a broad swoop high against her collarbones, where the material gathers and then dips in a V shape down the length of her back. I can't put a coherent string of words together in my mind as I watch her move across the room.

When she's within arm's reach of me, I catch her hand in mine and spin her into me.

"Charles!" she gasps with a laugh. "I've been looking for you all night. I didn't take you to be a wallflower. You look far too handsome in that suit to be standing in the shadows."

"I much prefer to watch you."

"Oh stop." She bats a hand at me.

I pull her closer to my chest and use my finger to lift her chin. She grabs hold of my black suit coat lapels and smiles. I kiss her pink-brushed lips until mine go numb and then I kiss her some more. My hands get lost in the contours of her body as the silky dress moves like water beneath my touch.

"Dance with me," I say into her ear.

With her hand on my arm, I escort her to the center of the crowded dance floor, my eyes never leaving hers. I turn her once beneath my raised arm, then catch her waist and hold her to me, breathing in the vanilla crème scent that dances along her skin.

The softness of her body pressed against mine, the welcoming blue windows to her soul, and the tickle of her hair on the underside of my chin as we sway to the beat of the music transport me to another place and time. In the Red Lounge, there is no war. In the Red Lounge, Poppy is not a British ammunition worker, and I am not the German spy tasked with hunting her. Here, we are simply Jakob and Poppy, two people falling in love on a late-spring evening in a crowded dance hall.

When Poppy told me she loved me in the pond, everything in my life crumbled and somehow rebuilt in the same moment.

I have yet to say the words back to her. I believed if I didn't say them out loud, Charles could hold them tight to himself and Jakob wouldn't feel them. I believed I could keep my heart in line until the end of my assignment in Beeston. I believed I could continue to spy on her without repercussion.

But in this moment, I know it's over for me.

This mission, Charles Andrews, my desire to transfer to the interpretation department after the war, my future with German Intelligence in any form. It's all over.

I will give it all up for a life with Poppy. I am now, and ever want to be, only Jakob Kirtchner, the man who loves Poppy Pemburton. I wanted to exchange my spy life for a stable life with roots and find a way to help Mutter escape Hans, but I see now that I don't need to work for Germany to have those things. I only need Poppy.

"I love you," I say against her cheek.

Poppy pulls back at my words and searches my eyes.

I don't know what she sees there, but after spending years of my life lying about who I am and what I feel, I hope that the one time I speak the truth it is evident.

"I love the fire in yer soul, the kindness in yer heart, and the passion with which you live life. You have utterly and completely wrecked me." I smile at her. "I was unsure of my future before. Of what dream I was going to follow and how I was going to get there. But I need you to know I love everythin' about you." I take hold of her face and draw her to me. "*You* are my dream." I'm unsure exactly how I am going to accomplish everything I want right at this moment, but I do know I cannot go one second longer without telling her how I feel.

Poppy wraps her arms around my neck and tilts her head to the side, a smile spreading across her face. "I love you too, Farm Boy." Her eyes are sincere and bright with hope.

I lean down to kiss her parting lips, when a couple, arm in arm, sidles past, and the woman bumps into me. The coy face of N18, Liza Humphries, winks at my upturned face, then nods with a discreet lift of her chin toward the exit before turning back to the man on her arm.

My hands turn to ice. Every muscle within my body flexes. Liza's heels click against the dance floor as she follows the man out the exit, each click an echo of a bullet exiting a gun. A blunt reminder of where I am and who I'm with.

"What's wrong?" Poppy's arms tense around my neck.

I wipe the panic from my face and will my muscles to relax. "Oh nothin'. I just remembered I need to run back to the post office. I was supposed to get somethin' ready to be mailed out first thing in the mornin'." I rub my hands over my face to hide some of the anger bubbling up within me. "I'm sorry to cut such a perfect evenin' short, but I have to get back there and get things squared away."

"I'll go with you. I can help," Poppy offers kindly.

I want to scoop her up and run far, far away with her. To keep her innocent of my crimes. To let her believe in Charles Andrews and start a new life together on a ranch in Texas. But I know I will need to tell Poppy the truth about who I am. I can't keep lying to her if I want a future with her.

"Thank you for offerin', but unfortunately, I'm goin' to be there for a good while, and I know you need to get home to Thomas and make sure he took his medication with his supper."

Her shoulders instantly droop at Thomas's name.

"Yes, you're right of course," she says. "Okay, then."

After ensuring Poppy is safely in the company of Annabelle, Nessy, and Sophia, I make my way to the post office in record time, knowing Liza is going to be there, ready and waiting to do some talking. She wouldn't be in Beeston otherwise.

"Good evening, cowboy," Liza croons as I flick on the light. "You had some pretty good moves tonight."

"I didn't dance," I say, throwing my cowboy hat on the counter she sits behind.

"I wasn't talking about the dancing." She winks.

My skin crawls at the thought of her watching Poppy and I, studying our every move.

"What do I need to tell you to get you to leave?" I ask her, walking into my back office, where she, unfortunately, follows me. I keep the conversation in English, mostly because I hope it irritates her, seeing how she despises everything about this country, but also because I can't chance anyone overhearing me speak German.

"Is that any way to treat the woman who's here to make sure you keep your job?"

"You're not my boss; you're my contact point," I huff.

In my office, Liza stands so close to me, the feathers on the black boa draped around her neck tickle the hairs of my arms, and the smell of her overdone perfume nearly makes me gag. Before I can tell her I no longer want the job anyway, she says, "No wonder Poppy is all giddy for Charles Andrews. Just look at the way your jaw line sharpens when you clench it. Yum." Her eyebrows pop, and she licks her lips seductively.

"Keep Poppy out of this. She has nothing to do with us." I take a step back from Liza, but she matches my movement with her own forward step.

"Oh, dear boy, that's why I'm here. She has everything to do with us." Liza draws out the *v* sound in *everything* and laughs gleefully. "She *is* our target after all, isn't she?"

My teeth clench inside my closed mouth, but I force myself to relax.

Liza draws her hands to her hips and purses her lips. "Oh no. Your cover hasn't been blown, has it? Please tell me you haven't made the rookie mistake of falling for the enemy." She rolls her eyes and continues, "She isn't even pretty. Certainly not worth the death penalty for deserting your post and betraying your country." Liza basically purrs the last part, and if I didn't know for certain that Gukenstein would have me hung for killing another agent, I would take her feather boa and strangle her with it.

All the same, panic that she might have glimpsed *Jakob* with Poppy tonight and guilt that I am indeed betraying Germany by falling in love with the enemy erupts through my insides. It's all I can do to keep my face neutral. Until I know what Liza's play here is, I have to keep my cards close to my chest.

"I would hate to be the one to tell Poppy that this is all a ruse," she gloats with an overly dramatic pout of her lips.

I know she's goading me, but I need to make her understand that she will have nothing to do with Poppy or the Chilwell ammunition factory.

"First off, Poppy is *my* target, not *our* target. And secondly, if you tell her, you'd blow my cover, and Gukenstein would have your head."

"That he would." She laughs. "But it would be so fun to watch Poppy scream with the hurt of your betrayal that it might be worth it. If I'm going to die for this job anyway, might as well go out with a show."

I can't help the snarl that escapes my throat even as the truth of her words burn my insides.

"That's what I thought." Liza clucks her tongue. "Gukenstein is going to love this turn of events. The target falls in love with the agent, and the agent falls in love with the target and can no longer be trusted to complete the mission. Gukenstein must send in a new agent," she points dramatically to herself, "to finish the job and earn the promised transfer after this messy war is all over and mopped up."

Liza wants the transfer? I feel my face pull in confusion, but I'm quick to mask it with anger, as though her desire to take the liaison interpreter job from me is all I care about.

"You have no idea what angle I'm working right now, Liza. You need to stand down. If my target loves me, then I've done the exact job Gukenstein sent me here to do, and that transfer will be mine—as promised. It's time for you to go," I say, moving past her and feigning nonchalance. "You do your job in Banbury, and let me do mine in Chilwell."

I walk back out to the lobby, move to the post office door, and hold it wide open.

"Goodnight, Charles," Liza purrs as she exits through the door with a wave of her black boa across my cheek. "This evening has been delightful and informative." And with that, she saunters off into the night.

Liza doesn't have anything concrete on me to report back to Gukenstein, but I do hope she's right about Poppy loving me. I hope that Poppy loves me enough that when I tell her the truth about who I am, she won't run.

Because it's time for Poppy to meet Jakob.

29

POPPY

BEESTON, NOTTINGHAMSHIRE, ENGLAND
JUNE 24, 1918

DANDELIONS AND WILDFLOWERS ARE IN FULL BLOOM, THEIR bright oranges, blues, yellows, and reds surrounding the pond's edge. Tall grass bends in the soft breeze of the summer day, and I can't help but tickle the blades with my fingertips as I walk to the dock. The sky above is the shade of my favorite forget-me-not flowers, and I resist the urge to spin and spin until I am sick with dizziness. Today is my first day off work in two weeks, and I'm eager to spend it with my love.

My love. Joy bubbles up within me.

After losing Luca, and now my father to the ails of his mind, I never believed I could be this happy again.

There are whispers of the war ending soon, and although nobody wants to raise their hopes and believe war gossip like that, particularly after four years of fighting, the higher rate at which we're producing ammunition makes the rumors more believable. Mr. Ashby now requires every factory employee to work all but two days a month as well as three overnight shifts. Between that and our weekly football matches, not only am I exhausted but I've also only seen Charles twice in the last month. Both visits were brief, and his mind seemed preoccupied with problems at work. It appears his post office duties have kept him as busy as my factory ones.

When I see Charles standing on the brown, wood dock, my face breaks into a smile. I run to him, anticipating a warm embrace, but when I reach him, his arms move around me with all the stiff awkwardness of a manipulated marionette.

"I have somethin' I need to talk to you about." He shuffles his foot back and forth against the strips of wood. His farm hat is noticeably absent as he mops his forehead with a handkerchief. Then he exhales in a manner that sends my heart racing.

Charles Andrews is never nervous. Is he going to propose marriage to me? My mind picks up my heart like a little baby bird and sweeps it away on wings of hope and desire.

"It's okay, Charles; you can tell me. I want to hear what you have to say," I say, resting a hand on his arm.

He doesn't speak for several minutes. His gaze finds the wooden dock beneath us, and he is quiet for so long, my hope wanes, and I have time to imagine every worst possible scenario I can think of: He has an incurable disease. He hates me. He's enlisted in the war. He's my relative. He wants to run away and join the traveling circus.

I need him to put me out of my misery.

I gently lift his face up to meet mine. "What is it, Charles? Please tell me."

He smiles with only his mouth and dips his head. When he looks back up, his eyes are heavy with emotion and . . . what else? Anguish? Fear?

Now I am certain this conversation is not headed where I hoped it was.

My palms grow cold despite the warm evening.

"There is something about myself I need to tell you." His voice is strange. Thick and strangled. His Southern American accent completely gone.

My lips quiver. "Okay."

"I am not the man I have led you to believe I am. I am not an American. I am not Charles Andrews."

My eyes narrow in confusion, and my heart pounds with so much force, I fear it will explode from my chest.

"What does that mean?" I manage to get out. I want to step away from him, but I've forgotten how to move my feet.

"My real name is Jakob Kirtchner. I am from Germany and am an intelligence agent for the German army."

Tingles erupt along the length of my arms and neck. My mouth goes completely dry. I don't understand what he is saying.

In my speechlessness, he continues. "Last month, I stopped sending information back to Germany regarding procedures and intel from inside the Chilwell ammunition factory. Instead, I focused all my efforts on pretending to scout the location of additional ammunition factories within England, telling my superior that after two years of digging into the same factory, my time in England would be better spent finding new ammunition factories for Germany to infiltrate. I have driven far and wide throughout this country over the last four weeks and misdirected their attention by providing false information on these supposed factory locations to keep their focus away from your factory and to ensure my superior would remain unaware that I am no longer an active member of his team."

An active member of what team? What is he talking about? Charles Andrews is not only German but also a spy?

That cannot be true. It makes no sense. I've known him for years. I *know* him.

I know that he only swears when he's tired, and that he prefers his farm boy hat to every item of clothing he owns, and that he has a soft spot for his mother and misses his father desperately, and that he worries about my well-being, and that I am the only person who can make him laugh so thoroughly that if he's sitting down he has to stand up in order to breathe, and that when I kiss him at the base of his neck, his fingers tremble. I know he loves me.

There is no possible way the man standing before me is capable of being an enemy to my country. An enemy to me! It's simply not true.

"I don't know what you're going on about, but you are not German, and you are certainly not a spy," I scoff.

"I terminated communication with my German contact the moment I knew I loved you, Poppy." His voice is quiet. Sincere. And *very* German. "The night at the Red Lounge."

All the blood drains from my face and limbs. Is my heart still beating?

I don't know, because I am weightless.

"You left early," I mumble, dazed, remembering back to that night. Remembering the slight bump of a woman against his side. The way he froze in my arms and his face turned white. The way he ran from the dance hall as though he were scared for his life. The way my instincts told me something wasn't right.

No. I stop that train of thought right there because Charles cannot be telling the truth.

He can't.

But yet . . . yet even as I dip into the questions and the denial begging for acceptance in my mind, the slow buzz of horror—of realizing that in only an instant your whole world is going to crash to the ground—is thrumming beneath the surface of every inch of my skin. The same way it did when I ran to the train station in the pouring rain on my thirteenth birthday to find an empty station. The same way it did when Charles handed me Luca's Killed in Action notification card.

My skin crawls as though a million tiny bugs are running the length of my body.

I manage to reach for the ring in my pocket.

Rub, rub, rub.

My breathing comes in gasps I don't know how to regulate.

I try to remember how to count, but the numbers don't make sense. I thump my hand against my chest over and over.

Charles stills my hand, and something about the touch breaks the spell of my frozen feet, and I jump backward.

"You don't need to be scared." He steps forward.

I scramble backward, my arms held out in front of me as if I could hold off an attack if Charles—wait, *not Charles*—wanted to hurt me.

My back slams into the dock's railing behind me. The force causes the air to momentarily leave my body, and that's when the realization of Charles's admission dawns on me.

This man has spied on *me*. On my friends. On our town. He doesn't love me; he is the enemy. He is *my* enemy. He was positioned at the post office, censoring every letter my fellow employees and I wrote. I gave the enemy locations to ammunition factories by disobeying the command given to *not* talk about our work. I gave him our secrets.

Panic erupts through me.

I step farther back from the German, my hands trailing the wood rail behind me to keep upright. How many secrets did I share because I trusted him? Will I be arrested for treason? What have I done?

I bring my hand to my mouth to ensure the bile spinning within my stomach stays put, but my extremities shake with a severity I can't control.

"Can we please talk about this?" Charles says, his arms cautiously outstretched as though he's approaching a cornered animal.

His strange voice rolls around me like images in the mirrors room of a fun house.

I turn away from him. Things I should have noticed as suspicious over the years but didn't cause rivers of guilt to stream through my memories: his sudden takeover as manager of the post office, his eagerness to drive me to the ammunition factory in Leeds to gather information for our safety protocols and then again to Banbury, the constant questions about my work, his warning in the pond to fear him.

My hands ball into fists so tight they lose feeling. I am so stupid! Did I ignore the signs? Perhaps I didn't want to see them. But I wasn't *looking* for reasons to not trust him.

"I thought I could do the job and go home, but then you happened," Charles says. "You came into my life, Poppy, and you turned everything upside down. You changed everything. The man I was. The man I want to be."

I spin back around, hot tears of fury streaming down my cheeks. "I trusted you," I scream at him.

The features of his face crumble, his head bobs forward, and he lets it hang where it falls.

"No. You do not get to hurt," I yell, walking back toward him, my finger pointing in accusation. "*You* caused this. You did this. You lied to me. Used me. Manipulated my feelings. You could have done your job without dragging my heart into it."

Charles reaches out to me.

"Don't you dare touch me," I seethe. "You will never touch me again. You will never look at me again. You will never speak to me again. Do you understand? I hate you."

"When I told you I loved you, I meant it. Every time," he whispers, and the words break me.

I lean over the railing and vomit into the pond, but my stomach is as empty as my heart.

"You fixed all the broken parts of me, Charles. Why did you heal me just to break me all over again?" I ask. "I let you in. Let you love me. I *wanted* you to love me. I wanted to marry you. Have children with you." A violent sob catches in my throat. "I wanted it to be you."

"We can make this work." He takes a step closer.

I turn and run into the field, leaving him alone on the dock.

"Poppy, please."

I turn back around at his plea but only to say goodbye. "War is war, Charles, or Jakob, or whoever you are. Nobody wins. Not you. Not me. Not the Allies. Not the Central Powers. We *all* lose. I loved Charles; I don't love Jakob. I don't even know who that is." Tears burn the backs of my eyelids. I lose everyone I love. Life has taught me that repeatedly.

Why do I never listen?

Charles nods his head as if agrees with me, but the sight of him makes me physically ill.

"Goodbye, Charles. Leave England, and do not contact me again, or I will turn you in to MI5."

"I understand," he says with his words. His eyes beg me not to walk away.

But it's too late. I'm already gone.

"I hope someday you will use the atlas I gave you," Charles calls out to my retreating back, but this time I don't turn around. "I love you, Poppy. I always will."

I keep running. All the men I love are ghosts.

~

June 28, 1918

CLARA SOOTHES MY HAIR BACK FROM MY FACE AND PLACES THE cold rag on it as I lay in her lap in my childhood bedroom.

"You're as white as a ghost," she whispers as she wipes then soothes, wipes then soothes. We must be quiet so as to not wake Father.

He cannot overhear our conversation. He can never know about Jakob the German. For my sake as well as Jakob's.

It's been four days, and I kept the secret to myself as long as I could, but I couldn't lie to Clara when she begged to know what had become of Mr. Andrews and me. And she swore not to tell Mrs. Fischer or the other canary girls the truth about Jakob's identity. While Annabelle would likely be enthralled by the danger of him and Nessy would feel sorry for me, Mrs. Fischer and Sophia would turn Jakob in to the authorities without a second thought.

Black or white. Enemy or foe. Right or wrong. That's all they see.

But our story is so much more than that.

Betrayer. Companion. Confidant. Enemy. Friend. Liar. Lover. Charles is all those things to me, even still. The lies don't erase the love I felt for him; they just put the knife into my heart, and the betrayal twists the blade.

Instead of the truth, Clara told the other women that Charles and I ended our relationship because he's going back to America soon and I'm staying here, so there was no point in continuing. This allows me the space to hurt without sharing any of the real details that would indict him.

How ironic, though, that I, too, am lying about a relationship I ended because of a lie. I snort laugh even though it's not even a little bit funny.

"There, there," Little Canary says as she strokes my brow.

"I'm sorry, Clara. I know you're scheduled to work the night shift tonight. You can leave whenever you need to."

"I told Mrs. Fischer I was unavailable this evening on account of an upset stomach, so she rescheduled me for the next round of required night shifts on Monday, July 1st. In fact, I signed both you *and* me to work, so you get to suffer through the long night with me." Clara winks at me.

"That's fine. I'm not getting any sleep right now anyhow."

Clara braids my hair quietly, and I relish the touch of her cool fingers against my flushed skin.

"Clara?"

"Hmm?"

Rub, rub, rub.

"What if my heart has shattered so many times I'll never find all the slivers? What if I am so broken the pieces of my heart will never fit back together again?"

Her hands pause mid-braid like she needs the stillness to think.

"After my father broke me," Clara says after a moment, "Mrs. Fischer taught me to find myself again by looking for the beauty in my brokenness. She pointed out the ways I was growing in strength, learning lessons, and overcoming difficulties through my sufferings." She continues braiding. "As we move through life's experiences, the shape of our heart changes, but I discovered that a heart doesn't have to be only one shape to be beautiful."

"What if your shape has cracks? What if it isn't whole?"

"As you slowly begin to pick up the pieces of your broken heart, if you discover there are missing slivers and your heart looks different than it did before, look for the beauty in what it looks like now. The cracks are what allow the light in."

"You are wise beyond your years, Little Canary." I squeeze her hand. "Perhaps someday I will believe my cracks serve a purpose."

"Think of the stained-glass mosaic window at the Beeston First Church of God," Clara says, undeterred by my doubts. "It isn't just one large sheet of glass. The image is made up of hundreds of differently shaped glass cuts. Some with sharp edges, some with dull edges; some large, some small; some that don't fit together exactly right. And yet somehow, the picture it creates when pieced together is beautiful. When the light from the sun shines between and around the cuts of glass, there is something magical that happens. It brings the window to life."

Clara looks down at me and holds my hands in hers. "In our brokenness, we find our beauty. I know right now all you can see is the dark—the cracks. But the light is within you, waiting for you to let it shine through your broken spaces and chase away the dark. When you find your light again, it will bring you back to life."

30

LUCA

PRISONER OF WAR LABOUR CAMP,
HENDECOURT-LÈS-CAGNICOURT, FRANCE
JULY 1, 1918

I LIE FACE DOWN ON THE COOL CEMENT FLOOR OF MY CELL IN the basement of the German guard building where those in solitary confinement are held and slowly finger the slivers I feverishly scratch into the cement day after day. This is how I keep track of the days I am in here so I don't succumb to insanity. There are no windows to note the passage of time, but they feed me once a day. When the food comes, I use my utensil to scratch another line.

Today, when they bring my food, I will mark the floor for the last time.

Line number sixty-four.

When Commandant held his gun to my neck the night of Sam's escape, his cold, empty blue eyes, filled with hate and death, stared back into mine for several agonizing moments until he said, "I change my mind. I am not going to kill you. Not today. My friends are going to take care of your friend out there." He chuckled as he waved his gun in the direction Sam ran. "But you? You I am going to break until you beg me to kill you," he whispered against my ear.

I would have begged him to do so right then, but I couldn't get my mouth to work.

Commandant has kept his promise with a stamina I doubted him capable of, and he has indeed won this fight. I am too weak, too tired, too gone to find a purpose to keep living.

Today, I am going to beg Commandant to kill me.

There is no more pride keeping me on my feet. I don't know if Sam survived the escape, and I haven't heard from Poppy in eighteen months. My ribs stick out of my body at odd angles. My cheeks have sunken inward. My skin crawls with bugs and lice. The German guard uniform I wore on my back the night of my attempted escape was stripped from my body as well as my drawing of Poppy and her last letter, with nothing given me to replace the clothing. The only thing still in my possession is my white feather, now dirty and brittle. I slipped the thinning, marred plume into my underwear the night they stole my garments, the itchy quill of cowardice a reminder to serve until I discover my heroic capabilities. But I am done trying to prove myself a hero to the world, to Commandant, to myself.

I am done fighting.

The echo of heavy boots and clanking of metal keys outside my door grabs my attention. I roll onto my back and push myself to a seating position against the back wall.

When the guard enters, I groan out loud to see it's not Commandant. I'm ready to die; no sense in putting off my death. This bloke is a newer guard at the labor camp and looks to be a few years younger than myself. He speaks near-perfect English. Since I've been in confinement, they've sent him in only twice to bring my meals, and both times he was with another German soldier for interpretation. Both times I got the feeling he would have rather been anywhere but in the room with me.

I don't blame him. The smell alone in here has made more than one guard lose the contents of their stomach.

Now he eyes me warily from the door. Alone. A bowl of something I won't eat sits on the tray in his hands. He glances over his shoulder and then moves into my cell before pushing the door shut behind him.

"Your food for today," he says, then places the tray on the floor in front of me. "I tried to add a crust of bread to your tray, but the cook took it off when he found out where I was headed with it." He straightens, and his hand immediately pinches his nose closed.

No German guard has ever tried to give me extra food. My mind wants to focus on that thought, but there isn't time.

"Where's Commandant?" I ask.

"Busy," he replies through strained nostrils. "You just have me today."

"I need to speak with him. It's urgent."

"Urgent? You're in solitary confinement. Are you sick?"

A course laugh escapes my lips.

"There was a brawl in the soup line that required extra guards, so I told Commandant I would handle prisoner confinement food delivery on my own today."

Something about his words makes the hairs on the back of my neck raise. The way he closed the door behind him. The way he's studying me from across the cell. The reason he came alone. Nothing about this sits right.

If he were going to kill me, though, he wouldn't have needed to close the door; nobody would care that I was gone. Except Commandant maybe. I think he wants my kill for himself.

Maybe it's better this way, though. If this guard kills me, Commandant doesn't win after all.

"Do it," I say and move to stand, but the weight of my own body is too much, and I topple forward, knocking the bowl of brown liquid off the tray, spilling its contents.

The guard walks over to me and helps bring me to a seat again against the cell wall. "Do what?" he asks.

"Kill me or whatever it is you came here to do."

He sits in a squat in front of me, our eyes level with one another. "I came to bring you food." His eyes shift to the liquid on the floor next to us. "Which I will now have to sneak you more of."

I drop my head. I just want this over with. I want everything over with. I am so sick of this charade. This game of life versus death. This challenge of wills.

With all the energy I can muster, I grab onto his shirt lapels and pull him so close our noses touch. "I. Am. Done. Do you hear me?" I scream at him. "Done. Kill me."

The boy studies me for a moment, and I pray he is forming a plan to end me, when he pries my fingers from his shirt and stands. He reaches into the pocket of his trousers.

I expect him to pull out a knife, or a sharp rock, or a handkerchief of some sort to fulfill my request. I do not, however, expect to come face to face with a small envelope. An envelope that I can see was white at one time. An envelope with my name written on the outside in a handwriting I recognize.

Sam.

I gasp out loud and tear the letter from the guard's grasp with a coursing energy I haven't felt in months. The seal is broken, so I know he has read it. I know many have probably read it on its way to me, but I don't care if the whole world read it before I did, because I have it now. And I can die knowing Sam is safe.

I hear the guard chuckle somewhere in the distance as I greedily unfold the paper, but all I can focus on is devouring the words in front me:

Dear Luca,

I don't know if this letter will make it to you, but if by some miracle it does, I want you to know I did it, brother. I made it past enemy lines and into friendly territory! It wasn't easy, and I nearly died at least one hundred times, as I'm sure you can imagine, but because you forced me to learn some German and gave me your pack before I left, I had exactly what I needed to survive until I made it safely away from enemy lines. It's a long story that I'll save to tell you when I see you again because I will see you again, Luca.

Sarah is safe and happy and sends you her unyielding love for what you have done for me. Luci is the most beautiful baby in the entire world, and believe it or not, her first word was Luca (Lu-la, but we know what she means). I have tried contacting Poppy, but I haven't received word back from her. I won't stop trying.

I've been restationed in France with a new unit. They're a bunch of wienies, but I'm trying to toughen them up. You know how it is. Just riding out this war until it's over. It's got to be soon, right?

I miss you like a ship misses the ocean, Luca. It's not the same without you here, always trying to be in my business and protect me, but I'm trying to do you proud.

Stay strong, Luca. One day at a time until this is over. Don't let them take away your fight. Don't let them change who you are.

Stand back up.

Forever your brother in arms,

Sam

The guard stands with one hand on the door of my cell, watching me, and I can't help but wonder why he brought me this lifeline. He's the enemy. Our people hate one another. Our countries are out for blood. Our will to fight is the only thing we have in common.

"Why did you give this letter to me?"

"I joined the war to defend my country, not to starve men to death in underground cells and strip them of their humanity. You and me," he points between us, "we are not friends, but our fight is not in here."

He makes to leave, but before the cell door slams closed behind him, he turns back and asks, "Do you still want to die, soldier?"

31

JAKOB

BEESTON, NOTTINGHAMSHIRE, ENGLAND
JULY 1, 1918

MY LIFE IN THE GERMAN ARMY IS OVER. FOR OVER A MONTH, I delivered misinformation about factory locations to N18 and Gukenstein and watched—listened—as they grew restless.

Two weeks ago, I went dark. I know my days in England are numbered. N18 knows exactly where to find me.

I'd hoped telling Poppy the truth about me would lead to the two of us running away together and starting a new life, but she was understandably angry. It's been a week, and she still won't speak to me. I can't stay in Beeston any longer, though; it isn't safe for me.

The day shift at the factory ended a bit ago, and I'm driving the Wolseley to Poppy's cottage to try and speak with her because I must try one last time.

"What do you want?" Thomas's words slur as he leans against the open cottage door for support. His right leg is attached to a foot that's shriveled and mangled, a gift from the trench foot I presume, and I do my best not to stare.

"Is Poppy home? I haven't seen her in several days, and I really need to speak with her. It's rather urgent."

He waves a finger in my face. "You that farmer boy? The one from America who works at the post office?"

I cringe at the reminder of Charles's identity. The day I arrived in England two years ago, Jakob was the only forgettable identity. Now, thanks to Poppy, I've experienced a restoration of life, and if I never hear the name Charles Andrews again, it will be too soon.

"The one and only." I try to smile.

"Stupid mongrel."

I can't help the way my shoulders flinch when he spits the words at me.

"That's what Poppy calls you." Thomas lets out a hollow, cruel laugh. "She sure is angry with you about something. She's been working shifts at the factory round the clock the past several days. I've hardly seen her. And when she is here, she's swearing your name backward and forward." Thomas hoots laughter again, but the laughter soon turns to wheezing, and the wheezes turn into a coughing attack.

I rub my hand down my face to bless myself with an added measure of patience.

When Thomas's lungs have returned to normal, I ask, "Is she home from her shift at the factory yet, sir?"

Thomas lets out a long burp, and the foul air blows directly into my face as he speaks again. "She didn't work today."

"She always works on Mondays."

"Not today." Thomas takes a long swig from the bottle in his hand. "She's working night shift. That's why I get to drink." He waves the bottle with proud victory in front of my face. "My daughter thinks she's the boss of me, but she's not as smart as her old man. I didn't fight the bloody Germans for a year and lose my foot to come home and be told what to do by my daft child."

I want to reach out and grab this man around the throat for the way he just spoke about Poppy, the woman who wanted nothing more than to see his safe return home and rebuild a meaningful life with him. The woman who, for reasons I cannot possibly understand even after my many conversations with her about him, loves the vile man standing before me with genuine care and concern. And yet he speaks about her like this?

Blood burns hot through my veins.

Thomas sways from side to side as he talks, nearly slamming his head into the wooden door frame as he loses his balance.

I reach out to steady him, or possibly strangle him, but he brings the glass bottle down hard on my hand to stop my touch. Pain shoots through where the glass cuts open my flesh, and a loud swear escapes my mouth.

Thomas's eyes grow big and round, and he stills.

I realize my mistake instantly.

I swore in German.

I close my eyes and pray he's too drunk to make anything of it.

He takes a step toward me. A deep line creases between his eyes as he glares at me. "What'd you just say?"

I shake my head as if it doesn't matter and try to redirect his attention. "The night shift doesn't start for a bit. Has Poppy already left for Chilwell?" If she just recently left on her bike, I could likely catch her in my auto before she passes through the security gates.

Thomas blinks over and over, as if he knows he was supposed to remember something important and is trying to bring it into focus but can't. He brings the whiskey back to his lips and slides down the length of the door frame, mumbling swears so rapidly I'm certain he no longer remembers I'm even here.

I slip away back down the walkway and take off toward Chilwell.

The summer evening air is deathly still tonight. Not even a leaf sways on a tree branch. The humidity causes my shirt to stick uncomfortably to my torso as I drive, but all I can think about is Poppy.

I exit the Beeston town limits and pass into Chilwell. The factory is only a few minutes' drive down this empty, dirt road, and the time is nearing seven o'clock, the start of evening shift.

As I get closer, I see a woman in a boiler suit walking along the side of the road. Between the amount of dirt kicked up from the wheels of the Wolseley and the distance she is away from me, I can't quite tell if she's walking toward the factory or away from it.

I move the car forward as quickly as the accelerator will allow, inching closer to the munitionette. When I pull alongside her, I see that not only is the woman walking away from the factory but she's none other than N18. I haven't seen or spoken to her since the night in the post office when she accused me of being in love with Poppy.

The hairs on the back of my neck stand on end, and I try to hide the way my fingers shake by gripping the steering wheel as the automobile comes to a stop.

"What are you doing at Chilwell, Liza?" I growl.

"Well, Charles Andrews as I live and breathe. Where on earth have you disappeared to the last several weeks? Oh, Uncle will be just thrilled I've found you." Liza's smile turns deadly. "He's been sick with worry," she says through clenched teeth.

"What are you doing here?"

"I could ask you the same thing, Cousin, but I think I know. And I think it might be too late," she says with a raise of her eyebrow and a knowing smirk of her lips.

"Too late for what?" My heart races, and my palms sweat with fury against the leather steering wheel.

"Did you know, Charles, that the Chilwell National Shell Filling Factory is the highest shell producing factory in England? Did you know that the Allies have turned the tide of the war in their favor because they are receiving loads more ammunition than our German soldiers are?" Liza steps up to my automobile and rests her forearms along the edge of the open window. "Did you know, Charles, that over the course of the last four years, the German army has sent one hundred and twenty intelligence agents in to Britain, and although sixty-five of those agents have been caught by MI5, you are the only one who has turned your back on your country? Did you know that you had the chance to provide our country with valuable intel, but because you chose the route of a coward traitor, I had to take matters into my own hands?"

"What did you do?"

"Oh, *I* didn't do anything."

"Liza!"

"I simply delivered some . . . *goods* from Banbury that Chilwell needed for their mixing house production line. Put on a boiler suit, show them your yellow hands and face, tell them you're carrying requested materials from another ammunition factory, and boom," she yells into the car, "they trust you. I waltzed right in and handed the special package from Gukenstein straight to an employee in the mixing house." She laughs. "Stupid Brits. It was too easy, really. They deserve what's coming. And I'll be back home in Germany before anyone understands what happened."

"We don't kill civilians," I snarl.

"We do when their jobs must be stopped, but no one tells us how," she snarls right back. "When you're here picking up the pieces of this mess, Charles, remember that you're the one who did this."

My face and body go numb with shock. I swear in every language I know as I shove the auto into gear.

"The party starts at 7:10, Mr. Andrews," she hollers as I accelerate toward Chilwell's security gate. "It's too late to stop it, but you can certainly still join. 'The more, the merrier,' Uncle always says." Liza's laughter fills the air behind me as I leave her behind in a cloud of dust.

The time on my Glashutte reads 7:04.

POPPY

CHILWELL, NOTTINGHAMSHIRE, ENGLAND
JULY 1, 1918

IT IS TWENTY MINUTES TILL SEVEN IN THE EVENING, AND THE rays from the rare ball of fire in the England sky today are relentless. There is not a flicker of wind nor cloud in the sky to provide relief from the thick heat that bears down. Sweat pours through every crevice of my body, my skin surrendering to the light's beastly beams, so much so that I can scarcely keep hold of my handlebars as I finish my bicycle ride to the ammunition factory for this evening's shift.

Once in the changing room, I swiftly strip my day clothes, relishing the freedom from the moist garments. I slide into my boiler suit, remove my hair pins, and secure my damp hair beneath a cap. I remove Jane's ring from my pocket, trading it for my face mask, and place the gold band in my cubby—the act of which becomes easier every day. After my rubber boots are on, I make my way onto the clean side, as it's called, and punch my work card into the time machine. Ten minutes till seven.

I meet the other night-shift munitions workers in the mixing house for our pre-shift instructions. Clara, who stands at the front of the group, is looking intently up at the supervisor who's speaking, and I nearly laugh out loud at the eager expression lining her face. Then, when the clock rolls to 7:00, we're dismissed to our assigned houses.

"It looks like they need extra help transferring the filled shells from the TNT mill into shipping crates, so we'll be working in the TNT stores room tonight," Clara says when she finds me in the back.

We exit the mixing house together, pass the melt house, and move toward the TNT stores building close by. "I'm tired already, Little Canary, and we have twelve hours to go," I say with a large yawn and stretch my arms around my body. "You're going to have to give me some of that energy you have buzzing around you if I am to make it through the night."

Clara laughs, and the brown of her eyes light up as if they're made of magic. "I can't help it. I'm feeling rather giddy because . . . I had my first kiss today," she squeals.

My eyes grow big, and I stop Clara in her tracks. "Clara! Who? When? Does Mrs. Fischer know?"

Clara giggles. "I wanted you to be the first one to hear about it, so I haven't told the others yet. I'll tell you all about it while we're working, but, oh, Poppy, it was amazing. I will never be the same girl I was before this kiss."

Clara swoons as we walk, and I hate that her words have my mind instantly turning to Jakob. I hate the way my heart pounds at the memories of him. The way my temperature rises at the thought of his touch. The way my soul aches when fear reminds me of his betrayal. I hate him so much I could scream.

Why is it so bloody hot today? I pull the collar of my boiler suit away from my body and fan myself.

"Clara, I'm going to run to the washroom and splash some water on my face. I'm feeling a little faint, but I think I'm just overtired and overheated."

"You are looking rather flushed." She puts a hand to my cheek. "Would you like me to come with you?"

"No; no need to fuss over me. Go on in and start. I'll join you in a moment." I smile at her.

"Okay. If you're sure." She spins around, her eyes glazed over and twinkly, a song humming from her lips, and an extra bounce in each step she takes.

My heart squeezes as I watch my little canary walk away. In her lies the goodness the world has somehow left behind.

I move quickly toward the washroom nearest the changing rooms, when, thru a small window that looks out toward the entrance gate to the Chilwell factory, I see what appears to be a scuffle on the pavement near the gated entrance. When the shouting voices of men become clear, I disregard the washroom visit and press my nose to the glass.

Uniformed entrance guards run amok, and bullets ricochet off the brick walls outside.

My heart lodges into my throat. Are we being attacked? *Clara!* I turn and begin to run back toward the TNT stores building, when a voice from the opposite end of the hall stops me in my tracks.

"Poppy!"

I whirl around. It's Jakob Kirtchner, and he's rushing toward me. "I know you don't want to talk to me, but you have to listen."

"What are you doing here? How did you get past the guards at the gate?" I look over his shoulder out the window to see factory guards running low to the ground with weapons drawn. I gasp. "Are they shooting at *you*?" How much longer until they realize he's in here? Do they know he's a German agent? Is that why they're after him? But why would Jakob lead them here?

There's a wild and crazed look in his eyes that freezes me to my spot. "Something is going to happen to the factory. You need to leave. Now." He's shouting at me, but I am still not used to the German accent in his voice, and it's as if my mind is trying to catch hold of a memory that no longer exists within me.

Then, he's running down the hall, throwing doors open and yelling at anyone who will listen. "Evacuate the building now! Run! Get out of here!"

But I'm still frozen in place, confusion mixing with panic. "Jakob. Stop. What are you doing? How did you even find me?"

He looks down at his watch, runs at me, scoops me up, and throws me over his shoulder as if I weigh nothing more than a sack of lace ends.

"Put me down this instant. This is ridiculous. How did you get in here?" I thrash and kick and pound my fists against his back, but Jakob continues to run down the hall toward the exit as he yells evacuation orders to every person he sees.

"Stop! Jakob, stop for a blasted second, and talk to me. What is going on?" Tears are streaming down my face now. I don't know if Jakob is telling the truth or not, but he is scaring people. He is scaring me.

He bursts through the door to the outside and shouts at me while continuing to run, "My superior ordered an attack on this factory. I don't know how or where or by what means; I only know it's happening now."

My blood freezes within my body. I'm simultaneously hot and cold. Shots are being fired at us as we run, but I guess they don't hit their mark because somehow my body is still hoisted above Jakob's, hurtling through the air.

I want to scream, but nothing comes out when I open my mouth. I want to move, but my limbs are paralyzed, as if I'm in a nightmare and can't save myself from the monster chasing me.

"Are any of the other canary girls here?" Jakob shouts.

Clara! Her name snaps my body out of its paralyzed state. I try to clamber down Jakob's shoulder.

"Oh no you don't," he says. "You're not going back in there." His fingers grip tighter around my waist where he holds me over his shoulder. "Who's in there, Poppy?" Jakob yells at me.

"Clara!" I scream.

Jakob swears and runs faster. "Tell me where she is, Poppy."

"You are not going back in without me," I yell. "I am not leaving this factory without Clara. Turn around right now! Go back! Go!" I am screaming so loud my ears are ringing. I claw against Jakob's back. I pull his hair, bite his flesh.

He lets out a string of swears, but he does not stop running.

"Jakob! Put me down. I will go get her!"

He passes through the wrought iron fence marking the factory gate entrance, and a noise so deafening I fear I will never be able to hear again erupts behind us.

My head snaps up just as the mixing house crumbles to the ground.

A plume of black smoke shoots into the sky where the mixing house caves in on itself. The earth shakes violently beneath us. Another explosion sounds and then another and another. The earth rolls in succession with each violent eruption, and my body flies off Jakob's shoulder.

I hit the earth hard on my back, and my breath is knocked from my lungs. I gasp for air against Jakob, who landed half on top of me and is non-responsive.

It takes a moment to catch my breath, but when I do, I scream Jakob's name over and over while shaking his shoulders until he lifts his head from where it lays against my chest.

A large gash across his forehead oozes blood.

"Clara," he utters. "I have to get Clara."

I move to stand with him as he rises, but the world swims, and my vision goes dark then light over and over until I fall to the earth and vomit with dizziness.

"Stay," he commands, and I have no choice but to listen.

From my prostrate position on the ground, I watch as Jakob runs in a zigzag back toward what is left of the buildings, back toward the continuing sounds of explosion, back toward the red blaze of fire that climbs the crumbling walls with ease.

And then he disappears behind the thick, black smoke billowing into the sky.

There is no sun to be found now, yet the heat is suffocating. The air tastes of smoke and despair, and gray ash falls from the sky like snow. My stomach rolls like an angry nest of rats.

Please, God. Please let Clara be okay, I hear myself pray as the earth holds me tight against it.

After what seems like hours, Jakob emerges through a backdrop of endless fog and hot flames that lick the sky, running with Clara tucked against his chest. His shirt is torn, the bottom half missing with the material now wrapped loosely around Clara's mouth and nose.

I try to stand, but my legs buckle. I roll to my knees and reach out my arms. I think I call to them, but the sound is lost before it leaves my lips.

Jakob's face is buried in Clara's hair, his blond locks a horrid shade of black and gray that match the sky. With Clara cradled in his arms, Jakob picks his way over blackened, charred faces and discarded limbs, past disfigured bodies strewn in every direction, and through the wails from the mouths of both the living and the souls of the dead, never stopping until he reaches me.

Jakob freezes when he's standing above me, Clara still held in his fierce grasp as if he's unsure what to do next. Tears pour down his cheeks, carving paths through the crusted dirt.

No!

"Jakob!" I grab hold of the leg of his trouser.

He won't meet my eyes. His head droops until his forehead touches Clara's.

"No! Not Clara!" I shout, sobs building in my chest. I pull Jakob to the ground, and he drops without a fight. Then he kisses Clara gently on top of her head before he lifts his eyes to mine.

"She is alive but not for much longer. She wasn't in the mixing house when the explosion occurred, but she was close by. The explosion must have knocked her to the ground and made her hit her head because she was unresponsive when I found her. She came to when I woke her, but she has taken in too much smoke." His voice turns coarse and low. "She won't survive much longer."

My fingers twitch to wrench Clara from his grasp and will her to live, to save her from this evil of war. I want to scream at Jakob that this is his fault. That he did this to her. To us. I want to tear him limb from limb and watch him suffer and die the same way heaps of people around me are dying. I want to allow the sobs catching in my throat the freedom to escape.

But then I look down at Clara's small body, tucked into Jakob's arms—her labored breaths, her limp form, the gentle heart shape of her face, and the flutter of her eyelids—and I know I will do none of those things. I only have minutes, maybe seconds, to tell my little canary goodbye.

"Clara?" I say softly. I rub her arms and kiss her cheek.

Clara stirs in Jakob's arms and turns toward my voice.

"Poppy." Clara barely makes out the word, but her eyes flutter open.

I bury my face in Clara's neck, trying so hard to be brave. To be strong for her in this moment. To be strong for both of us.

But when she whispers a soft, "I love you," my resolve shatters.

"Please don't leave me, Little Canary. We'll get you to a hospital. We will get you help. Just hold on a little longer, okay?"

"Tell Mrs. Fischer I love her too," Clara sputters. "Tell the canary girls they were the only family I ever had or wanted." Her lungs erupt in violent coughs, and I try to soothe her.

"No, no, no, Clara. You are going to tell them yourself. We're going to help you. You just had your first kiss, remember? You're going to fall in love, and get married, and have babies, and live a long, beautiful life. You're going to be just fine. Right, Jakob?" I look to him for confirmation, but he only chokes on a sob, rolls Clara into my arms, and walks away to the iron fence behind us.

I press my nose to Clara's cheek and caress her face with my hand. If only I had let her come with me to the washroom. If only I had talked to her for a few moments longer. If I had made a million different small choices over the course of the last two years, would Clara still be dying in my arms right now? Could I have saved her life? Did I do this to her?

"Poppy," Clara breathes out, "it's time for me to go."

She closes her eyes for the last time and exhales slowly, her last breath leaving her perfect body. Her head lolls into my chest, and I curve myself around her as if I could shield her from the angel of death.

But I have no shield and wield no power.

There is no power stronger than death.

33

LUCA

THE LOCK ON MY CELL DOOR RATTLES AS IF SOMEONE'S jamming a key into the lock, and I jump at the sound. I have already had my daily food ration brought to me, so even though I didn't eat it, there should be no reason for another visit today. *Tonight?* I hope it's a new bowl of soup. My stomach rolls with hunger, and although the liquid tastes terrible, it provides enough nourishment that I don't starve.

Only a few hours have passed since the young German guard was here, and I have spent each of those hours rereading Sam's letter and pondering the guard's parting words: *Do I still want to die?*

The lock rattles once again, and this time I hear the key click into place. Commandant pushes the young guard into the room and walks in after him. I use every ounce of strength left within me to stand before them.

The young guard is holding a tray with a bowl, and I can't believe how grateful I am for what can't even be described as food worthy for animals.

Commandant speaks quickly in German, but I can't follow any of his words. When the boy doesn't translate right away, Commandant smacks him hard on the back of the head.

The boy's face reddens, and he speaks to me without meeting my gaze. "Commandant says because you spilled your last bowl of food, he has brought you another. There was only a cup of broth left this evening after the other prisoners ate their supper, so he added . . ." The boy pauses, and his gaze sweeps to the commandant's. "Some things to make it go further," he mumbles.

At that, the tray is shoved into my chest, and the brown liquid sloshes over the sides of the bowl. The liquid that remains is hardly enough to cover the large handful of dismembered body parts that apparently make up my meal.

I take the tray into my hands.

"Sag danke," Commandant orders.

I close my eyes and mutter, "Thank you", through clenched teeth.

Commandant laughs. "Fressen."

I look at the boy, questioning.

"He wants you to eat it up," the boy tells me.

I clear my throat and pick up the spoon. My stomach curdles at the thought of eating another human being. I gather a spoonful of broth—avoiding the swirling fingers and toes—bring it to my lips, and that's when I smell it: human urine and feces.

I glance up, but the boy's gaze is glued to the floor.

Commandant howls with joy, holding his sides as though he might combust with laughter.

I let the tray and bowl clatter to the floor. The contents spill and spray over both of their black boots, bringing Commandant's laughter to an abrupt stop.

Commandant takes a step closer to me. His beady, blue eyes bulge out of his square face. "Leck es von meinen schuhen."

He repeats it, but I don't know what he's saying.

Commandant grabs the boy by the collar, swings him forward, and shakes him at me. "Übersetzen," he yells in the guard's face.

The boy licks his lips and shakes his head before translating words that slither up my spine.

"Commandant says you need to lick it off his shoes."

I hate that I almost bend over to do as I am told. Years of punishment from Aunt Elizabeth has engrained that abusive obedience into me. Instead, I reach into my underwear and pull out the singular feather I have carried since the day I decided to enlist. The symbol of the dozens I collected in the green vase on Aunt Elizabeth's mantle and my reminder to keep fighting against cowardice.

I spin the feather in my fingertips, and as I watch the wispy ends, I realize this feather has become more of a crutch than a source of encouraging power. It represents years of guilt, shame, and loss that I've fought to let go, but its constant reminder is only keeping me prisoner to the past.

"No." I crumple the frail feather between my palms, then blow the pieces directly in Commandants face. The white bits stick to his sweat-lined upper lip and the black dirt smeared across his face.

He sputters at the feathery wisps and recoils. I smile with grave satisfaction.

"Do your worst, you filthy Boche. I will never kneel before you." My lips shake despite the confidence of my words.

The boy eyes me warily before translating my words, then shakes his head as if he knows I have just signed my death sentence.

I know the message was received as intended when Commandant slams my body into the brick wall behind me, knocking the air from my lungs.

His forearm presses heavily against my chest, pinning me beneath him, his face inches from mine. He grabs a fistful of my matted hair and yanks my neck at an angle that causes me to nearly lose consciousness. A punch lands against my concave gut before his fist swings back again and then meets my left eye.

My vision blurs, but before I can dive into the swimming black stars encroaching, a fist lands against my mouth. I smell the blood before I taste it.

Commandant speaks to me in German, his voice a quiet whisper, his jaw clenched so severely that when he speaks, his teeth grate together. Bits of feather dance on his face as the muscles in his cheeks twitch.

When he's finished speaking, he takes a step back, and the boy translates: "Commandant wants to know if you think you're a hero for helping your friend escape. He says you aren't a hero. You are a weak boy with nothing and no one to live for. You will die alone here, and nobody will care."

Words I've told myself in repeated measure spring from his mouth as if he's reading the dialogue straight from my pained soul. The taunting message assaults every decision I've made to push beyond my past. To let go of the guilt and shame. To discover something deep within me worth saving.

I am locked in a cage I will likely die in. My body waste seeps into every breath I inhale. My tears of loss and bitterness taste like salty ocean water. The absence of love in my life weighs more than the pack of every soldier in my squadron combined. And with these thoughts, I can't help but realize Commandant is right about me.

I nearly drop my head in supplication and open my mouth to beg for death, when my eyes flick to the boy. "*We are not friends*," he had said, "*but our fight is not in here.*"

Our fight. *My* fight.

In that moment, I realize the truth of what I've been missing all along. The truth buried so far beneath layers of false beliefs, ideals, and ignorance that it took nearly losing my life for me to see it.

Fighting *people* isn't what makes you a hero.

It's fighting evil in all its forms that makes you a hero. It's fighting against the demons that hold you back and keep you from believing in who you truly are. It's facing the worst parts of yourself and finding something within you that's still worth fighting for. It's standing back up when all you want to do is surrender. That is what makes you a hero.

I finger the scar beneath my chin. I am *not* a coward. I have always had strength and bravery within me. Unfortunately, it took coming to the brink of death to find it. I will either die in this cell with dignity or live every day of my life bravely.

The one thing I will not do is surrender.

The end of Sam's letter repeats in my mind: *Don't let them take away your fight. Don't let them change who you are. Stand back up.*

I look at the pieces of white feather littering my cell and feel a power I've never experienced flow through me. I have everything I need to survive inside of me.

I push off the wall and take a meek step forward. My legs are weak and wobble beneath me, but I know I can eventually turn the weakness I feel there back into strength. Until Commandant kills me, I will rebuild the muscles in my arms and legs. I will rebuild the strength in my hands and feet. I will rebuild the thoughts in my mind.

Commandant pushes my shoulder with hardly any effort at all, and I fall into the wall behind me, the sharp brick cutting the flesh along my elbows. He howls with laughter and wipes tears from beneath his soulless eyes.

I mask my face, but rage boils beneath my skin. That is the last time Commandant will push me down.

Commandant is still laughing when he exits my cell. But before the boy follows suit, he reaches into the pocket of his trousers, where the sharp corner of something white sticks out.

At first, I think it's another letter, but when I see that the white plastic package is an army food ration, my heart soars. Right now, I need food even more than I need words.

Without so much as a glance my direction, the young guard slips it into my hands from behind his back and walks away.

34

JAKOB

BEESTON, NOTTINGHAMSHIRE, ENGLAND
JULY 1, 1918

THE NIGHT SKY IS A BLACK CANOPY OF SPILLED INK ABOVE OUR heads as Poppy and I make our way by foot through the hordes of people pushing along the streets between the Chilwell factory and Beeston. Family members of those who work in the factory search for their loved ones, medical and emergency personnel rush with wheelbarrows through the streets to claim the bodies of those in need, survivors run frantic for home.

If the stars dot the sky tonight, they do not shine. If the scent of summer permeates the evening air, it is hidden by the stench of death and despair. If the crickets chirp nighttime lullabies, they are drowned out beneath the wailing nightmares of the survivors.

We don't know the body count as of yet, but we couldn't leave Clara lying on the ground to be trampled or thrown in a wagon like so many other victims we saw.

Poppy carried Clara out of the rubble, through the factory gates, and to the edge of the Chilwell factory property line in effort to transport Clara's body to Mrs. Fischer, who Poppy said will ensure Clara has a proper burial. Only once did Poppy stop to sit along the side of the road and sob. She wouldn't even place Clara in an offered wheelbarrow and push her; Poppy refused to let go of her. When Poppy's arms trembled beneath the weight, I could only wrap my arms beneath hers and offer support.

At the edge of the factory property, we unexpectedly found Mrs. Fischer, who had come straight from the dormitory the moment she heard the blast. Poppy passed Clara's body over to Mrs. Fischer and promptly collapsed into my side, her eyes glazed over and vacant. She hasn't uttered a word since.

I know she won't want to be left alone with her drunk father at home, so we are finding our way to the church in search of Preacher Jones. I am hoping that if anyone might be able to bring Poppy a sense of peace, direction, or guidance right now, it will be him.

As we walk, I am astonished by the reach of the factory's explosion. Windows are blown out of homes and buildings along the entire route home from the ammunition factory. A fine layer of ash coats the streets, the leaves of the trees, and the bodies of every person within reach of the explosion.

Anger boils within me followed swiftly by icy guilt. Is this my fault? Did Gukenstein order this attack because I stopped sending information back? Did N18 organize this purely because she's trying to usurp me? To punish me for falling in love with the enemy?

If I had stayed the course, let Gukenstein pull my puppet strings, and pushed my feelings for Poppy away like a good German spy, would this still have happened?

I want to think this planted explosion was a preplanned notion. I want to believe this was always Gukenstein's end goal so I don't have to carry the weight of at least one hundred deaths —and countless more injured—on my back. But I suppose I will never know for certain.

It's better that way. But the very fact that this happened without my knowledge tells me I'm on Gukenstein's radar for desertion at best and treason at worst. Either way, I know I'm living on borrowed time now.

Just inside the doors of the chapel stands a cloaked man, his hands clasped together in prayer, his lips muttering toward the heavens.

I lean into his space. "Preacher?"

"Preacher Jones and Mabel are at the ammunition factory, praying over the victims and sending their blessed souls to the afterlife," the man says, his face never leaving the ceiling.

Poppy doesn't so much as blink next to me. While we wait for Preacher's return, I suppose she can clean up and rest at my flat in the back of the church.

Once inside my humble home, I help Poppy to a seat on the floor of my washroom and place a folded towel on the floor beside her as well as a pair of my trousers and a white cotton shirt. The clothes won't fit, but it's the best I can do given our situation.

"Bathe," I say. "You will feel better when you wash off the ash, and dirt, and sweat."

She gives me a look that says she won't but doesn't say as much, and I leave her to herself.

Silence stretches out for so long, I worry she's fallen asleep right on the floor where I left her, but as I move toward the washroom to check, the sound of water pumping into the tub basin fills my ears.

I don't want Poppy to feel rushed, but I, too, need to clean off the blood and soot that covers my body. I make my way to Preacher's living space on the opposite side of the church. I'm sure Preacher won't mind the intrusion of his space given the circumstance. Poppy might stay in the bath all night, and I can't wait that long.

My plan was to leave this evening. I won't do that now—not until I know Poppy is stable—but by morning, I must be on the first train out of Beeston.

Within twenty minutes, I head back to my side of the church, but when I step inside, screaming wails of grief seep beneath the washroom door. Poppy's sharp cries claw their way up my spine as if her fear is searching for a new host and my soul is ripe for the picking.

I shouldn't have left her alone.

"Poppy!" I burst through the door, careful to keep my back to the tub. "Are you okay?" I shake my head. "That's a ridiculous question; of course you're not okay, but is there something I can do? Maybe you should get out of the bath. I don't want you to get hurt."

Her breath comes out in heaving sobs that tremble through her chest. When she finally speaks, she whispers, "It's too late for that," across the space between us.

"I know." My head falls forward, and I stuff my hands into my pockets.

There is no fixing this. There is no apology that takes away the myriad of sins I've committed against this woman. There is no payment in the world that fills the demands of justice for my actions. No mercy for a man like me.

Shame blossoms from the depths of my stomach through my chest, and my cheeks heat with embarrassment. I was a fool to think I could ever truly be with this woman. Maybe in another life we could have loved one another. In another time. In another world, where we weren't destined to be enemies.

I'm leaving tomorrow, and when the war ends, it's Luca who will come home to her.

I'm not certain if I find consolation or anger in that thought. Perhaps both.

His mate from the war wrote a letter to Poppy, looking for her and asking her to write Luca. I almost missed it. I'd let down my guard at the post office—stopped filtering through the mail once I decided to end my intelligence career. Luca hadn't written in ages. I naively assumed he was dead. Gone from our lives. One less thing to worry about. But he's still alive, placed permanently in a solitary confinement cell in France for an attempted escape from his prisoner of war camp.

From behind me, drops of water drip in steady rhythm onto the floor, indicating Poppy has stepped out of the tub.

My body freezes.

A small puff of air tickles the back of my neck as she whips open the towel I left folded on the floor. The sound of cotton folding around a body fills the gap between us.

Then I sense her walking toward me in the small space, and the air changes between us. Thickens with tension that causes my heart to swell and warm in the same moment.

Slowly, I turn to face her.

Her eyes are puffy and swollen, her face stricken with grief, and my insides twist with agony.

"I am so sorry," I say. "For all of it. Everything."

My stomach aches. At the guilt from the secrets I kept. At the ways in which I manipulated her feelings. At the death of Clara. But it's the secret I'm *still* keeping, the one I know I must tell her eventually, that is intensifying my distress. Yet I can't tell her the truth now. Not when she just lost Clara and the factory —the steady rocks of her present life.

"You will never know how sorry I am," I say instead.

She places a finger on my lips and quiets me. "I don't want to talk about it anymore. I can't." She breathes. "I am so tired of hurting, Jakob. So tired of feeling pain. I don't want to feel anything anymore. I want to be numb. I want to vanish into another world that isn't full of loss and sorrow, if even for just a moment." Her fingers brush mine with intimate purpose. "You want to know what you can do for me? Make me forget everything, Jakob." She runs a hand along my arm and up the back of my neck. "Please."

In the next moment, her lips are on mine. Her other hand trades the grip of her towel for the strands of my hair. Her soft body presses intimately into mine, and in between kisses, she pleads with me to make her forget.

My chest thuds at the desperation in her voice, at the feel of her beneath my grasp, at the sound of *my* name, and I neglect to recall anything except how much I want to comply with her wishes.

And so I do.

POPPY LIES NEXT TO ME IN THE BED, CURLED AGAINST ME, finally asleep after hours of making love intermixed with screams and tears. It's the wee hours of the morning now, but I will myself not to fall asleep for fear that I will miss even a moment of her skin against mine. Am I foolish to hope this road for us is just beginning? To hope that last night wasn't a final goodbye to what could have been.

I know our being together was only a way for her to forget her pain. I know that. But after the night we shared, I can't keep my thoughts from slipping into the enticing, grand delusion that Poppy feels something more for me than just a way to escape. That when she wakes, she might be able to move past my mistakes and build a future with me. That in a few hours, when I run far away from Beeston, she will run with me.

We can collect Mutter and go anywhere in the world. It could be a new start for all of us. Together.

I let out a long, slow sigh, and Poppy shivers next to me as my breath trickles over her bare shoulder. I need to tell her the truth about Luca. Telling her is the right choice to make. The trustworthy thing to do.

But . . . But.

But after our night, I have hope that didn't exist before, and I don't know if I can do the *right* thing when the *wrong* thing could give me everything I want.

35

POPPY

JANE'S RING! WHERE IS THE RING? I BOLT UPRIGHT IN CHARLES'S bed, gripping the sides of my naked thighs as if there's a pocket there I'm forgetting about.

My brain is a frenzy of activity as I try to remember where I last had the ring. Is it in my boiler suit on the floor near the tub? I leap from the bed and run into the washroom, frantically searching the pockets of my uniform, when the realization sets in as a sinking ship into the silent ocean.

I won't find the ring here, or at my cottage, or at the ammunition factory, where I tucked it safely into my locker twelve hours ago before my night shift began.

Jane's ring is gone.

I grip the edge of the tub basin and remind myself, step by step, how one breathes.

Jane's ring is *gone*. Forever.

"Poppy?" Jakob says softly from behind me.

I jolt and snatch the discarded towel from last night and wrap it around my body.

He stands in front of me, a pair of khaki trousers and a white cotton shirt sitting slightly skewed on his body as though he hadn't quite had time to dress.

"I—I—I have to go," I stammer, needing desperately to be alone. I don't know where my feelings for this man fall. Twenty-four hours ago, I never wanted to see him again. But last night he saved my life. How do you hate somebody who does that?

He tried to save Clara. Rescued her from a building engulfed in flames as it crumbled to the earth, which provided me the opportunity to say goodbye.

She's the only person in my life I have ever been able to utter that word to.

"I need to go home and check on Father. I need to assess the situation at the factory and speak with Mr. Ashby and Mrs. Fischer to see what needs to be done now."

"Marry me, Poppy."

The emotions that threatened to overtake me only seconds ago freeze in place, and my tongue becomes thick and hot as if I'm chewing on cotton. *Marry him?*

"Run away with me. I must leave Beeston. Right now. Come with me."

In my stunned silence, Jakob pulls me toward him and wraps his arms around my waist.

"We can go anywhere you want. We can start a new life. Get married. Have babies. Create the family you've always wanted. You can meet my mutter." Jakob presses a kiss to the corner of my dropped-open mouth. "I love you, Poppy. Say yes."

His words are a balm to my broken spirit. His offering of escape like a stick someone is holding above the quicksand that's pulling me under. Could grabbing on save my life? Is marrying Jakob how I take the next impossible step forward? Is the promise of a family—and a mother who could possibly love me —the way out of this endless pain of war and loss? The thought makes my palms zing with anticipation. I loved Charles; perhaps I love Jakob too.

Jakob's golden-brown eyes plead with me to say yes, to follow his lead, to run away for love. But love always comes at a cost. If I reach out and accept his offering, what do I lose?

Father's drunken face and bum foot flits through my mind. Who will take care of him? Who will make sure he eats and sleeps? Who will provide for him since he can no longer work?

And the canary girls! Could I truly walk away from them without a word? They broke through my barriers—my walls of defense—and showed me it was okay to let people in as we came together in an impossible time. Can I leave them alone to pick up the pieces of a crumbled factory and broken spirits?

If I leave now with the factory in ruins and rubble instead of staying to help rebuild and ensure the Germans don't get the final say, will Clara's death have been in vain?

My stomach sickens at the thought.

She was too good for them, but they took her anyway. I cannot allow that. I have spent my life wishing others chose to stay. Now it's my turn to make that choice.

"I wish I could," I whisper against his chest. And I mean it.

Because the truth is, I do want to run away. I want to curl up in a ball and die.

But I need to live. For Clara. For the life she no longer has. And there is only one way for me to do that.

I step back out of Jakob's touch. "I have to stay."

Jakob nods his head, his jaw tight, his golden-flecked eyes like smoldering amber. "I want you to know, I am prepared to face the consequences of my choices. If you feel you need to turn me in, I will respect that."

I consider his words. Jakob did not plant that bomb at the factory. He did not kill hundreds of innocent men and women. Although turning him in to the hands of his own wolves might have been appealing a week ago, I am ready to put this behind me and move forward.

"A life for a life," I say with a solemn dip of my head.

Jakob takes a deep breath and stuffs his fists into his trouser pockets. "I hope you find everything you're looking for, Silent Canary." His gaze is filled with misery. Maybe regret? Shame? But

I don't want him to suffer any more than he already has for his choices. We all make mistakes.

I move swiftly to him and place a kiss upon his cheek. "You too, Farm Boy." I bite hard against the flesh of my bottom lip to keep tears from falling as I dress and flee the church. Because despite everything, I know there's a part of me that loves this man.

~

I SMELL FATHER BEFORE I SEE HIM, ALCOHOL PERMEATING OFF him in waves.

"Good heavens, Father, it's not even eight in the morning." I step around his motionless body in the sitting room, and my eyes flit to his—which are glazed and bloodshot—as I move into the kitchen to begin his breakfast. "Where did you find liquor anyhow? I thought I got rid of it all."

He grumbles past me and demands coffee.

"We're out of coffee rations."

"After all I've done for you," he laments, "you can't make me a darned cup of coffee when I need it?"

After all he's done for me? I know better than to start a trip down memory lane, particularly on this unwelcome morning when I am held together with only a thread of dignity and compassion and a mirage of sanity, but I can't keep quiet.

"You have quite literally, never once, done a thing for me since Jane left, Father." I retrieve my apron from the cupboard.

"Oh, you want to talk about Jane?"

"No." I tug the apron over my head.

"You want to talk about Jane. About how much better she is than me? Jane left us, Poppy. Left you. On purpose. She never wanted to be a mother."

"Stop." I yank the apron strings into a knot behind my back with a bit more force than I intended.

"I went to see her, you know," Father says before taking a swig of the bottle he's nursing.

"No, you didn't."

"Took a trip to America, February of 1916. Found that little wench. Told her we missed her. Begged her to come home."

February 1916? That's when he left for France to serve in the war. I'd feel sorry for his confused state of mind if he weren't driving me so batty. "No you didn't, Father. That's when you enlisted and went to France. You've lost your mind." I cut a slice of bread off a loaf and place it on a plate with half a boiled egg and a cut of cheese.

"You know what Jane did when I found her, Poppy? She laughed at me." He throws his hands in the air. "Laughed! Told me that we were such darlings for missing her but that it was quite pathetic I was still pinning after her all these years later. Then she thanked me for coming to visit her and said she'd certainly have her secretary present me with an autographed photograph of herself on my way out and didn't so much as ask after you."

I don't know why he's goading me right now, pushing this clearly made-up story onto me. All because of what? The fact that we don't have coffee?

He's been wildly unhinged since he returned home, but he never, ever brings up Jane. In fact, I can't remember him so much as uttering her name in the last decade, and now he's done so four times in one minute.

Whatever his reason is for doing so, I'm too tired to care. "That didn't happen, Father." I deposit the plate of food in front of him and bring my hands to my hips. "You're delirious."

But my refusal to believe his story doesn't deter him. "I returned home from my little visit and the next week saw a deplorable advertisement for her American picture show posted near the theater, her face laughing front and center." Father sobers. "It was like she was laughing at me all over again. Like I wasn't good enough—man enough—to love her." His face falls, and his voice drops a level. And in that one movement, I know Father is telling the truth.

My heart plummets.

My fingers shake against the folds of my apron as the realization comes in sharper focus. "The two weeks in early February when you told me you were traveling around Scotland for work to pick up parts for The Weir, you were in America?"

Father nods, his eyes hollow.

"You saw Jane." The words come out of me slow and soft. I wish they hadn't, but even as the truth I've avoided believing for years rings through me—*Jane doesn't love me, never did, and will never return home*—my heart aches with jealousy. I can't believe he went for her without me. Saw her. Spoke with her.

Father's face turns indifferent once again, and he brings the bottle back to his lips. "I walked straight from the theater to the war office and enlisted."

"And left me the very next day," I say, finally understanding the secret behind his enlistment.

"And you were better for it. You don't need me, Poppy. You never have."

Fury burns beneath the surface of my skin at his ridiculous words. *I've never needed him?* I was thirteen and lost my mother! Had I known twelve years ago that I was going to lose Father the same night I lost Jane, I would have staved off hope of bonding with him over our loss and saved myself the pain of gaining a new scar.

Unfortunately, I don't have the time nor the desire to discuss our failed relationship now. Not after the twenty-four hours I have had. Right now, there are people at the factory who need me more than I need my father's validation.

"I can't do this with you today, Father. There was an explosion at the factory last night. A lot of people were killed or badly injured." I force myself to swallow down the lump that bulges in my throat. "I need to go help with the cleanup." I untie my apron and return it to the cupboard.

"An explosion at the factory? That must be what that awful sound and all the shaking was about. Knocked me right out of my bed. Thought we were having a bloody earthquake. Didn't keep me from climbing right back up and sleeping off the alcohol like a baby, though." He laughs as if this were nothing more than a joke to be shared amongst friends, and I hate him for it.

"It was the Germans."

Thomas spits liquid from his mouth, and I watch it dribble down his chin. He stands—well, sways really—and raises his arms around his head, going off about the "filthy Germans."

I shouldn't have said anything.

"I already took care of one of those bird-brained fools. Bloody German spy trying to pass as a stupid American farmer," he hoots. "I won't be able to make them all pay, but I sure as night took care of that one."

All the blood drains from my face. "Which one, Father?" But even as I ask the question, I know.

"I wasn't certain at first when he came looking for you yesterday—that fellow you've been spending so much time with," Father says. "He doesn't look enough like the ones I spent a year facing off with, but when he swore in German, I knew." He smiles wickedly. "Could have taken him out myself, but this bum foot of mine would have given out on me, and he might have gotten away. It was better that I waited until I sobered up and could make my way to the bobbies this morning.

I gasp. "You didn't."

"I certainly did. Then I got myself a little treat on the way home for doing my patriotic duty." He shakes his bottle of liquor in front of his face and lets out an atrocious laugh.

"They'll kill him." My entire being buzzes, every nerve ending coming to life at once.

"They'd certainly better, or I will find him and do it myself," Father huffs.

I have to warn Jakob.

My feet hit the cobblestones so fast, I scarcely feel the stones beneath me. The smell of death and ash still hangs ever present in the air, reminding me what I've lost, and I force myself to face the truth that life and death are, in their simplest form, the nature of the earth. While you cannot have life without death nor death without life, one does not negate the other's purpose for being. When people leave me, either by choice or by the essence of Earth's wishes, I must be enough for myself, or I will always find myself alone, heartbroken, and sad.

It was never Jane who needed to change. To love me enough to stay.

It wasn't Thomas with his secrets, or Luca with his absence, or Jakob with his lies who needed to change.

It was always *me*.

I need to be enough for myself.

And that is a truth I must cling to, for when I round the corner of the church, a gunshot rings out across the meadow. Seven magpies take to the sky at the sound, drowning out my scream.

I will never forgive my father.

36

LUCA

PRISONER OF WAR LABOR CAMP, HENDECOURT-LÈS-CAGNICOURT, FRANCE JULY 6, 1918

"Every Saturday morning, Commandant and his crew of officers head down to the river to bathe," Dietrich, the young German guard, explains to me as he helps me to stand in my cell. "During this bathing ritual, the rest of the guards eat breakfast. It is at this time each week that I will fetch you from your cell and bring you outside to the back of the building for a few minutes to allow you some fresh air and maybe a wash."

He pulls a set of handcuffs from his trouser pocket and dangles them in front of me. "You are to remain in handcuffs the entirety of the time. If you try anything, I will blow my whistle, and every guard in the camp will be here within seconds. The camp guards have been ordered to shoot you on sight if they see you outside of your cell."

He motions for me to put my hands behind my back and asks me if I understand.

I nod my head in agreement.

Dietrich has brought real food to me every day this week. It isn't always much or delicious, but it is edible—and sanitary—and for that I am grateful. With the increased nourishment, my legs don't consistently buckle beneath me the way they did five days ago.

The young guard places the metal cuffs on my hands and walks out of the cell, motioning for me to follow him. We do not speak. He moves quickly through the dark, damp, unfamiliar walkway. I was unconscious when Commandant brought me down here the night of my escape attempt, and this is the first time I have been outside my four walls in two months.

I can't keep up with Dietrich's pace, but I am determined not to give up. Determined not to stop and lean against the wall so my aching legs can rest.

He glances over his shoulder at me only once but doesn't slow.

My lungs burn with exhaustion, but the desire to feel air on my face and see anything besides cement walls fuels my tired steps onward.

We climb a tall flight of stairs with a steep incline that takes me as long to climb as it used to take me to run from my cottage to Poppy's. I can only walk the first couple steps before I must fall to my hands and knees and crawl like a newborn calf up the remainder.

When we reach the door that opens to the outside, Dietrich grips my elbow and pulls me through.

The morning sun is so bright, I close my eyes to keep them from burning, and even then, I hold a hand over them because my eyelids ache beneath the light's rays. My naked skin absorbs the heat, and I can't help the tears that come at this small taste of freedom.

I take a long, deep breath in and allow my lungs to fill with fresh, clean air.

When I can finally open my eyes without the sun blinding me, I take in my surroundings. I'm not planning an escape anytime soon; I wouldn't make it past this building without being killed in my current physical state. But knowing where I'm being imprisoned within the camp grounds me. Helps me feel a sense of identity and control.

"Let's go," Dietrich says gruffly next to me, and I know our outdoor adventure has come to an end.

"Thank you, Dietrich."

He doesn't respond, but as I make my way back to my cell, I feel something akin to hope budding deep within my belly. I am careful to keep it down low where it belongs, though. Hope in a situation like this can save your life, but it can also inspire you to make choices that could kill you.

If it's possible, Dietrich moves quicker on our return trip. I want to cry out in pain when my knees buckle at the speed with which I'm trying to push them. But when I lie on the floor of my cell once again, I know every ache left in my arms, every spasm in my chest, every scream of my muscles is worth those few moments outside these walls.

It's as if the light from the sun woke something dark and dormant within me: a reminder of why I'm still here. Still fighting to survive. Fighting to get stronger every day.

And with that, a new sense of determination surges through me.

I will do push-ups on the floor of my cell until I'm blue in the face. I will run in place as fast as I can until I collapse. I will squat down and stand back up over and over until flames lick my body. I will eat everything I'm offered.

Because I know the choices I make alone in the dark will show what I am capable of in the light.

37

POPPY

CHILWELL, NOTTINGHAMSHIRE, ENGLAND
AUGUST 8, 1918

"WHERE ARE THEY?" I DEMAND.

Mr. Ashby sits alone in his office, perusing papers behind his desk, but his head jerks up at the sound of my voice. He removes his spectacles from his face and kneads a hand across his eyes as if he hasn't slept in days.

He likely hasn't.

Despite the terrible destruction and the extreme shock that riveted the heart of every employee, repairs were swiftly carried out overnight after the explosion, enabling some of the next morning's day shift to start work again. All but twelve of the surviving workers were back at the machines the following day. Not only did the factory have to keep up a sense of morale for the public but we wanted to be here. We wanted the enemy to know we wouldn't be stopped.

Now the factory rebuild is nearly complete, and I know Mr. Ashby has been involved in every exhausting step.

"Who, Miss Pemburton?"

"The Commission of Enquiry investigators."

His white mustache twitches as he frowns at me. "The British Home Office officially closed the case last evening, Miss Pemburton."

"But they didn't solve the crime."

"They kept the case open for a month. They searched, investigated, interviewed, and harassed our employees for information. They did everything they could, but there was no concrete evidence of espionage. Nothing to keep the case open. Nothing and nobody to pin it on. No leads to follow. No trace of a strange women planting something in the mixing house." He raises his brows. "The only man who could have told us anything further, Charles Andrews—or whoever he was—is dead. There is nothing else Scotland Yard, the Enquiry, you, me, or the Minister of Munitions, Mr. Winston Churchill, can do. Scotland Yard was called off and sent home, and now the Enquiry has closed their report."

"I want to see the report."

"You can't." Mr. Ashby breathes out a long slow breath. "It's classified as 'SECRET.' Not even *I* am privy to its contents."

"What then? They're just calling this horrific event an accident? The explosion that we *know* was planted by the Germans and that killed Clara Whittaker and over a hundred other men and women is being called an accident? An accident caused by what?" I can barely contain my voice.

"First off, we don't *know* anything. Mr. Andrews told you an explosive was planted, but there's no proof he was telling the truth and nobody of consequence to corroborate his story. For all anyone knows, it was Mr. Andrews himself who planted it before 'he grabbed you and ran out,' as your testament states. Or at the very least, he was working with the supposed young lady who did plant it by creating a diversion at the gates. We simply don't know. There are too many unknowns to definitively declare what happened as espionage."

A large huff explodes through my chest, but before I can say anything, Mr. Ashby holds up his hand to stop me from speaking. "I'm not saying he wasn't telling the truth, but nobody saw or heard anything out of the ordinary that day except for Mr. Andrews running through security."

"That is ridiculous," I seethe. "Jakob Kirtchner did not kill over a hundred civilians. He would have never done that to Clara. To me."

"If it was the Germans, they got away with it. But the more likely explanation, if you don't want to believe Mr. Andrews was involved, is that it *was* an accident. After speaking with many of the surviving munitions workers and studying shell filling trends and war demand for more ammunition, the authorities believe the explosion was likely due to a combination of increased pressure on you ammunition workers to produce the shells at rapid rates and the employees becoming lax about safety procedures. Those things, mixed with the unprecedented hot July day, made for a lethal combination, and an unfortunate accident took place. I'm sorry to say, Miss Pemburton, that it's not an implausible notion." Mr. Ashby simply shrugs his shoulders.

"The bloody papers didn't even tell the truth about how many people died. Sixty!" I yell at Mr. Ashby, "The papers say only sixty people lost their lives in a Midland explosion. At the very least, can we not honor every single one of the one hundred and thirty-four lives that were lost that day?"

"They can't tell the truth, Miss Pemburton!" Mr. Ashby pushes up to a stand so quickly the chair behind him flies backward. He places his palms on the desk and leans toward me. "We can't give our location away in the papers, and it would be bad for war morale if British citizens knew the truth about the devastating numbers. I am as angry as you are about it, but our hands are tied. It's over."

I take a step forward and place my own palms on the desk across from him. "Make no mistake about it, Mr. Ashby; this is far from over."

I make my way to the building that houses the changing rooms to prepare for shift, my thoughts spinning and twisting with reckless abandon. It's been five weeks since my entire world fell apart. For the second time. And my father, the one person I hoped would be there for me when I returned home from Clara's funeral in Cardiff, was drunkenly absent.

For a year, I've tried to help heal Father's mind, body, and spirit, but as it turns out, Father doesn't want to be healed. I suppose he saw too much, or was hurt too severely, or was pierced too deeply by things I could never possibly see, but I have come to an understanding: Father didn't come home to bring our family back together. He came home to drink himself to death.

The day after Jakob was killed, I moved out of the cottage and back into the lace factory dormitory. I still check the cottage from time to time to make sure Father has food and is still alive, but I will never forgive him.

I squeeze my eyes closed at the memory of the seven magpies in the sky above the meadow near the church. The angry trill of their cries. The image of two bobbies running past my frozen body on the cobblestone street, Jakob Kirtchner's lifeless form held between them.

Hot tears burn beneath my lashes.

I wipe them away with forceful fingers.

Father made a choice that wasn't his to make. I may not have loved Jakob the same way he loved me, but he certainly didn't deserve to die.

After I change into my uniform and clock in for my shift, I enter the danger house. It's abuzz with tense energy. Tonight is our last football match of the season before the championship qualifying matches begin later this month, and frenzied discussions circle the room: Who will Mrs. Fischer choose to play center forward in Clara's stead? How can we even play without her? We must win this match in her honor!

Once the room settles a bit, I call the canary girls over to my station and recount the information I received from Mr. Ashby. The women are as outraged over the outcome of the investigation as I am.

"When do we get to tell the truth, then?" Nessy asks. "When do we get to truly pay tribute to those who died here?"

"How many days did it take us to start production again at Chilwell after the explosion?" I ask the women.

"Less than twenty-four hours," Annabelle boasts.

"News of the closed investigation doesn't mean we have to accept the outcome. It doesn't mean Scotland Yard and the Enquiry get to tell the end of our story. It doesn't mean the Germans won," I say.

"But they did win. They killed and injured hundreds of us and won't pay," Nessy says.

"So we *make* them pay," I say, "with an allied victory. We put so much ammunition into our boys' hands the Germans won't be able to break through our lines." I walk through the group of listening girls. "On June fifteenth, our factory earned a shell filling record."

"Four thousand, seven hundred twenty-five shells. The most shells filled in a twenty-four-hour period in all of England," Sophia spouts.

"My fingers burned through the torn gloves, and my hands ached for three days after, but it was the best twelve-hour shift I've ever worked." Annabelle smiles.

"If we could do that, how many shells can we fill in one week for Clara?" I ask them.

"How many shells can we fill in honor of the one hundred and thirty-four men and women on the night shift who did nothing more than clock in to work on July first to serve their country?" Sophia asks, grabbing the hands of Annabelle and Nessy.

"The canary girls of Chilwell National Shell Filling Factory No. 6 are going to show those Germans exactly who they messed with," I say, pulling the girls into a circle.

We wrap our arms around one another's backs.

"We are going to assemble the most shells ever produced at an ammunition factory in one week," I say. "We are going to end this war, ladies. Are you ready? I am *done* being the Silent Canary. It's time we show everyone how loud a canary can sing."

From behind our closed circle, a commotion from the danger house entrance catches my attention. Mrs. Fischer fights against the door, her arms seemingly full to the brim with piles of something. She rushes into the room, her face alarmingly white, her eyes bulging behind her spectacles.

As she gets closer, I realize she's holding what appears to be hundreds of dirty, old envelopes.

"Mrs. Fischer, is everything alright?" I ask in alarm.

The girls spin around to face our supervisor, who stops directly in front of me, out of breath, her lips trembling only slightly more than her hands.

"He's alive, Poppy," Mrs. Fischer says, her voice a choked whisper.

"Who?" I ask as I peer into her crazed eyes.

"Luca." She shakes the envelopes at me. "Luca Whelan is alive."

38

LUCA

PRISONER OF WAR LABOR CAMP, HENDECOURT-LÈS-CAGNICOURT, FRANCE AUGUST 31, 1918

ONE HUNDRED AND TWENTY-FIVE MARKS ARE SCRATCHED INTO the floor in the corner of my cell. I finger them as I count them over and over. One hundred and twenty-five days since Commandant threw me down here to slowly die.

I would be dead if it weren't for Dietrich. We still are not friends, as he promised we would not be. We don't talk other than passing words and phrases when he brings my daily meal and on Saturdays for my five minutes of fresh air. But he is the closest thing to human interaction and hope that I have, and I relish our interactions.

The familiar click of the key in the cell door sounds, and I jump to a stand. I know from my markings that today is Saturday, and I am eager for release.

"Hurry," Dietrich commands as he swings open the door.

He places a tray of food on the floor. I see a small piece of bread about the size of my fist sitting next to a bowl of what appears to be cooked animal meat, and my stomach rumbles with hunger.

Sometimes I eat first and then we go outside, but today, Dietrich pulls my arms in front of me and places the cuffs on my wrist. He exits the cell and begins racing down the corridor toward our exit without so much as looking back to make sure I'm following. I have no trouble at all keeping pace with him anymore, and while I wonder what the rush is today, I don't much care. The blood pumping through my veins as I run up the stairs is euphoric.

"Wash quickly," Dietrich says as he points to a bucket of water and a small sliver of soap on the ground. He paces along the brick wall, keeping watch, but his fingers are fidgety today, and he can't seem to keep any part of his body still. For a young boy who's usually rather stoic, his behavior is unsettling, but I'm thankful for the cleaning supplies anyway.

When the air has dried my skin off enough that I'm no longer dripping with water, Dietrich ushers me back inside and down to my cell.

At this point, he usually closes the door and leaves me until Sunday, but today, he pushes his way through the door behind me, looks back down the hall from where we just came, then closes the door, enclosing the two of us inside.

"I have something for you today." Dietrich reaches up and removes his cap from off his head. He rests the cap in the palm of one hand, and with the other hand, he uses his fingernail to cut a thin piece of string that I can see has been sewn into the lining of the cap to keep it in place. "A guard searches me before I come down to the cells," he says as if it explains his actions.

Once the loose stitching comes undone, he peels back the lining from his cap and pulls out an envelope. "I found this in a garbage pail inside the commandant's barracks when I was clean-ing," he says and shoves the envelope into my hands. "I think you will want to read this."

There is writing on the outside, but it's smudged, so I can't make out anything except faint, blurred lines of black ink. I peer into the already opened envelope and pull out a thin sheet of paper.

When I unfold it, my breath catches at the sight of her penmanship.

August 9, 1918

My Dearest Luca,

Where do I even begin? How do I find the words to tell you the horrors I have experienced these last two years? I feel as if I have lived one hundred lives in the time since I last wrote you. I have not stopped shaking since last evening, when I found out you were not dead, as I have believed you to be—as I was told that you were through a Killed in Action notification two years ago—but that you are very much alive, or so I hope.

Your letters to me over the years were stolen and hidden from me in the cuckoo clock at the post office. Thank goodness for the new post office manager who noticed the bird wasn't cuckooing on the hour and called someone in to fix it. Apparently, the maintenance worker popped open the backboard of the clock, and your letters came pouring out.

I received the lot of them all together just last evening. But your writing appears to have stopped earlier this year, and I hope beyond all ability to hope that you no longer write to me because you are not allowed, as a letter from Sam notified me, and not because something has happened to you. Not when I so desperately need you to be okay after just finding out the truth.

If this letter has, by some miracle, found its way to you, please know how much I love you. From my yellow head down to the tips of my toes.

I have so much to tell you, Luca, but for now I will just say that every part of my heart beats for you. If you can find some way—any way at all—to let me know you are okay, I would be so relieved and maybe, possibly, believe that it is true.

My heart is yours,

—Poppy

When I look up from the letter, Dietrich is gone, but a small square paper and a charcoal stick lie on the floor near the door.

39

POPPY

CHILWELL, NOTTINGHAMSHIRE, ENGLAND
OCTOBER 3, 1918

I RUN SWIFTLY THROUGH THE ALLEYWAYS AND BUILDINGS THAT lead from Mr. Ashby's office to the danger house, clutching the thick, white certificate in my hand. The certificate we have waited over a month to receive.

Mr. Ashby was delighted to present the award to me on behalf of the women. He congratulated me on being the driving force that pulled the factory together in a time of turmoil and great despair to achieve this incredible goal. This award sets our factory apart from every other factory in England. He even swiped a tear or two from beneath his spectacles as he shook my hand and thanked me for my service and leadership.

By the end of August, we knew we had slaughtered the record for most shells filled at a single factory in a week's time, but to see the official document with a signature by Mr. Churchill himself is going to send the canaries to the moon.

A large yawn escapes my mouth, and I'm forced to slow to a walk. I blink a few times to bring my surroundings back into focus and roll my neck slowly from side to side. I can't believe how tired I feel in the early afternoons these days. We put so many extra hours in to accomplish our filling goals that I suppose I'm still trying to catch up on rest.

I am sleeping rather well at night now, though, especially since I discovered the truth about Luca. It's as if everything is finally right side up in my upside-down world. This war has taken so much from me, but it has given me back Luca, even if just in letter form. Although I have yet to receive new word from him, just knowing he possibly exists in the same world I do has made my life more manageable.

I round the corner of the danger house and burst through the doors. The room is warm with the hazy afternoon sun streaming through the open windows above us, and chatter buzzes vigorously throughout the room as the women work. Metal pings echo throughout the space as employees hammer pins into the tops of the shells. Trolley carts packed with filled howitzer shells that are prepped for delivery roll past, and I relish the cacophony of sounds that have become music to my ears.

I stand on a large table filled with random shell parts in the middle of the room and wave the white paper in the air above me. "It's here! It's here!" I shout.

The women gather 'round at the spectacle I'm making.

"Get down from there at once," Mrs. Fischer scolds, but her smile eases the harshness in her tone.

I'm overjoyed she's here today to witness this recognition award from our country's leaders, as she recently accepted part-time work at the Oxford hospital in London. She works in Chilwell the first two weeks of every month and at Oxford the last two, laboring as a nurse alongside her old professor to help heal the thousands of soldiers returning home.

I oblige her request and step down from the table, then hold the certificate directly in front of me.

Several of the women slip off their safety face masks to see better and remove their TNT powdered gloves as they inch toward the paper.

"Isn't it beautiful?" I ask. Another yawn slips from my mouth, and I quickly move my hand to cover it.

Mrs. Fischer narrows her eyes at me, but I dismiss her look with a shrug of my shoulders.

Annabelle fingers the seal on the certificate, and Nessy reverently places her yellow-tinged hand on the large printed block numbers that read 275,327.

"Two hundred seventy-five thousand, three hundred twenty-seven," Nessy whispers. "We did that."

"Two hundred seventy-five thousand, three hundred and twenty-seven in one week," Annabelle shouts. "We bloody did that!"

A cheer rings out through the room.

"Where should we hang it?" Sophia asks.

"How about next to our football championship certificate there?" Nessy suggests, pointing to the wall opposite the entrance door. "They are both in honor of Clara and the women and men who died along with her."

"I can't think of a better spot for it," I agree, and we make our way to the wall.

The victory we felt as a team winning the football championship in Clara's name last week, was unlike any victorious feeling I have ever experienced. We gave everything we had within us that night on the football pitch and then stood up and gave more. Knowing each player left a large piece of her heart on the pitch that evening with the common goal of playing for our little canary, of saying goodbye to her in our own special way, bonded us in a way that will never be undone.

"Love is the strongest motivation in the world, isn't it?" Nessy says as she adheres the white award next to the football certificate.

"The night Clara died," I tell them, "I was certain there was no power on earth stronger than death, but perhaps I was wrong. Perhaps love is the greatest power of all."

Mrs. Fischer nods. "Love has built armies but destroyed countries. Built families but destroyed individuals. It all depends on where you focus your love: on the people or the power." She looks at each of us. "The key I've learned throughout my sixty years is to remember what love is and what it isn't."

"And now is when Clara would clasp her small hands beneath her chin and say, 'What is love, Mrs. Fischer?'" Nessy says, and we all laugh, knowing that's exactly what our little canary would say if she were here.

Mrs. Fischer slides her spectacles from her nose, folds them, and tucks them into the pocket of her sweater. "Well, Little Canary," she pauses to wink at Nessy, "love is both soft and loud. It's saying hello but also goodbye. It's opening your arms but knowing their strength. It's a forgiving heart but also a noble one that knows its own worth. Because before you can truly love anyone else, you must love yourself."

Sophia clears her throat and adds, "Love is knowing you were better for having that person in your life, no matter how long or short they were there for."

"Love is the light in the darkness." Nessy tucks her arm through Sophia's. "Love was Clara."

"Love is a brand-new pair of gorgeous, lace-up black leather boots but also your favorite worn-in ones that conform to your feet perfectly," Annabelle says with a happy sigh.

"Love is familiarity," I say as years of church roof memories and the safety and protection of Luca's arms warm my thoughts. "But also discovery." I think of Jakob. The way we were together. His large, captivating personality and larger ego. His gentle eyes that hid a conflicted soul.

Over the last several months, I have come to recognize his faults and mistakes for the horrifying choices they were while accepting the complicated, albeit real, feelings I did develop for him. Jakob manipulated my feelings and lied to me over and over again, not only taking the knowledge of Luca's life to his grave for reasons I will never know now but also consciously deciding to watch over and comfort me as I mourned Luca's death. Yet I cannot deny that there was a part of me that loved him. As Charles, yes, but also as Jakob.

While one hundred thirty-four people did lose their lives on the day of the explosion, Jakob saved hundreds of other workers' lives that night, including my own, by running through the building, screaming evacuation orders. He tried to save Clara. He betrayed his own country for love.

While he was rather misguided, I want to believe his heart was good. That the wrong choices he made were for the right reasons.

My stomach grumbles then with embarrassing force. My hand flies to my belly as if I could possibly hide it.

Annabelle chuckles. "Didn't you just eat, Poppy? Goodness, you have an appetite these days."

I laugh and roll my eyes. "I always have an appetite, but what I wouldn't give for a Fry's Five Boys chocolate bar right now."

"Oh, me too!" Nessy laughs.

"Alright," Mrs. Fischer says, "enough talk of chocolate and love for today. Back to work, ladies." She claps her hands over and over at us, as if she's trying to scare away pesky chickens. "Congratulations on an incredible job done, but let us not relent in our efforts. Back to work you go."

I turn to leave, but a gentle pull on my wrist makes me look back over my shoulder.

"Poppy, follow me please," Mrs. Fischer says quietly.

"Yes, ma'am."

Mrs. Fischer and I exit the danger house and move in silence through several outdoor corridors that connect different work-houses, the canteen, and the storage facilities until we come to a one-story building of offices near the back of the factory property.

The longer we walk, the more my senses spike. Where could she possibly be taking me? And why?

We enter a small room hardly bigger than a closet. The room is empty other than a square table and one chair in the center of the room.

"Sit," Mrs. Fischer commands as she pulls a string hanging from the ceiling. A single dangling bulb flicks to life.

I obey and hold my fingers still in my lap, confusion and perhaps a little fear surging through me.

Mrs. Fischer stands in front of me and places her hands on her hips. "Are you with child?"

My eyes bulge in disbelief. "Excuse me?"

"Are you with child?" She repeats and points to my stomach.

"Absolutely not. How could you say such a thing?" I am so flabbergasted at her blunt and frankly rude accusation I can hardly produce words.

"Stand up."

"No." I grip the sides of the chair firmly. "I have done nothing that should allow you to think—"

Her hands grab hold of my shoulders and pull me to a stand, interrupting my defiance.

"Mrs. Fischer!" I balk.

"How much sleep are you getting?" she asks as she moves her hands along my abdomen.

"Plenty." I try to push her hands away, but she persists.

"And is your sleep sound or agitated?"

"I . . . I don't know."

"Are you rested in the morning when you awake but rather exhausted in the middle of the day and evening?"

"Well yes, but—"

"How is your appetite?"

"Normal."

"Incorrect. When was your last menses?"

I look at her aghast. "Not that that's any of your concern, but I haven't had regular monthly bleeds since I was a youth. And I haven't had a *mother* to confer such matters with."

"Have you experienced unexplainable nausea the last several weeks?"

"I have experienced *explainable* nausea," I counter. "I've inhaled copious amounts of poisonous powders and sleep odd hours due to working both day and night shifts. My body is all discombobulated, but I am *not* pregnant. It's . . . well, it's just not possible."

She takes a step backward, and her hands return to her hips. "You shared a bed with Mr. Kirtchner the night of the explosion, did you not? That was twelve weeks ago."

How could she possibly know that? I told one person. *Sophia*.

My breath hitches, and my heart beats wildly, the reality of what her accusation means causing panic to sear through every inch of me.

"Well yes, but it wasn't . . . I mean we didn't . . . well we did, but I couldn't be." My voice lowers, and it feels as if I'm speaking with a mouth full of marbles. "It was one night. It didn't mean anything." The numbness that coursed through me, the desperation to feel anything but pain that evening with Jakob resurfaces now.

"Your ovaries don't care if your heart was into it or not, Miss Pemburton."

My hand finds my stomach, and I press my fingers against my abdomen as I shake my head from side to side. "I can't be, Mrs. Fischer. I cannot be pregnant. Not now."

40

LUCA

PRISONER OF WAR LABOR CAMP,
HENDECOURT-LÈS-CAGNICOURT, FRANCE
NOVEMBER 16, 1918

SCREAMS ERUPT AND BLEED THROUGH THE WALLS OF MY CELL. At first, I think it's my nightmare. But when I pull myself awake, the noise seeps beneath and around the tight seal of my chamber door like a poisonous gas.

Guns are firing. Men are shouting, their muffled voices blurring together. It sounds as though a revolution is commencing outside my cell.

My heart thuds so hard my ears ache and my stomach trembles. What's happening out there? How long has this pandemonium ensued? What did I miss?

My cell door unlocks, and I fly upright, ready to defend myself. The door swings open, and Commandant steps through the doorway. Surprise flicks across his face as he takes me in. He hasn't seen me since he left me nearly dead and weaker than a mouse after the feather incident months ago, but he masks his shock quickly.

"Germany signed the armistice with the Allies five days ago in a railcar in the Forest of Compiègne," he says in his thick, German accent.

"Kaiser Wilhelm II abdicated?" I ask, unbelieving.

"The war is over, yes."

I fall to the floor and finger the mark I made before I last fell asleep: two hundred and twelve. Two hundred twelve marks carved into my cell floor. For seven months, I have lived within these four walls. I have been abused by German guards and seen the soul of Satan. I have found the bottom of the world and crawled my way back to the top. Within these walls I have lost and I have found Sam, Poppy, God, and myself.

And now it is time to go home.

Sobs heave within my chest, and I can do nothing to silence them. Freedom comes at a price, and mine has been charged, fought for, and paid.

I wonder if Dietrich will let me hug him goodbye. Although he is adamant we are not friends, he saved my life in here, and I have nothing to thank him with except the overwhelming gratitude in my heart.

As for the sorry excuse of a man and human being standing in front of me, I have nothing to say to him. Without wiping my tears, I stand and move to walk past him.

His arm whips outward, and the mouth of a rifle grazes my forehead.

"The war is over for everyone but you." Commandant's voice is thick with rage, and the gun clicks against my flesh.

No. No. I did not survive seventeen years with Aunt Elizabeth, two and a half years of war, eighteen months of receiving no word from Poppy, one life-threatening escape attempt, and seven months in solitary confinement to die now.

"If you kill me, you will be charged with murder," I say.

"Nobody will know."

"I will know." Dietrich walks into the cell and stands in front of me, his own weapon drawn and pointed at Commandant. "Put the gun down."

Commandant lowers his weapon and begins chuckling. Soft and jovial at first, then evil and menacing. He reaches into his breast pocket and pulls out a small envelope. He waves it in the air like a white flag, still laughing.

I catch Poppy's script on the outside and lunge for it but miss.

Dietrich was able to bring me writing tools only twice, but I don't know that either of the letters I wrote Poppy were sent or delivered. And other than the one I received from her telling me she'd believed me to be dead, I have had no word from her. How many other letters has Commandant discarded?

Commandant pulls a thin paper from the envelope and unfolds it while making tsking sounds with his lips. "War isn't for lovers," he sneers, following it with a tempest of laughter that rips through his body. He shakes the letter at me and snarls, "You will never be free of me. Free of *us*."

Then he brings out a single match and strikes it forcefully against the cement before bringing it to the paper.

I watch as flames of burning red consume Poppy's script. Commandant catches the falling ashes of paper in his cupped hands, then blows them into my face. Just as I did to him with the feather.

Fiery hot waves unleash within me, rage consuming me from the inside out. I could kill this man with my bare hands, and I find that every part of me desires that outcome. But when I look at Commandant, his eyes are watching me, amused at my reaction. I refuse to allow him to burrow himself so deep within my soul that I will never be rid of him.

"The war is over. Your people lost. *You* lost, Commandant," I say, and without another thought, I lunge for the opening in the door.

I don't know who fires first, but bullets erupt in the tiny cell behind me.

I turn to look back into the cell just as Commandant falls to the floor, his hand clutching his chest. His weapon clatters to the ground, and blood spills from more than one place in his body.

Dietrich's chin is raised, his shoulders pulled back, a small, satisfied smile on his lips. For the first time, he looks older than the seventeen years he is.

I see then that his right shoulder and left leg have been hit.

He follows my gaze to his shoulder, then looks back up, his face white.

I catch him right before he hits the floor.

"Stay with me, Dietrich. I'm going to get you help." I put pressure on the wound in his shoulder with my hand, the only thing I have, and drag Dietrich—half his body leaning against mine—toward the stairs, noting far too many British prisoners dead on the floors of their cells and along the hallway as I move through the building and outside.

Beneath the morning sun, German soldiers mill about, smiling, talking, and celebrating the war's end with German beer and wine, as if there weren't a massacre happening just below their feet.

"Help!" I cry out. "This guard has several gunshot wounds that need to be attended to."

Two German soldiers run forward and retrieve Dietrich's body from my grasp. I flinch when their hands graze against mine, but none of them pay me any mind.

The war is truly over then.

Most of the British prisoners have already left camp. A breeze blows past, tickling my naked skin, and I hope someone has left a few clothes behind.

One guard lays Dietrich on a table, while the other wraps a stiff cloth around his upper arm and ties it off.

I squeeze Dietrich's good shoulder, and he offers me a slight nod of his head.

"Friends?" I ask before I leave.

"Nein," Dietrich says through clenched teeth.

"You saved my life twice. I think that constitutes some sort of friendship, Dietrich."

A small smile forms on his lips before a guard slips a tool into the wound in Dietrich's leg and retrieves the bullet. Dietrich lets out a strangled cry.

"You British, you're so needy," he says after a few gasps for air.

"Good thing I'm Italian, then," I say, winking at him.

He chuckles at that and then braces himself as the guard moves to remove the bullet in his shoulder. After several deep breaths, Dietrich's head rolls to the side, and he studies me for a moment before speaking. "Good luck, Whelan. Safe travels home."

"Why did you shoot Commandant for me?"

Dietrich's jaw clenches, and his face reddens. "I did that for me."

I nod my head in understanding and toss a goodbye into the air.

"Freunde?" I yell back at him over my shoulder.

He just shakes his head and chuckles, and I realize it's the first time I have heard genuine laughter since before Sam left. The sound is glorious.

"Amis?" I say in French, still walking. Laughter spills from him, making him sound like the youthful boy he is. And I hope that Dietrich gets to go home and be a kid. That the war didn't rob him of his final years of childhood.

"Amigos?"

"Go home, old man," he yells from his spot in the guard's arms.

I don't know what troubles I may find along the way or how long it may take me, but that is exactly what I'm going to do.

41

POPPY

CHILWELL, NOTTINGHAMSHIRE, ENGLAND
DECEMBER 3, 1918

FIVE MONTHS WITH CHILD, AND TODAY IS THE FIRST DAY I rose without the need to rush to the lavatory. I inhale the crisp winter morning air as I walk toward the Chilwell ammunition factory, relishing the calm of a settled stomach and my growing little belly.

My body hardly shows the wonder within me, which Mrs. Fischer says is likely due to the severe nausea I experienced the first several months and the fact that this is the first time my body has carried a child, but that suits me just fine. Baby Canary and I get to share this secret, just the two of us—and Mrs. Fischer—for a little longer before the rest of Beeston has the opportunity to weigh in on my circumstances.

I opted not to tell the canary girls about my situation until I, myself, could come to terms with the news. It took weeks before I truly believed Mrs. Fischer's diagnosis, and once I did, I spent the next weeks coming to accept it while processing my feelings.

Do I hate Jakob for leaving me with a baby? *It wasn't his fault alone; I made the choice too.* Do I hate myself, then? *No. Maybe a little.* Should I write to Luca about the baby? *No, I want to have that conversation in person.* Is Luca going to hate me? *I don't think so.* Hate my baby? *Who could hate a baby?* Will he accept us? *Hopefully.*

Was spending that evening with Jakob a mistake? *Yes.* A blessing? *Also yes.* Am I grateful to Jakob for this gift of life within me? *Absolutely.* If I am, does that make me a bad person? *No . . . I hope not.*

I smooth a hand across my slightly swollen abdomen as I approach Chilwell Factory, and my heart flutters with gratitude. "I love you, Baby Canary," I whisper to my stomach for the hundredth time today.

The war ended three weeks ago, but I have yet to hear from Luca. I wrote him nearly every day after receiving the news he was still alive in hopes that at least one of my letters would make it through to him.

Sam and Sarah Davies have exchanged several letters with me over the last few months. Our correspondence has lifted my heart, and the stories Sam tells of Luca and him in France has helped Luca feel closer.

The ammunition factory is finishing up the last of the ammunition production and then Chilwell National Shell Filling Factory No. 6 will officially close its doors at the end of the year. Mrs. Fischer has allowed the twenty women staying in the old lace factory building dormitory to continue their stay until then, but on January 1, the dormitory will resume its previous factory status and begin operating lace again under her direction.

In October, upon Mrs. Fischer's great insistence, I moved into her apartment on the top floor of the lace factory building. *"How can I look after you and the baby if you're not under my roof? You're moving in with me, and that is that."*

I smile at the memory of Mrs. Fischer taking the greatest care to prepare the guest room for me, of her addition of five down pillows to make sure my growing hips don't ache, and of her gentle fussing over my nutrition. I round the corner of the factory gates, laughing to myself over her insistence that I do not, under any circumstances, ride my bicycle until after Baby is born, when the profile of a tall man leaning against the factory gate stops me dead in my tracks.

Luca.

My breath catches in my throat.

He looks the same, only sharper somehow. Cheeks that were soft are angled and sunken. While his shoulders still sit broad beneath his white cotton shirt, they slope forward. His face is still handsome but weathered. Aged.

His head turns my direction. His eyes wander over me. When they catch mine, they turn to pools of emerald that hold me in a fierce embrace.

How Luca can touch me without *touching* me makes my heart race with reckless abandon.

His cheeks grow pink as he surveys me. And then he smiles.

Everything I have lost, every experience I have missed having with him over the last two years is forgotten behind his smile. Everything that has gone wrong is made right beneath the warmth of his gaze.

I don't know who moves first, but in the next breath, I am in his arms, and we are—both of us—sobbing like children who have found their home after wandering the streets lost and alone.

His mouth presses kisses to the corner of my eye, the middle of my forehead, the tip of my nose, and every inch of my yellowed cheeks.

I shake in his arms like a leaf before the first winter storm, trying desperately to hold on to this moment in fear of what is coming next and where the approaching storm will take me but also ready to be free of the past that has tethered me down.

"Firebird," he whispers, his voice as familiar to me as my own, his nose tickling my ear, "I know we have a lot to talk about, but right now, everything I want to tell you I fear words would only cheapen. May I kiss you?"

I wrap my arms tight around his neck at the same moment he brings me into him. My lips collide with his, and while his body appears tired and worn down, his soul is alive and buzzing with an energy that brings color and dizzy excitement into my world. My hands tremble at the feel of his skin beneath me, and as he deepens our kiss and runs his hands up my body and into my hair, my spine prickles with remembrance of all that we were. Of all that we had. Together.

"I love you too," I say as we pull apart for air.

Luca laughs. "I'm glad you understood the message."

His hand trails down my side, and deep within my body, something leaps within my womb at the touch, bringing me back to the present.

I take a step back and lace my fingers together. "There is something I need to tell you."

Nerves race within me. My throat becomes heavy and hard to speak through. Confidence I had moments ago withers with the words sitting on the tip of my tongue.

"What is it, Firebird?" Luca's eyes narrow in on me in concern.

Fear tiptoes across my heart, leaving tiny footprints behind that imprint the words *You could still lose Luca* right into the fleshy organ beating wildly in my chest.

I take a breath and count backward from ten over and over until the fear has settled enough for me to speak.

"I am with child."

Luca's head recoils, and his brows furrow together, causing his left eye to squint. "What?"

I take a deep breath and grip the edges of my loose cotton dress to pull it taught against my middle. "I am five months with child."

Luca stares at my belly and takes a step back from me, his head shaking with vigor. "No. Poppy, you can't be. No. No." His head drops, and his eyes don't leave the ground. "What happened?" His voice is quiet. Soft. Broken.

"Jakob Kirtchner happened. Or you might remember him as Charles Andrews. He wasn't an American postal worker. He was a German spy." Fresh anger at all that Jakob's lies took from me threatens my dry eyes, but I force my tone to remain calm. "He manipulated me. Faked your death. Hid your letters from me." I pause, not sure how much information to give, how little to leave out. I've rehearsed this conversation a million times so I'd be prepared for the day Luca came home, but now that he's standing in front of me, staring at me as though I'm a stranger, I can't remember a thing I practiced with Mrs. Fischer.

Words begin to pour out of me with reckless abandon. "Then, in July, he saved my life during a factory explosion that killed and injured hundreds of people. Clara died that night. She was only sixteen. I couldn't handle losing any more people I loved. I couldn't be alone to face the pain of the world anymore. I wanted to die that night. I needed to do something to forget everything." I take a breath. "Then my father turned Jakob in. I heard the shot that killed Jakob. And now I'm left to raise this baby." I place a hand against my stomach. "And you should know that while my feelings for Jakob are . . . complicated, I love this baby very much."

I wait for what seems like hours for Luca to talk, but his lips remain closed, pulled taught. He is stoic. His face unreadable and colorless.

"Please, Luca, say something."

"I . . . I . . . I'm sorry," he finally sputters out. "I can't do this."

My heart sinks, and I close my eyes against his rejection, refusing to accept it. "You can't do what?"

He motions to my middle. "I can't do that, Poppy. I can't stand in as a father to a German child. Not after what I've seen. Not after what they did to me." Luca's eyes glaze over, and his hands tremble at his sides. "I can't love the child of my enemy. You created a family with the man who told you I was dead? I can't raise the child of the man who did that."

His words cut so deep, the guilt coats my conscious like blood as I realize the depth of what I'm asking Luca to do—the path I'm asking him to walk. I can't ask this of him, yet I hear myself doing it anyway: "You haven't tried yet," I say softly, hoping there's a world in which Luca can see the three of us together. "Can you give us a chance?"

Luca brings his fist to his mouth and bites down on his knuckles.

He turns away from me and lets out a loud cry. The frustration in his yell to the heavens—the evident anger at having to make what must seem to him an impossible choice—shatters my soul. "I can't try, Firebird. I have nothing left in me. I thought I was coming home to Poppy Pemburton, the girl I've loved for my whole life. The *you* I said goodbye to two years ago. But I don't know where you went."

I see him slipping away from me. The refusal in his turned back.

I spin his shoulders to make him face me. "I'm right here, Luca." Frustration fills my voice, the tears I'd kept in now seeping through. "I'm right here, standing in front of you, begging you to see me. Me *now*, broken and whole, scarred and healed. Not the girl I was the day you boarded the train and left me behind. That girl believed her worth was dependent on the love of others. That girl believed that when she let someone into her heart, they would leave her, betray her, and break her.

"This girl," I point to myself, remembering the lesson Clara taught me not so long ago, "knows that brokenness is what allows the light to shine through. I was betrayed by a man I trusted, but I will never betray the gift he left me by turning my back on an innocent child who is not at fault in this." I raise my chin and lower my tensed shoulders. "I am the girl whose picture you sketched that night on the roof. The girl I couldn't see yet but you believed in all along. You don't have to find me, Luca." I place my hand on top of his beating heart. "I am right here where I have always been."

Luca takes hold of my hand, and his thumb slides across the inside of my wrist as he gently removes my hand from his chest, the touch igniting my skin as if his fingers are laced with fire. He swipes a finger along his scar, and that's when I know.

Luca is going to walk away.

He loves me but not enough to shoulder the pains of his past.

"I will always love you, Luca. I never stopped. Even when I believed you to be dead. My heart doesn't know how to do anything else." I shrug. "If you look on me laden with the child of a German spy and choose to walk away, I cannot fault you. I will be sorry to watch you leave us," I say as I place a protective hand over my belly, "but I will not stop you. Baby Canary and I deserve to be loved fully and completely."

"I'm sorry it can't be me." Luca's lips tremble. "Goodbye, Poppy. I'm glad you finally found the family you were looking for." He affords me one last lingering gaze before turning and walking away.

LUCA

BEESTON, NOTTINGHAMSHIRE, ENGLAND
DECEMBER 23, 1918

THE SMELL OF CINNAMON PRICKS AT MY NOSE AND ALERTS MY senses, slowly waking me in a familiar sweet haze. Before I open my eyelids, I listen for the bustle of pots and pans below and am greeted with the clanging I've grown accustomed to in the early hours before dawn breaks.

Upon my return from France, Mrs. Fanny Christmas provided me the same room in her apartment above her Sweet Shoppe that I'd stayed in after the cottage fire and my same job making chocolates until my move to Italy the first of the New Year. Although the air outside is cold and damp with winter moisture, the air in my small room is warm and smells of yeast, sugar, and spices.

A knock on my door sounds, and Mrs. Christmas's voice calls through, "Mrs. Fischer is here to see you, son."

My eyes fly open.

"Mrs. Fischer? It's not even six in the morning yet!"

"The early bird gets the worm, or something like that." Mrs. Christmas mutters as if she's no happier about the intrusion than I am.

If Mrs. Fischer is the early bird, that makes me the worm. Somehow that's not comforting at all.

After dressing, I make my way down the stairs and through the dining room of the Sweet Shoppe, and I spot Mrs. Fischer's sharp bob, which ends at the top of her thick, black overcoat. She stands by the glass door, impatience rolling off her in waves. Her hands are placed on her hips while her right foot taps the floor in rapid succession.

"Good morning, Mrs. Fischer."

She spins to face me. "Get your coat, Luca."

"Are we going somewhere?"

"Would I ask you to retrieve your coat if we were not?"

I nod my head in submission and move quickly to gather my coat and scarf from the hook behind the counter. I follow Mrs. Fischer into the cold morning air and bite back a swear as a gust of wind freezes my nose.

"Wouldn't you rather speak to me inside the shop? With a nice warm glass of hot cocoa or tea?"

"I have time for neither warmth nor tea," she bristles.

"Okay." I nod, wondering who doesn't have time for warmth. "May I ask what this is about, then?"

We make our way halfway down the deserted Main Street toward the Square in the center of town under the soft glow of the oil lamps before she speaks again. "I have never believed you to be a coward, Luca. Not when you avoided water and swimming as a child. Not when you never stood up to that troll Aunt Elizabeth of yours. Not when you chose to stay behind when all the other Tommies your age were suiting up and enlisting at the start of the war." Cecilia's eyes narrow at me, and her chin juts forward. "But this," she gestures outward toward the vacant street beside us, "this walking away from Poppy and her unborn child; *that* makes you a coward. Being too afraid to let go of your hurt and anger, being too afraid to find it in your heart to move beyond the past and let yourself finally, truly love *all* of her and be happy; that is what makes you a coward. You spent your whole life trying to run from your past—trying to hide it—afraid that the story of your family's death made you a coward, only to overcome all of that and run now."

Mrs. Fischer's words swarm around my head like buzzards trying to peck every last piece of life from my body.

My first instinct is to take offense. To lash out at Mrs. Fischer for seeing only one side without considering what the cost has been for me as well.

But beneath the layer of frustration, a question pushes through my guarded heart: is she right? In trying to protect my own heart from anger and fear that I could never love the baby Poppy carries within her, am I running?

Mrs. Fischer stops walking and faces me. "Do you love her?"

"Always," I answer without pause.

"Then don't run, scared of what-ifs and past choices that were made based on false realities. Poppy loves you too."

I shake my head and blow out a forced puff of air between my lips. "Jakob stole our plans. His choices altered the course of our lives."

"Yes, he did. He created a mess of *both* your lives, but Poppy has decided not to let somebody else's choices define her future. Now you must decide, Luca, how much more you are going to let that man take from you. He stole two years of a life with Poppy; are you going to let him steal a lifetime?"

I shudder at her question and grip the ends of the scarf around my neck, needing something to squeeze. The moment I walked away from Poppy, I wished I'd turned around. Wished I'd had enough gumption to stay. To forgive Jakob, the Germans, and Commandant in order to be what I needed to be for Poppy. But I didn't know how to turn back.

When I think about her with Jakob or about raising a German child, my chest constricts with panic, and my thoughts turn to the battlefield. They turn to Commandant's snide remarks, cruel punishments, and his many attempts to take my life. I want a life with Poppy. I don't want Jakob to decide my future. But I don't know how to have either of those things.

"Poppy made one mistake that has since turned out to be her greatest blessing. A gift from God that pulled her from the ashes. You wish that baby had been yours? *Your* gift to her? That together *you* created a family?" Mrs. Fischer's brown eyes glisten behind her spectacles. "Then put down your pride, Luca. You still can."

I inhale the chill in the air and twist my foot back and forth against the peppered snow-white cobblestone walk. Is it as simple as that? Put down my pride. Don't run. Take back my future.

Perhaps this child within Poppy is a chance to let go of the unfairness of it all rather than a reason to hold on to it. Could that be my *how*? Although that's certainly easier said than done, a small bubble of hope rises within me all the same.

Mrs. Fischer silently pulls me forward to continue our walk, and when we come to the corner opposite the Beeston First Church of God, Mrs. Fischer tucks her hand in the crook of my arm and guides me across the street, walking until we're directly in front of the large stained-glass window. I let my eyes flicker upward to the church roof. The secret haven there that belongs to Poppy and I is hidden from view here where I'm standing, but I imagine us up there together, and I can't help the memories of us that follow. There's no denying that every good, happy, worthwhile part of my life includes Poppy. *Is* Poppy.

My heart softens.

"If I can believe it's not too late," I say, "if I can find it in my heart to look past what Jakob did, how do I look upon the child and not feel anger? Malice? Hate toward a babe who is not of my own flesh and blood but that of my enemy?" I look at Mrs. Fischer. "I'm terrified I won't be able to love the child, and I won't do that to Poppy. I won't marry her and then turn my back on her offspring."

"The babe is Poppy's child just as much as it is Jakob's," Mrs. Fischer says. "Do you really think you could ever hate a person who quite literally shares a heartbeat with the woman you love?

If your heartbeat is tied to Poppy's and this baby's heartbeat is connected to that same string, are you not already a family?"

My heart swells at her words, gooseflesh rising on every part of my skin. An uncontainable shot of adrenaline shoots through my body, my hope no longer contained in the low parts of my belly. I swoop Mrs. Fischer up into an embrace and swing her around in circles.

"Luca!" she cries. "What has gotten into you? Put me down this instant. This is highly inappropriate behavior."

Laughter bubbles up from my insides, and when I set Mrs. Fischer down, a smile beams across her face before she can cover it with her gloved hand. The laughter in her eyes, however, she cannot hide, and warmth careens through my body as if it were a summer's day.

Mrs. Fischer smooths her overcoat beneath her hands and then does the same to her hair before addressing me again. "Once you have calmed yourself, you may enter the Lord's house." She gestures to the church doors. "There will be no yelping, hollering, or swinging of people about inside that sacred place of worship, but there is someone inside waiting to see you. Merry Christmas."

If Mrs. Fischer did things like wink, the smirk on her face lets me know this would be one of those times. I would give anything to see a certain redhead standing just inside the doors when I walk through them. And if she's dressed in white, I won't object.

The doors swing open easily beneath my touch, but it isn't a beautiful girl with red hair who greets me. It's a rather short girl with mousy brown hair, simple features, and large dark eyes. She holds a small child of maybe two years on her hip, a girl from the looks of it, with identical big eyes. A small bump protrudes from the woman's middle, testifying to another child on the way.

"Hello, Lu-lu," the small child says to me, and the unknown woman smiles.

A smell wafts off them, and it takes me a moment to place it. *Fish*.

Sam walks up next to the woman and wraps an arm around her. "Luca, I'd like to introduce you to my family. This is Sarah and Luci."

I've never been happier to see his ugly face. I pound a fist against my chest and burst into laughter while crossing to them in one bound. I swoop them up in a hug, my heart racing with joy and shock.

"Sam, mate, how are you here? I can't believe it!" I place a kiss to Sarah's cheek and then Luci's, then bring Sam in for another embrace.

"Merry Christmas, Luca. Poppy arranged for Sarah, Luci, and I to spend the holidays with you. She didn't want you to be alone, and I couldn't wait for you to meet my girls."

I nearly swallow my heart and pray there's still time to correct the biggest mistake of my life.

43

POPPY

BEESTON, NOTTINGHAMSHIRE, ENGLAND
DECEMBER 25, 1918

HOW MANY LIVES CAN ONE LIVE IN A SINGLE LIFETIME? Father used to tell me that for every book whose pages I opened, that world became a part of me. Another life I had the opportunity to live. But what of our real-life stories? The ones where *we* fight the wicked army, nearly lose our life to the cause of freedom, slay the dragon, and rise from the ashes of those who have fallen?

I believe those stories change and shape us the way words on a page have the power to do. But what if you lose more than you gain? If your story doesn't have a happy ending, does it still matter? Do those stories still inspire? Or are they just more lives added to the chaos of the billions of stories swirling around both our real and imaginary worlds? Perhaps stories are nothing more than an endless collision of joy and pain.

"Merry Christmas, Preacher Jones. We're looking forward to this evening's Christmas service," Mrs. Fischer says to Preacher, interrupting my spiraling thoughts as we approach the Beeston First Church of God's wide-open double doors arm in arm. The large wood doors are adorned with evergreen wreaths and vibrant, red ribbons tied in pristine bows. Preacher stands at the door, welcoming in his flock, and beams at us.

"Mrs. Cecilia Fischer and Miss Poppy Pemburton, welcome, and a very Merry Christmas to you both." As he shakes our hands, the sounds of "Silent Night", sung by the church choir, trickle softly through the open doors along with the ringing of Christmas bells and melodious harp music played by Mabel Jones, Preacher's wife, in the background.

Sam, Sarah, and little Luci Davies enter through the doors a few steps ahead of us, and I can't help but look around to see if Luca is nearby. I wish my heart didn't ache for him as desperately as it does. I know I made the right choice in saying goodbye to someone who can't accept all of me, but Luca wasn't just someone. He was *the* one.

"He won't be here," Mrs. Fischer says, patting my arm.

"I know," I sigh. "It'll take some time before my brain accepts that, though." I'd hoped when I'd arranged for Mrs. Fischer to bring Luca to the church to meet Sam's family two mornings ago that being near *our* place would have inspired a slight change of heart within him. Perhaps that was a romanticized, girlish thought, but as Luca walked away from me that day, I found myself desperate to turn back time.

Luci gives me a little wave goodbye over her mother's shoulder as she disappears into the church, and I'm sad the Davies family is leaving after the service. I've enjoyed listening to Sam's stories and getting to know Sarah for the past few days they've been in Beeston when they weren't spending time with Luca. Thankfully, we are already planning a time in the spring to get together again.

"Mrs. Fischer, I invite you to find a seat inside." Preacher motions toward the chapel pews and then he turns to me. "Miss Pemburton, would you follow me, please?" he says and makes a show of offering his arm.

"Follow you where?"

"If you would, please." Preacher smiles at me and nods his head at his extended arm, offering no further explanation.

Confused, I look to Mrs. Fischer for clarification.

She simply shrugs her shoulders, but there is a twinkle in her eyes as she waves goodbye and walks inside the chapel.

Intrigued, I take hold of Preacher's arm and allow him to guide me down the concrete steps, around the corner, and down a long stretch of winding pathways that lead to the far backside of the church where, behind a large grove of trees, the brick wall covered in vines is that leads to the hidden flat portion of the church roof. Has Preacher discovered our secret hideaway? After all these years, is he going to chastise me for using a sacred house of God for recreation?

But when we exit the throng of trees, my jaw drops, and I'm rendered speechless.

All the vines are gone. Completely removed, leaving behind only a large, naked, red and brown brick wall. There are no more thick, twined brown branches covered in thorns, pinecones, and lush green leaves. No climbing vines that provide footholds for a quick escape to the top.

But even more shocking than the brick being stripped of the climbing green is a set of wooden stairs somebody has built that extend from the ground to the small opening on the roof. A long, narrow piece of wood has been attached to all the steps trailing up to the roof, a handrail of sorts so that the stairs are blocked in on one side by a guardrail and on the other side by the large brick wall.

Preacher chuckles next to me and motions to the bottom step. "Go on."

"I . . . I don't understand."

"Go on." He urges me forward. "It won't be daylight much longer."

My hands tingle as I take a shaky step toward the wood boxes. "Where did these stairs come from? What happened to the vines?"

Preacher places a gentle hand on my back and moves me forward. "The vines weren't safe anymore. They built these yesterday. Worked all Christmas Eve. I tried them myself. They are sturdy enough for you, but be careful, you understand?"

No, I don't understand at all. "They who?"

A large smile breaks out across Preacher's face, and he points upward. That's when I notice there is more to see here than just a new set of stairs. A small piece of white paper is affixed to the large brick wall about three stairs up from the ground.

I look over at Preacher, and he appears as giddy as a school-girl.

"Well, I have a sermon to preach, don't I now? Merry Christmas, Miss Pemburton," he says and tips his hat before turning to leave me alone.

I carefully move up the first three steps, and when I reach the paper, chills dance up my arms and neck.

It's a painting.

The strokes are imperfect, the dimensions not to scale, the colors slightly off, but I know instantly what the scene is, and tears well in my eyes. A young boy with dark hair and green eyes stands across from a young girl with red hair and blue eyes (*then blue will always be my favorite color*), a Ferris wheel lit up behind them and a night sky so dark the stars twinkle with joy. A white bow is tied in the girl's hair and trails loosely down her back.

The bottom of the paper reads:

The night I told you I loved you

I move up the next few stairs to another painted scene painted nailed to the brick. It's the floral couch that sits in my cottage, a fire blazing to the left of it, a girl with red hair and a white bow weeping upon its cushions. A young boy with dark hair stands next to the fire, one hand putting a blanket around the girl's shoulders, his other one holding Jane's goodbye note over the flames.

The night I vowed I would always protect you

Our church roof is painted next. A man and woman stand in an embrace beneath a canopy of green leaves. Flowers bloom along vines that wind around the couple, romanticizing the scene. The girl wears a blue dress that compliments the boy's black trousers and stark white shirt. She's whispering into the boy's ear, and scrawled above his head are the words: *I. LOVE. YOU.*

The night you changed my life

Next is a simple charcoal sketch of a man alone inside a cement block cell. He's naked but for a pair of white undergarments around his bony frame. He sits, his back curved against one wall, his head in his hands. Beside him, hundreds of lines are carved into the floor.

The time I found the depths of hell

I reach the next picture, and a sob catches in my throat. A woman in a boiler suit is kneeling on broken ground, a young girl with a heart-shaped face slumped in her arms. The woman's face is etched in pain as she looks toward the heavens, holding the girl tight to her chest. In the background, buildings are engulfed in flames.

The night you did too

Two more steps take me to the image of a man who looks as though he's weathered a storm standing across from a woman in front of the gates of the Chilwell National Shell Filling Factory, their hands clasped together. She is strong, her face determined, sure, happy. The word *home* is written in the shape of a heart on the woman's chest.

The time I found heaven

The next picture is a painting of a woman's profile. She is dressed in a long, flowing white gown. The paint is thick, the texture of the gown rich with movement and dollops of paint that make it seem as though the dress might fly right off the paper. Tendrils of red hair tumble behind her, and tiny, white flowers don the length of her short locks. Her face is tilted upward to the sun. Her arms cradle her protruding middle.

The time you did too

The paper that follows is the sketch of a woman, her head bent down, one arm reaching out to a man who's walking away from her. His arm is extended behind him, their fingers inches apart, his face contorted and his heart—or is it hers—on the ground beneath his foot.

The time I made the biggest mistake of my life

The next work of art is an explosion of color. A dark-haired man is bent over a large table with a paintbrush in his hand. A smattering of paints, charcoal sticks, brushes, and stacks of paper dress the table. Ten finished works of art lay on the floor by his feet.

The time I tried to make it right

I take a shaky step up to the last stair, and the picture on the wall takes my breath away. A woman walks up the newly built wood stairs, taking in the pictures placed along the brick wall. One hand is placed over her heart, and one hand caresses her stomach. A man stands at the top of the stairs gazing down at the woman.

The day I asked you to marry me

My mouth goes dry, and my heart thuds within my chest.

I step onto the roof, and Luca is standing in front of me. It's dusk now. The winter sky, purple and pregnant with heavy clouds, sits as a beautiful backdrop behind Luca, who's dressed in a handsome black suit, his jawline sharp and smooth, his green eyes set and serious. A red firebird feather is in his hand.

Soft flakes of snow start to fall between the brown tree branches above our head, landing like first kisses on our skin.

"Luca—"

"Poppy," he says at the same time, and we chuckle awkwardly.

"Please." I motion for him to speak first.

Luca's hands shake before he stuffs the one not holding the feather into his pocket, and his lips tremble when he says, "Oh, okay." He smiles, although he looks as if he might cry, and takes a deep breath.

"We have been through a lot, you and I. Both together and apart. Our story is long, difficult, and complex but also beautiful, adventurous, and . . . and not long enough." His voice breaks, and he presses a closed fist to his lips as he tries to compose himself. "A whole lifetime with you would still not be long enough for me. Poppy, I love you." His voice grows louder, his confidence growing. He steps closer to me and continues, "You are the perfectly freckled-face girl who has held my heart in her hands since the moment I met you. We have had different experiences over the last few years, but we have learned the same thing: to love ourselves. To accept all the parts that make up our whole.

"And I am not whole without you, Poppy. Without *all* of you." He takes another step closer to me and holds my hand in his. "I'm sorry it took me some time to figure out where my heart was, but I know I can love the child growing within you because I love you. I have seen a lot of things over the last few years that make my head spin when the images and memories flit through my mind, but I vow to you and this baby that I will never let those come between us.

"If you will have me, I will never stop choosing you. I will never stop counting your freckles or kissing your lips. I will never stop reaching for your hand or chasing you around this church roof. I will never stop painting our lives or coloring your world. I will never stop losing myself in the wonder of your eyes or finding my soul tangled with yours."

Luca holds my left hand in his and runs the firebird feather slowly down the length of my ring finger. Tingles race across my skin, shooting fire in every direction at the play of the soft, feathery strands of red along my fingers.

"Marry me, Poppy Pemburton," Luca's deep voice says. "Marry me, and let me have the honor of caring for, loving, and serving our family the remainder of my days."

Our family.

I slide the feather from his hands and wrap my arms around him. "Nothing would make me happier than becoming your wife."

44

LUCA

BEESTON, NOTTINGHAMSHIRE, ENGLAND
MARCH 8, 1919

THE CANOPY OF LEAVES ABOVE MY HEAD SWAYS EVER SO gently in the soft, rainy breeze as I stand, sure-footed and eager, in my designated groom's spot on the church roof. The Saturday afternoon sky is a slate gray with the promise of heavier rain to come, but for now, the clouds remain swollen with little relief.

Preacher Jones stands at attention directly to my right, suited up in his Sunday best, tears already brimming in his shiny, black eyes, even though my bride has yet to arrive.

"Nervous?" Preacher leans over and whispers.

"Not even a little bit." I smile.

Preacher's wife, Mabel, sits behind us, playing beautiful, soft melodies on her harp—an instrument that required no less than five men to haul up the narrow wood stairs Sam and I built together. I was sorry to cut down the vines, but they had become thorny over the years and no longer safe to climb, especially for a woman with child. I'm an artist, not a carpenter, so the nailed-together boxes aren't anything to boast of, but they are sturdy and made with the passion of a repentant man, if nothing else.

The plucking of Mabel's fingers against the strings in this small, intimate space bounces off the trees and branches above us, and the soft roof catches the sound, holding it like drops of glass tinkling around us. The music echoes against the beat of my heart—the rain, the soft wind, and our memories, hopes, and dreams creating a beautiful, unique sound. Like sheet music for our love story.

I look around the small, square space in front of me in to the smiling faces of our closest friends, and I am overwhelmed with gratitude. Mrs. Fischer, the canary girls, and Sarah Davies transformed the roof into a place so beautiful I can hardly believe it's the same space that's been Poppy's and my refuge for years. A small aisle created from a white cloth strip stretches from one end of the flat roof to the other. Three rows of simple, white chairs with bold, dark-red ribbons tied around their backs flank the aisle.

In the first row, Sam and Sarah Davies sit on one side of the isle with baby Samuel—born just last month—in Sarah's arms. Opposite the isle sits Luci Davies, a big three-year-old who requested her own seat next to Mrs. Fischer. The older woman holds Luci's small hand in hers and reminds her every few moments to sit still. Behind the first row sits Annabelle and Sophia on one side and Nessy and an empty chair in Clara's honor on the other. In the final row, Mr. and Mrs. Fanny Christmas are on the left side, and Mr. Ashby and his wife are on the right.

Small bouquets of deep-red and white roses interspersed with white sweet peas and sprigs of green leaves sit in clear glass vases along each side of the aisle. Velvety red and white rose petals, scattered liberally by Luci, dance throughout the space. White candles glow with soft light inside tall, rectangular lanterns that have been placed on each side of the aisle at both the beginning and end of the white cloth. More lanterns sit on small tables that have been set up in different corners of the roof to provide extra light.

In the canopied trees above us, white lace is loosely draped through the branches and leaves, creating an ethereal beauty unmatched by anything I have ever seen.

The harp begins playing Mendelssohn's "Wedding March," and chairs squeak as people shift in their seats to look back toward the roof opening.

She's here.

In time with the slow rhythm of the harp's melody, Poppy moves down the aisle toward me. I catch her eyes, and my heart stops beating. Her beautiful hair and deep-red lipstick set off her blue eyes and long, white dress with such striking intensity all the oxygen within me leaves my body at once. Preacher grabs onto my shoulder and gives me a quick squeeze, which, thankfully, holds me steady.

In her hands, Poppy holds a bouquet of flowers similar to the ones that line the aisle she moves through, only the one she carries is larger and includes white calla lilies and the red firebird feather I asked her to marry me with. The feather sits right in the middle, snuggled between a white rose and a calla lily.

Every magical story begins with this feather, Luca.

Poppy's dress—made of tussar silk with floating, intricate white lace panels down each side and up her bodice—is one she designed, created, and sewed herself, with a little help from Mrs. Fischer and the canary girls. Covering Poppy's arms is a thick, white fur cloak, and the dress beneath it flows freely about her form as she moves. When she reaches the end of the aisle where I stand, she curves her arm around her belly.

I reach my hand out, and she grabs hold of it, her fingers calloused yet delicate as they latch onto mine. "Happy twenty-sixth birthday, Firebird."

"I can't think of a better gift."

"No? I guess I'll have to see if Mrs. Christmas will take back the one hundred Fry's Five Boy chocolate bars I bought for you, then."

"One hundred?" she gasps.

"One for every year of our new life together in Italy." I can't keep the smile from my face. This woman has made every one of my dreams come true. I only want to give her the world in return.

Poppy hands her bouquet to Mrs. Fischer, then stands on her tiptoes, wraps her arms around my neck, and says, "A whole life-time with you would still never be enough."

"Then thankfully I am yours for eternity."

Poppy looks at me then the same way she did on this very day thirteen years ago, standing in front of the Ferris wheel, excited but sincere. "My heart is yours, Luca."

My heart flips the same way it did that day as a fourteen-year-old boy after hearing her say those words. "Forever. Forever and always, I will love you," I vow.

45

POPPY

WHEN THE PAINS COME, THEY COME SHARP AND FAST.

Angry fists twisting in my stomach as if nails are clawing my insides out, and a burning between my legs so severe I'm nearly blinded by the pain. Mrs. Fischer lifts my skirt while Nessy slides gloves over her hands, Sophia reminds me to breathe, and Annabelle passes out in the corner.

"It's time to push," Mrs. Fischer commands me now, hours of tumultuous labor behind me.

I should be relieved, but I am so tired and sore I can hardly move.

"Where's Luca?" I shout as searing spasms shoot daggers into my lower back.

"I'm right here." Luca's muffled voice sounds from outside the closed bedroom door that separates us. "I'm right here, Firebird. I'm not going anywhere."

I scream as fire rips through me from my breasts all the way to my toes.

"Breathe!" Sophia takes me by my shoulders and holds me down firmly against the bed. "You have to breathe through the pain. Stop trying to fight it." She brings a cold, wet rag from the basin beside her to my cheeks and I calm slightly.

"Okay, push now," Mrs. Fischer yells from between my legs. "I can see the head. Give me two more good pushes, and this will all be over."

"Remember that time you pushed Frank Boyd down in the schoolhouse?" I hear Luca shout through the door. "He was three times as big as you, and smelled like boiled cabbage, but he made fun of my terrible English, and you pushed him straight to the ground. Do you remember?"

I look at Nessy, speechless, trying to convey with my eyes that I'm going to murder Luca if he speaks again.

"She remembers, Luca. Thank you," Nessy says. To me she whispers, "Men," with a huff.

"Push like that," Luca's muffled encouragement continues. "You are the strongest woman I have ever known." I hear a heavy thud against the door then and imagine Luca's head pressed forward against the wood, his gorgeous, dark hair falling forward, and his worried, green eyes hidden behind closed lids as he speaks in earnest. "You are about to bring life into this world after this world has taken so much life from you. I will never cease to be amazed by your strength."

And now I'm crying. Big, fat tears of emotions. Agony, love, desire, desperation, fear, longing, and hope all mix together as Luca's words wash over me before another stab of labor squeezes my abdomen.

"Big breath in now," Mrs. Fischer coaxes, and I obey. "Big breath out, and push as hard as you can, Poppy."

Again, I obey.

"Good; very good. One more time. Baby is almost here."

Baby. *Our* baby, I think—mine and Luca's. Our gift from Jakob. And the thought sends courage coursing through me. I can do this.

Sophia breathes in and out with me and squeezes my hand as I bear down and push, every muscle within me working together at the same time to help bring this soul into the world and provide it a body in which to live.

Sweat beads down my forehead, my back, between my breasts, and in the creases of my arms, and all I can think about is how strong Luca believes I am. About how strong I know I am. About Jakob, in heaven, passing this babe from God's arms to mine.

And then there's crying.

Within moments, Mrs. Fischer places a screaming, small body wet with blood upon my bare chest, and Nessy wraps a warm blanket around the two of us. A head of light-strawberry hair rises and falls against my skin.

As the baby quiets, my heart explodes with a love I have never known. This is the only person in the universe who truly knows what every beat of love within my heart sounds like.

"It's a girl," Mrs. Fischer whispers as she watches us. "A very tiny but perfectly healthy baby girl." Tears roll down her weathered cheeks. "You are a mother now, dear girl. Congratulations."

"Her name is Clara," I announce softly. "Clara Whelan."

Nessy nods her head in approval, her eyes growing moist. "That's perfect," she says.

"A beautiful name for a beautiful girl," Sophia says from my side.

Annabelle has yet to rise from the floor.

After I spend some time with baby Clara curled against my bosom, Nessy removes her from my hold, washes and wipes her clean, and wraps her in a soft cloth. Mrs. Fischer cleans me and helps tie a soft robe of red around me.

When Nessy carries Clara back to my side, I gasp at the color of my baby girl's skin. *Yellow*.

"Yellow from the TNT powder," Mrs. Fischer says. I look up at her, unable to form words of understanding. "It has happened to many of the women who've worked at the ammunition factories for years," she continues. "Their babies have been notably small and underweight and are tinged with the yellow skin of their mothers but otherwise perfectly healthy. Most babies' yellow skin has faded over time, as your own has, and I have heard no reports as to any of the babies suffering any other side effects or long-lasting consequences from the TNT. The yellow will fade, and her weight will increase as you feed her regularly."

"Let's ensure you both get something to eat now," Nessy says. She teaches me how to feed my baby properly, and Sophia brings me a plate of bread and fruit.

Once both Clara and I are cleaned up and fed well enough, Mrs. Fischer opens the door of the bedroom.

Luca's hands are pressed against the frame, his knuckles white as if he hasn't moved from that spot since the women brought me in here when the pains first started in the early, dark hours of the morning. His hair stands on end as though he hasn't stopped running trembling fingers through it.

His eyes find mine, and they are wild with fear.

"I am okay," I tell him with a smile. "Your baby girl is okay too."

Air rushes out of him and then he gasps. "Girl?"

Luca dashes to my side, scoops our little bundle into his arms, and smothers her with kisses before doing the same to me. A joy comes alive within me that's so huge I feel as if I've created an entirely new level of happiness no word has yet been invented to describe it.

The light is within you, waiting for you to let it shine through your broken spaces and chase away the dark. When you find your light again, it will bring you back to life. Clara's words dance in front of me. I close my eyes and let them seep into the deepest parts of my soul.

Luca sits down carefully on the edge of the bed. "Poppy, I have seen you hurt and hollow, happy and free. I have seen you in your angriest moments and in your loveliest. I have seen you dressed in factory black uniforms and in a gorgeous, white wedding dress. But you have never been more beautiful than you are in this very moment."

A smile spreads across my face. "I can't wait to start our lives together in Italy, Luca. Just the three of us. The Whelan family."

Love has the power to hurt, to destroy, and to break you so small you fear you will never be whole again. But it also has the power to heal. To create something within you more beautiful than you have ever known. Love mends the broken, brings peace to your soul, and creates unmeasurable joy. The key is to keep searching until you have found the love that does exactly that.

46

POPPY

BEESTON, NOTTINGHAMSHIRE, ENGLAND
JUNE 20, 1919

I HOLD TIGHT TO LUCA, MY LEFT HAND IN HIS.

I walk next to him, trusting myself unwaveringly.

He is my rock, solid and sure. And I am his.

Baby Clara is tucked safely into the crook of my right arm, sleeping peacefully amidst the chaos at the Beeston train station, which bustles with life and noise in the welcome afternoon summer sunshine.

Men smile beneath top hats and mustaches. Women in traveling dresses gossip behind newspapers. Children with lollipops and popcorn spilling from their hands weave in and out of an endless stream of white steam billowing across the platform.

I stroke the soft, smooth skin of Clara's chubby arm beneath my finger. Warmth wraps itself around my enlarged heart and calms me. Clara is just shy of three months, but she has fattened up deliciously. Mrs. Fischer is certain Clara is going to outgrow all her clothing by the time we arrive in Italy, so she brought a small suitcase just for Clara to the station today.

"It's full to the brim of frocks and rompers of all sizes," Mrs. Fischer tells Luca and I as she snaps open the case's buckles and runs her hands through the clothing. "The canary girls aren't seamstresses quite yet," she laughs, "but these were certainly made with . . . excitement." Mrs. Fischer's eyebrows raise with warning. Annabelle, Nessy, and Sophia began working at the Beeston Lace Factory when Mrs. Fischer reopened in January, and their thoughtfulness warms my heart.

With the exception of the gifts from the canary girls, Luca and I are bringing only one travel case a piece, with a few clothing items each, Luca's art materials, the firebird feather, and the atlas Jakob gifted me for Christmas two years ago.

I almost left it in the cottage, ready to leave the past in the past, but as my thumb haphazardly flipped through the pages before I tossed it back into the drawer, a page with the corner bent down caught my attention. A map of the southern portion of Germany.

I looked closer and saw the smallest drip of an ink dot above the printed city name of Munich. *Is that where Jakob was from?* It could have been a misprint on the page, so slight was the mark. And I would have believed that to be true had it not been *Germany* that was earmarked and had I not then found the name Johanna Kirtchner printed along the stitched binding in tiny letters. *A sister or his mother, perhaps? But why leave a name at all?*

I would never have those answers now, but whenever Luca and I decide to tell Clara the truth about her heritage, I will ensure those markings mean something to her. While Jakob had his faults, I pray the courage and compassion with which he lived his life are characteristics he passed on to our daughter.

"Are you ready then?" Mrs. Fischer asks, glancing up at the tracks when the sound of an engine huffing its way into the station alerts us that it's time to say our goodbyes.

"Ready as we'll ever be, I suppose," Luca says.

"And you are certain you do not want ownership of the lace factory?"

I take hold of Mrs. Fischer's hand. "Thank you for the offer. It was the hope I held onto after I found out I was with child and would be on my own to provide a life for the two of us. But now . . ." I trail off with too many thoughts and not enough words.

"Now there's too much weight in Beeston. Too many difficult memories," Mrs. Fischer says, filling in the spaces I don't know how to.

Luca wraps an arm around my shoulder. "We want to create new memories together as a family in a place that doesn't remind us of all we've lost. All we've suffered."

"We need to move forward, and Italy is where we want to do it." I lean into Luca, and he presses a kiss to the top of my head.

"Let's get you three on that train, then," Mrs. Fischer says with conviction, but I'm not oblivious to the sorrow in her voice.

"Come with me my little Clary Canary," Luca says using his favorite nickname for our little yellow baby and plucks Clara from my arms. He gives Mrs. Fischer a one-armed hug, offers a goodbye, and walks onto the train, giving me a moment alone with her.

"Goodbyes are always hard for me. I've never said a goodbye to someone that didn't hurt in the very depths of my soul," Mrs. Fischer says. "That's how you know it was real, I suppose."

"I guess no amount of love can make a person stay if it's their time to go. All we can do is cherish the moments we had with them and hope our paths cross again." I fidget with the ends of my black shawl.

"Ours will cross again, Poppy. I know it." She smiles, but it doesn't reach her eyes.

"Mrs. Fischer, it's not that I care—not really, because he doesn't deserve a minute of my concern, and I will never forgive him, but—" I chew my bottom lip, not sure how to ask for this ridiculous favor.

"I will check in on your father often," she says resolutely.

"Thank you," I manage to whisper. My eyes flick around the station, but Thomas isn't here. I'm not surprised, but my lips quiver anyhow. "Tell him goodbye for me, please."

Mrs. Fischer leans close, and her arms come around me. My body presses into hers as she grabs onto me in an awkward hug.

I do not cry when she lets go of me. I do not cry when she tells me to be a good girl and to take care of her darling Clara. I do not cry when she pats my hand or presses a kiss to my cheek. I do not cry as I tell her that I love her or that I will write her soon. I do not cry as I turn and step between the train doors.

"Poppy," Mrs. Fischer calls out before the doors close.

I turn back around.

A large family of six climbs onto the train at the same moment, and as they maneuver around my frozen form, Mrs. Fischer mouths the words, *I am so proud of you.*

That is when I cry.

Several months ago, I wondered how our stories change and shape us. If, despite their endings, they matter.

Clara did not get the happy ending she deserved, but she taught the world how to love. That matters.

Jakob didn't get a chance to see his story fulfilled, but he left a beautiful child filled with light to carry on in his stead. That matters.

She matters.

Mrs. Fischer's story, Luca's story, even Jane's and Thomas's stories—they all matter because I wouldn't be standing here today without them.

Perhaps that is the beauty of life. As humankind we are connected and intricately weaved together with those who love us, those who break us, those who leave us, and those who change us. Each connection creating a unique piece of the tapestry that is our life masterpiece.

The train car doors squeal shut in front of me. I press my face to the glass window, but she's already gone.

The small cry of a baby whispers its way to my ears through the noise of the passengers finding their seats. Several rows away, Luca stands with our daughter cradled in one arm, his other one holding up her arm and waving it at me in the most ridiculous manner, as if baby Clara is excited beyond belief to see me.

Luca's eyebrows bounce up and down above eyes that dance with anticipation over new adventures.

I love that look of Luca's more than any other. It reminds me of our childhood. It reminds me of *us*.

Laughter bubbles up through me as the two of them make complete fools of themselves just for me. When I make my way back to them, Luca enfolds me in an embrace and kisses the top of my head.

"I'm nervous, but I'm ready," I say, knowing now that fear is not something to be controlled by, but it is also not to be avoided. Because while fear should be challenged, it is also a gift that keeps us safe. Cowardice is not the presence of fear within us; it is the absence of strength to question the fear when it comes.

"Take me home, Luca."

"Count with me," Luca says with a wink.

"Ten, nine, eight, seven, six," we chant together between bouts of laughter, "five, four, three, two, one."

Then we are off, the train barreling forward and our past falling behind the future that awaits us.

THE END

AUTHOR'S NOTE

On my desk sits an 8x10 white wooden picture frame. Inside the frame is a gold foil print of the silhouette of a Miss Elsie Lavinia Gibbs who lived from 1901-1918.[1] Above the line art are the words, *Thank you for telling my story*—the work of art a gift from my sister, who knew I was going to want to give up on writing this story every single day. Who knew my self-doubt, insecurities, and failures along the way would likely get the best of me sometimes. But who also knew I had been drawn to tell this story in one of those hair-raising, belly-swooping, instinctually spiritual moments, and I would need something tangible to motivate me to keep going. Every time I wanted to walk away from this project because it was too hard, I would look over at sweet Elsie's face and remember *why* I was writing. I couldn't give up on her or the one hundred thirty-four people who lost their lives in the Chilwell Ammunition Factory explosion whom her face had come to represent for me.

As you may have guessed, the real-life Elsie Lavinia Gibbs inspired the fictional character Clara Whittaker in this novel. The backstory behind Clara's arrival at the factory for employment is entirely fictional, as is her past and upbringing, but like Clara, Elsie did, in fact, begin war work at the age of fourteen.

While there are no recorded details as far as my research provid-ed that specify why Elsie began employment at the factory at the young—and illegal—age of fourteen, many young women in England were drawn to war work with promises of large wages—some jobs even with food and board provided—or because they sought adventure, or because they desired socialization. Perhaps Elsie had one of those reasonings, or perhaps it was something else entirely. The unfortunate truth was, however, that the War Office was so desperate for bodies to fill positions in factories, they would often turn a blind eye to clearly fabricated ages on the paperwork.

As my research into the Chilwell factory explosion unfolded, my heart broke to learn that on July 1, 1918, only two years after her arrival at the factory and five months before the end of the war, the beautiful, young Elsie Gibbs would lose her life, shy of her seventeenth birthday, for doing nothing more than clocking in to work at 7:00 pm for the evening shift. The moment I came across the picture of Elsie's face, every hair on my neck stood on end, and a physical urgency pulled at my spirit in a way I have never experienced. My heart would simply not let go of the image of the heart-shaped face of this young girl from Cardiff. Instantly, the character of Clara Whittaker began to take shape in my mind, and it is my greatest hope that through Clara, I have brought honor to Elsie and shed light upon her brave and noble work as a munitionette.

I deliberately used the real town of Beeston[2] and street names found on 1915 maps of the town rather than create a fictional town, as the setting for large portions of the story, which include scenes at the train station, post office, Poppy's and Luca's homes, the church (although the name of the church in the book is fictionalized; to my knowledge there was no Beeston First Church of God in the early twentieth centu-ry), the Sweet Shoppe, The Humber Bicycle Factory where Luca works, the Weir at the Beeston Lock and Canal, and the lace factory where Poppy is employed at the beginning of the novel, which then serves to become the women's dormitory. Although the real location of each of these specific places may not have been exactly where they are detailed to be in the novel, they did exist in the town at that time. Many of the women who would have been employed at Chilwell National Shell Filling Factory (NSFF) No. 6 did, in fact, come from Beeston since the small town was located less than three miles east of Chilwell. Prior to war, if the women were employed, they largely worked doing lace or textile work. Unfortunately, the need for lace and textile work plummeted after war broke out, and many women throughout the town lost their jobs. It felt authentic to the story to place the characters in Beeston and pay tribute to the citizens of this town who either worked at the Chilwell factory at some point during WWI or who if they, themselves, did not work there, very likely knew someone who did. The factory at Chilwell would have affected the lives of all the Beeston townspeople in some way, and I wanted to acknowledge that.

Chilwell NSFF No. 6 was commissioned in August 1915 at the instigation of David Lloyd George, the head of the Ministry of Munitions, due to the "shell scandal" that broke a few months earlier in May 1915. Allegedly there were not enough high-explosive shells to overcome the superior German firepower on the Western Front; therefore, the Ministry of Munitions was created. Two months later, the Munitions of War Act was passed, which provided the government the power to construct national factories to speed up and control production of large caliber high-explosive shells with TNT. Responsibility for the construction and operation of the new factory was given to Viscount Godfrey John Boyle Chetwynd,[3] a man with no previous experience in handling explosives. All my research into this man taught me that although he had no practical knowledge in regard to ammunition, he was tremendously resourceful, always moved about with a sense of superior urgency, and was a nonconformist who despised red tape. He demanded, and essentially got, a free hand to design and create the factory without any political intrusion.

It can be tricky to use real historical figures' names in a work of fiction, so rather than use Lord Chetwynd's name and risk misrepresenting this historic, noble man, I chose to create the fictional character Mr. Ashby for the role of owner. I combined his role to be owner *and* manager of the factory in this novel for the purposes of pacing; however, the Chilwell NSFF did have a Works Manager by the name of Arthur Bristowe. I attempted to use a combination of the bold, passionate characteristics Lord Chetwynd was widely known for and the bravery of the site manager, Mr. Bristowe (who was an absolute hero in regard to his efforts in the aftermath of the explosion, receiving the Edward Medal[4]—the industry equivalent of the George Cross —for his heroism), to inspire the fictional character of Mr. Ashby.

Chetwynd signed off on the site acquisition in Chilwell on August 29, 1915. Construction of NSFF No. 6 started on September 5, 1915. The first shells were filled on January 8, 1916, and the first batch was tested at Shoeburyness firing range on January 23.[5] Supply to the army commenced in April of 1916, just one month before Poppy becomes employed there. I tried to adhere closely and accurately to the timeline of the Chilwell ammunition factory construction and the manufacturing of shells as I worked with the fictional plot of the story. It was important to me that the factory was represented with as much accuracy and authenticity as possible throughout the entire novel.

As Luca references in the story, the property of NSFF No. 6 was incredibly large, spanning over two hundred acres![6] The shell store was the largest building on the land. Its floor area covered nearly nine acres, and the structure could hold up to 600,000 filled shells and 100,000 empty shells.[7] By war's end, the factory had employed approximately 10,000 workers, many who were women due to the men being gone on the front lines.

As is mentioned in the book, despite the factory's large size, only those who worked there truly knew exactly where the factory was located. The War Office forbade the location of factories from being printed in any form in effort to keep the site locations from falling into the enemy's hands. When accidents occurred at the factories, the newspapers would often not report the incidents. They didn't want to dampen war morale by noting that citizens were being harmed in their war efforts, and they couldn't report where the accidents occurred, as it was illegal to divulge factory whereabouts. On the occasion that something *was* printed in the papers, the numbers of deaths and injuries was always minimized and only a general location of the factory was provided. For example, in the instance of the factory explosion here at Chilwell, the media hid the truth of the magnitude of devastation that occurred by reporting that only 60 were feared dead in a Midlands explosion.[8] The truth about the horror that occurred there, the number of lives that were lost, and the extent of the damage caused would not come to light for decades.

Canary girls, as women munition workers throughout England were affectionately called, came to be known as such due to the bright yellow staining upon their skin. The discoloration was caused from handling the picrate/picric acid explosive found in TNT.[9] Although employees were provided uniforms, the actuality of their protective clothing was deplorably deficient, as proven by the many deaths, injuries, and illnesses these women suffered. Their hazardous work with explosives and toxic substances caused a range of health issues, from skin complaints and discoloration to bone disintegration. Other reported symptoms included vomiting and stomach pains, changes in menstruation, heart palpitations, hair turning green or falling out altogether, chest pain, breast deformation, weakening of the immune system, anemia, migraines, and fertility problems. There were multiple cases reported of munitionettes giving birth to yellow children, as Poppy did. One "baby canary," Gladys Sangster,[10] was one of Britain's yellow born babies because her mother worked in a munitions factory in Banbury. She remembered that in her town, most children were simply born that way, and doctors told the mothers that only time would fade the discoloration.

To contend with the health challenges they faced, the women working in factories began to play football during lunch breaks. Football matches helped raise money for wartime charities, and larger matches would draw tens of thousands of spectators.[11] As far as my research allowed, I could not find proof of an organized women's football team at Chilwell NSFF. Although this specific portion of the story (a women's factory football team at Chilwell) was fictional, the playing of women's factory football was not, so I chose to add in a storyline that showcased a positive part of ammunition factory life amongst the daily hard and dangerous labors they performed.

An estimated six hundred people were killed by accidental explosions during the course of the First World War. The greatest loss of life occurred on July 1, 1918, at 7:10 pm, when the ammonium nitrate plant, also known as the amatol mixing house, at the National Shell Filling Factory in Chilwell, Nottinghamshire, exploded, resulting in the loss of 134 lives and injuries of hundreds more.[12] "This gave the Chilwell explosion a prominence which derived from the fact that this was the largest loss of civilian life in a single incident on the Home Front during the First World War. That alone made it a subject of particular interest."[13]

Due to the ferocity of the explosion, witness accounts state the blast was heard anywhere from twenty to thirty miles away. Only 32 bodies of the 134 who died could be positively identified. [14] As soon as the explosion occurred, everyone on site knew it was a crisis. Calls were put out to all the emergency services, ambulances, fire brigade, police, doctors, nurses, motor cars, and even wheelbarrows within a close proximity. Chilwell had only one fire engine but within ten minutes of the blast, three hundred members of the St. John's Ambulance were on site, rendering first aid. They were later congratulated by the speed with which they arrived to begin bringing aid to those who had suffered. Other local people rushed to the site to assist. Chetwynd was not at the factory that evening; he was at Winthorpe Hall, the family home near Doncaster, in bed with influenza—the Spanish flu, as it became known. Despite being ill, as soon as he received a telephone call telling of the blast, he immediately drove to Chilwell and was on site by 10 p.m. to find that the clean-up was already in full swing.[15]

Regardless of the extensive damage and the workers' extreme shock, repairs were swiftly carried out overnight, enabling some of the next morning's dayshift to start work again, where all but twelve employees returned to work.[16] That number is astounding to me. The bravery of these men and women is inspiring! Within four days of the explosion, the factory was up and running, and by August the factory was fully restored.

The first thing that Chetwynd did post-explosion was contact the Chief Constable of Nottinghamshire to arrange for an inspector to come from Scotland Yard to take witness statements. These were subsequently part of a Commission of Enquiry set up by the British Home Office. Chetwynd told the Enquiry he was convinced it was sabotage and indeed was said to have named a possible culprit. The Enquiry took forty witness statements from those who had been on the previous shift which had finished at 6:00 p.m. Of course, there were no surviving witnesses in these areas to provide oral evidence as to what might have actually happened in the lead up to the explosion.[17]

Most citizens, as well as the Home Office, believed the blast to have been accidental. It was coming up on the offensives of the summer of 1918, and the pressure was on the workforce to produce as many shells as possible as quickly as possible. Everyone just wanted the war to end! The factory was running twenty-four hours a day, seven days a week, three shifts per day —hence the reason in the later chapters of the book, Poppy mentions not having seen Charles in weeks. That would have been a very accurate representation of a relationship at that time, as they were quite literally working around the clock. In addition to increased labor, July 1, 1918 was a hot, torrid day, and witnesses said ice was brought in to try to keep the TNT cool. Not to mention, something certainly could have happened when amatol was being moved to the Press House. Ultimately, though, there was no conclusive identifying cause of the explosion—sabotage or otherwise.

Scotland Yard inspectors who had previously arrived at Chilwell on July 8, 1918 to look at what was to be found and conduct interviews subsequently returned to London. The British Home Office Committee of Enquiry closed out its report of the explosion on August 7, with no specific recommendations made, and the report was classified as SECRET.[18] It is probable that Chetwynd, himself, never actually saw this report.

Upon Scotland Yard's return to London and the close of the unsolved investigation, Winston Churchill sent a telegram to the factory saying:

> "Please accept my sincere sympathy with you all in the misfortune that has overtaken your fine Factory and in the loss of valuable lives, those who have perished have died at their stations on the field of duty and those who have lost their dear ones should fortify themselves with this thought, the courage and spirit shown by all concerned both men and women command our admiration, and the decision to which you have all come to carry on without a break is worthy of the spirit which animates our soldiers in the field. I trust the injured are receiving every care."[19]

A memorial monument stands on the north side of Chetwynd Road, near where the factory's Mixing House stood, at or near the seat of the explosion. It commemorates all those killed at the factory, in addition to the 134 killed in July 1918. There is also a mass grave where the remains of most of the victims of the explosion are buried in St Mary's Churchyard, Attenborough, near Nottingham.

Despite the devastation of the explosion, the Chilwell ammunition factory became Britain's most productive shell filling factory, supplying more than half of the high-explosive 60-pounder and 15-inch shells used by British troops in the Great War.[20] In the factory's two years and nine months of production, Chilwell filled 19,325,959 shells, representing more than half of all the shells filled in the numerous factories throughout the country during the same period.[21] Just two months after the fatal blast, the factory filled 275,327 shells in one week—a record number.[22] This was a fascinating fact I came across in my early research of the Chilwell ammunition factory before I even began writing, and I knew I wanted to include it in the story. Even without the notoriety of the explosion, those output figures significantly enhanced Chilwell's reputation.

Still today, it seems that the truth of the Chilwell National Shell Filling Factory No. 6 explosion is far from clear. There is every reason to conclude that human error was the likely cause of the explosion, but since sabotage was never conclusively disproven—only not able to *be* proven—when I came across this story, I couldn't help but wonder . . . what if?

What if it *wasn't* an accident? What if Chetwynd was right? What if it was sabotage? Who would have desired an outcome of that nature? An outcome that killed and injured hundreds of civilians. A disgruntled employee? Someone with a political agenda? The Germans? Did someone know the truth and choose to stay silent? What is in that SECRET report that not even the owner of the factory was likely privy to? My mind started to spin with possibilities of culprits and their motives. When the thought entered my mind, *What if one hundred thirty-four people lost their lives that day because a German spy fell in love with the enemy,* The Silent Canary was born.

So now I ask you, dear reader, what do *you* think happened?

[1] https://livesofthefirstworldwar.iwm.org.uk/lifestory/7671618

[2] http://www.beeston-notts.co.uk/default.htm

[3] https://www.westernfrontassociation.com/world-war-i-articles/chilwell-the-vc-factory-explosion-1-july-1918/

[4] https://heritagecalling.com/2018/06/29/the-chilwell-catastrophe-fatal-explosion-on-the-home-front/

[5] https://www.westernfrontassociation.com/media/6533/2019-42-jun.pdf page 12

[6] https://www.westernfrontassociation.com/media/6533/2019-42-jun.pdf page 6

[7] https://www.heritagegateway.org.uk/Gateway/Results_Single.aspx?uid=1085832&resourceID=19191

[8] https://blogs.nottingham.ac.uk/manuscripts/files/2014/06/Nott-Guardian.jpg

[9] https://issuu.com/designraphael/docs/munitionettesflyer_book_07final pages 34-35

[10] https://www.dailymail.co.uk/news/article-2561630/The-war-children-born-YELLOW-How-women-working-explosives-factories-sparked-clutch-Canary-Babies-WW1.html

[11] https://spartacus-educational.com/Fmunition.htm

[12] https://www.heritagegateway.org.uk/Gateway/Results_Single.aspx?uid=1085832&resourceID=19191

[13] https://www.westernfrontassociation.com/media/6533/2019-42-jun.pdf page 8

[14] https://heritagecalling.com/2018/06/29/the-chilwell-catastrophe-fatal-explosion-on-the-home-front/

[15] https://www.westernfrontassociation.com/media/6533/2019-42-jun.pdf pages 12-13

[16] https://www.bbc.com/news/uk-england-nottinghamshire-44658982

[17] https://www.westernfrontassociation.com/media/6533/2019-42-jun.pdf page 17

[18] Maureen Rushton, Canary Girls of Chilwell (Newton Books: Nottingham, UK, 2nd Edition, 2016), page 65

[19] Haslam, M. J. (Captain, RAOC) (1982). *The Chilwell story, 1915-1982 : VC Factory and Ordnance Depot.* Chilwell: The RAOC Corps Gazette. Pages 45-46

[20] http://www.greatwarci.net/journals/34.pdf page 4

[21] https://www.westernfrontassociation.com/media/6533/2019-42-jun.pdf page 9

[22] https://heritagecalling.com/2018/06/29/the-chilwell-catastrophe-fatal-explosion-on-the-home-front/

SOURCES

I had the absolute privilege of poring over many primary and secondary sources while researching this project. Journals, personal diaries, handwritten letters, first-person voice recordings of personal histories from ammunition factory workers in WW1, books, articles, British newspapers, advertisements, online file archives from the Imperial War Museum, and archived film footage from inside the Chilwell ammunition factory were invaluable in bringing to life the characters and story of *The Silent Canary*. It was my greatest intention to stay authentic to the details and facts of the Chilwell ammunition factory, the explosion, war along the Western Front, and the historical time period. This is a fiction novel; therefore, some liberties were taken with historic details in effort to tell the story in an engaging and fluid manner, and any mistakes or errors within the pages of this book are entirely my own.

If you care to further research the Chilwell National Shell Filling Factory No. 6, ammunition factory life, canary girls, the Chilwell explosion of 1918, war along the Western Front, POW camps, or the personnel mentioned in the Author's note, here are some further books and resources I found helpful in my study and research.

Enjoy!

The Canary Girls of Chilwell: the story of No. 6 Shell Filling Factory, Chilwell, Nottinghamshire by Maureen Rushton
The Chilwell story: VC factory and ordnance depot by Haslam, M.J. and Berragan, G.B.
Never Let Anyone Draw the Blinds by Lottie Martin
Canary Child by David Field and Alan Dance
Canary Girls by Jennifer Chiaverini
As Dawn Breaks by Kate Breslin

https://www.bbc.co.uk/programmes/p0202530
https://www.bbc.com/news/av/uk-england-nottinghamshire-44602259
https://www.iwm.org.uk/
https://www.historic-uk.com/HistoryUK/HistoryofBritain/White-Feather-Movement/
https://www.theguardian.com/world/2008/nov/11/first-world-war-white-feather-cowardice
https://spartacus-educational.com/FWWfeather.htm

https://archive.org/details/protectiveclothioogrearich/page/8/mode/2up

https://journals.openedition.org/apparences/1355?lang=en

https://alphahistory.com/worldwar1/west-munitions-factory-1916/

https://www.donmouth.co.uk/local_history/great_war_football/great_war_footbal
l.html

https://downloads.bbc.co.uk/england/ww1/bbc-world-war-one-at-home.pdf

http://www.nottshistory.org.uk/articles/mellorsarticles/toton2.htm

https://cdn.nationalarchives.gov.uk/documents/education/letters-from-the-first-
world-war-1915-3-trenches.pdf

https://the-past.com/feature/the-men-behind-the-wire-british-pows-in-the-first-
world-war/

https://sites.google.com/site/echoinmyheartsite/

For a complete list of names of the fallen and information about the Chilwell
National Shell Filling Factory employees, these two sites will be helpful:

https://rollofhonour.nottinghamshire.gov.uk/Memorial/Details/215

https://livesofthefirstworldwar.iwm.org.uk/community/2400

ACKNOWLEDGMENTS

"In the end, though, maybe we must all give up trying to pay back the people in this world who sustain our lives. In the end, maybe it's wiser to surrender before the miraculous scope of human generosity and to just keep saying thank you, forever and sincerely, for as long as we have voices."

—Elizabeth Gilbert

The book you hold in your hands would quite simply not exist without the tireless efforts, brilliant mind and endless cheerleading of Alena Divis. From our first two-hour conversation ten years ago in the Provo, Utah, Kneaders about the plot and characters I was dreaming up in my head to reading literally Every. Single. Draft. of this story (reader: you would not *believe* how many drafts there were even if I told you the number), to every call, text, visit, and Marco Polo that kept me from burning this manuscript alive. Alena, while I pray you never have to read this book ever again, I hope you see your fingerprint on every page of this story.

I owe much of the success in achieving this accomplishment of publication to the Storymakers organization for connecting me with the most amazing authors and mentors who played a part in helping transform my writing and build up my proverbial toolbox of writing skills, particularly J. Scott Savage, Lisa Mangum, Jen Geigle Johnson, Mindy Burbidge Strunk, Martha Keyes, and Lyndsay Condie. A huge warm hug to each of you for your kindness, patience, and invaluable feedback on my pages and query letter at the beginning of this journey, as well as for the classes, workshops, and mentoring you provided to this newbie baby author. You gave me wings, then taught me how to catch myself and try again every time I failed to fly.

My never-ending gratitude to the incredible authors who have allowed me to overwhelm them with questions about publishing, marketing, and social media: Cindy Steel, Kortney Keisel, Karen Thornell, Kiri Patterson, and Rachel Scott McDaniel. Thank you will never be enough for all you've taught me. Each of these women have written handfuls of books that will make you laugh, cry, swoon, and discover. Find their books! Read their books! Thank me later!

I had the great fortune of working with two wonderful editors on this book: Rachel Garber of rachelgarber.com, and Aubrey Parry of Ravishing Revisions. Ladies, thank you for getting me to the end and pouring your individual knowledge and passion into this work. Rachel, I am in awe of your talent and the depth to which you not only understand but also love the language and power of storytelling. Aubrey, I am endlessly grateful for your attention to detail and the gentle finesse you have as an editor to navigate a story and pull out the best parts to make them shine. I consider myself the luckiest author to have worked with you both!

I am convinced Kiri Patterson and Kylie Birch are both made of story magic, and I had the privilege of being a bystander as they flooded that magic with their whole heart and soul into this manuscript. Thank you from the bottom of my emotional heart for every moment you spent with these characters and their journey. The book is so much better for it.

Thank you to the many, many bookstagrammers and

reviewers—with an extra special thanks to Kayla @klas.fa-vorite.reads and Holly @hollys_book_musings for supporting me, carrying me forward and introducing me to so many wonderful people—who have taken a chance on little unknown me and the book of my heart and soul. Bookstagrammers, your willingness to give this book your precious time and your excitement in sharing it with others make my heart explode with gratitude in ways you can't possibly understand. Book people are the very best kind of people, and I am truly blessed to be a small part of this incredibly supportive online community.

And to you, dear reader. Without you, these pages would stay lonely and sad. The people whom this story is about deserve to be remembered and honored. So thank you for opening this book and giving this story life, purpose, and meaning. Thank you for taking a chance on a debut author and spending your time with me and these characters. Readers, you make the world a better, kinder, more compassionate place to be. Keep sharing your love of books!

To all my sweet neighbors and friends near and far who have asked how my writing is going, sent me an encouraging text, laughed with me over dinners, chatted books with me, shared my content, commented on a post, sent me a DM, encouraged me on this path, and shown a level of excitement for this book that has at times brought me to tears, THANK YOU. There is not enough paper available to me to list you all individually by name, but please know I love each of you to the depths of the deepest ocean and wish you unlimited amounts of chocolate and reading time for all of your days. Writing is an endless stream of self-doubt. Knowing people are in my corner means the world and keeps me from slamming my head into my keyboard.

To my darling Young Women: Savana, Andie, Brittin, and Amanda, who pretended to be asleep at our winter overnight as I told every detail of what I wanted this story to be to, Ashley (who, at 1:00 am, very patiently listened to every detail when I'm sure she just wanted to go to sleep!). When I got to "the end", you all immediately "woke up" and shouted, "I want to read that!" Your excitement in those early stages of my writing meant everything to me. Each of you are grown women now with glorious lives of your own, but I took your goodness, your strength, and your faith and put a little of each of you into these characters. Girls (because you will always be my girls!), I hope you see yourself in these pages.

Tyler, Miles, Hyrum, Jared, Corbin, Keagan, and Kaiden. Thank you for whisper shouting while playing video games all summer so I could—kind of—concentrate on writing, for crowding around my writing desk and chatting about your lives while I *pretended* to concentrate on writing, and for being the absolute coolest knucklehead teenagers that exist.

Luci, Wendell, Mary, Rebekah, and Nathan: your compassion and excitement for this story has buoyed me up over and over. Thank you for caring about what happens next, asking after me, reaching out, and all of your love and encouragement! I am truly blessed to have each of you.

Grandpa Olson, thank you for letting Poppy share your birthday. Grandma, I hope you smile every time you open chapter one and look at the heading. Thank you both for the phone calls and the check-ins. I love you!

Cheryl Nelson, Alisa Ence, Amanda Beirdneau, Giselle Nelson, and Alena Divis (insert sobbing emoji times five). Thank you for being my constants in a world that is anything but. Your encouragement, suggestions, feedback, support, and out-pouring of love over me and these pages over the last ten years of writing them has meant the world to me. I treasure each tear, laugh, and heart swoon this manuscript inflicted within you. How lucky am I that get to have each of you in my life for eternity? Thank you to Chris, Skyler, Craig, Ty, and Tyler for being men that inspire the writing of fictional heroic leading men everywhere. Y'all are the good ones.

Tyler, Kylee, Addy, and Livy, thank you. Thank you for knowing the worst parts of me, the tired parts of me, and the overwhelmed parts of me and loving me anyway. Thank you for popping into my office with hugs, mugs of Dr Pepper, teenage drama that needs unfolding, and reminders to cook dinner. You are resilient, you are kind, you are loyal, you are understanding, and you embody love. I hope you see yourself in the best parts of every character in these pages. You are my four greatest accomplishments, and I am so proud and thankful to be your mom.

Bobby. There are no words sufficient to explain what your support, love and encouragement mean to me. You are the first person I told about my crazy dream to write a book. You looked at me, and without missing a beat, said, "You absolutely should; you would be an amazing author." You have held me while I've cried in frustration over these pages, opened the computer and sat me in my chair after I announced I was giving up, and celebrated every milestone—big and small—right alongside me. You are every good piece of this story, every good quality reflected in my characters, and every goodnight kiss I want for the rest of my life. My heart is yours.

And above all else, I thank my Father in Heaven for guiding me through every page of this manuscript and every step of this journey to publication. I have been abundantly blessed, and my gratitude to Him for the gifts He has seen fit to bestow upon me knows no end. Glory to God.

ABOUT THE AUTHOR

Angela Bricker was raised in Houston, Texas, where she gained a love for country music and Blue Bell ice cream. At the age of seventeen, she moved to Utah to attend Brigham Young University and fell in love with the mountains, the snow, and NO humidity, so she never left! Bricker currently resides in the heart of Utah with her husband and four children. When she's not researching history and writing love stories, you can find her kissing her toddlers' boo-boos by day, tracking her teenagers' phones by night, and planning epic parties all hours in-between. Her energy to write is fueled by overflowing mugs of Dr Pepper and an admiration for historical women who choose to misbehave.

Let's be friends! I would love to hear from you.

Email: authorangelabricker@gmail.com
Website: https://angelabricker.com
Instagram: https://www.instagram.com/angelabrickerwrites/
Goodreads: https://www.goodreads.com/author/show/55794441.
Angela_Bricker

www.ingramcontent.com/pod-product-compliance
Lightning Source LLC
Chambersburg PA
CBHW030239120726
47903CB00005B/1541